BOOKS IN THE IMMORTALS SERIES

The Others
Hold On

The Others

Immortals Book 1

EMMA WOLF

ISBN-13: 978-1-73346356-1-4

Cover design by: Warren Design
Printed in the United States of America

DEDICATION

Dedicated to Richelle Kohler who never let me give up and my family who put up with me during the process.

PROLOGUE

"I don't dance."

The words were a brittle defense against the radiant force of her, her eyes catching the light of the moon and shining with such mischief that Talus felt his resolve eroding. Around them, the gala was a blur of silk and ambition, a sea of "important" people who held the keys to his life's work. He should have been networking; should have been extolling the virtues of his plan for a new world. Instead, he was captivated by the girl with the rose-petal lips and a quirky smile that always drew out his own awkward grin.

"How about I lead then? Come on, dance with me." She held out her hand to him.

"I assure you, even if I were a puppet on strings I would be incapable of dancing." Another day he would have indulged her. Another day he would have grabbed her and danced her around the room without a moment's hesitation, just to keep that smile on her face. But the stakes were too high; he couldn't afford to look like a fool.

"Puppets do not dance. Take my hand Talus, please." The smile was fading a little and at that moment he knew he was beat. Despite himself he smiled when he felt the familiar tingle as their hands touched. She seized the opportunity, as he knew she would, and pulled him close to her.

Soft violin and piano drifted among lighted pillars covered in flowers. A secret garden come to life in a courtyard that just yesterday had been nothing more than an office patio. She started slow and easy, just a gentle sway with a step here and then a step there. She was

1

taunting him, begging him to take the lead.

He shook his head and wondered if there was anything she could not talk him into. His arm wrapped around her waist, pressing into the soft teal fabric that brought out the fire in her red hair. She rested her head against his chest and he was gone. The people around him, the people he was so desperate to impress, faded away.

The music grew louder and the tempo increased. He spun her—awkwardly, stumbling over his own feet—but she laughed, a sound so rich with life it felt like a physical warmth. He remembered the year he'd wasted being afraid of this feeling. A year stealing glances at her from afar, making light conversation, making 100 different excuses a day for why he should not get closer to her.

It all ended one chilly October day, she wore that blue sweater that fell just off her shoulder. Just one ordinary day she walked straight up to him as he sat drinking his coffee. She placed her hand on the table and leaned in close with a smile. "Life is too short to wait any longer for this." With that she pulled him out of his chair and gave him a kiss.

From that moment he had been lost in her. He had two things in his life that really mattered, his work and her. But as they spun around this room, As he dipped her, nearly dropping her in his enthusiasm, he felt a surge of desperate devotion. His work; his grand, secret mission to conquer time and entropy, was all for this. He wanted an eternity of these stumbles.. To be dancing under the moonlight with her for all time. To listen to her whisper in his ear

"I love you Talus."

"And I will forever love you, Lily."

✷ ✷ ✷

He rose from his bed. His breath coming in short gasps, his eyes squeezed tight.

He clutched the edge of the mattress, his knuckles white, anchoring himself against the violent tide of grief that threatened to pull him back under. Talus tried to slow his breathing, tried to push the memories away. The dream had been so vivid he could still smell the jasmine on the breeze. Every awakening was a fresh bereavement, a jagged reminder that the "eternity" he had sought had been granted in the cruelest way possible.

He stood, his legs trembling, and made his way to the surface lift. The silver tube hissed as it ascended, a sterile coffin rising toward a graveyard. He had to move on, he had to find a way to stop these dreams. And yet…he knew he never would. He clung to them even more than he tried to push them away. For just a moment she was real again. For just a moment she was more than a wisp of memory in the back of his mind. He could feel her warmth in his arms, see her bright smile and hear her laughter.

The doors slid open to a cool, biting breeze. He breathed deep and closed his eyes. If he was honest with himself he could understand why some were so desperate to return to the surface. But things would never be like they were. The buildings, landmarks, and people were all lost to them. Just as she was lost to him. All he had wanted was eternity by her side and what he got was an eternity haunted by her memory.

He started walking the same worn path. The bright moon and stars above helped to light his way and his eyes quickly adjusted. The town where they had lived before moving into the underground lab was not far. Walking there was something he did frequently when his dreams became too hard to face. Or was it that he wanted to face them? Did he revisit those places in order to make the memories and the dreams stronger, to make sure that they always kept coming back?

Broken buildings stretched along the horizon. Some barely looked worse for the wear, others were crumbling and still others were completely gone. But as he walked through the town that he had spent decades in, the buildings shifted and repaired. He saw it all as it once was, as it should be, as it still might be if only he had never come along. A foolish dreamer with little sense of the world.

On the corner, crumbling tables righted themselves, small folding chairs reappeared and the coffee shop that he visited every Tuesday morning rebuilt itself. And there, on the top floor, right in the perfect spot to smell all the fresh coffee and pastries, was her

3

apartment. The window that she would look down and smile from. He could hear her then "Back again? Grab two cups, I'll be right down."

It was nearly always perfect timing. By the time he was seated at one of the tables, she'd appear and reach for her coffee. He used to joke that all he was to her was a free cup of coffee. Lily was not above using her looks and charm to help make ends meet and get the little things she could not always afford. Like gourmet cups of coffee. He never minded though, and he doubted the others whom she conned into a sandwich or a drink ever did either.

He kept walking. Building after building rose up and shared their memories and their secrets. The park where he first introduced Cary to Lily. Where she had pushed him into the lake in response to a cheeky joke. He sat on the grass and just listened to the laughter in the breeze, the hum of people talking, the rustle of the trees. Somewhere a dog barked, a child cried and when this moment was real, he had overlooked it all. Now he relished every little sound. Every little memory made the image in his mind clearer. The trees grew stronger, the colors brighter and she was louder. She was so loud. So loud that there were times Cary would joke she should hand out earplugs to everyone who stood within 100 feet of her.

He laid down on the grass and as he looked up at the moon and stars. The facade around him fell and he was just alone. Completely alone in the spot where he could distinctly remember feeling her laying in the crook of his arm. There was something comforting about the moon and the stars. It was the same moon that had shown down upon her face the night they danced. The same moon that was high in the sky when the first bombs fell. The same moon that shown through the night when the dust had settled to reveal what was left of their world. His eternal companion. They were the same in many ways, never changing, just watching the life around them go on.

There in the grass, in the light of the moon, he turned his head and felt his nose get wrapped up in her hair. She was back with him once more. He breathed deep and listened to her sigh as she snuggled closer to him. He closed his eyes and let the moonlight wash over him, a hollow king in a kingdom of ruin, waiting for sleep to bring back the only world that mattered.

1

Anya

"Anya!"

The voice echoed down the narrow hallway, bouncing off the reinforced titanium ribs of the base. Anya stopped mid-stride, her boots clicking against the perforated metal flooring. She took a steadying breath, pushing aside the prickly impatience that came with being grounded, and turned to see Ryan jogging toward her.

"Ryan! What are you doing here? I thought you were on comms tonight."

Ryan came to a stop, his dark features became shadowed as he frowned at her.

"I am on comms. Funny thing about comms," he said, his voice dropping to a cautioned level. "I can use them to track where people are, make sure they're where they're supposed to be." Before she could retreat, he reached out and caught her wrist, hoisting it up to illuminate the sleek, black device wrapped around her forearm. "This comm, for example is restricted to quarters."

Anya yanked her arm free, the metal of the device feeling like a cold shackle against her skin.

"I've been restricted to quarters for days! I need to get out Ryan, you'll have to lock me up to stop me."

"I'm sure you'd like to see me try." Ryan challenged.

"I'd like to see anyone try."

"It's easy. All I have to do is place Mr. Wuggles on the door to the elevator."

He pulled a wide, transparent cylinder from his belt. Inside, a large, fuzzy spider scuttled across the glass. Anya felt a genuine shiver crawl down her spine as the creature reached up a thick, multi-jointed leg and pointed directly at her. She was certain the malevolent thing was marking her for later.

"Oh come on! Why do you still carry that thing around with you everywhere?"

Ryan raised his brow in an expression that clearly meant he thought the reason was obvious.

"If you aren't trying to stop me, then why are you here?" she asked, her curiosity finally winning out.

"I have something for you."

Her eyes lit up with excitement but the rest of her expression remained passive. "Something for me? Why would you have something for me?"

"Well they've been developing it down in the lab and they wanted you to have the first prototypes. They've been waiting till your reinstatement next month but I knew you were never going to last that long."

He reached into his pocket and produced several matte-black spheres, each the size of a plum and pitted with small, precise holes. Anya took them, feeling the surprising weight of the high-density tech in her palm.

"They're called Plasma Globes, and they are designed to take out groups. Press the recessed button to arm it and then throw. On impact, the electric charge triggers, stunning every immortal within a ten-foot radius."

She placed the balls into her own pocket. The "or more" part was a little disconcerting but if she was going to use something like this, things probably were not going well for her anyway.

"Plasma Globes? Really? That's the best they could come up

with?"

"It's some joke about old tech." Ryan shrugged.

"How long does it last?"

"10 minutes at least."

"Impressive, but I won't be in a position to use them tonight."

"If anyone is going to have a chance it's you."

"You should get back before someone comes looking for you."

"And you better get back before morning. I won't be able to hide your absence from Captain, and I'd hate to leave Mr. Wuggles in your room."

"You wouldn't!"

"I would." His eyes softened, the teasing gone. "Just don't take any risks okay?"

Anya bowed with a theatrical flourish of her arm, turning to continue her trek toward the surface lift. As Ryan turned to walk away, she smoothly pulled a hollow straw and a red blob of adhesive goo from her pouch. With a sharp puff of air, she sent the projectile flying. It splattered perfectly against the back of Ryan's neck.

"Ugh! You know that doesn't wash out!" he yelled, reaching back to find his hand covered in scarlet slime.

"Threaten me with that spider again and I'll use lavender next time!"

"Not pastels! Anything but pastels." Ryan grumbled, though she could hear the faint chuckle in his voice as he walked away, smearing the red goo further into his collar.

Anya's footsteps transitioned from a click to a dull, echoing clunk as she reached the main observation gantry. From this height, she could look down into the dizzying vertigo of the base's central shaft. Tunnels branched off like the veins of a titan, forming a massive subterranean city designed to shield the remnants of humanity from the toxic atmosphere and the endless wars above.

To most inhabitants, this hallway was a dead end—a path to a forbidden world. But as a scout, Anya was a rare breed. She was one of the few who had seen the sky without a screen and felt the unfiltered heat of the sun.

She unclipped her breather mask, sliding it over her face with a practiced click. It hissed as the filters engaged, cleaning the stale, recycled base air before it hit her lungs. The built-in HUD flickered to life, bathing her vision in a soft green night-vision glow. She checked the weight of her Fulgar at her hip and ensured the extra power charges were seated in their slots.

Reaching the airlock, the heavy mechanism engaged with a powerful swoosh of equalizing pressure. It was the sound of impending freedom. She stepped into the small, circular elevator. With a low, mechanical groan and the comforting grind of ancient gears, the lift began its ascent.

When the lift stopped, a small display screen beeped, showing the exterior thermal feed of the mountainside. Anya watched the heat signatures for several minutes, ensuring no patrols or hostiles were loitering near the exit. Satisfied, she pressed the release.

The rock face, disguised by seamless holographic and physical plating, slid aside. Anya stepped out into the biting chill of the surface. As the door hissed shut behind her, vanishing back into the crags of the mountain, she breathed deep.

Alone in the vast, dangerous silence, she felt the weight of life as a ranger scout lift from her shoulders. Here, there were no reprimands, no restrictions, and no walls. Just the wind, the stars, and the beautiful, lethal unknown.

Anya had been taught about fear her whole life, taught to overcome her fear of the enemy while knowing that there was no way to beat them, no way to win. All they could do was hide and hope for survival. It seemed to be enough for everyone else, they all seemed to accept it. But for some reason she couldn't or maybe she wouldn't, because there had to be something more for them. Something more than fear and waiting for death.

Under the oppressive weight of her mask, Anya's face was covered in obsidian greasepaint, which matched the jumpsuit she wore for night missions. Anya's feet crunched against the ground as she made her way across the treacherous, rocky scree that wound between the mountain's ribs toward the skeletal remains of the valley city. This town, once a thriving hub for the base's builders, was now a grid of shattered asphalt and crumbling brick, a monument to a civilization that had been forced to trade the sun for survival.

No matter how many times she walked through the rubble of the small town the sense of unease never lifted. She could not imagine what life would have been like there, what stories there were, how they lived, what it was like to live beneath the sun. Maybe today she would find some sort of answer among the abandoned buildings.

She kept low to the ground as she drew nearer to the town's remains. The further away from base, the better her chances to encounter one of *them*. While an immortal had never been spotted in the town, they were coming closer. Night and day watches had been doubled, all just waiting for the inevitable.

Anya crept forward to the streets that had once been full of people. The quiet town was nestled between several towering mountains. Captain said that this settlement had grown in the middle of nowhere, perfectly hidden, just a place for workers to stay while they built the base. There were many little towns like this scattered about rural areas.

She placed her hand on a bit of wall beside her. Small shards of debris twinkled down like raindrops and she enjoyed the simple sweet sound. She heard it again and smiled, until she realized that the sound was coming from further away than the wall beside her.

She looked down at her forearm and activated the map for just a moment, refusing to risk too much light, it confirmed what she already knew. Her fellow scouts were nowhere near the direction of the sound. She froze, the rough gravel biting into her knees as she watched a run-down store. Anya peeked up from behind the wall. Staying low was her best chance of going undetected. She remained motionless.

Nothing.

She was still.

Absolutely still.

Whatever was out there, she could not risk being seen by an immortal this close to base.

They were harder to see at night. She had only known them to wear dark gray clothing. It made them much easier to avoid during the day, but in the darkness they were nearly invisible.

As time crept slowly by without another sound she started to relax. Probably just a rat or another part of the building deteriorating.

Her breath caught.

A gloved hand reached out from the deep shadows, gripping the rotting door frame. Because the building was still largely intact, the immortal remained hidden in the darkness inside.

She waited.

The immortal stepped into the cold light. He was a towering figure in a long, tattered gray coat, his brown hair lashing against a face that looked carved from marble. His eyes burned a cold, unnerving blue, stripped bare of any human spark.

His eyes looked to the sky above before he turned to enter the next building, a former grocery store. Anya had never seen one intact before but the refrigerators against the back wall and the rows of shelves with deteriorating food packages made its past life obvious. Many times, against orders, she had walked through those aisles. Picking up scraps of wrappers and reading the labels trying to figure out just what a candy bar might have tasted like or what the obsession had been with something that came in colorful plastic bottles.

No matter how many pictures Anya looked at or how much time she spent reading the old histories, it never seemed real to her. All just a wonderful fantasy world where the only thing people had to fear was getting hit by a bus before they had a chance to die of old age.

She heard rustling and banging come from inside the building. The immortal wasn't here to browse, he was looking for something. What could an immortal want with an old grocery store, or an old human town at all? Was he searching for proof that a base had been built nearby?

For over an hour Anya trailed him, watching as he tore through rubble and grew angrier and angrier at his lack of success. It was obvious that he had been expecting to find something very important, perhaps something even more significant than a human base. She continued after him.

The sun was going to creep over the horizon in less than an hour. Anya wasn't dressed appropriately enough to trail him during the day. The immortal reached the edge of the town and Anya followed. She had to see what he would do next.

Would he leave now? Look back through the town? Where had he come from? She cursed as he started walking away from the city limits through the mountains. There were few rocks for her to hide behind once he got to the pass. But trailing him through that narrow pass out of the mountains was not her only problem. She knew what was hidden at the opening. Directly in front of her was a large rock that did more than mark the entrance.

"Night team, check in and return to base. Day team prepare to head out." Her comm relayed the message that she had been dreading.

Don't move, Delta. Don't move. Her comm let her know just who was behind that rock, and prior to her suspension he had never been on scout patrol. He was about to have his first encounter with an immortal.

Watching the map on her wrist she saw the other scouts heading back. They could make their run back to base without being seen. There was just one scout that needed to stay completely put –

A blur of movement.

The immortal turned toward the left to face the rock.

She cursed silently.

"Delta, check in. Come in Delta." The voice spoke again.

Delta was now hiding on the opposite side of the boulder, she could see it all lined up in front of her

The immortal was still facing the rock. He had heard something.

Just keep going. Keep going. Let me bring him home. Anya knew then that she was the only one who could help Delta. His survival was up to her. She was much farther from the scene than she would have liked but she could not risk exposing her cover until she knew.

"Anya, Delta isn't responding. You both need to return to base."

She reached for one of the balls that Ryan had given her. If it worked the way he said she could activate it, toss it and take the immortal down so that Delta could run.

The immortal took another step toward the rock.

Delta remained still. His hands were shaking as he clasped his Fulgar, upside down in his fist.

Anya took a deep breath. She dropped the ball back down into her pocket. She did not want to risk frying Delta too. She would have to do this up close.

The immortal took another step. He was close enough to touch the rock now.

She pulled her Fulgar and sprinted.

The immortal spun, his hand disappearing into his coat for a weapon, but Anya was a blur of movement. She collided with him, wrenching his wrist behind his back with a sickening pop. She slammed the Fulgar into the base of his skull and pulled the trigger.

A violent surge of electricity buckled them both. White light seared her retinas as the charge spent itself into the immortal's spine. His body went limp, collapsing into the dirt like a puppet with its strings cut. She looked down at him, his eyes looked back with nothing but anger behind them.

She inhaled deeply and went to the other side of the rock. Delta was still there trembling. She motioned for him to stand. His legs were weak beneath him and Anya could only shake her head. They could not risk sending out rangers like Delta.

"Anya," Her comm screeched in her ear again. "Captain will have you hanging from the waste tubes if you do not get him back before sunrise!"

"Can you run?" She looked over to Delta, he was pale and sweaty.

He looked back at the body on the ground and then up at her.

He nodded.

"Good. Do not stop and do not look back. Go!"

"Delta and Anya returning to base. Immortal down at location A7. Day scouts be advised." She said into her wrist com.

She pushed Delta forward and watched as he disappeared between the jagged rocks of the mountains. With one last look toward the immortal seething on the ground she burst into a run as well. She made sure Delta stayed ahead of her, keeping him in her sights as he followed a winding path. As long as she could see him she knew he would make it to base, and if the immortal regained muscle function…well at least he would reach her first. She wasn't sure that would be such a bad thing. The immortal could only kill her, the captain could make her miserable for the rest of her life. He might put her on kitchen duty for this one.

The sun was stretching into the sky by the time she saw Delta's small frame disappear into their mountain. She breathed a sigh, she was definitely going to use bringing him home safely as leverage against disobeying the captain- again. How could anyone accept a life beneath the surface once they had been outside, among the wind and the light and the stars? There were children that had yet to walk beneath the sun.

Anya looked back down the path. She had heard nothing and there was no chance the immortal would have seen where they went or which mountain was their home. She looked toward the light from the rising sun that was coming over the mountains. Captain would really have her this time and it might just be her last chance to feel the warmth on her face. She decided to climb.

The mountain was weathered but she made her way up the craggy edge. She reached a small section of rock that jutted out just enough to stand on.

Across the wide empty expanse the sun was greeting the new day with ribbons of pink and orange. A soft breeze blew but she could barely feel it through her mask and suit. More than anything she wanted to live beneath that sun, to see the bounty of the earth, hear the crash of ocean waves.

The giant orb was calling to her, a shining beacon that told stories of life upon the surface. The beautiful sun had seen humanity at its peak striving toward an impossible future, only to destroy it all. *Well if this is my last chance out here for a while, I might as well make it worth it.* She slipped her thumbs underneath her mask and pulled it off.

The black paint on her face felt itchy and stiff, but the wind was still a cooling embrace unlike any other that she had ever felt. Technically the air was now breathable, technically they should be able to go without the masks. Protocol dictated that they remained in use and they were still useful for night missions. She breathed the fresh air that had blown over the oceans and across the sands. The smell and feel of the wind filled her with peace and anger. The two emotions feuding against each other, one wanting to relish the moment and the other furious over the fact that it could not be permanent.

This was nearly worth it all, this one moment. At Phoenix she would never have been granted a moment like this. She was never given even an inch of freedom. From the moment they realized her destiny, she belonged to them. Her family turned her over like nothing more than a toy they had outgrown. Then it was all over, no more childhood, no more friends, just life training to be among the best Rangers in the world. A year before she was to complete training, her outspokenness, her conviction, and her heart caused her to lose her home and the only person she had left – Mamoru.

"Ranger Anya, you are hereby expelled from Phoenix and you will not be allowed to continue training as a Ranger at this base. Your refusal to follow orders and commit to protecting your fellow humans has shown that you have no place among us."

She stood tall in the Great Hall as her Captain berated her in front of everyone, the other Rangers, the people of the base and even Mamoru. She would not give him the satisfaction of breaking her. If her family leaving the base without even a goodbye did not break her, her own exodus from Phoenix would not either. But that did not mean she would go quietly.

"I will protect the people of this base and any other with my life! But that is a living, breathing, person that you are torturing in that room! How can you expect anyone to be a part of it?"

Captain Grayson leaned in close to her, his face in its usual scowl. "You think you are so high and mighty. That Fulgar you carry, how do you think we learned it would work? How do you think we learned about regeneration times? You are so willing to take advantage of everything we have gained and yet you can't stomach what it takes. You will never be a Ranger and I hope no other base agrees to take you. I hope you are lost out on the surface so one of those bastard creatures can shoot you through your pathetic bleeding heart."

Four years later and those words still rang through her head. They still forced her on, forced her to prove him wrong. Maybe if she was strong enough, if she was fast enough, if she could find a way to stop it all, she could prove that torture was never the answer.

"Anya. Get back now. Captain knows you're out…and he's being very quiet. It is kinda scary, like a dog that you know is all bark, who suddenly sneaks up and bites your hand off." Anya smiled. She gave a sigh, normally it would be Captain yelling through her head for her to get back, or do her job or listen. He was never quiet with his anger, either something else was wrong or he was going to hang her out to dry this time. It would be much easier if she could just be like the others and accept this life. But something inside her would not let her stop fighting for a future that offered so much more.

2

Talus

Talus stood upon the mountain's jagged spine, a solitary gargoyle carved against a sky of bruised violet and sulfur. Below him, the horizon didn't just stretch; it bled into an infinite, flat expanse of desolation. Miles of scorched earth, once the vibrant heart of a continent, were now reduced to a pale, shimmering sand that stung the eyes. Here and there, pathetic tufts of mutated green clawed through the ash—nature's desperate, ugly attempt at a comeback. From his perch atop the solitary mountain he could see everything around him. He tried to see things as they once were, the way he saw them before it was all gone.

In the wavering heat, he could almost see the ghost of the old world: the skeletal ribs of skyscrapers that once pierced the clouds, monuments to a species that thought it had conquered the heavens only to be buried beneath them. Now, the only "conquest" left was the subterranean hive beneath his boots. A tomb for the living.

He pulled out a metal case from his pocket. He flipped it open, avoiding looking at the picture inside as he grabbed a cigarette. He liked the irony of cigarettes, even if they were before his time and having them now was as much a testament to his ingenuity as his current state of being. He held the soft brown paper tube in his hand for a moment, smelling the tobacco within. It was sweet and fresh.

"There you are."

The voice was a familiar anchor, dragging him back from the precipice of memory. Talus didn't turn to know that it was Cary.

"Yes, here I am."

He lit his cigarette and held it in-between his fingers, just letting the smoke waft in the breeze. Watching it twist and twirl in the wind was somehow normal and peaceful in a way that few things were anymore.

"Those things will kill you, you know. Nothing but a damned barbaric custom that we were good to have done away with. Like high school dances, whoever thought those were a good idea."

Talus gave a small smile despite himself but it quickly turned to a frown. He pulled the cigarette to his mouth as if the movement suddenly took much effort. He took a deep breath, trying to calm those emotions, push back the memories that still haunted him. Countless years of death and still there was still one that haunted him more than all the rest. It was a long moment before he could answer Cary.

"Why else would I have them? What if the answer is 300 years of these things? Then you will have a great deal of catching up to do my friend."

Talus watched the smoke swirl up toward the clouds and clear sky, as if the small bits of tobacco were trying to escape the desolation below. Even the damn cigarette had a way out, while he still had none. He was left here, to watch over the end that was still sure to come.

"No. I could not bear it if she were right about another bloody thing. But…she was right about everything else." Cary held out his hand for one of the cigarettes still cradled within the gold case in Talus' black coat pocket.

They were hand rolled with the tobacco Cary grew for him. Cary had never even seen a cigarette until Talus showed him one when they were still in college. Used to be all the rage he said, one of the ways people used to kill themselves. Which meant it used to be something Talus would have avoided at all costs.

Talus slid a second cigarette from the gold-lined case. His fingers lingered on the paper—caressing it like a rosary—before handing it over. He clicked the lighter for Cary, the blue flame illuminating the deep lines of weariness on both their faces.

"Why are you here? I am supposed to be left alone up here." Talus knew Cary was trying to avoid telling him something.

"I know, but the satellites are picking up communications. There is someone else out there. We are not the only ones. Isn't that bloody fantastic?" Cary's small smile showed the lack of real emotion behind his words.

Talus scoffed, a jagged sound that tore through the quiet. "We knew they survived, Cary. If the cobalt bombs didn't scrub the planet clean of us, they didn't scrub them either. All they did was kill the world and everyone on it who was worth a damn."

Talus sucked hard on his cigarette and caught the falling ashes in his palm. He crushed them slowly until the embers dimmed and turned his palm black. He looked out over the plains, the day was hotter than he had remembered a day being in decades. The sunlight caused the pale sand to shine bright enough to fatigue his eyes.

"Leave me be Cary, I do not come here for company." Talus flicked the cigarette down over the edge of the cliff and watched it slowly fall down to the ground.

"You can be really freaking dense. I know there are others out there, others like us. We all know that. But Kit has been listening to everything she can get from the satellites. Most of it is from them but there are others Talus. Even if you want to wallow in your lab for all eternity the truth is there may still be a war going on over there."

Talus placed his case back into his pocket and started making his way down the mountain. There were plenty of camouflaged handholds and foot pegs that made going up and down easy work. However, it did not make for an easy getaway as Cary was able to lean over the side and watch as he tried to leave the conversation. Perhaps he was still a bit immature after all these years but this was not a conversation he wanted to have…again.

"What the hell do you think you're going to do Talus? Run away? To Where? We live in the same underfecking ground lab. There's not even any doors that you can lock that I cannot open!"

Cary did have a point. A really good point. And yet Talus knew he would have at least a few moments alone as Cary was a much slower climber than he was.

Talus reached the large square entrance long before Cary was even halfway down. The gray staircase revealed below him was a glaring contrast to the tan sand around it. He was glad to hear the entrance swish shut before Cary could enter. Not that Cary would struggle to find him. There were only a few places that Talus liked to be.

His boots clunked loudly against the metal as he walked briskly to his quarters. It had been his home since before the war and very little had changed. It was a simple rectangle space off of his lab. Just a bed, chair and desk. There was only one real reason why he came to this room.

Talus threw himself in his chair and pressed the palm of his right hand to his eye. Slowly he trailed his fingers down his face to look at the picture that still sat perched on his desk.

"History repeats itself once again. It repeats itself even when there are so few left to repeat it. Perhaps it is the only thing the people on this planet know how to do anymore." He had confided in her for years, long after she had rotted away to dust. She was not even his in life and in death she was nothing, yet still he talked to her.

"I was never supposed to be making these decisions. But then you always knew it. You always knew that if I played God once, I would be playing him forever. It is all my fault and yet they still come to me like I have the answers. But I do not Lily, I never did."

He knew the other immortals wanted him to tell them what to do. Ever since he became the first it was like he made the decisions for all of them, forever. No matter how many mistakes he made, how many bad decisions, how many lives he cost, they still came to him. He felt no wiser or older than when he was a scared little boy on the sidewalk looking at a man who had frozen to death in the cold. Yet here he was leading the last of what had once been one of the most powerful countries on the planet, though it was little more than rubble.

"At least it's not so hitto hot down here."

"Hitto?" Talus questioned, as expected Cary came into the

room, but with much less fight than Talus had been anticipating.

"Finnish. I'm on the 'H's for the swear-word-of-the-day calendar."

"Charming."

"One for every day of the new century." Cary continued with the joke, but there was little laughter behind it.

They sat in silence for a few moments, both knowing what they needed to talk about but neither one wanting to start the conversation. It had all gone wrong every other time and yet to do nothing just seemed so…

"They are out there Talus, they've been out there this whole time. This whole time that we've been sitting here just existing. I don't know how we've missed their communications for so long but they're being hunted."

"We have not missed their communications. We have always heard them. I just kept it from you. I was not aware that Kit had taken to listening in."

Now Talus braced himself for the fire that was certain to come. Cary clenched and unclenched his fists as he leaned against the metal desk. His lips were set in a firm line.

"So you made your decision then? We just ignore them. Let them all be hunted to extinction? Why wouldn't you even tell me? Tell anyone?"

"What else would you have us do? You want all of us to travel halfway around the world with no more answers and no more to offer than they already have? Last time we tried to save the day we did a pretty poor job of it." Talus stood up and walked around the corner to his lab.

Long open metal shelves gleamed in narrow rows, overflowing with vials and containers of various sizes. Talus ran his fingers across the smooth metal as he walked across the chilly room. Talus opened the fridge at one end and pulled out a vial of red liquid. He swished it around for a moment before throwing it against the wall. The glass shattered, and the red liquid sprayed across the white paneling like a fresh wound.

Cary came up beside him, his eyes on the blood that had splatted across the far side of the room.

"We have never sent any communication out before. Maybe they have answers we don't. They're still fighting, Talus. That has to mean something."

Over 100 years of war and still that man had astounding levels of optimism. But this time Cary did not know as much as he thought he did. He was making a very big assumption. It would not be the first time that they had tried talking with the humans. But there were some questions that Talus had not been able to answer that he knew the humans could.

"The planet cannot survive another war." Talus said.

"Apparently, the war never stopped. What good is the planet if there is no one left?"

"Spoken like a true environmentalist. Pretty sure Professor Norken is rolling about in his grave now that his best student said those words. And in case you have forgotten, we would still be here."

"That's not the life any of us want to live, Talus."

"So immortality is only worth it when we get to watch people die?"

"That's not fair, Tal. No, it is only worth it when there is something left for us to live for. What do we have now, Talus? I'm not even sure we have each other. Consarn it!" Cary stopped, his breath hitching. When he spoke again, the fire was gone, leaving only a hollow vulnerability. "I don't have the answers. But letting them die in silence... I won't accept that. And the man you used to be wouldn't have either."

They were once again in silence. Talus could not remember the last time Cary's voice had been so soft. Was it when they had to make this decision before or was it when Cary told him Lily was gone?

"I have work to do. We can discuss this more tomorrow CarCar."

Cary winced at the old nickname, a relic from a movie they'd watched a lifetime ago. "Stupid movie," he muttered, the insult holding no weight as he turned and left Talus alone in the red-stained dark.

The lab felt smaller with Cary gone, the silence rushing back in like a rising tide. Talus stood before the long, gleaming rows of metal shelves, his eyes scanning the glass vials with a vacant intensity. He wasn't sure what he was looking for anymore. He had become a master of the stall; every chemical reagent, every concentrated toxin, and every serum he developed achieved nothing more than a temporary, dormant stutter in the fire. The blood would go quiet for a few moments, teasing him with the prospect of an end, before the cells found a way to warm themselves back into their relentless, immortal rhythm.

He looked at the specialized refrigeration unit in the corner. He had a new plan—one he wouldn't dare inflict on the others. He had observed his own blood samples under extreme cryogenic stress; they didn't just sleep, they froze in a way that defied regeneration.

Talus had thought of this experiment more than once. He had first seen the reaction of his blood to extreme cold decades ago. His mind told him that all he would get would be a dreamless sleep for the first time since that day in his lab. He told himself that over and over again, that the answers he might get would be worth the discomfort. Just a little cold, a little nap and then some nice warm blankets to bring him back. He still could not bring himself to do it. All he saw was two sky blue lifeless eyes staring at him any time the thought passed through his mind.

He went toward his latest notebook and flipped through the pages once again. Talus had tried all the obvious answers, every poison he could manage, every manner of death he could test on the blood he had taken. Creating eternal life had been the easy part, taking it away was the real challenge.

His lab was one of many but it was once just a secondary lab, a much larger one was just down the hall. That one had been the laboratory where all of them used to work together. But now this lab was enough for him and had everything he could think of. With plenty of geothermal and solar energy he could stay in the room and work throughout his entire life and never have to stop. He never wanted to stop. After all this was what he wanted wasn't it? To live a life without fear? How was he supposed to know it was also going to be an eternity without life?

"You should come and eat something Talus."

Kit's voice drifted in from the doorway, light and airy, cutting through the sterile chill of the room. He didn't look up. He had no patience for her today. She stood there in the doorway, still trapped in the physical form of a sixteen-year-old, her blonde curls catching the harsh light.

"The strawberries are ripe and there is more wheat so there will be bread again. Can you smell it? There is nothing like the smell of fresh bread. Come share it with us please? Please? Talus you must be hungry."

Talus finally looked at her, his eyes dark and recessed. "I am not hungry and neither are you. Do you even remember what it feels like to be hungry? To feel anything?"

Kit did not back away from his gruff response. She was the only one that had not learned the way of things around here, the way of him. Her pale hands stroked a long blonde curl but still her eyes shone with that damned happiness.

"No, I do not remember hunger. I do not remember what the world was like before, except in pictures of course. But despite all that is wrong and all that we are, I can still feel. I can still enjoy the day, I can still relish every moment as best I can. If this is all that is meant for us, why do you insist on making it a prison?"

She had no idea what she was talking about. She never did. She was all hope and flowers and sunshine. Kit was undoubtedly one of those people who would have gone to church and believed that God was going to save them.

"Because it is a prison!" he roared, the sound echoing off the metal vials. "You have no idea what real loss is. Everyone you have ever loved is in this bunker, and they will be here until the stars go out. Up there?" He pointed a jagged finger toward the ceiling. "Up there is my fault. The only blessing in this whole cursed disaster is that I finally got what I wanted: a life without fear. And look at it. Look at the eternity of nothing I've built for us."

"You are a fool if you think you are living without fear Talus." Her sweet demeanor swiftly turned dark. "You are as afraid of success

24

as you are of failure."

Just as easily as her dark facade had come, it disappeared. She broke into a gentle smile once again. "Head to the dining hall when you are ready to eat. I'll tell mom to expect you. Don't make me come back here and bring it to you."

She skipped away down the hall. Talus watched her go. He hoped that it would be a long time before they crossed paths again. Lily would have told him to be patient, to give the girl a chance, but she was no longer here to be his conscience. Lily...his mind started drifting toward hazy memories. A bright smile lighting up the darkness, red hair shimming down her shoulders in perfect little spirals. Green eyes the color of the summer grass after a morning rain. He slammed his hand hard against the metal desk, glad that he could still feel pain. Glad that he had a way of pushing those thoughts to his mind. Glad that his human survival instincts were still there, still wanting to fight against the perceived threat, even if there would never be a real one again.

3

Anya

Anya took one last look at the rising sun and pulled her mask down, the seal hissing as it locked, severing her connection to the world above. Climbing down she tried to memorize the feel of the sharp rock digging into the creases of her hands. The sound of her fingers sliding along the rough surface. To know the breath and scent of the wind and have it fossilized in her memory. It would likely be a long time before Captain trusted her with access to the surface again, whether or not she had saved Delta.

She reached the door and stiffened at the familiar groan of the elevator as it opened on the side of the mountain. Taking a deep breath she boarded and took one last look toward the blue sky that blossomed over their ruined world. Another groan and it was all lost to her. She rested her back against the smooth cool metal wall.

The elevator arrived at the platform she had left just hours before. Anya headed straight for the Captain's office, for two reasons. The first was that she wanted to get her punishment over with and the second was that she had to pass his office to get down to her quarters. Sneaking past in the middle of the night had been easy. Going by unnoticed now was impossible.

Stairs at designated points along the circle platform would take her down to the ranger's quarters. At the lower levels there were hallways that would lead her to other parts of the base, but the top floor was the Captain's. He resembled a bit of an aging hero, with a

26

strong physique and graying hair.

Outside the Captain's door, the air felt charged, heavy with a static she couldn't explain. Through the frosted glass, she saw his silhouette, a broad-shouldered pillar of a man. He was unmoving, his voice a low, indistinguishable rumble. Something was definitely going on. She ran over a number of scenarios in her mind, trying to pinpoint the right thing to do.

"Anya."

Standing next to the Captain's door was a ranger who looked much like Delta but older. She carried herself with strength and confidence.

"Alright Rena, how much trouble am I in?"

The woman gave her a small smile. Anya got the feeling that everyone was in on something that she was not. Last time she had gone out when she wasn't supposed to, Captain was waiting for her at the elevator. He had set her working on the farms with no ranger duties for a month, a fate that nearly sent her surrendering to the other side.

Rena didn't scowl. Instead, she offered a thin, unsettling smile. The kind people gave to those who didn't know they were standing on a trapdoor. "The Captain's barely mentioned your little excursion. I think his mind is... elsewhere. He told me to put you in the conference room."

"Well...better get this over with." All of this was leading up to bad news, and she was trying to plan for every scenario she could think of as she continued along the platform. They had nearly reached the conference room when Rena grabbed her arm.

"Delta told me he was going to be exposed anyway, they were going to see a human no matter what...and at least you brought him home safe."

So that was it then. An immortal had seen two of them in close proximity to the base, so the rangers were thinking that they were going to evacuate. Anya certainly hoped the Captain did not think that such a small encounter would warrant moving the entire base.

Anya nodded to Rena and then headed to the conference room. She opened the metal door and looked around. There was a large table surrounded by chairs. On the wall was a large monitor turned on to the map which was dotted with little red circles. Many were covered with x's. She stood up and looked at all the little x's that represented lives lost. For each one she pictured Delta's face, or Ryan's or Mamoru's…rangers gone before their time. Gone before they truly had a chance to live.

She was still looking at the map when she heard the door open. She sucked in a breath through clenched teeth hidden behind her pink lips. When she turned to look at the Captain, the older man's face looked weathered and chiseled like the rock she had just climbed. The expression of sadness on his face warned her that whatever had arisen him so early this morning, it had little to do with her going on the surface.

He motioned to the chair beside him. Anya didn't sit. She yanked off her mask, letting her red hair spill across her face in a wild tangle, and leaned against the edge of the table. The metal was ice-cold under her palms. In the silence her dread only rose.

Captain looked at the map and then to the door. Part of her just wanted to shake him and tell him out with it. The other part of her, the part of her that knew what he was about to say, wanted to relish the last few moments of ignorance. There were a hundred other things that he could be upset about, but she could think of only one that would have them alone in this room with that look on his face.

"Phoenix was attacked."

She grimaced. Faces arose before her eyes. An entire base, the one where she was born, raised, trained, gone. Anya's hands gripped the edge of the table and her mind wandered to the sunrise she had just watched. To the gentle caress of the wind against her cheek, pushing back her hair. That moment of such beauty while those she knew lay dying.

She looked up at her Captain, the one who had continued her training, took her in and gave her the opportunity to prove the fight could be won without sacrificing their humanity. The cold edge of the metal table pressed deep into the thin black gloves she still wore. She could picture them all, picture the halls, eating dinner all together in the great room, the laughter that would ring out through the gathering room in the rare moments when there was nothing to do. It was all playing though her mind like a montage in one of the old movies Ryan had her sit through in the archives.

Through it all her mind and her mouth could only focus on one name. She knew the protocols, she knew what would happen, but she still had to ask. To try, to see if there was any chance that she would see him again. It was nearly Earth Day, they were supposed to celebrate, the way that they used to. She was going to show him everything, maybe even convince him to stay.

"Mamoru?"

"There have been a few Rangers at the checkpoint mostly the scouts, it seems most of the civilians got out but…" He looked at the door again, he spoke without looking at her. "The base was attacked at night; they had very little time to get the civilians out and they were probably ambushed trying to bring down the system."

Perhaps this was punishment for her moment in the sun. Maybe it was time she had to listen to the rules and just find a way to survive and die on her own terms, not theirs. But then Mamoru had always been great about following the rules and look where it got him. A lonely burned out death while she stood miles away watching the sunrise.

There was a chance he was still alive. Even if he followed protocol he might be leading the last of the civilians out or pinned down by immortals somewhere or being his usual stubborn self and giving his life to protect some useless data. But despite the lack of value the protocols put on the lives of Rangers, there was a chance…a chance she had to act on.

She felt the Captain lean against the table alongside her, his arms crossed in front of him. He was her commander but he had still taken it upon himself to look after her. Take her in when no one else would and put up with her insubordination much more than he should.

"I can't leave him to die." Anya said, her voice ringing with a sudden, terrifying clarity. "I know that it is all we are meant for in this life. To try and survive until they find and kill us. I know that, but I can't accept it. I've never been able to and you know that. Just this once I am going to make sure that it doesn't have to be that way. Today I am not going to just accept death."

She felt the Captain shift beside her. His fingers twitched against his arms, his jaw set in a hard line of internal conflict. He had taken her in when Phoenix cast her out, and had suffered her rebellion because he admired her spirit.

"Anya, the protocols—"

"To hell with the protocols!" she snapped, her eyes blazing. "If there's even a ghost of a chance he's out there, I'm going back."

The Captain looked at her then, seeing the fire that Phoenix had tried to extinguish. He didn't yell. He didn't call the guards. He reached for his wrist comm, his thumb hovering over the activation switch.

"Rena, the supplies I asked for. Bring them to the conference room immediately."

The Captain's voice was like grinding stone. Anya felt the weight of the command settle in her chest. This was a suicide mission, yet her Captain had already known exactly what her choice would be and had planned for it.

"You will have several Fulgars with full charges, first aid and several nutrient injections. You will also need to change your boots. If they see you, or you get caught, you cannot leave the markings of our base. They must think you are from Phoenix." Captain looked at her resigned and Anya nodded.

She had to be Mamoru's protector now. She had to believe that the one reason that she kept fighting, would keep fighting himself.

"And I started the day thinking the worst thing I'd get was kitchen duty," Anya said, her voice cracking with a forced levity. "Sending me on a suicide mission is a pretty creative way of getting me out of your hair, Captain."

He stood up abruptly, the humorless movement cutting her off. The long, deep lines of his face hardened, outlining a jaw that looked as though it were bracing for an impact. He didn't find the joke funny. He didn't find any of this funny.

"You have been with us for four years, Anya," he said, his voice dropping into a low, dangerous register. "You have fought and lived with my rangers. You have spat on my orders more times than I have gray hairs. Do you want to know why I haven't banned you? Why I haven't tossed you into the waste tubes?"

Anya was not sure if she was going to like this answer. One reason was that there was nowhere else to go. None of the other bases had offered to take in a discarded ranger.

"You fight because you believe that one day if you fight hard enough you and everyone else will get to live. You are rough around the edges, most people here do not get along with you, but somehow you still give them hope. I have turned you from a ranger no one wanted into a ranger that I can use to keep people from giving up." He looked away from her then and walked to the map on the wall. He drew a small x over the circle that marked the location of Phoenix base with his finger.

"I would have you stay Anya. I would order you to stay. But what would you do if I did so? What would you do if I confined you to quarters under guard?"

She would fight the whole base if she had to and he knew it. She was no use to him as a traitor but as a martyr? If he wanted a martyr, a martyr she would be, at least she would go down fighting for Mamoru.

"I am not going to stop you, but do not suggest that it is I that wants you on this fool's mission. You can do much more good here than dying in Phoenix trying to save someone that is already dead."

The words stung worse than a Fulgar strike. Anya pushed away from the table, taking a sharp, jagged breath. "I'm not trying to be a hero or a martyr for you, Captain. I just want a better life than this. I'm tired of losing the only people who make this hell worth it."

"Then get suited up," he said, his back still turned. "Stay in the dark gear. Take the service tunnel as far as it goes. Phoenix will have cut their power to ghost the base, and remember—until the survivors know who you are, you'll have enemies on both sides."

Anya nodded, her jaw set. As she turned to the door, the Captain spoke again, his tone shifting back to the familiar, gruff authority that felt like home.

"You do know that when you get back, I will still have to discipline you for breaking out again?"

Anya managed a small, bittersweet smile. "I know. But I'll probably just do it again."

"I know."

"I go crazy being cooped up down here," she added. "Besides, you need me. Your new boy Delta was shaking like a leaf out there."

"I know."

"Rena thinks the rumors are true. That we're evacuating because of the town encounter."

"I know."

"We shouldn't," Anya said firmly. "It was one Immortal. It doesn't prove anything." She pointedly left out the detail of the creature snooping through the old grocery store.

"I know."

Anya couldn't help but smile at her Captain, he was done being of any use to her. He was back to just the Captain.

Rena opened the door then carrying a new belt that was fully loaded with Fulgars and clips all the way around. A back pack fitted with a repelling line and a few extra supplies was on her shoulders. Rena also carried a pair of boots with soles marked with the current insignia of Phoenix. The boot marks were their unofficial way of communicating when on the surface. Anya traded boots and belt and then took the back pack from Rena. She was starting to wish she had at least got a full night's sleep.

"Be smart. Be strong. Be swift. And come back Anya."

4

Talus

"So it should be ready then?"

Talus held his left hand up to the harsh laboratory light, flexing his fingers in a slow, rhythmic sequence. He watched the play of tendons beneath his pale skin, wondering if this was the final time he'd feel the fluid grace of his own anatomy. It was not a bad appendage after all, he was right handed and this was his left—but it was a fine piece of biological engineering nonetheless, and he felt a sudden, sharp pang of preemptive mourning for it.

"It should be," Raina replied. He gestured toward the modified industrial freezer. "The pressurized seal around the outer rim is designed to cut off circulation entirely. It'll trap the hand in a vacuum while preventing the cold from escaping. Are you certain?"

Talus gave a stiff, mechanical nod. He refused to let the tremor in his gut reach his face. He knew this wouldn't kill him but he knew it was going to hurt with a ferocity he hadn't felt in decades. He remembered the coldest winter of his youth, when the air had turned into a blade that flayed the skin off your face. But the cold wasn't the enemy; it was the thaw. The agony of blood returning to frozen vessels was a medieval torture he was about to willingly invite back into his life.

Talus had been working with Raina through the night to see just

33

how cold they could make the freezer go. It was a completely insane idea, to freeze his own hand. He just had one more problem to solve that was proving to be trickier than he thought.

"This is going to be brutal, Talus," Raina warned, packing his specialized wrenches into a canvas roll. "Even for someone like you. The transition in and out of cryo-stasis…" Raina shook his head.

"Pain I can handle."

"Well, you're a braver man than I." Raina shouldered his pack, his eyes lingering on the hand-sized aperture in the freezer door. "I hope you find your answer.

"It is not a matter of bravery Raina."

He knew Raina would not understand him. No one in the base did, except for Cary. And even Cary was not likely to understand this time.

"I will be off then Talus. Should I send someone to make sure you are alright at the end of this? Maybe they could figure out how to get the blood you need."

Raina was trying to be helpful, everyone around him vacillated between offering assistance and avoidance. It was not too much unlike himself. For all he knew it was a side effect of the life they led.

He walked back to his tiny living quarters and sat in the chair. He weaved his fingers together and just looked at them. Then he looked at Lily's smiling picture on his desk. He wondered what she would think of his idea. Probably the same thing she thought about his other crazy ideas and which were often voiced, and followed up later by a round of I told you so's. Talus was the only one left to remember her that way. The only one who could picture her smile when she was really happy. The only one who could still clearly see the way her eyes would light up when she could help someone. She was such a godly thing, a trait that he often saw as a fault but not with her. Perhaps there really was a God just like she believed and he had found one hell of a way to punish the wicked.

"I'm running out of options, Lil," he whispered, tapping his condemned left hand against the cold metal desk. "Wish me luck."

He gave the picture a small salute that felt foolish. Yet it was no more foolish than talking to someone that had died decades before. He took one last lingering look at her.

"Tal, I'm back" Cary's voice exploded into the room, vibrating with a frantic, forced cheer. He framed himself in the doorway, his lanky frame leaning heavily against the steel casing. "and I hope you have a better answer for me than you did yesterday…and what is this bullshit about freezing your hand off? Raina seems to think you have kept him up all night just to engineer a new way for you to torture yourself."

The perplexed face of Cary invaded his quiet space, his two hands rested on the door frame as his body pressed into the room. Cary was a lanky sort of fellow with a bit of what they used to call a "boy band" look to him. But instead of picking up a microphone he had picked up a packet of seeds and tried to save the world.

Talus looked up at him and simply shrugged, his arms rubbing against the square edges of the chair he was resting in. "It is just another idea. Maybe if we freeze the cells to where they cannot move, then they cannot regenerate. It might be useful or it might not, either way it will be interesting." He stood and motioned for Cary to follow him into his lab.

"See here is the fridge, I will just put my hand in. Let it freeze for as long as I can stand and then pull it out. I am just debating the best method of testing the effectiveness."

Cary leaned down to get a look at the fridge that now had a thick, rubberized cuff protruding from the center of the door, designed to form a vacuum seal around the limb.

"What about cutting your hand and testing how long it takes for the cut to heal? It is not a perfect experiment since the stem cells would be trying to warm and revive the hand as well. But it could give you an idea of how much it would slow down the regeneration process, if it does not stop it entirely. Do you have something against your left hand that you have decided to do this?" Cary took Talus' left hand in his own. "It looks perfectly fine to me. Bejabbers, what did it ever do to you?"

Talus yanked it back, a flash of irritation crossing his face. "You didn't blink when I took a hatchet to it last year. Why does the freezer bother you?" He subconsciously rubbed his wrist, where the faint, silver line of a perfectly healed amputation remained.

"Because we don't know the variables this time," Cary snapped. "What if the cold shatters the stem cells? What if it doesn't grow back?"

Talus walked around Cary to reach for a scalpel from the shelf. He motioned to Cary to grab the timer that was on the wall behind him.

"It is the idea of the day Cary. Tomorrow I plan to strap some explosives to my chest and see what happens. You are the one that wants to help the humans, and to do that you need answers. We have no idea how to stop the Others. Ready?"

"Yes I am ready. But why the left hand?"

He pressed the scalpel into his palm, tracing his life line with a steady hand. He watched with clinical fascination; the wound didn't even have time to weep. The edges of the skin simply reached for each other, knitting back together in a blur of hyper-accelerated mitosis.

"Well the right hand is slightly more useful and I have terrible balance so losing a foot would be problematic."

"Three seconds, not bad. I wonder if I could do better? Shall we have a regeneration face off?"

Talus shot him a withering look. Cary always tried to use humor in situations where he felt uncomfortable. It was a trait that Talus had never particularly enjoyed.

"Alright so we will compare the frozen hand…once I can cut into it." He took a deep breath. He really was not sure what he was so scared of, he had hurt himself many times over the decades trying to find a weakness or any sort of answer to the mysteries surrounding their existence.

"You sure this is going to turn out alright?"

"Nope. All I know is that it is going to be cold and it is going to hurt."

Talus took one last look at his hand and then looked toward the small freezer once again. He shrugged. If he was not so sure that he would live he would not be doing this. But since he had that belief… he undid the seal on the hole and quickly shoved his hand in. For the first sixty seconds, there was nothing but a dull ache. Then, the needle-points of the cold began to flay him. It felt as though his skin were being scraped off with a rusted rasp, the chill burrowing into the marrow of his bones.

"Tal! Talus, it's getting cold in here. Why is it so cold? You didn't fecking mention I was going to freeze too!"

The pain began traveling up his arm, past where the seal should have been. Some part of his brain realized that he must not have closed it. He pushed himself forward toward the fridge and his shoulder crushed against the button. Instantly suction wrapped around his arm and pulled his hand in.

Soon his breathing slowed, the pain decreased. He started to feel nothing at all.

"So what now?"

"Give it time"

"How much?"

Talus shrugged. He was not sure but he did know that he was in no rush to remove his arm. The pain had moved past the screaming phase into a dull, terrifying void. His breathing slowed. His vision narrowed to a single point of white light. He felt his hand go from a part of his body to a heavy, senseless weight. Just a block of meat.

"Snookerdookies."

Talus raised an eyebrow. "What now?"

Cary shrugged. "Nothing else to do, thought I would try it out."

"So running out of curse words and thought you would make up your own?"

Cary nodded.

"That… is all the incentive I need… to end this," Talus gasped.

He punched the release. The vacuum hissed, and he wrenched his arm free. The second his hand hit the ambient air of the lab, he screamed. It wasn't a sound of anger; it was a primal, gut-wrenching shock. Pure fire erupted through his veins. His blood, warm and frantic, was trying to force its way back into a limb that was now a solid, translucent white, turning a bruised, necrotic black at the wrist.

"Tal…your hand…"

Talus barely registered Cary's words. He tried to shut his whole body down and escape. His eyes were pressed shut, his teeth clenched and his good hand was gripping the frozen one as if the extra support would stop the pain. It was all useless. The blackness was reminding him of why he was enduring this folly.

Slowly he peeled his eyes open, his teeth still clenched tightly. His hand up to his wrist was a brilliant white, turning gradually to black where the frozen tissue transitioned into an undamaged arm. So much dead tissue, did it stop the stem cells in his blood from being able to heal his body?

"Cary…the scalpel. Do it now!"

"Why I'd thought you'd never ask." Cary muttered.

Talus was too busy trying to go to a happy place, any place without the throbbing in his arm. He had been so wrong. When it came to cutting his hand off, the pain ended quickly and so did the regeneration. But this agony was unending, the blood felt like acid trying to burn its way into his frozen extremity. He pressed his back into the cabinet behind him, rolling back and forth. The movement and pushing his back and shoulder of his frozen arm into the hard cabinet was a minute distraction.

He heard Cary's steps and was glad that his friend was going to do the experiment because he was still not able to fight his way out. He felt his hand being lifted and he gasped at the touch. He clenched his teeth again. When he felt the chunk of loose flesh against his tongue, he realized his lip must have been caught between.

The actual pressure of the scalpel was barely noticeable and he wondered if the skin was still too frozen to penetrate. Forcing his eyes apart he looked down at his arm, half expecting the black arm to just be forced off since the flesh was dead. Instead he saw the black was turning to a pale purple…the stem cells were reviving the dead flesh.

"Tal I got through, I made the cut. But the blood underneath, it's red. Either it was never affected or the warm blood has already begun to heal your hand. Talus, don't screw with me you still owe me. Can you hear me?"

Talus did not need Cary to tell him that his warm, healthy blood was fighting his way through his hand, as if a war was pulsing through his veins. Hundreds of tiny soldiers were hacking away at the frozen flesh and he could feel every swing of every sword. The pain reached an apex at the tip of his fingers, one moment where it exploded throughout his entire arm causing him to scream in shock and agony. His eyes flew open and he began gasping trying to calm his body from the panic, but then it began to recede, leaving in waves of intensity.

He looked at his abused hand. The bright white warmed to the pale color that he knew so well. The black of his arm was gone and he could watch the colors disappear as if someone was taking an eraser to the last bits of cold and ice. Finally, when there was nothing but a dull ache, he stood up.

"Cold and pain. And you were worried. Next time do not doubt me." Talus tried to smile but the experience had left him a bit weak. He leaned back against the cabinet for support.

Cary glared at him. "Okay, I will never doubt your stupidity again you dunderhead. You did manage to slow down the healing though, took nearly two minutes."

Two minutes? That was something but they already knew that the more severe the wound the longer it took to heal. One of their kind had their legs blown to pieces and still managed to regenerate fully functioning legs. Talus had often wondered why only the needed legs regenerated. What prevented each half or each section of the body from regenerating into a full human? He thought it had something to do with the heart or the head but he had no way of testing it without risking someone's life or sentencing them to an even worse eternity.

"How long has it been since I put my hand in there?" Talus was still staring at the appendage in shock. He had honestly expected it to freeze solid and either fall off or require amputation.

"About 30 minutes."

30 minutes…this was yet another dead end. Sure it could slow someone down and maybe if the whole body was frozen it would stop

regeneration. Maybe if they asked nicely they could get the other immortals to stand still long enough to build a giant super freezer around them.

"So how did it feel?"

"Worse than having my hand cut off. It was hard to think or even breathe. All that to learn nothing except that it is even more pointless than we thought."

"Well don't do it again. That was fucking painful to watch."

"No...I will not be doing that again. Next plan was explosives remember?" Talus flashed a small smile at his friend.

"That is not funny Tal, you have no effing way of knowing the consequences."

"Isn't that the point? To find out?"

"The solution doesn't have to mean dying. You cannot keep torturing yourself for the choices the world made."

"If I wanted to kill myself do you think I would be here? Would any of us?" Talus grew quiet and turned away. He looked at all the vials lining the shelves, at all the notebooks filled with scribbles. He had one good idea all his life, one success followed by an eternity of failures. "There are people dying out there, dying because beings like us are slaughtering them. They are out there desperate for help and I have nothing. I am the one that is supposed to have the answers Cary!"

He knew it was out there, it had to be. If there was no answer then the true end of the human race would happen. All that would be left would be beings like them going on forever and trying to rebuild a planet in order to live out eternity alone. He walked through the room to where her picture rested. He stared at it as he gripped the desk. Lily always had the answers before, always knew the right thing to do, why wasn't she giving them to him now?

"I always hated your arrogance, Tal. Even back when we were kids. You actually believe you're the protagonist of the apocalypse," Cary continued, his voice echoing in the hollow lab. "For fuck's sake, man, you could barely pass English Lit. You're a brilliant chemist, but you aren't a god. You aren't capable of ending the entire world on your own, no matter how much you want to take the blame for it."

Talus sighed, his expression a mask of weary defiance. "Then who is responsible, Cary? If not the man who unlocked the door?"

"The people outside are still fighting," Cary said, stepping into the room. He gestured vaguely toward the surface. "They've spent a century learning how to wound the unwoundable. They've hunted our kind, they've damaged us in ways we didn't think possible. Maybe they've found the weakness you're too close to the project to see."

"Reach out to the humans. See what they need but don't tell them who we are, they probably would not trust you if you did."

Talus knew that much from experience.

5

Anya

Anya sprinted toward the transit tubes, her boots ringing hollow against the corrugated metal of the maintenance deck. She knew the tunnels wouldn't take her all the way to the heart of the disaster, but the surface was a graveyard of open sky and scanning eyes. Underground was the only way to move fast without becoming a target. If the immortals were attacking a base, then they would have plenty of cover both above and below the surface. They were very paranoid for creatures that could not die.

"Anya, Anya are you there?"

The voice crackled in her ear, warm and frayed. She smiled despite the iron tang of fear in her mouth. Ryan. He was still at the comms, probably vibrating from too much caffeine and a complete lack of sleep, refusing to let anyone else take his shift while she was in the wire.

"I'm here, Ry. Don't tell me you're still awake."

"I'll sleep when you're back. Listen, I know I'm not supposed to do this, but I've hijacked the mag-rail override. I've activated a high-velocity transport burst toward Phoenix. It's a dirty signal, and the system is going to throw a fit, so the tunnels will still be dead-sealed when you arrive. You have to jump before you hit the terminus wall or you're going to be a very flat Ranger."

She could picture him, hunched over the computer, whispering as he not only stayed past shift but broke protocol. The system was supposed to be offline now, lest the immortals figure out how they got around the tunnels so easily. It was technology that they did not plan on sharing. Despite that he still took time to state the obvious, she smiled to herself.

"Got it. Jump before I go splat. Stop mothering me, Ryan."

"Just get there, Anya. Magnets engaging in three... two... one..."

Anya snapped a high-tension clip from her belt and looped the wrist-strap tight. She hooked the carabiner onto the overhead guide-rail and stepped onto the lower mag-pipe. She felt the sudden, violent tug of the magnets locking onto the steel plates in her boots. A low hum of electricity vibrated through her soles, then—force.

The world vanished into a strobing blur of concrete and shadow. Ryan had pushed the magnets to their absolute limit. The wind whipped her red hair into a frenzy against her mask, the friction heat rising until the air smelled of scorched metal. She was a human bullet screaming through the dark.

Suddenly, the red emergency lights of the Phoenix terminus wall flared in the distance, rushing toward her at a terrifying speed.

She slammed the release on her belt. The magnets died instantly. The momentum threw her forward; she tucked her chin to her chest, hit the deck with a bone-jarring thud, and rolled. She came to a stop inches from the sealed blast door, her lungs burning, every muscle screaming in protest.

"Anya, I can't open the gate now but if you get to the other side without being followed I can override it and let you out. But without knowing what's out there..."

No sense risking the immortals finding this tunnel or ambushing her. She checked that her mask was completely secure before looking for surface access. Anya found the ladder carved into the rock wall. It was a jagged, vertical climb that led to a narrow maintenance hatch. She ascended with practiced silence, her heart hammering a frantic rhythm against her ribs.

She cracked the hatch just an inch. An immortal stood ten feet away, his back turned, his long gray coat fluttering in the mountain wind. He was scanning the horizon, bored and arrogant. He didn't think there was a human left alive with the spine to challenge him.

She pulled her legs up to the highest rung of the ladder that she could. She tried to slow her breathing, just waiting until he turned just enough that he would not see where she came from. He was going to be down for a while but he would know exactly what happened to him.

She surged out of the hatch in a single, explosive movement, launching herself onto his back. She wrapped one arm around his throat and slammed her Fulgar into the side of his neck. The device unleashed a savage blue arc of electricity. The immortal's body went rigid, his eyes rolling back as he slumped to the dirt.

"One down," she hissed.

"The other sentry is a mile south, near the primary ridge access," Ryan reported.

She refrained from telling Ryan that Phoenix was where she had grown up, she knew where the damn access panels were.

"I'm going silent now, Ry. I'll ping you if I'm alive to need a ride home."

"Just make sure you come back Anya. The halls are lined with the blood of martyrs, don't be one of them."

"Been saving that one have ya?"

"Read it in a book and memorized it just for you."

She shook her head and shrugged. There were worse quotes that she could inspire in people…and better ones.

She ran across the broken terrain, staying low in the scrub. She reached the second sentry just as he was turning to investigate a sound. She didn't wait. She dove through the air, rolled through a spray of gravel, and delivered a sweeping kick that took his legs out. As he hit the ground, she pressed the Fulgar to his neck and emptied the charge.

Two stuns. She had half an hour, maybe less, before their regenerative systems shook off the shock and they alerted the rest of the hive.

Anya dropped down into the access. The whole tunnel was clouded with smoke. It was common procedure to destroy anything

44

that might have useful information. It was a dangerous process but it was quick and it kept working even after the people had fled. Anya walked slowly, she had no idea what her plan was. She did not even know how many she was up against or where they were. She had never come to a base during an attack before. Protocol dictated that the Rangers first evacuate and then destroy data. Their first stop would have been the barracks so that would be hers too. She would not leave without finding him, one way or another.

Anya placed fresh charges in both Fulgars. With luck she would not pass many of the immortals before reaching the clusters of barracks. A few more steps and the whole of Phoenix opened up before her. It was built in a similar fashion to Tigris, tunnels branching out from the center hole.

Her steps slowed. Her movements became much more deliberate. Bodies lined the floor, all of them rangers. They had all laid down their lives to give others a few extra minutes to escape. She looked at each face as she passed. Names and memories floated to her mind. Anya pushed back the emotion with so much force that it felt like the lump in her throat had been punched.

As she neared the Captain's quarters, she heard voices. They were cold, resonant, and devoid of empathy. Immortals. They were in the Captain's quarters, probably trying to salvage the very data the Rangers had died to burn.

"Human!" a voice barked from behind her.

Anya spun. An immortal stood on the stairs, his pistol raised.

"Nightmare." she spat back.

Anya dove down among the bodies as the first bullet was fired. That was going to make things harder since she had no doubt that the others would have heard that. She grabbed the ankle of the immortal.

She pulled him down. There was only time for a quick shock. Others would be on the way.

The stairs down to the barracks were going to take far too much time. Anya took her rappelling line and clipped it to the pole concealed just under the platform. She dropped three levels in a terrifying freefall, the friction of the cord burning through her gloves.

She kicked off the wall, swinging onto the barracks landing.

More dead rangers.

More memories.

More anger.

No Mamoru.

She wondered how many immortals had fallen here, how many humans did they take down with them? To die in order to stun an immortal creature for the length of time it took to make breakfast was a waste of life.

No guards on this floor, they were all too busy up above. Some might see it as an oversight but the only way to escape the barracks would be to go up or down, and immortals were waiting in both directions. These bases were not built to be able to escape an invasion.

Opening the door to the first barrack Anya walked past all the doorways that led to each family's living quarters. Instead at the end of the long hallway was a wall. She pulled off her glove and pressed her hand to a slight discoloration on the surface. The door slid open. Empty.

She hung her head. She was not sure what she had been expecting, Mamoru would not be hiding in any of these rooms if there was even a chance of getting civilians out. She walked back to the main platform and decided to head down to the Ranger barracks. Mamoru was often dispatched to assist the younger Rangers because he had a certain knack with them. It was how they had first met and he felt compelled to take her under his wing to calm her rebellious nature.

There were a few bodies on the Ranger platform but it was largely deserted. Most of the Rangers had lost their lives defending the upper level of the base, or trying to get out through the surface exit.

He must be down on the lower levels somewhere. If that had been his assignment he might have been able to get up to the escape tunnels before he was pinned down or wounded. She took a step toward the stairs to the next platform when she heard a whimper. Her entire body froze and every centimeter of her body tensed. She turned around and took one quiet step in the direction of the sound.

A sniffle.

A shush.

Somewhere there were people hiding. She knew every inch of the Ranger barracks and headed toward the storage closet. She pressed her ear to the door and heard a muffled voice within. Perhaps Mamoru was hiding in there, waiting for the right moment to get a child out. It would be hard to tell when the pathway was clear.

She slid the panel open and bit her lip to hide her disappointment. Inside were three children, two girls and a boy. They looked barely old enough to be in the Ranger program, probably only recently tossed away by their families. The children looked up at her in fear, each one clutching a few toys. She gave a small smile. That was why the children were in the storage closet. It was where they had hidden the toys they were no longer allowed to have. She knelt down in front of them and widened her smile.

"Hey, don't be frightened. I am here to rescue you. No one forgot. I came back all this way to make sure you get out safely."

She knew what it was like. Knew the hopelessness, knew feeling completely alone and unloved. These children had no one and now they had been left behind to die. She couldn't abandon them, they had been abandoned enough to last a lifetime. Instead she would give them hope that somewhere out there was someone who would care for them, just like Mamoru had cared for her.

The biggest girl looked to the others and they both nodded to her. They each dropped their toys and stood up.

"We are ready to follow you Ranger Ma'am."

All three children gave her a solemn salute and it caused a familiar anger to well up in her. She removed her pack and shoved the toys the children had been carrying into it. It was bigger and bulkier than she would have liked but it was worth it.

"None of that now. Just call me Anya. I'm going to get you out of here and then later the four of us will have some fun at my base okay? Just because you are a Ranger now doesn't mean you can't be a kid too. Follow closely and obey every command and we'll be safe in no time."

They each nodded and Anya motioned for them to follow her

back the way she had come.

As they reached the rappelling line, a sharp pain blossomed in Anya's side. She stumbled, her hand going to her waist. It came away slick and crimson. Shot. She hadn't even felt it.

"Human!"

The immortal from the upper deck had recovered. He stood above them, aiming down. Anya didn't think. She reached into her belt and pulled out a prototype Plasma Globe. The new technology Tigris had not yet tested in the field. She could only hope it worked as Ryan has promised. She hurled it at the upper gantry.

The world turned blue. A massive discharge of static electricity filled the shaft, screaming like a dying god. The immortal collapsed in a heap of twitching limbs.

"Go! Up the stairs! Now!" Anya shoved the children toward the upper tunnels. Every movement sent a fresh spike of agony through her side, but she kept them moving.

"Anya…what…how…?" The oldest girl questioned.

She motioned to her ears to let the children know that she didn't want the immortals below overhearing.

The oldest girl nodded and took the hands of the other two. Anya motioned for the children to come to her side. Grabbing the free hand of the small boy she held it up. "Don't let go of each other."

They nodded and Anya reached into her bag for some smoke grenades. She threw one in each direction and then pulled the children through the growing smoke toward the tunnel.

"Ryan open the tunnel. Activate transport ability on my command. We're heading to the Phoenix rendezvous."

"All clear Anya? You sure?"

"Not if you waste time. Open the damn tunnel!"

He quickly obeyed. Anya pulled the children through. She did a quick check in the hazy light to make sure all three were still with her.

"Close the tunnel and activate the magnets to the rendezvous" Anya gasped out as the adrenaline started to fade and her wound made itself known.

"Anya?" Ryan asked.

"Do it Ryan, I'll be fine."

The tunnel closed just as quickly as it had opened. She stared at it for a moment trying to force away that sense of dread. She would be coming back, she just had to get the children to the rendezvous first.

The Phoenix rendezvous was underground two miles away from the base. It was meant as a stopping point so the survivors could find the safest base to turn to, or head back home if it turned out to be a false alarm.

She put the children on the tubes ahead of her so that she could watch them. This was a journey that everyone started practicing from the moment they could hold on to the pipes. It was only a few minutes away but her mind imagined Mamoru's fate for each second of those minutes until they arrived.

The four of them jumped off the pipe and walked towards a solid wall. The secret room was well hidden and the doorway betrayed nothing of the massive space within. As they approached the door opened and they were greeted by Burion, a Ranger from Phoenix.

"Anya? What are you doing here?"

She was surprised that Burion recognized her because he had barely entered the Ranger program before she had been expelled from it. He was still very young but obviously one of the lucky few Rangers to escape.

"I went to Phoenix to see if I could help and to find Mamoru, but I found these guys instead."

She knelt down beside the three children and removed her pack. She delivered each child their treasured toy and stood back up.

"Did you know where Mamoru was?"

"Anya..." Burion looked at her sadly and reached out to touch her shoulder. "Even if he did survive somehow you don't have time to find him before they blow up the whole base. I saw them placing charges as we were getting out."

Anya pressed her lips together, biting down on them to keep the sob inside of her where it belonged. All this, and she still did not have what she came for. Well It was a suicide mission anyway; she might as well take it all the way.

"Get the rest of them to Tigris. I'm going back."

"You've been shot, you are going to be slow and you won't be able to find him before the whole base explodes."

"The place is full of stunned immortals. They will not blow the place with them inside."

"Of course they will, they're immortal. They'll all regenerate by tomorrow with nothing more than a headache."

The others started to disappear down the tunnel. Anya was glad that at least her attempt to get Mamoru was not entirely in vain. There were some who would live because of her efforts. Now all she had to do was get back down there and find him. Dead or alive she had to know.

"I'm going Burion. Your duty as a ranger is to get all the civilians to safety. Take them to Tigris." Anya left no room for discussion. Her side was throbbing. The black suit did a good job of hiding most of the blood, but the gaping hole left by the bullet was hard to miss.

"Well if this is goodbye." Burion held out his arms for a hug and moved toward her. Anya could do nothing but raise an eyebrow as the boy she barely knew wrapped his arms tightly around her.

"Lucky for you Fulgars don't just work on immortals."

6

Talus

Talus sat alone on the jagged spine of the mountain, a solitary figure etched against a sky the color of a bruised plum. He drew deeply from his cigarette, the acrid, familiar smoke tantalizing his nostrils before curling away into the thin, freezing air. Below him, the world was a patchwork of scars and shadow—a silent testament to the devious evolution of human warfare.

Cary would be making contact with the other bases soon and he had some idea of how it would go, but perhaps Cary would have better luck. Most of the underground bases that had been built before the war were in the Southern Hemisphere, which was thought by scientists of the time to be the place with the best chance of surviving a nuclear holocaust. But little of the world had been spared as the bombs had gotten bigger, stronger and much more devious than any scientist could have predicted. Such was the curse of scientific advancement; it was born from logic and reason and then controlled by emotion and greed.

He looked down at the gold cigarette case resting in his palm, the metal worn smooth by decades of restless thumbing. He wondered how much the humans truly knew of their own history. The real genesis of immortality was likely a ghost story now, lost to all but the few who had stood in the epicenter of the miracle. The proof the world never wanted: that death was the very thing that defined the soul.

After all these years it never ceased to amaze him how agonizingly clear those memories still were. Decades could pass from one recollection to the next and it was just as if he were perpetually watching a high-definition reel of his own failures. Perhaps that was what made it so hard to get over her, and so hard to see humans again.

She had a bleeding heart that went beyond anything he had ever seen. A complete stranger could come up to her and ask for a favor and Lily would find a way to make it happen. Far too often she arrived late to a date or a party because she had stopped to get a poor man some food or help a child find their mother. At first, in his youthful cynicism, he'd chalked it up to a calculated bribe for her God—a down payment on a heavenly mansion. But as he'd watched her, he realized she didn't want a reward; she simply couldn't help but pour herself into the cracks of the world. He would have loved her until the stars burned out if he hadn't been the one to strike the match that set the world on fire.

"What do I tell them, Lily? How do I help them? You always knew that this was not the way that people were meant to live. Yet you offered no answers and no solutions, just trust, trust that your imaginary friend would use his mythical powers to make everything alright. You wanted us to defy everything we know of science and the universe and trust in God. What God would allow this? Would allow all his people to suffer just to punish one man?" He took his first draw from the half burnt cigarette and leaned back against the rock behind him.

He had no tangible weapons to offer the Rangers, no serums to grant them the strength they lacked. He had only theories, violent, desperate theories with little hope of success. He thought of the dark ideas in his notebook: stoking the fires of a volcano, overloading the bio-electric energy within their own stem cells until they detonated, or the crude simplicity of high-yield explosives. He had never tried the worst of his theories because there was always the chance of subjecting someone to a living hell in a destroyed body or one in eternal pain.

"I wish I could believe in your God, Lily. Success would mean so much more if it meant that I could spend eternity in heaven with you. Make good on that promise to love you forever."

Emotions were rarer for him now but when he thought of her, they came back. He knew without a doubt in his mind that it was Lily that preserved what humanity he had left.

"Talus! Talus Marin! You brain-dead jellyfish, stop moping around here. Cary sent me to get you." Talus felt a firm arm on his shoulder and turned to see Kit. Her energy was a jarring contrast to the stagnant air of the peak.

"I have no desire to talk to them." He knew Kit was rolling her eyes at him.

"Are you not the least bit curious?" she countered, stepping around him to face the horizon. She looked sixteen, her blonde curls dancing in the gale, but her eyes held the weight of centuries. "Think about it, people with expiration dates, fighting against people who have none. You have got to wonder how they survived this long, how much they have seen and overcome…you could not write a better story."

Talus' hand shot out, slamming against the stone ledge with a crack that should have shattered bone. "And tell me Kit, in your little story what am I? The hero? The villain? Or just the architect of the prison?"

Kit paused for a moment. When he looked she seemed to actually consider his question.

"That would depend on what you do next I think. After all, your story is not done yet either, just because it is a veeeeeery long one doesn't mean that you can't change the ending." Kit moved closer and looked out toward the horizon. "You still love her so much. If she were standing here right now, in the middle of this mess, what role would she play? Would you be brave enough to join her?"

Talus looked up at the sky and then to the gold cigarette case he still held in his palm. It was an easy guess where Lily would be in this battle. She'd be in the trenches, tending to the wounded, probably scolding an immortal for their lack of empathy while she bandaged a human's hand, but he also had no doubt that she would not want him by her side. She had made that obvious enough when she was alive. But he never would have let her fight such a battle on her own, especially not one that he had such a hand in creating.

His fingernail slid into a groove in the cigarette case. "You have the same ability to talk me into things I have no desire to do. Do you know that?"

"I will take that as a compliment." Kit chirped.

"Take it how you will, but know that even she wasn't good enough at it to save me from myself." His lips were set in a firm line as his eyes bored into the picture.

"Well then I will just have to be better." Kit said, turning to head back down the mountain path. "I grow weary of the same life Talus day and day out. I want to travel and actually have something worth seeing. I want to meet new people, experience new things. I have all the time in the world but so little of it actually matters."

Talus watched her silhouette retreat into the mountain's shadow. His mind drifted back to the 'before'—to the smell of old library books, the frantic energy of a university lab, the terrifying, exhilarating rush of falling in love. Kit had never known those things, despite her immortality. She was a frozen moment in a world that had moved on. Perhaps it was time for the world to change again, though he knew better than anyone that one stone cast into the water created ripples that never truly stopped.

Talus left the wind-scoured peak behind, descending the steep, rocky trail that wound down into the subterranean belly of the sanctuary. He deliberately steered away from the sector housing his personal quarters and his beloved laboratory, instead taking the long, echoing corridors that led toward another area of the base. His side of the complex was a sprawling graveyard of empty rooms and dormant consoles. A silent remnant of a time when the base had been teeming with researchers, engineers, and families. Now, the dust lay thick and undisturbed on the floor plates, rising in tiny, silver motes wherever his boots broke the silence.

He told himself he liked the quiet, liked the separation. He had never been good with people anyway. But the lie always cracked against the nagging, unyielding silence. The hours stretched out in a suffocating vacuum, punctuated only by the rhythmic hum of the base's geothermal generators. The quiet reminded him of his absolute isolation, ticking away the centuries much like a heavy grandfather clock used to ring out the hours in a past life. Before the war, his lab had been a chaotic symphony of clinking glass, murmuring voices, and frantic, late-night debates. It had never been silent.

At the end of a long, dimly lit corridor, he pushed open the heavy blast door of the communications hub. The room was surprisingly small, cramped, and archaic. It bore a striking resemblance to the tactical communications bunkers depicted in twentieth-century war films—the kind they used to broadcast on history networks before the world lost its history. Knobs, analog dials, and bulky cathode-ray monitors lined the workstations, chosen specifically because their primitive circuitry was impervious to the sophisticated EMP pulses that had fried modern electronics.

Cary was already inside, hunched over a main terminal beside Elan. Elan's fingers were a blur across a mechanical keyboard, his eyes reflecting lines of glowing amber code. Elan was the base's quiet miracle; he could dismantle, rewrite, or repair any digital architecture they managed to break. It was a skill born purely of necessity. Once, in the decades immediately following the collapse, Elan had been the worst offender in the base for accidental system deletions and hardware malfunctions. But time and survival had driven him to mastery, proving that necessity was indeed the ruthless mother of invention.

"Has there been any response?" Talus asked, his voice cutting through the steady clacking of the keyboard.

Cary and Elan both looked up simultaneously, their faces pale under the harsh fluorescent tubes.

"No," Cary said, leaning back in his swivel chair and tossing a stylus onto the desk. He gestured sharply toward Elan. "Because shortstop here refuses to open the transmission channels without your official authorization. Remind me, Tal, when exactly did you get appointed Commander-in-Chief? I don't recall us holding an election down here."

Talus walked into the room, a faint, wry smile touching his lips as he looked at his oldest friend. He gave a brief, respectful nod to Elan. "Really, Cary? I'm hurt. Everyone else was there. We threw a massive party, tons of fanfare, speeches... I'm fairly certain Kit brought balloons. Maybe you were just too busy pruning your hydroponic flowers to notice."

Cary let out a soft grunt, shaking his head as a bitter smile ghosted over his features, though his eyes remained tight with irritation. "Hilarious. At least I actually have communication access now, your Excellency."

"Here are the military frequencies we've been intercepting over the last forty-eight hours," Elan interrupted, his voice flat, his gaze snapping instantly back to the amber monitor. He didn't have time for their banter. "I've decrypted roughly eighty percent of the traffic. The operators keep cycling the encryption keys every six hours, but the structural algorithms barely change. Both sides are completely oblivious to the fact that the other is listening, yet their code structures are remarkably similar to the pre-war military encryptions used by the old North American coalition. It's lazy. It's like they aren't even trying to hide it."

Talus dragged a heavy metal stool over to the primary console, seating himself at the edge of the workstation. He turned his back to Cary and Elan, staring at the cascading walls of text. "There was a time, Elan, when you wouldn't have been able to solve a child's Sudoku puzzle in a Sunday paper, so I wouldn't judge them quite so harshly. Those people haven't had centuries of idle, empty time to sit in a climate-controlled bunker and study mathematics. They've been entirely occupied with the exhausting business of trying not to starve or bleed to death."

Cary's chair screeched against the floor plates as he stood up. "Talus, you utter zounderkite!" he shouted, the old, archaic insult dripping with genuine anger. "How long have you been sitting on this data? How long have you been quietly listening to their radios while they fight, scream, and die out there?"

Talus inwardly cringed at Cary's words. His friend was like Lily in many ways, they both believed that one person could save the world. When in reality all it took was one fool person to destroy it, and the latter was far more likely.

"I never stopped." Talus said quietly.

Cary slammed his fist down onto an empty, dark terminal beside Elan, the metal casing rattling violently. Elan didn't even flinch, his fingers maintaining their steady, rhythmic typing. Talus couldn't bring himself to blame Cary for the outburst. His friend had every right to be furious that the ongoing survival of the human race had been kept a secret from him for decades. But Talus shielded himself with a colder truth: what good would the knowledge have done? They had no cure for immortality. They had no weapon to balance the scales. They had nothing to offer then, and they still had nothing to offer now.

"Why have we been sitting here doing nothing when they've been dying?"

"What could we do, Cary? Tell me!" Talus spun his stool around, his eyes flashing with a rare, sudden heat. "What could we have possibly done to alter the outcome? And stop acting so incredibly naive. You knew just as well as I did that the global sanctuary networks were being hollowed out of these mountains decades before the first missile left its silo. You knew they were engineered to sustain human populations for generations. Did you honestly believe they all sat empty when the sirens finally wavered? Did you think the species just politely vanished because it was convenient for your conscience?"

"After all these years have you learned nothing about playing God?"

"I have learned the consequences of a war between people who cannot die!" Talus roared back, standing up to meet Cary's glare.

The tension in the small room was thick enough to choke on, the air heavy with decades of unspoken resentment and shared guilt.

"If you two can manage to stop bickering for thirty seconds, I can give you the translation of the latest packet," Elan said. His voice was chillingly calm, a detached anchor in the storm of their argument.

He struck a final key with an authoritative click. The cascading code vanished, replaced by a single, stark line of translated text at the top of the amber screen.

Talus and Cary broke their stare, both leaning over Elan's shoulders to read the glowing letters.

PHOENIX BREACHED. PROTOCOL FOLLOWED.

"That was the last message?"Talus murmured, his anger instantly evaporating into a cold, hollow dread. He reached out, his fingers hovering just above the screen as if he could pull more context from the glass.

"Sent in the middle of the night. Hardly time to get everyone out before protocol." Talus muttered, his mind visualizing the panic, the dark tunnels, the screams of children echoing in the steel corridors of Phoenix base.

He turned away from the terminal and walked toward a massive, dark screen that dominated the far wall of the communications hub. He placed his right palm against the bio-metric interface at the base of the frame. The scanner whirred, a green line tracing his skin before the screen erupted into brilliant, blinding color.

A high-resolution topographic map of the planet materialized, its continents crinkled with mountain ranges and valleys, completely overlaid with a galaxy of tiny, colored pins. Cary walked up behind him, his anger temporarily subdued by the sheer scale of the data hidden from him for so long. Talus knew the question his friend was tracking, and rather than waiting for the accusation, he simply pointed to the map.

"Red is for active sectors," Talus explained, his voice hollow. "These are the sanctuaries where we have confirmed human populations living entirely underground. Most of these communities have been isolated for at least two generations, developing their own cultures, their own laws, and their own armies. The blue pins... those are the ghosts. Those are the bases that have been completely wiped off the network. Yellow indicates potential human construction—scouts digging new outposts or trying to salvage old surface ruins. And the black pins..." Talus paused, his finger tracing a cluster of dark, jagged markers near the northern ridges. "The black is where our logs indicate the Others are operating."

"What is their objective, Talus?" Cary asked, his voice dropping into a whisper as he stared at the heavy scattering of blue and black across the hemisphere. "Why are they hunting them?"

"Even with Elan decoding their military channels, we don't know," Talus admitted, his shoulders slumping. "The Others don't use radios. They don't transmit data. They move like a virus, and they leave no records behind."

"And what about the protocols?" Cary asked, pointing to the text on Elan's monitor. "What does it mean when a base says 'protocol followed'?"

Talus was silent for a long moment, the weight of his historical knowledge pressing down on his chest like a lead weight. He knew exactly what the protocols were; he had read the military survival blueprints before the concrete had even cured.

"The human bases in this sector; and likely across the other continents, are linked together by a massive, undocumented web of sub-surface transit tunnels," Talus said, his voice dropping into a clinical, detached rhythm to keep his emotions at bay. "Most of them were excavated during the final years of the resource wars or immediately after the fallout cleared, meaning there are no official maps in the old government archives. They were engineered so that the survivors could migrate between bases to escape localized cave-ins, trade hydroponic yields, or hold council without risking surface radiation or radio interception.

"The protocol," Talus continued, swallowing hard, "dictates that the moment the human scouts detect the presence of the Others approaching a base, they initiate a total evacuation of the civilian tiers. They pack what they can carry into the transit lines. As the rearguard retreats, they are ordered to systematically demolish every terminal, burn every server, and collapse the entry arches. They leave nothing behind that could reveal the location of the neighboring sanctuaries. Once the primary vault is fully breached by the enemy... the engineers detonate the main transit tunnels. They seal the blast gates from the outside."

Cary's face drained of color. "They blow the tunnels? Even if their own soldiers are still inside fighting?"

"They leave people to die in the dark," Cary whispered.

"What other choice do they have, Cary?" Talus snapped, turning to face him. "They are outmatched, outgunned, and fighting a nightmare entity that regenerates from a bullet wound before the casing even hits the floor. The only strategy they have left is total information denial. They sacrifice the few to keep the network hidden from the hive. So far, it's the only reason the species hasn't been completely extinguished. The Others only seem to stumble onto these bases by accident or through sheer proximity during surface sweeps."

"While we sit in the shadows and do nothing of course." Talus could feel the heat of Cary's anger but he still stood by his decision. At least he had until an arrogant little girl err young woman showed up on his mountain. He had accepted that humans did not want their intervention. That they would never be able to trust him.

"If you want that equation to change, Cary—if you genuinely believe you have a strategy that doesn't end in us being hunted by both sides—then be my guest," Talus said, throwing his hands out in a gesture of bitter invitation. "But understand this: they will not trust us. The moment they discover what we are, the moment they see a wound heal on our skin, they will turn their guns on us. If we open that door, we have to tell them a story. And it had better be the most convincing lie we've ever told."

"And then what?" Cary asked, his defiance faltering slightly as the practical weight of the problem settled on him.

Talus threw his hands up in sheer exasperation, letting out a sharp, mocking laugh. "Look at you! You spend an hour screaming at the way I run this sanctuary, calling me a tyrant, and the moment I offer you the wheel, you immediately defer back to my lead. You want to be the savior, Carebear, but you don't want to design the cross."

Talus walked toward the heavy steel exit door, his hand resting on the cold brass handle. He stopped, his gaze lingering one last time on the sprawling, scarred map of the world, the blue pins representing thousands of lives that had gone out in the dark.

"Elan," Talus ordered, his tone shifting back to the quiet authority of a director. "Send a tight-beam, low-frequency communique to the coordinates for Tigris base. Keep it brief. Tell them we are an independent survival outpost and that we want to assist with logistical data and agricultural supplies. Tigris is currently the largest active hub on the red network; if Phoenix has fallen, Tigris is the next logical target in the line of march. They are going to need help the most."

He turned his eyes to Cary, his expression deadly serious. "Cary, whatever you do during that transmission, whatever narrative you construct to get them to trust you... do not mention my name. Even if you lose your mind and tell them the absolute truth about what we are, ensure they never find out that Talus Marin is alive down here."

Talus knew that the names of who had worked in this base had been removed from all records. But he had no idea if there were still some that might know his name, who he was. They might one day trust an immortal, but if they knew his history they would never trust him. Cary and Elan both watched him in silence, their heads nodding in a slow, solemn agreement.

Talus pulled the heavy door open, stepping back out into the freezing, empty corridors of the dead wing. He walked quickly, his coat billowing behind him, eager to return to the only place in the entire ruined world where he felt any semblance of peace: the quiet, sterile loneliness of his laboratory.

"What? Done already? I was just coming with some popcorn."

Talus looked up at the vaulted concrete ceiling and inwardly cursed his luck. Or perhaps he cursed Lily; because if there was such a thing as an afterlife, a lingering consciousness somewhere in the ether, sending Kit to disrupt his brooding was exactly the sort of playful vengeance Lily would orchestrate.

He turned toward the corridor to see Kit leaning against the door frame, balancing a deceptively large ceramic bowl heaped with freshly popped kernels. The rich, buttery scent cut right through the cold, metallic tang of the underground base. It was an uncanny sight; despite centuries of isolation and the collapse of global supply chains, some human traditions stubbornly persisted among them, maintained like sacred, domestic rituals.

Talus sighed, rubbing the bridge of his nose. "You have some sort of obsession with food."

"And you avoid it like it has the power to kill you," Kit retorted, stepping into the hallway. She tossed a kernel into the air and caught it expertly in her mouth. "If you would just sit down and eat a proper meal once in a while, our tech team wouldn't have to keep boosting the base's internal energy output just to keep your cell-regeneration stable. Now, don't try to slickly change the subject. I thought you were supposed to be in there talking to them."

"I gave Cary and Elan the data. I told them exactly who to contact and what to say—or, more accurately, what not to say," Talus muttered, crossing his arms over his chest. "Is that not sufficient?"

"First contact with the human survivors in decades... an absolutely historic moment... and you're leaving it entirely up to Cary and Elan to make a stellar first impression." Kit looked at him with a sharp, knowing smirk, her ocean-blue eyes dancing with amusement. "Cary, who genuinely behaves as though every curse word invented between the sixteenth century and the apocalypse is a necessary piece of sentence structure, and Elan, who fundamentally communicates in monosyllabic grunts. It's a flawless plan, Tal."

A dry chuckle threatened to break past Talus' lips despite his best efforts to maintain his solemn facade. It was infuriating how easily she did that. His thoughts were constantly attempting to drift back down into those pitch-black valleys of guilt and history they visited every single night, and yet, with a single snarky comment, she managed to hook his collar and pull him right back into the present.

"You are being incredibly unfair," Talus said, his voice dropping into a tone of mock defense. "Cary was a remarkably eloquent speaker back in our university days. He holds a doctorate." He paused, his conscience forcing him to add, "Granted, it's in botany."

Kit let out a soft, melodic laugh. "See? I rest my case. But fine, if you say they'll handle it, I suppose they will. I'll just pop my head in and see how the diplomacy is going."

"They probably won't even receive a response right away," Talus said, trying to inject more certainty into his tone than he actually felt. He leaned back against the cool, damp concrete wall. "The Rangers might just ignore the signal entirely. They have no idea who we are, and frankly, telling them the truth about our little immortal sanctuary wouldn't exactly inspire them to trust us any better."

"Quite right." Kit nodded, her expression softening as she stepped closer. She took another handful of popcorn, the sound of the crunch loud in the quiet hallway. "I guess I'll just go in then, and you can slink back to the safety of your dark laboratory. I'm sure one of us will bother to fetch you if the world starts ending again."

She reached out, her fingers wrapping around the cold brass handle of the communications door.

Talus' gaze flicked down the long, empty corridor toward his laboratory. A place of absolute silence, white light, and ghosts. Then his eyes drifted back to Kit and the steaming bowl of popcorn. The warmth of it felt intoxicatingly real, a sensory anchor pulling at memories of an era when life was measured in years rather than centuries. If he just took a single bite, he could close his eyes and pretend that none of this was real. He could pretend the world outside was whole, and that they were all just sitting in a darkened theater, watching a beautifully tragic science-fiction movie.

He reached his hand toward the bowl, his fingers extending, but Kit caught his movement. With a swift, fluid motion, she pulled the bowl entirely out of his reach, holding it close to her chest like a prize.

"Nice try, Talus," she teased, a brilliant, triumphant smile breaking across her face. "But if you want a taste of the good life, you're going to have to actually go in there and speak to whoever answers that radio."

Talus let his arms drop to his sides, giving a dramatic, heavy sigh of defeat. "Why are you the only person in this entire base who talks to me this way? Who actually tries to give me orders instead of constantly relying on me to carry the weight of the world?"

Kit's smile slowly faded, replaced by something much deeper, a rare moment of vulnerability that caught Talus completely off guard. She leaned her shoulder against the door frame, looking up at him through her lashes.

"Perhaps it's because you clearly need someone to talk to you like a human being, Talus. You've looked completely lost out here these last few years," she said softly, her voice carrying a wistful, delicate weight. She looked away, staring into the middle distance of the empty corridor. "Or perhaps... perhaps it's because I'm the only person in this sanctuary who wasn't alive before the war. I don't remember the skyscrapers, or the oceans, or what it felt like to watch a sunset without ash in the air. I'm completely alone in that respect, and I'd prefer not to be."

She looked back at him, her upper lip tucked slightly into her mouth, her vibrant blue eyes searching his face. "I just want the chance to make my own memories. Something real to keep me company when the nights get long."

Talus crossed his arms tightly, deliberately breaking eye contact to shield himself from her unsettling gaze. "Unless those memories just end up reminding you how desperately alone you really are."

The silence returned, stretching between them like a physical barrier. Talus' features slackened, his defenses crumbling for a fraction of a second as his mind took him back. He was sitting on a plush, velvet couch. His arms were wrapped tightly around Lily's shoulders, pulling her small frame against his chest to ward off the sharp chill of a November winter night. A roaring fire crackled in the hearth, casting long, amber shadows across the living room walls. Soft, low jazz wafted from the speakers in the corner. There was a bottle of cheap wine on the coffee table, a bowl of fresh popcorn between them, and an endless stream of laughter and effortless conversation that lasted until the sun came up. If he could have chosen a single pocket of time to freeze, a single memory to inhabit for his eternity...

He violently wrenched himself away from the thought, slamming the door on the past before the grief could choke him. This was neither the time nor the place to get lost in the graveyard of his mind.

"Come on, then," Talus said, his voice suddenly crisp, welcoming the sudden rush of practical urgency. "If you want me in there so badly, let's go. I need the distraction."

He reached past her and gripped the handle, swinging the heavy blast door open with a sharp jerk.

He didn't even have time to take a step forward before he found himself nearly colliding with Elan, who had been on the verge of rushing out. They stopped so abruptly their noses were practically touching, separated by a mere fraction of an inch. Both men froze, their eyes locked in identical, wide-eyed expressions of sheer shock, neither making any immediate attempt to move or break the bizarre proximity.

After a long, agonizing beat, Elan managed to force his voice past his throat. "I... I was just coming to find you."

"What is it?" Talus asked, keeping his voice low, though curiously, neither he nor Elan made any effort to step backward. They remained nose-to-nose, a strange vignette of tech-room tension. "Have you made contact with Tigris?"

"Not as of yet," Elan muttered.

"Then what could you possibly need that required you to nearly take my teeth out?"

Elan's eyes darkened, the frantic energy returning to his face. "The Others. Their army has altered its trajectory. I think they know about Tigris base."

Talus went completely rigid, his gaze drifting past Elan toward Cary, who was standing by the primary terminal, his face grim. Talus let out a long, ragged sigh that felt as though it came from the very bottom of his lungs. The calculus had changed. If he chose to remain silent now, thousands of innocent people could die in the dark. But if he spoke, there was absolutely no guarantee the human survivors would even listen to the warnings of a ghost.

"Can you bypass their security and slice directly into their internal communications network?" Talus demanded, stepping past Elan into the hub.

Elan gave Talus a look that was overly cocky for someone who still blushed at the sight of anyone with breasts. "Do you know who you are talking to? I could slice into Cavalk's encrypted planetary arrays from this prehistoric terminal if you gave me twenty minutes."

Talus shook his head, a grim smile touching his lips. "Let's start with just Tigris."

As Elan's fingers returned to the keyboard in a furious, synchronized ballet of keystrokes, Talus paced the small room, desperately trying to map out the dialogue in his head. He had to calculate the exact weight of every word. If he said too much, the human command might panic, rushing out into the ash in a careless, chaotic frenzy that would leave them exposed to surface sweeps. If he said too little, they would dismiss the warning entirely, remaining stubborn until the blast doors were breached. The sooner they began their preparations, the more organized the evacuation would be, ensuring the Rangers could guide the civilians through the subterranean transit lines without leaving a trail for the Others to hunt.

"Talus?" Elan's voice cut through the room, sharp and urgent. "I've bypassed their firewall. I have their Captain on a secure, direct channel."

Talus halted his pacing. He took one deep, stabilizing breath, stepped up to the microphone console, and pressed the transmission toggle.

"Tigris Command, listen to me very carefully," Talus said, his voice carrying the cold, clinical authority of a director. "Your perimeter has been fundamentally compromised. The immortals have pinpointed a high-density human signature in your geographical sector. You need to initiate immediate emergency protocols for a total civilian evacuation. Now."

There was a long stretch of crackling white noise over the speaker, the audio cutting through the tense atmosphere of the hub. Then, a voice filtered through the static; a voice deeply weathered by years of hardship and conflict, but entirely unbroken by them, carrying the immovable weight of a leader.

"This is Tigris Command," the Captain responded, his tone hard and suspicious. "I am currently housing thousands of refugees from the Phoenix breach, alongside hundreds of critically wounded soldiers. I have entire generations of civilians under my direct care. We simply do not pack up an entire base and evacuate on the anonymous whim of a stranger over an unverified frequency."

"You will have an entire generation of corpses if you choose to stay," Talus countered, his voice remarkably calm, though his knuckles turned white where he gripped the edge of the console. He knew exactly what the man on the other end was experiencing, the paralyzing logistics of fear. "We have intercepted the internal tactical channels of the immortals. They are actively hunting the coordinates for Tigris. They are coming, Captain."

"Who the hell are you?" the Captain's voice barked back, the static flaring with his rising anger. "How do you possess deep-network access to our internal military protocols?"

There it was. The exact precipice Talus had feared. The turning point where a single sentence could mean life or death for thousands. The Captain was undoubtedly sitting in his command bunker, assuming this was a psychological ploy by the immortals. Some sort of cruel trick designed to force the humans out of their fortified bunkers and into the open where they could be easily slaughtered. And historically speaking, the Captain had every logical reason to believe exactly that.

Talus closed his eyes, letting out a slow, heavy breath. He did the precise thing he had explicitly ordered Cary and Elan not to do. He threw away the lie. It was the only way to prove he was on their side, that he always had been, or at least always tried to be.

"I know your protocols, Captain, because I am the man who sat in a room and helped to draft them," Talus said, his voice echoing in the small communications hub. "If you open the inside cover of your physical command manual you will find an archived authorization signature. The name is Talus Marin. You can choose to believe that I am a ghost, or you can choose to believe I am an enemy, but the fact remains that I am on your side. I always have been."

The radio line fell entirely silent, save for the rhythmic hiss of atmospheric interference. Over the channel, Talus could hear the distinct, faint sound of papers shuffling, the heavy thud of a binder being pulled from a shelf on the other end of the world. He could picture the old Captain, surrounded by his officers, wiping the dust off a worn, leather-bound manual that had survived the firestorm.

When the Captain's voice returned, the anger was gone, replaced by a cold, terrifying awe. "If you are truly the man listed in these archives... that would mean you are one of them. Why should we trust you?"

"I know you are reluctant to trust me and you are right to be wary. But the mathematics of your situation don't care about your trust, Captain. Whether you believe in my intentions or you despise my existence, you have to get those people out of that mountain."

Without waiting for a response, Talus reached down and slammed his hand onto the kill-switch, severing the transmission and plunging the communications hub back into an abrupt, heavy silence.

He slumped back onto his stool, burying his face in his hands. He could feel his fingers trembling against his skin, a sudden rush of adrenaline hammering through his veins. He had absolutely no idea if he had just saved them or if his words had just delivered the final blow to Tigris base. But it was something. It was a stone cast into the water, and as he sat there in the quiet room under Kit's watchful eye, he could only hope the ripples would buy the humans enough time to live another day and for him to have one less nightmare on his conscience.

7

Anya

Anya slowly peeled her heavy eyelids open. Her muscles ached, and her first conscious realization was the unforgiving, rigid stiffness of the mattress beneath her. As the blurry geometric shapes around her coalesced into focus, she took in the scene: pristine white bedsheets, stark white privacy curtains, blinding white walls, and a seamless white floor that reflected the fluorescent tubes overhead like polished ice.

She was still in the Medbay.

It was the kind of infirmary where, if a soldier weren't already driven mad or dying upon arrival, the sheer monotony of the environment would finish the job before they were discharged. The aggressive brilliance of the room assaulted her senses, making her head throb with a dull, rhythmic pulse that made her brain want to leap entirely out of her skull. Honestly, a physical migraine might have been a welcome reprieve; for the last forty-eight hours, her unguarded mind had dwelled on absolutely nothing but cinematic loops of Mamoru.

For two days, Anya had remained tightly cocooned in the bleached linen sheets, shedding silent, hot tears into the fabric as a torrent of memories eroded her defenses. She remembered the day her parents had signed her life away to the Ranger program—surrendering her to the military with little more than a detached, perfunctory nod and a curt, clipped goodbye. She had been a terrified, hollowed-out child until Mamoru stepped forward out of the bunker's shadows. He had greeted her with a warm, easy smile and an encompassing hug that instantly drove the chill from her bones. From that exact moment on, the circle of his arms became the only territory in the ruined world that felt like home. He was only four years her senior, yet back then, he had seemed vastly older, wiser, and larger than life. Her undeniable constant in her frightening new life as a ranger.

Mamoru came to her aid whenever she messed up, worked with her when she fell behind in training and taught her the tricks that had her flying through the ranks. But she kept falling backwards as her rebellious streak only grew. Despite her problems, Mamoru had helped her become one of the top Rangers in her class, which allowed her to get away with even more. At least until her final year when she refused to obey a direct order and complete her training. Not even Mamoru could save her then, and she was so angry that she wasn't even sure she wanted him to.

Once again, she pushed the thoughts away and wiped another tear with the damp edge of her bedsheet. The sooner she healed and moved on, the sooner she could get back to being a Ranger. She needed the distraction. She needed to know what happened. She needed to stop sending everyone away. Most of all, she needed to get the hell out of this colorless cage. It was not helping her mood at all.

"First order of business when I break out of here," she muttered aloud to the empty, hum-filled room, her voice raspy from disuse, "is to locate my heavy dye launcher and paint this entire room. Bright, chaotic blue and deep forest green. This white-out is a localized hell on Earth."

"A little extreme, white is supposed to be calming or make you think the place is sterile, can't remember which."

Anya swung her head toward the doorway, the sudden movement sending a sharp lance of pain through her temples. Captain Tennant stood framed in the entrance, his broad shoulders slumped under the weight of his uniform, his face lined with an exhaustion that ran far deeper than simple sleep deprivation.

"It needs a mirror because without one I can't tell which one of us looks worse. I'm pretty sure it is you though. Which is bad for you because I've not only been shot but electrocuted." Much more bite than she thought came out at the last word. She still needed to go back and show Burion that turnabout was fair play. He needed to learn his place.

"Stow that anger Ranger. He saved your life. They blew the base Anya, there was no way you could have gotten to the ground floor and back out before the detonation. It was gone before the others even made it back here. They likely wanted to try and stop the escape so they destroyed it, even with their own people inside."

Anya crossed her arms tightly over her chest, the stiff hospital gown scratching against her skin. She deliberately turned her face toward the blank white wall, entirely unable to look him in the eye. And even though the heavy silence in the room already gave her the answer, the desperate, childish part of her soul simply had to voice the question aloud.

"Mamoru?"

Captain Tennant didn't answer immediately. He let out a slow, deflated breath and solemnly shook his head, his eyes fixed on the floor plates.

A heavy, crushing weight descended onto Anya's chest, threatening to cut off her air supply. She kept her eyes downcast, staring fixedly at a tiny scratch in the white paint of her bedframe.

"How are you holding up?" Tennant asked, deliberately steering the conversation away from the dead. "The bio-tech lab was able to replace your kidney and things are progressing well."

Screw the damn kidney, she thought bitterly. The failing organ felt like a trivial, insulting punishment compared to the absolute failure of her entire life. Maybe if she hadn't insisted on going out to the surface that day. If she had just stayed at the base like she was supposed to, she could have gotten to Phoenix sooner. She could have dragged him out herself..

"The cellular matrix won't be fully structured and ready to function completely on it's own for a few more days. And even then the doctors say you will need to take it easy. You are lucky they were able to grow a replacement in the lab." Tennant continued, his tone shifting into an accusatory, parental strictness. "We could have easily postponed this entire medical delay. We could have secured your replacement kidney once our caravan reached the coordinates of the new southern sanctuary. But your remaining kidney isn't functioning anywhere near the parameters it's supposed to. It's failing under the stress, Anya. Why didn't you get this corrected the moment it was flagged on your medical files?"

Anya swallowed hard, a dry, bitter lump forming in her throat. At the time, her reasoning had seemed perfectly sound. The regimented base doctor had noticed the slight congenital decline during her standard enlistment physical a year ago, but because her primary kidney was processing impurities well enough and her overall endurance scores were off the charts, he had left the choice of elective surgery up to her. She had declined it out of pure stubbornness; she didn't want to spend two weeks sidelined in a recovery ward while her peers were out on the line. Now, that choice was a ball and chain, pinning her to a stiff mattress in a blindingly white room.

Anya rolled her eyes, the cynical gesture sending a fresh ripple of pressure behind her temples. "If this is your nice, diplomatic way of getting around to saying that I'm stuck in this damn Medbay for the foreseeable future, Captain, you can just forget it."

"The doctor explicitly ordered total bedrest, Anya," Tennant said, his voice dropping into a stern, unyielding cadence. He didn't flinch under her glare. "Any elevated heart rate, any unnecessary physical stress, and that remaining kidney could shut down entirely before the bio-techs are even done growing your replacement. You aren't going anywhere."

"If I have to rest, I would vastly prefer to do it in my own bed, in my own quarters," she muttered, shifting her weight slightly and instantly regretting it. "This place leaves a hell of a lot to be desired."

"You can't be moved. The monitoring equipment is attached to the wall."

"I feel like I ran full-speed into an Iron Maiden," Anya groaned, letting her head sink back into the unforgiving pillow. "And honestly, I'm not entirely sure if that wonderful feeling is from the Fulgar blast or from the firmness of this bed."

Her entire body felt completely locked down, a cage of sore muscles and rigid joints. Her skin felt uncomfortably tight across her torso, and every shallow breath she took caused a sharp, painful tug against the stitched lacerations at her side. Her neck was throwing a violent tantrum, its muscles knotting up and screaming loudly up into the base of her skull. It was feeding a migraine that she was absolutely positive would sit itself behind her eyes for at least the next three days. None of these physical symptoms boded well for her chances of breaking out of the ward.

Tennant's hardened features softened just a fraction, a ghost of a smile touching his weathered lips. "Medieval torture references? I see your mandatory recreation hours in the historical video vaults were not entirely wasted." He paused for a moment and then sat down in the chair next to the bed. "You saved those children, Anya. You did a good thing. Good things are hard to find these days and when they happen it gives people hope. You gave people hope, Anya. They will fight harder now."

Instead of continuing, Tennant parted his lips to speak, hesitated, and closed his mouth again. He shifted uncomfortably in his chair, his eyes finding the floor plates before flicking back to her face. He was clearly looping his thoughts, trying to calculate the exact phrasing, or perhaps he simply didn't know what order to deliver the news in. All Anya knew, based on her years in the service, was that when a commanding officer hesitated like this, the upcoming brief was going to be bad for her.

It was probably going to be a hell of a lot worse than a few days of forced bedrest in a room completely devoid of color. Just yesterday, she had thought she was thoroughly sick of the dull, oppressive metal bulkheads that lined the lower sectors of Tigris base. Now, surrounded by this chalky white-out, she desperately missed the familiar, honest gray of the shiny stuff.

Yet another conversation that was building toward a terrible ending. Anya stared at the ceiling, wondering how much more structural trauma her psyche could take before it fractured completely.

The destruction of Phoenix base, the loss of Mamoru, getting shot by an immortal monster, getting electrocuted by a fellow ranger, and now more bad news? Dear Universe, she thought bitterly, sometime in the near future, I would highly appreciate a brief intermission. Not a long one—let's just shoot for a couple of hours. Just long enough for a dreamless nap and a single cup of hot, artificial coffee.

"We're evacuating Tigris, Anya," Tennant said finally, the words falling flat and heavy into the silence of the room. "I already have the logistical relocation teams organizing the transport manifests and generating new base assignments. None of the hidden outposts within marching distance have the cubic footage or the hydroponic yields to absorb our entire population. Tigris is being permanently split up."

That was it. Another home down the drain.

"Is it my fault?" She asked.

It was a dumb question the moment it left her lips. It shouldn't matter who drew the line at this point; the tactical reality was already locked in. They had to abandon the sector, and Captain Tennant was not the kind of leader who would displace over two thousand civilian souls without an absolute, airtight reason. His brilliant strategic leadership was the sole reason Tigris had expanded to become the largest active base in the sector. Every refugee, every soldier, every child in these tunnels depended on his calculations. They needed him. She needed him. He was exactly the type of steady, protective Captain she had always desperately wanted back during her turbulent days at Phoenix base. Not to mention he was the only commander willing to take a volatile chance on her career.

"While you were here, our comms hub intercepted a strange, tight-beam communication," Tennant explained, leaning forward. "The operators were claiming to broadcast from a sector deep in the North. They stated they had successfully sliced into the internal tactical channels of the immortals. According to their data, the enemy has officially determined that a high-density human base is operating in this mountain range. They explicitly ordered me to execute our emergency protocols and evacuate."

Anya's eyes widened, her physical pain briefly sidelined by a sudden jolt of excitement. "People in the North? Genuine survivors all the way up in the northern zones? Captain, if there are organized outposts managing to survive that deep in enemy territory, maybe there are more human populations out there than our scouts ever realized. If we could establish a line, mobilize the sectors together, we could finally figure out a weapon to—"

Tennant silently raised his right hand, a simple, authoritative gesture that instantly cut off her frantic rambling. He stood up from the metal chair, his boots scraping against the floor plates, and walked over to a stainless-steel tray near the wall, aimlessly toying with a pair of diagnostic instruments.

A heavy dread sank into her stomach. Great, she thought, this is the exact part of the movie where the commander tells the broken soldier that her war is officially over. That they found a major threat and she's just going to be left behind to rot in this white shroud of misery. What the hell was wrong with the design of this room anyway?

A bizarre, morbid thought crossed her mind. Wait... maybe that's the trick. Maybe I didn't survive the gunshot at all. Maybe I'm already dead. Crap, if this sterile, blinding white-out was the actual afterlife, she might actually have to reconsider her stance on the immortals, because so far, eternity wasn't shaping up to be very comfortable.

"They were not our people, Anya," Tennant said, his back still turned to her as he set a metal tool down with a sharp, resonant clink. "The broadcast didn't come from a human outpost. They were... immortal."

Anya froze, her breath catching in her throat. "What? That's not possible if you said they knew protocols. If the immortals knew our protocols we would all be dead by now."

"They didn't just happen to know the protocols, Anya," Tennant said, turning around slowly to face her, his expression grim. "The voice on the channel claimed he was the person who wrote them. The emergency survival protocols were drafted and authorized before the first missile ever left its silo. Before the war, Anya."

Anya felt her jaw drop open, a completely ridiculous, stunned expression taking over her face. For a brief second, she was actually grateful that the Captain had diverted his gaze toward the plain white wall beside her bed. She wondered idly if she should feel insulted that a stark, unpainted surface was more visually appealing to him than looking at her right now. Maybe her face really did look worse than his.

The tactical implications began to collide in her mind like a series of cascading detonations. If these northern entities had written the foundational survival manuals for the human race, and they were immortal, it meant one of two terrifying things: either the enemy had always possessed their exact operational blueprints and had simply been playing a cruel, prolonged game of cat-and-mouse with the survivors, or... the voice on the radio didn't belong to the group that was hunting them.

Could that even be a possibility? Could there actually be two entirely different factions of timeless entities operating on the planet? Every single piece of archived historical data she had studied during her training suggested that the immortals had fought as a single, terrifyingly unified front during the collapse. A force that eventually seized absolute control over the remnants of the surface. There was never a single mention of a civil war or an internal schism within their ranks. Unless... unless that was the real reason the Northern Hemisphere had been hit so hard during the nuclear exchange? Maybe the primary faction had used the atomic firestorms to completely annihilate a secondary group of their own kind?

"So... you don't trust the source of the transmission," Anya said slowly, her voice trembling as she tried to piece the puzzle together. "And yet, you are evacuating our entire base and following the protocol anyway?"

The captain threw down the tool he was examining and started pacing.

Captain Tennant abruptly threw down the diagnostic tool he was examining, the metal clattering loudly against the tray. He began pacing the narrow width of the white room, his hands clenched into tight fists behind his back.

"What other choice do I have, Ranger?" he barked, his

professional composure cracking just enough to reveal the raw panic beneath. "They know exactly where Tigris is located; that much is completely undeniable. They have our geographical signature. Even if this northern broadcast is a psychological trick engineered by the enemy... we are absolute sitting ducks if we stay inside this mountain. If I split the base, scatter the divisions, and run the civilian caravans through separate transit lines, then maybe—just maybe—some of our people will have a chance to survive."

"Or you will lead them right to every single base in the area." Anya's voice was solemn, dropping into a shaky, thin register that betrayed just how physically drained she truly was. She felt weak, her muscles trembling beneath the white linens, but deep down in the core of her chest, a sudden, bright fire was beginning to kindle. It was a dangerous heat, sparking a reckless idea—one she was absolutely certain the Captain would categorize as treasonous, but one she felt a desperate, driving urge to pursue anyway. The only tactical question left floating in her mind was how. How could a bed bound, broken soldier possibly execute a plan from inside a medical cage?

"So you would have me leave everyone here to die? Were you not the one that just risked everything to save the people at Phoenix and now you want me to leave them to the same fate here?" He paused. "I am sending everyone on roundabout paths. The journey will take two or three times as long as normal and we'll camp in safe rooms to make sure we're not being followed. I will not leave this entire base to die and you will not question my decision further, Ranger."

He marched back toward the threshold, his broad frame cutting off the light from the hallway as he stared out into the bustling, panicked corridor.

Anya hesitated for a fraction of a second, swallowing down her own frustration. When she spoke again, she intentionally softened her delivery, letting the venom drain from her words. While her stubborn pride refused to let the Captain walk away without hearing her opinion, she also didn't want to destroy the fragile bond she shared with him. She didn't want to lose yet another home, even if the circumstances dictated that Tigris base was already doomed.

"No, Captain, I am absolutely not suggesting we leave anyone behind to die," she said quietly, her eyes tracking the rigid silhouette of his shoulders. "I am asking what if we choose to trust the immortal who reached out to us. If he truly wrote our protocols before the world burned, then at some point in our history, someone who desperately wanted to keep the human race safe chose to place their faith in him. They trusted him to design the exact, do-or-die defenses that have kept us alive in these holes since the end of the war."

Finally, Tennant turned completely back to face her. At long last, he looked directly into her eyes, but the expression settling over his weathered features was a far cry from the understanding she had hoped to find. The hard, deeply etched stress lines on his face twisted into a mask of pure, unadulterated anger and disgust. It was a dark, hostile look that didn't suit his fundamentally protective nature at all.

"An immortal, Ranger!" he spat, the word dripping with an ancient, generational hatred. "They traded away every ounce of their humanity simply to escape the natural grace of a peaceful death, and in that exact same breath, they sentenced the rest of humanity to die. They cannot be reasoned with, they cannot be trusted, and they cannot be treated as anything other than parasitic demons. That is quite enough of this, Ranger Anya. I am the commanding officer of this base, and my orders are absolute. If you possess any desire whatsoever to remain a uniform-wearing Ranger when this war moves south, that is the absolute last syllable I will hear from you on this topic."

Well, Anya thought bitterly as she sank a fraction deeper into her stiff mattress, that officially confirmed her darkest assumption. He would never, under any circumstances, authorize her to initiate a line of dialogue with the northern entity. He would never allow her to investigate whether these timeless creatures might be structurally distinct from the monstrous entities hunting them down from the ridges. Was it possible that this specific broadcast harbored a remnant of the compassion and empathy that the primary hive had completely cast aside? Maybe...

She took a slow, painful breath and shifted the trajectory of the conversation. "So when do we leave?"

Tennant's left hand slowly closed around the thumb of his right, his calloused fingers wringing his own fists together with a slow, grinding friction, as if he were trying to twist the moisture out of a wet towel.

"Tomorrow," he murmured, his voice sounding suddenly small, stripped of its command-deck volume. "Tomorrow morning, the entire base packs what they can carry into the transport frames. I am personally commanding the largest civilian division. The remaining Rangers are being split across the groups, and everyone has been handed their individual base assignments. The tunnels don't bridge the entire distance to the southern mountains; we are going to be forced to travel across the surface for part of the way."

He stopped wringing his hands, letting his arms drop heavily to his sides. "We will have to maintain a steady pace, Anya. The medical staff informed me that any undue physical strain or sudden impact on your torso will cause that remaining kidney to shut down. The medics will not have the equipment to save you if the kidney fails. They told me explicitly you wouldn't survive the first mile of the trip."

Anya swallowed hard, a dry, heavy lump forming in her throat as the cold reality of the medical brief finally crystallized in her mind. She understood now. She understood exactly what this entire, somber visit had been leading up to. She was being benched. She was being left behind to die in an empty mountain while the rest of her world marched away.

A dark, cynical thought crossed her mind: maybe this would actually work out beautifully in the Captain's favor. She could become the great, tragic martyr for the Tigris cause. The brave, broken Ranger left in the tomb to spur the surviving soldiers onward into the next battle. An inspiring memory to give them that hope they hadn't possessed since the war started.

"Ever had one of those days where you realize you really should have just stayed in bed?" she asked, a faint, humorless smile touching her lips. She genuinely had no idea how else to process her own abandonment. But beneath the numbness, a sharp realization flickered to life: if she was being left behind in an evacuated base, she was being

79

left behind with an entirely functional, deep-network communications hub. If only she lived long enough to use it.

"I'm sorry Anya. You will have to stay behind but as soon as you are able and away from the base I will give you the rendezvous point." He gave her a small smile. There was little chance of her making it out alive if the immortals breached the base while she was bed bound, but he was trying to give her hope. The hope that he thought would get her to fight harder.

Anya opened her mouth to respond, a sudden wave of emotion threatening to break through her cynical exterior. She wanted to tell him that despite his stubbornness, he had been an incredible Captain to her. She wanted to remind him of how much she had genuinely valued their late-night debates over cups of terrible, scorched artificial coffee; how they used to share quiet laughs while watching the green recruits struggle with simple logistics because they were too arrogant to ask for guidance. She remembered the long, grueling winter nights training side-by-side in the armory while the rest of the installation slept beneath the rock. She even missed the stern, exhausting lectures he delivered whenever her rebellious streak got the better of her. At some point across the years, without her ever realizing it, those moments had become her definition of home.

She barely talked to anyone but the Captain and Ryan and that was only because they would not take no for an answer. There were times that he almost seemed to push her toward disobeying orders just so he could use it to show the rest of the base how much of a hero she was. She wasn't half the hero he wanted her to be or a tenth of the hero he wanted everyone to believe she was.

She opened her mouth to speak but still the words were trapped in her throat. They were there, just waiting to be said but the lump in her throat seemed to be pushing those words down. Her chest was tight and it was painful. She vividly remembered her very first day entering Tigris base—how he had greeted her with that aggressively formal, bone-crushing handshake and a rigid welcome, a calculated display of authority designed to break a young Ranger who had been explicitly red-flagged as a liability rather than an asset.

Finally, a few words forced their way out but they were a weak imitation of the grand goodbye running through her mind.

"Thank you Captain…Good Luck."

He deserved more than that and she wanted to give him more but all that came out of her mouth was silence. No amount of pushing and shrugging of her shoulders could get the other words to come out.

"Anya! Thank the sky, you're finally awake!"

The heavy medical door hissed open as Ryan Avery burst into the room, entirely bypassing the Captain's rigid posture. With a dramatic flourish, he tossed a massive, crudely constructed fake spider made of frayed wire and black insulation tape directly onto her lap. "Mr. Wuggles was completely inconsolable without you!"

Anya let out a sharp, genuine yelp, her survival instincts flaring as she scrambled backward against the pillows, frantically swatting the wire monstrosity off her legs. The sudden, violent twisting motion caused a white-hot lance of agony to rip through her stitched side, making her catch her breath. "Damn it, Ryan! You and that godforsaken spider are quite literally going to finish me off before the enemy does!"

"Ranger Ryan Avery, cease these ridiculous shenanigans immediately and report." Captain Tennant barked, his face instantly hardening into a classic command-deck scowl.

Ryan instantly snapped into a crisp, if slightly theatrical, military salute, though his vibrant eyes remained bright with an irrepressible energy. "Captain, I have successfully finalized every single transport manifest you assigned to my division. I am just heading down to the residential tiers to help a few more families secure their cargo crates, and then the column will be entirely locked and loaded."

Ryan's demeanor was oddly cheerful for a soldier who was currently organizing the total abandonment of his home while simultaneously preparing to leave his best friend behind. But as he looked between Anya's pale face and the Captain's grim expression, he seemed to finally read the bleak atmosphere of the ward. The manic energy softened, and he flashed his trademark, wide, "everything is going to be perfectly fine" smile.

"Come on, you two," Ryan said, stepping closer and dropping his hands. "This isn't some grand, tragic ending. We are going to see each other again in a matter of weeks. The enemy doesn't even possess our exact coordinates yet; that tactical blind spot should buy our caravans at least a few days of lead time. And even if everything hits the fan, well the solar-glide plane is fully fueled and primed in the launch chute, Captain. I give you my absolute word as a Ranger: I will fly her out of this mountain before the enemy so much as touches our outer walls."

Anya gripped the edges of the metal bedframe, attempting to haul her upper body into a higher sitting position so she could look him dead in the eye, but the torturous pulling sensation across her abdomen forced her back down against the mattress.

"Ryan, follow the others, Captain will need all the rangers that he can get to get everyone out."

"Are you completely out of your mind?" Ryan countered, his grin broadening into the manic, unhinged expression of a wild cat. "I have been actively dying for a practical excuse to field-test that solar plane over a long-distance trajectory for six months, and this evacuation finally gives me a reason to be reckless enough to actually do it."

At this, Captain Tennant seemed to step out of his dark thoughts, his presence returning fully to the clinical reality of the room.

"I will be seeing both of you at Tressle base in a few weeks. Or sooner. If that plane is ready to fly I want you to get her out of here the second you get a hint of trouble Ryan. The medical team assures me her muscle tissue is capable of healing on its own, but any excessive structural strain or sudden movement before the new cellular kidney is properly anchored will destroy the matrix and cause lethal systemic shock. The medics on the rearguard will demonstrate how to safely disconnect the life-support leads when the time comes. Your single hardest objective, Ranger Avery, will be keeping this stubborn girl completely still. Regardless of whether the blast doors are breached or not."

Captain Tennant was much calmer and more collected when he was giving orders. It was what he was meant to do. Meanwhile Anya could not help but sneer a bit at the tubes that kept her tied to the machines around her bed.

"Captain Tennant! We need you on Tier Three immediately!"

A frantic, muffled shout echoed from the corridor outside, followed by the hurried clatter of boots. Anya saw her Captain close his eyes for a brief second, shaking his head in a quiet flash of annoyance before his military mask slid back into place. She offered him a small, supportive smile.

"I will officially report back for active duty in a few weeks, Captain," Anya said, her voice steadying. "You have my word."

Tennant offered her one final, heavy nod before turning on his heel and vanishing into the chaotic swarm of the corridor.

The heavy door hissed shut, isolating the room once more. Anya turned her full, narrowing attention onto Ryan, who was already leaning over the edge of her bed, idly picking up his wire spider.

"Alright, Avery," she said, her voice dropping into a sharp, low whisper. "Tell me absolutely everything about this solar plane of yours. Have you genuinely managed to bypass the battery failure, and is she truly rigged to fly?"

8

Talus

"Still no further word from the humans. I suppose your prediction was accurate," Cary said, leaning heavily against the industrial steel frame of the laboratory door. His arms were crossed over his chest, his voice carrying a trace of the long, exhausting silence that had settled over the compound since their last transmission.

"I usually am," Talus responded. He didn't look up from the ocular lens of his microscope.

Beneath the glass, he was carefully tracking the cellular mutation of human stem cell strains in a simulated natural environment. He adjusted the fine focus with a gloved thumb, watching how the microscopic structures warped and ruptured when subjected to an influx of the aggressive new carcinogens he had spent the last three months synthesizing. It was tedious, chilling work, but it was the only resistance he could offer against a dying world.

"Elan does have something specific he wants you to look at, though," Cary continued, straightening up. "One of the main strongholds belonging to the Others is expanding, and it's happening abnormally fast. According to the satellite photo, it's already eclipsed the layout of their surrounding outposts by a significant margin."

"How massive is the footprint?"

"At least two square miles, likely more," Cary said, his expression darkening. "It's difficult to establish an exact boundary line. They're deliberately obscuring our satellite sweeps by venting columns of thick black smoke across the perimeter."

"What could they be building? Another new weapon? Something even stronger because their last attempt was not a success?" Talus stood up from his stool, a deep, familiar dread settling behind his ribs. He paced toward the center of the sterile room. "They will see the planet destroyed at this rate. Sometimes I don't even think it is the humans they want to kill, but us."

It was an intrusive, deeply unsettling thought, one that had occupied the margins of his mind for years. Yet every time he attempted to figure out the cold logic of it, the pieces refused to align. If their own kind truly sought to erase them from the map, their methodology was unnecessarily prolonged.

"We stopped them once, we can stop them again. He is not the only one that has been making improvements." Talus said.

"If only they were not so sparse with their communications we might know more." Cary muttered, running a hand through his hair. "Elan is losing his mind trying to crack their shifting internal encryptions. Half the time, he can't even isolate their shortwave signals among the background radiation. He thinks the Others might have launched a proprietary network of low-orbit satellites that our arrays can't even detect."

It was classic Elan—always inventing a dozen terrifying scenarios where the enemy was a hundred steps ahead of their position. For decades, Talus' faction had remained at a total strategic standstill, confined to these hidden mountain ridges, while the primary hive of the immortals moved forward by leaps and bounds. None of this data boded well for the survival of the remaining human colonies.

"We cannot waste time on foolish speculation. We have to find a way to get in there and get the information. Otherwise we are just waiting for them to attack us or destroy every last human in existence. Neither of which we can allow to happen. Go back to the comm hub, Cary. Tell Elan to keep hammering the satellite arrays. If he needs to reassign a few communications technicians from the primary grid to assist with the decryption."

Cary nodded grimly and slipped out of the lab, his boots clicking softly down the concrete corridor.

Talus did feel like the leader of the base but that was the last thing he wanted to be. If anyone else was up for the job he would gladly pass on the responsibility. But they all simply deferred to him. Perhaps it was because he had worn the mantle of an immortal longer than anyone else in these tunnels, or perhaps it was because his hands were the ones fundamentally responsible for the initial spark that escalated the war. He had made this world; he may as well be a part of what happens to it next.

He crossed the laboratory to his primary desk, his fingers brushing past neat stacks of medical journals before pulling out a series of physical satellite photographs captured several months prior. It had been the first time their standard passes had managed to catch a semi-clear frame of whatever massive structure the Others were building.

He bent over the glossy paper, studying the dark, geometric shapes. He still wasn't entirely certain if the dense soot billowing from those towering, industrial smokestacks was an actual byproduct of heavy manufacturing or simply a tactical smoke screen deployed specifically to blind their surveillance sweeps.

Slowly, he traced his index finger along the faint, black lines of the exterior conveyor systems that snaked out from the monolithic main buildings. He stopped at a small, recurring distortion on the belt. They were mass-producing something in immense, uniform quantities, but no matter how many times he subjected the image to high-density enhancement, the physical geometry of the objects remained unrecognizable. He could identify the uniform rows of what appeared to be living quarters, and perhaps a massive center structure that resembled an administrative hall or a wide-open staging arena. But the true, frantic expansion was restricted entirely to the fortified perimeters surrounding the smokestacks. Whatever secrets the enemy possessed, they were buried deep within the dark zones they didn't want the satellites to see.

Perhaps the most perplexing riddle of all was the complete lack of surface movement. In fifty years of automated satellite observation, they had almost never witnessed an immortal physically exiting the boundaries of that valley. They had observed heavy armored transports arriving at the primary gates, but once those iron thresholds closed, nothing ever emerged. The vehicles remained parked in rigid, rusted configurations across the outer courtyards like monument markers. It was one of the biggest mysteries he had ever encountered and just like his other mysteries he was nowhere near solving it.

Given the absolute absence of surface traffic entering or exiting the valley, Talus heavily suspected that the Others were utilizing an intricate tunnel network. Similar to that of the humans. But if that assumption was correct, it raised an immediate contradiction: why did the enemy's ground forces always seem so completely stymied whenever a human settlement managed to seal its primary blast doors and collapse its transit tunnels? One would logically assume that an immortal, technologically superior force would possess identical subterranean entry protocols.

He frowned, turning away from the dated prints. He needed to see how the valley's architecture had expanded over the last month if he wanted to calculate what their old brothers were hunting for. He spun around to head toward the main communications hub, only to nearly collide with Cary, who had returned from relaying his message to Elan.

"So you were already tracking that base, that's why you didn't seem surprised. I knew you'd look into it as soon as I turned my back." Cary noted, a faint, lopsided smile on his face.

Talus nodded, sliding the photographs back into their folder. He didn't acknowledge that his friend was correct in his assertion of Talus' behavior. There was no one who knew him better.

"Elan states that the physical footprint is expanding, but we are still completely blind regarding the structural purpose of the facilities. I am heading down to the comm station to pull the raw daily imagery from the morning pass. There has to be something we are overlooking."

"You know, all this abstract talk about the humans and their supply lines actually got me thinking about the old days," Cary remarked casually, falling into step beside Talus as they exited the lab and entered the dim, vaulted corridor. "Specifically, how much I desperately miss the taste of real, seared meat. I can't even remember the last time anyone in this mountain actually bothered to spin up that rakehell bio-synthesis process."

The idea of meat made his mouth water just a bit. He still vividly remembered the existential debates he used to have with himself regarding the ethics of becoming a strict vegetarian. But that was back when meat still required the systematic slaughter of living, breathing animals. In the modern era, the creation of animal protein was a simple matter of genetic sequencing and cellular manipulation inside a standard culture vat. No killing, no blood. And yet, despite the technology, their entire colony had voluntarily transitioned to a utilitarian, plant-based diet; food had lost its social texture and emotional appeal to them over the years, serving as nothing more than a necessary chemical charge to sustain their biology. The immense time and power required to run the synthesis vats simply wasn't worth the return. Kit's mother might have undergone the task if she was more of a cook than a baker.

"I wonder who I could talk to about making meat. Maybe if I did something absodamnlutely great for Elan he would go use that mojo of his on Tom. I mean Elan's charms are hard for anyone to resist so if anyone can get Tom willing to make some meat it's Elan... Yep You're not even listening to me."

Talus wasn't. His thoughts were entirely fixed on the valley as they approached the reinforced iron doors of the communications room. There had to be an observational blind spot they could exploit to gain a closer look at the installation's interior. Perhaps if they cross-referenced the layout of the valley with the smaller, isolated outposts scattered along the southern ridges, a structural pattern would emerge. An industrial buildup of this magnitude, spanning several decades and utilizing millions of tons of steel, made absolutely no logical sense for a race that didn't require food, sleep, or territorial expansion. The Others had been executing this massive engineering project for over half a century, yet it was only within the last fifteen or twenty years that they had suddenly deployed their ground divisions to aggressively hunt down the remaining human sanctuaries. What was the catalyst?

They reached the communication room with Talus remaining only vaguely aware of Cary's ongoing monologue, which had shifted toward a prediction that the entire base would likely throw a literal ticker-tape parade the moment the human refugees arrived at their gates. As uncomfortable as that emotional display sounded to his old sensibilities, his mind simply lacked the capacity to focus on social logistics right now. .

"Elan," Talus called out, his voice instantly cutting through the steady chatter of the room. He walked directly toward the primary console near the entrance. "You mentioned this specific complex has been aggressively expanding its borders. Do we possess the raw frames from the morning pass? I know we instructed the automated arrays to remain locked onto those coordinates in the event the prevailing winds cleared the smoke screen long enough for a high-definition capture."

Elan nearly leaped out of his swivel chair at the sudden sound of Talus' voice, his fingers slipping across his keyboard before he managed to steady his posture. He offered a quick, nervous nod, clearing his throat as he scrambled to clear his monitors. Nothing quite initialized an entry like the old commander getting straight down to operational business.

"Uh, yes, sir. Absolutely. Let me pull up the uncompressed files for you right now," Elan stammered, his fingers flying across the input deck. "I have been getting pictures of it at least once a day since that one was the closest to Phoenix and Tigris. I thought maybe we could get a heads up of when they were rolling out for the attack."

Elan had been his link in the communication room for about 50 years now. He barely acknowledged the others who managed communications because honestly Elan was the first person he saw in the room (he sat closest to the door) and he was very good at what he did.

Together, the three of them crowded around the glowing monitor, scanning through the sequential series of morning photographs. There was frustratingly little to see; the images were dominated by billowing, charcoal-colored clouds that obscured the ground level, revealing only occasional, tantalizing glimpses of moving structural components on the exposed sections of the conveyor belts.

"Wait. What exactly am I looking at right there?" Cary asked, his humor vanishing as he leaned forward, pointing a calloused finger at the lower left quadrant of the display.

Talus focused his gaze where Cary indicated. A brief, violent downdraft in the valley had torn a temporary tear through the black smoke screen, exposing a sharp, perfectly geometric dark square cut directly into the rocky earth. He knew from their older topographic maps that there were no buildings or foundation walls designated for that specific sector of the courtyard.

"Isolate those coordinates and enhance the contrast, Elan," Talus commanded.

Elan's fingers moved across the interface, zooming the digital lens into the gap. As the pixels resolved, they could clearly discern the clean, vertical drop of concrete retaining walls and the unmistakable shadow of depth. It was an access shaft.

Talus let out a slow, cold breath. His hypothesis was correct. The Others possessed their own underground transport infrastructure, allowing them to move entire divisions across the continent without ever exposing their numbers to satellite surveillance. But that single confirmation still failed to answer the fundamental question: where did those tunnels terminate, and what were they actively hauling out of the dark?

"Do you have any more pictures from this day?" Talus asked, his pulse quickening. He hoped the automated camera had captured whatever was entering or exiting that threshold before the smoke closed back in.

"The satellite stays over the base for an hour so let me see what other pictures it took." Elan explained, his face pale in the green glow of the monitor. "Let me run the chronological sequence."

Elan advanced the pictures further and with jerky movements the picture came to life. Black clouds filled most of the images. He was a paranoid one and always had been, but by all accounts, he had won…so what was he so afraid of? The smoke moved back and forth and a vehicle jolted its way out of the tunnel. There was more smoke in the pictures, likely to cover up what was in the vehicle. Whatever it was they really wanted to make sure that anyone that was spying could not see. But the winds were in their favor and even though the vehicle disappeared for several pictures, it reappeared for one perfect shot.

It looked like a troop carrier. The vehicle's open-air bed was lined with two rigid rows of human beings sitting shoulder-to-shoulder on bench frames, their heads bowed. More bodies were visible crammed into the narrow central aisle, some lying down in exhausted, motionless heaps.

"When were these pictures taken?"

Elan's mouth was slightly agape and Talus knew that his likely was as well. Cary was leaning in and squinting at the picture curiously. Elan shook his head out and managed to find his voice.

"The day Phoenix was attacked. This is not long after the base was blown up." His voice was hoarse.

All this time he had thought they were blowing up the bases to prevent the humans from coming back or to destroy anyone trapped inside or maybe just because they were monsters. He never thought that they were blowing up the bases so that the humans would never realize what wasn't there that should be.

"I don't get it what has you both so spooked. It is just a truck full of the Others right?"

Both Talus and Elan slowly shook their heads back and forth. The people in the troop carrier were not wearing the long dark coats that the Others were known for, instead they were wearing the Ranger's signature jumpsuits.

"Those are not immortals, those are Rangers. The Others are expanding their army and they are using humans to do it."

9

Anya

The Tigris base was silent. So profoundly, hauntingly silent. Without the familiar, ambient hum of the geothermal ventilation grids or the distant, reassuring rumble of thousands of civilian lives moving through the lower tiers, the vacuum of sound felt like a physical weight pressing down on Anya's eardrums. She could feel herself steadily spiraling into a localized insanity. White. Quiet. There was absolutely nothing to tether her mind to the waking world. The medical team was gone. Her community was gone. She was entirely done with this sensory deprivation. This sterile ward was Hell. The absolute, pure definition of—

"How are you feeling today Anya?"

She instantly shot imaginary laser beams directly out of her eyes, thoroughly frying Ryan Avery to a smoking crisp right where he stood in the doorway. At least, she was pretty sure she had; after all, that was the only logical, self-defense response to the person who had voluntarily kept her trapped inside this white room of absolute, maddening isolation. Did anyone actually recover or get better in a place like this? She was convinced this was the specific black-site room where command sent people when they wanted them to die quietly, or where they brought enemy scavengers they intended to torture for logistics. There was simply no other rational explanation.

"Anya? Are you okay?"

Apparently, she did not, in fact, possess weaponized laser beams in her retinas. Well, that was deeply disappointing.

"I need to get out of this room immediately, Ryan," she rasped, her voice sounding raw and foreign in the empty space. "It is just completely horrible here, and the silence is entirely too loud."

Ryan looked at her with a sad smile.

Ryan looked down at her, his usual manic energy replaced by a heavy, somber expression. He offered her a faint, sad smile that lacked its typical warmth. "I hate to break the news to you, but it's quiet everywhere now, Anya. The whole base is gone."

"Which is exactly why we are heading down to the primary communications terminal right now."

Bracing herself, she forced her upper body off the pillows and intentionally ignored the immediate, sickening pulling sensation at her flank. Gritting her teeth, she gripped the edge of the metal frame and swung her bare feet off the side of the mattress, letting her toes hover over the cold concrete floor plates.

"Anya! What the hell do you think you're doing?" Ryan lunged forward, his hands flaring out in a panic. "You are going to pull your stitches out! I am telling you right now, I am far too squeamish to witness that much blood. Not to mention terrible with a needle and thread so I couldn't put you back together again."

Ignoring his protests, she pushed off the bed, took a few tentative steps, and steadied her trembling posture. The flesh across her torso was incredibly tender, but the pain wasn't entirely unmanageable. She knew that with Ryan's physical support, she could manage the distance to the comm deck. They could be forced to execute an evacuation at any given second. She wanted to make absolutely certain she could isolate and reactivate the exact tight-beam frequency Captain Tennant had used to speak with the Northern broadcast earlier before that happened. There were massive, generational answers that she wanted, and for the first time there could actually be someone out there who could answer them.

But as she shifted her weight forward to take another step, a sharp, unyielding tug at her side dragged her back to reality. She looked down, hit by the frustrating realization that she was still physically chained to her medical prison.

Dozens of clear plastic lines and bio-metric tubes were snaking directly into her flesh, connecting her to the massive, humming life-support apparatus positioned to her right. The automated machine was continuously cycling synthetic nutrients and specialized medicines into her system to help cultivate and stabilize the bio-tech kidney matrix currently developing within her torso. The organ itself had been surgically attached to the arterial network, but it was still far too small and immature to properly filter her blood on its own. Consequently, the thick, dark-fluid tubes running out of the opposite side of her body were performing the heavy renal filtration that her native biology should have been handling. She wasn't just weak; she was structurally immobilized. Unless, of course, Ryan could find a way to unhook the auxiliary lines just long enough for a brief trek down the corridor.

"I have been pinned to this horrible mattress for a days now, Ryan, and my brain cannot stand the alienation for another minute," she said, her voice dropping into a dangerous, unyielding register. "I need to go to the communications room. You are either going to lend me your shoulder and help me walk down those stairs, or I am going to rip these leads out and crawl there entirely on my own."

Ryan was suddenly right beside her, his hands firmly but gently pressing against her shoulders, using his weight to force her back down onto the pillows before she could tear her stitches.

"Can you at least tell me why we are going to the communication room?" Ryan reasoned, his eyes wide with concern as he held her in place. "If you want to talk to the Captain I am sure you can still reach him on wrist comm."

"Before he left, the Captain admitted to me that an entity, someone he strongly suspected was an immortal, had patched directly into our encrypted frequencies to warn him that Tigris base had been compromised," Anya explained, her breathing shallow as she sank back into the linens. "The Captain cut the feed and refused to trust the source because of what they are, but I am not entirely convinced it was a trap. If that entity wrote our emergency protocols before the war, I want to talk to him myself. I want to know why an immortal is trying to help us survive."

Ryan nodded calmly and Anya knew he had likely gotten the same debrief she had. He slowly turned his head to look at the chaotic jungle of tubes, bags, and monitors flanking her bed.

"Fine. But you are not going anywhere. If you won't stay away from the network, then I am going to dismantle the comm tier and reconstruct the system right here in this room. We are not moving you and we are absolutely not disconnecting those life-support leads until I know that your kidney won't fail and you won't die in the elevator."

Anya parted her lips to deliver a fierce protest, but she quickly closed her mouth, realizing she wasn't going to negotiate a better deal out of him. Mostly because, deep down, she knew his assertion was entirely correct. But she still desperately wanted to throw a brick through the blinding white walls of her room.

Ryan vanished into the corridor, and over the course of the next few hours, he periodically returned to the ward, his arms loaded with heavy, scavenged components extracted from the main communication decks downstairs. Anya watched from her bed, marveling at his reckless technical ingenuity. He was systematically transforming her sterile room into a chaotic command outpost, hauling in several micro-processors, miles of colorful copper wiring, heavy signal transceivers, and a dozen industrial components whose names she couldn't even begin to guess.

He became so entirely consumed by his work, so intensely focused on splicing lines and bypassing network encryption gates, that he didn't utter a single syllable or look in her direction for the rest of the afternoon. That suited her perfectly; between the heavy waves of post-surgical exhaustion and the continuous chemical drip of her IV, she found it incredibly difficult to keep her eyes open for more than ten minutes at a time, let alone summon the cognitive energy required for mundane conversation. She lay back in the quiet, watching the green status lights of the stolen computers begin to flicker to life.

When she next drifted awake, Ryan was sitting in the metal folding chair right beside her bed, looking every bit as physically and mentally exhuasted as she felt. His eyes were bloodshot, fixed in a glassy stare at the chaotic, improvised rig he had spent the last several hours constructing. In his lap, his hands loosely held a pair of battered, heavy-duty comm headsets.

"Are you absolutely certain about this, Anya?" he asked quietly, his voice lacking its usual theatrical spark. He didn't look up, instead tracing a thumb along the foam padding of the earpieces. "What if the Captain's assessment is right? What if whoever broadcast that message can't be trusted?"

"What is there to lose? The base is evacuated, we are the only ones here. If things go south, we hop in the plane to the next base and we are no worse off than we were. But if they can be trusted then maybe we can get some answers and figure out a way to stop the immortals who are trying to render us extinct."

Ryan let out a slow, deflated breath, finally lifting his gaze to meet hers. "Well when you put it that way. It still sounds like a crazy plan and one hell of a longshot. And something the Captain would not be happy about."

A thin, cynical smile touched Anya's lips. "Which is exactly why it is an incredibly good thing that we currently have the entire base to ourselves."

"Well, that's just classic Anya behavior right there," Ryan muttered, a ghost of his trademark grin finally breaking through his exhaustion. "Always looking on the absolute bright side of an apocalyptic abandonment."

"Go ahead, say it," Ryan teased, lightly nudging the edge of her mattress with his boot. "I bet you are really glad you have a tech-genius like me keeping you company right about now."

Anya offered a brief, reluctant nod. It was the unvarnished truth. She never would have possessed the physical strength to drag her broken torso down to the main communications tier on her own, and she definitely wouldn't have known how to configure the routing protocols once she got there.

"Yes, yes stow that ego. Find the signal from the North, it should be the only one without an identifier."

"Thanks for the tip." Ryan replied dryly.

Anya deliberately ignored the fact that he was dramatically rolling his eyes at her as he slipped his headset on. She was used to being the one giving orders or at least the one leading the way. Captain Tennant was always in command at the base, but out with the rangers, they followed her.

Ryan tapped a final sequence into a salvaged keyboard, pointing to a blinking cursor on the display before slipping a secondary headset over Anya's ears and adjusting the microphone arm.

"A heavy, static-laced hiss filled her ears. She swallowed down the dryness in her throat and leaned toward the receiver. "Hello? This is Tigris base calling on a secure channel. Is anyone currently monitoring this frequency?"

For a long, harrowing string of seconds, the only response was the empty, white-noise crackle of the upper atmosphere. Anya shifted uncomfortably against her pillows, the motion causing a dull throb behind her ribs.

"Are you sure it is the right signal? Are we broadcasting only to them?"

Ryan gave her the most profoundly frustrated look she had ever seen him manifest. Without a word, he aggressively spun the main monitor and the keyboard around on the bedside table, angling them directly into her lap. "If you would like to take over, be my guest. This is the same connection that the Captain had and swore never to contact again. See? It even says right there, never communicate with again."

"Now that's not exactly fair." a voice suddenly crackled through the speakers, slicing through the static with startling, crystalline clarity. "All we did was warn you about your imminent death and you block off all communication?"

Anya froze, sharing a look of absolute, paralyzed shock with Ryan. The breath caught in her lungs. They had done it. They had actually successfully initiated a direct line of dialogue with the immortal and they seemed...normal?

"That... that was our Captain," Anya stammered, forcing her voice to stabilize as she gripped the bleached edge of her bedsheet. "He

97

does not place his trust in immortals. Under any circumstances. But for what it's worth, he did take your advice. We are the only two souls left operating inside this base."

Her voice felt thin and fragile, trembling slightly despite her best efforts. She had spent her entire life being trained to fear and destroy these timeless entities.

"That is to be expected I suppose." the voice replied, his tone shifting into a relaxed, almost conversational cadence. "But why did you get left behind? No one wanted to be your moving buddy?"

Ryan and Anya exchanged another quick, bewildered glance. The entity on the other end of the line sounded almost jovial—a bizarre, casual demeanor that was the absolute antithesis of the silent, predatory monsters that hunted them through the ruins of the surface.

"She was wounded getting people out of Phoenix before it blew." Ryan answered for her, leaning into his mic. "I stayed behind with her while she grows a new kidney."

"Well, now, that is mighty chivalrous of you and of her I guess. It's an honor to meet two willing martyrs. Might as well introduce myself. I am Elan. Talus will be here once someone manages to find him. He seems to have wandered off again."

Anya reached out with a trembling hand, her fingers searching the control deck until she found the master mute toggle. She pressed the switch down, cutting their outbound audio feed, and spun her head toward Ryan.

"What do you think?"

Her voice was soft but her mind was running in every direction. She had no idea what to think, for the first time since she found herself completely alone at Phoenix, she was lost. She had no plan and no idea of what to do.

Ryan simply shrugged his shoulders, his expression just as shocked as her own.

With a tight nod, Anya flipped the master toggle back up, restoring the link. The line remained quiet for a long moment. Anya figured that whoever this Elan character was, he was deliberately holding his tongue until Talus arrived at the terminal.

"Hello. This is Talus," a new voice suddenly announced. It was deeper, carrying a measured, clinical authority that immediately commanded attention. "To whom exactly am I speaking?"

"I am Anya and this is Ryan. We are all that is left at Tigris base."

A prolonged, heavy pause settled over the line. Anya didn't realize she was actively holding her breath until it finally escaped her lips in one long, ragged gasp. She couldn't even identify what was making her so intensely nervous; she had faced down enemy plasma fire without her heart rate spiking this severely.

"Anya..." Talus murmured, his voice trailing off as he seemed to ponder the designations. "Why does that name... what?" There was a sudden, muffled scratching sound on the audio feed, followed by the distant cadence of voices, as if someone on their end had hastily cupped a hand over the microphone. A moment later, Talus returned to the channel. "Ah. Yes. Right. You were the one who explicitly disobeyed my structural evacuation protocols and re-entered the lower tiers of Phoenix base after the structural breach occurred. That action is to be commended for its bravery, or severely admonished for its foolishness, I suppose."

"You suppose?" Ryan barked, his protective instincts instantly flaring as he leaned toward his mic. "She took a high-velocity slug to the torso while dragging a group of civilian children out of the rubble, and now we are left stranded in an abandoned base, hoping her biology regrows a freaking kidney before we're attacked!"

"That is an unfortunate complication," Talus responded calmly, entirely unbothered by Ryan's hostility. "But if you are truly alone in that facility, and severely wounded no less, why are you spending your time attempting to initiate contact with us?"

Ryan raised his hands in a helpless gesture, turning his face toward Anya to let her take the lead.

"Because when the Captain informed me about his initial conversation with you. I just thought... maybe you might actually possess some real answers for us," Anya said, her voice growing stronger as the internal fire returned to her chest. "Maybe you know a definitive way to fight back against them. If you are truly the same species as the monsters hunting us down, then you must know their weaknesses. We cannot just spend the rest of our lives using Fulgars to stun them for a few minutes. We win some battles, but we are systematically losing the entire war."

"Wait... did you say you are able to stun them with your devices? I would very much like to know the exact parameters of how those mechanisms operate."

Anya frowned, a chill running down her spine. The question was deeply strange. Did their curiosity imply that none of the northern immortals had ever experienced the effects of a human stun weapon? If that was the case, it meant they weren't simply a faction of enemy soldiers who had suddenly experienced a crisis of conscience and switched sides during the conflict. Could they be a separate lineage of immortals entirely? Ones who had never been on the wrong side of the war in the first place? She had read vague, fragmented accounts of such anomalies in the ancient pre-war histories stored in the archives. But as the nuclear escalation reached its climax, all formal mention of a secondary faction had ceased entirely. Their existence became largely attributed to rumors.

"It's a localized high-voltage arc delivered directly to the neural cluster in the neck," Anya explained, leaning closer to the receiver. "The electrical disruption completely paralyzes an immortal's motor functions for a brief window. Not very long but long enough to get away."

"Of course! The biological nervous system!" Talus' voice broke back in, his clinical detachment completely melting away into pure, scientific fascination. "The synthetic pathways were always significantly more sensitive to localized overloads, but I never once considered utilizing the frequency for total motor paralysis! It isn't exactly the cellular solution I was actively searching for, but that deployment is certainly inspired engineering."

"Talus, before you go back to your lab and electrocute yourself, how about we finish the conversation?" Elan interrupted, his tone laced with amusement. A moment later, his voice focused back on the humans. "So, assuming your base is breached, what exactly is your escape plan?"

"We have a solar plane that we can use to meet up with the others once Anya is ready to travel." Ryan answered for her.

Silence descended over both sides of the transmission. Ryan reached down and muted the outbound audio once more, turning his face toward her. His expression looked significantly more exhausted and drawn than it had when they first started the conversation. They knew very little more than they had ten minutes ago, and yet... what did they really have to lose by continuing? The rest of their people were already gone, marching along separate paths; the coordinates of the primary evacuation remained as safe as they had ever been.

"Sharing information could be useful for both of our endeavors. Would you consider redirecting your flight path north?"

Anya quickly slapped the outbound toggle back on. "You mean... you want us to fly directly to your location?"

Ryan began shaking his head 'no' with a violent, frantic intensity, his eyes wide with warning. But for the first time in the entire conversation, Anya felt her mind locking onto a single, clear destination.

"Prior to the Others discovering the geographical signature of Tigris base, we 'might' have considered sending a dispatch team to your coordinates," Talus explained, his voice turning somber. "But as your circumstances have changed and you find yourselves without a home... you would be welcomed here."

Ryan was still vigorously waving his hands, signaling a total refusal, but Anya had all but made up her mind. Even if she had to navigate the distance by herself, even if she had to drag her bleeding body across the surface on foot—for the first time in her entire generation, the human race had an actual, mathematical chance to move onto the offensive.

"The Others?" she questioned, picking up on the term.

"That is the designation we use to refer to the other faction of immortals," Elan answered softly. "The ones who... well, the ones who did not turn out like us when the transition occurred."

"So there are a lot of you there…and you are all immortals?"

"There are currently five hundred of us operating within this mountain complex, and yes, we are all immortal," Talus stated flatly. "If you choose to navigate to our position, I will transmit our secure landing coordinates and link our primary comm network directly to your plane's navigation computer. If you choose to decline, then we strongly suggest you do not remain inside the Tigris bulkheads a single moment longer than necessary. The Others are closing in on your automated perimeter grids. Their scout units are actively searching the secondary tunnel systems right now."

Anya pressed the mute button down again, turning her body to face Ryan. The dull ache in her side was steadily morphing into a sharp, burning heat, but if Talus' intelligence report was accurate, their escape window was shrinking by the minute. It would take a few days of continuous travel to reach the northern territory, even with the solar plane. The aircraft was engineered for endurance, not raw speed, after all.

"This is madness Anya." Ryan whispered, his hands trembling as he gripped his headset. "We do not even know if we can trust them. What if they are luring us to our death?"

She raised an eyebrow at him. "Really? They have killed thousands of us just by raiding bases and yet they are going to go through all this trouble just to kill two lousy humans? Come on. You have to be dying of curiosity about this. Who knows what kind of data archives we might find up there? Maybe they know how to permanently kill an immortal. That single piece of information would change the status of this entire war."

In her sudden burst of excitement, she accidentally raised her hands to emphasize her point, instantly triggering a sharp, white-hot tug against her abdominal wall. She grimaced hard, her breath catching in a painful gasp as she clutched at the specific point where a clear fluid tube was still surgically sewn into her flank. She pulled her hand away, checking her palm; there was no fresh blood, meaning the internal stitches had managed to hold against the strain. Just a few more days of total immobility, and her biology should have been back to operational status.

Ryan was on her in a split second, leaning over her frame to examine the entry site of the tube and checking the flow lines on her IV rack. He shook his head, his mouth set in a firm, unyielding line.

"If you want me to actively pilot that plane into enemy territory, Anya, then we are making an absolute, non-negotiable deal right now," he said, his voice dropping into a rare, parental strictness. "Two days. You stay pinned to these pillows, you rest, and I will handle the logistical prep for the aircraft. But we are not launching out of that chute until I have verified proof that your new kidney is stable and that your stitched side won't completely tear open. I don't possess the medical supplies or the technical know-how to start cultivating another organ from scratch if you ruin this one."

For a fraction of a second, Anya's stubborn, rebellious streak flared, tempting her to argue the timeline. But as she looked at the genuine terror in her friend's eyes, she forced the impulse down. She needed his skills to fly the plane, and he was right. She wouldn't last a single day if she started bleeding to death internally while they were thousands of feet in the air in the middle of nowhere.

She took a slow, regulating breath, reached out, and flipped the comm switch back to active. She leaned in toward the microphone.

"Send the coordinates," she commanded. "We launch in two days."

10

Talus

Talus held the pictures in his hands, going over them again. He wondered how long this had been going on, how many extractions had he missed? Why hadn't they been paying closer attention? He could not even remember how long the Others had been blowing up bases. Perhaps fifty years ago? Or was it seventy? The decades had a seamless way of bleeding together when death no longer kept time. Elan likely still had the pictures saved from the other bases and they could get a closer look.

Gathering the loose documents into a disorganized stack, Talus turned on his heel and marched out of the lab, his heavy boots echoing sharply down the concrete tunnels toward the communications tier.

He had underestimated his enemy. He had underestimated Cavalk, and he had swore to himself that he would never let that happen again. As he navigated the dark, vaulted corridors, his thoughts became a chaotic, shifting vortex of past and present, memories of pre-war steel structures swirling together with the stark reality of their current underground exile until nothing made logical sense.

He reached the threshold of the primary communications hub and threw the heavy iron door open with a forceful, impatient yank. The sprawling room was silent, dominated by the rhythmic, low-frequency hum of radio towers and the pale green glow of inactive monitor banks.

The main command consoles were empty. Well, mostly empty.

A lone figure was hunched over the auxiliary shortwave array in the far corner. A technician he had barely exchanged a dozen syllables with over the course of their long confinement. How was that even possible after so many years stuck underground together Talus did not know.

"Where is Elan?" Talus demanded, his voice cutting sharply through the static-laced quiet.

The figure stiffened, spinning her swivel chair around with a startled gasp. "Asleep in his quarters, I'd reck'n," she said, her voice carrying a thick, slow Southern drawl that hit Talus' ears like a sudden bucket of ice water. She squinted at the wall clock. "It's purt near three in the mornin', Talus. Whatcha' needin' from the deck at this hour?"

"Satellite photos from immediately following other base attacks but before the explosions."

She nodded and leaned back in her chair.

The woman nodded slowly, leaning back against the mesh padding of her seat. "Elan keeps those specific high-security files locked down tight on his personal mainframe. He ain't even puttin' those images on our local server for the rest of the crew to browse. I ken getcha into his terminal, though. Just give me a sec to bypass his local lock."

She stood up, her movements casual and unhurried as she walked over to Elan's primary command station near the door. Her fingers danced across the interface with practiced ease, clearing the security prompts and initializing the encrypted directory where the photos were archived.

"He's the only one who truly understands the folder organization in this terminal," she noted, stepping back to grant him access. "So I'm hopin' you can actually decipher what yer lookin' for in there."

"Thank you, Betsy," Talus said, offering a tight, formal nod as he stepped forward. "You are becoming remarkably proficient with these network routing systems."

He had absolutely no idea if that statement was accurate, but it felt like a significantly kinder option than admitting he had spent the decades completely ignoring her existence.

"Aw, bless yer heart for noticing," Betsy replied, her face lighting up with a brief, genuine warmth. "Elan's been helping me out a bit 'ere and there when the lines are quiet."

With a soft murmur, Betsy returned to her auxiliary station, leaving Talus alone in front of the primary monitor.

A familiar, low-level anxiety rippled beneath his skin as he stared at the glowing interface. He was still nervous every time that he got in front of a new computer, ever since his first experience with his new computer in this base. The sadistic computer was always working against him.

He began scrolling through the massive data directories, his frustration mounting within seconds. He had no functional understanding of Elan's cryptographic filing system. The directories were labeled with endless, seemingly random strings of alpha-numeric code—numerical sequences that could signify coordinate parameters, orbital paths, or data classifications. There were thousands of individual sub-folders nested within the mainframe; if he attempted to manually audit every image file himself, he would be pinned to this computer until the geothermal systems failed.

Logic dictated that he should simply abandon the terminal and wait for Elan to return to his post at dawn, but the raw desire for answers burned too fiercely behind his ribs. Besides, if he was being thoroughly honest with himself, he had absolutely nothing else to occupy his thoughts during the dark hours of the night. With a heavy, defeated sigh, he clicked open the first directory in the sequence and began scrolling.

Time lost all meaning. Talus moved from folder to folder, his eyes burning as the black-and-white topography of destroyed bases became a seamless, exhausting blur. He lost all track of the chronological count.

At some point during the night, Betsy had departed her station, offering him a soft pat on the shoulder and a quiet, sleepy "bless yer heart" before slipping out into the residential corridor. She had been replaced on the rearguard shift by Ben—a remarkably young, brilliant immortal who had quickly become something of a celebrated icon among the underground laboratory circles for his work on shortwave frequency modification.

"Hello? Anyone there?"

The voice filtered through the ambient static of the room, thin and fragile. Talus kept his eyes fixed on the screen, his fingers continuing their rhythmic tapping across the arrow keys.

"Hello?"

The second transmission arrived a moment later, and this time, the voice broke through Talus' hyper-focus, pulling his eyes away from the screen. It was the girl. The human Ranger from Tigris base.

Ben paused at his neighboring console, his hand hovering over his headset as he looked over at Talus. "You want me to take it or you?"

Talus looked over to Ben. That was a good question, did he want to talk to her? He didn't know. But he knew with absolute certainty that he did not want anyone else to talk to her and risk the human pair changing their plans.

"I will take it." Talus said, his voice firm.

Ben nodded understandingly, turning back to his own diagnostic monitors without another word.

Talus reached over, lifting the heavy leather headset and slipping it over his ears. He adjusted the adjustable microphone arm, positioning it a mere fraction of an inch from his lips; he had no desire for their conversation to become public currency among the night-shift, and eventually Cary and Elan.

"This is Talus." he spoke into the microphone, keeping his register low and measured. "Are you in need of assistance?"

A long silence stretched across the tight-beam channel. The white-noise hiss of the upper atmosphere was so intense that Talus began to wonder if her transmission had experienced a terminal encryption failure, or if whatever medical complication she was hiding had suddenly taken a ruinous turn.

"Couldn't sleep," her voice finally crackled through the earpieces.

His face twisted with confusion. He had no idea what that had to do with him or why that meant she needed to get on comms to call him.

"And?" he prompted, his tone tilting toward his standard clinical detachment.

"Ryan is asleep in his quarters. It's too quiet here with everyone gone."

Once again he wondered what any of this had to do with him. His eyes drifted back to the monitor screen, which was currently rendering a high-contrast photograph of an empty ridge that offered absolutely nothing of tactical value. It was becoming increasingly apparent that he would accomplish nothing of substance before Elan returned to find the right files.

"Can I ask you something?"

The voice was back and he frowned. He had a suspicion that whatever she wanted to ask was not going to have an easy answer.

"You can ask," he replied cautiously, leaning back against his seat. "But I cannot promise an answer."

"Who are you really?" The questions began to erupt out of her, her cadence accelerating with an intense, desperate curiosity. "Where do you come from? How old are you? Are you someone we can really trust? Where have you been all this time? Did you fight in the war? How do you survive? Do you even eat or sleep? Did you used to be one of the Others? Why don't you pick a side?"

He tried to follow her onslaught of questions but knew that most if not all would have to wait.

"Let's start with just one question and go from there." he said softly, his voice dropping into a calming, deliberate rhythm.

Another prolonged, heavy pause hung over the line.

"Can I trust you?" she asked.

The words were stripped of their military bravado, revealing the raw, unvarnished vulnerability of a soldier left behind in the dark. Talus' frown deepened. He had no idea how to answer that. She had no reason to trust him and he had nothing that he could say that would convince her to trust him. After all he was just a voice on her comm, a voice coming from a creature that had killed countless numbers of her companions.

"I have no way to reassure you that you can" Talus answered honestly, "No one here will harm you but we are by our counterparts, creatures that you cannot trust. All I can logically offer you, Ranger, is an invitation to have faith."

"Faith seems like an incredibly archaic concept now," she murmured bitterly. "Like something from an old history file."

"Organized religion might have faded but never faith." Talus countered gently. "Faith is a biological imperative, Anya. It will always manifest in some form or another, so long as a conscious mind is breathing."

"I don't even know what to have faith in anymore."

The soft sorrow in her voice caused Talus to hit the power toggle on Elan's monitor, plunging the complex directories into darkness. He leaned back in his chair, letting the silence of his own hub surround him.

People," he said quietly into the microphone. "There is always faith to be had in people."

"Does that include you?"

He let out a long, slow breath. "That depends on the day and who you ask. Personally, I have always found it harder to have faith in myself than in others."

"Yeah," she sighed. "I get that."

"There are many individuals within these tunnels that I place my absolute faith in," Talus continued, his thoughts drifting toward Cary, Elan, and the rest of his fractured collective. "And I continue to maintain a foolish, stubborn faith in those who have proven they do not deserve it. Furthermore... I am beginning to find faith in you, Anya. Already, you and your companion have demonstrated more raw courage and willingness to trust the unknown than many of my own kind have shown in years."

"Perhaps because I am the only one that sees that we are

running out of options," she countered dryly.

"Or it is because you have faith."

Silence reclaimed the channel. Talus found his thoughts drifting to the young woman preparing to travel an immense distance into the unknown on the off-chance that she could save an entire civilization. It was cocky and bold, two things that he found he admired in her.

"Why are you different?" she asked suddenly.

It was the question he had known she would ask and one she deserved the answer to, even if he did not quite know how to answer it.

"Ask me when you get here," he replied.

"Is that your insurance that I'll come?"

"It is a conversation that I would vastly prefer to have in person," Talus explained, his voice softening. "I want you to see me and see the rest of the people here before you know the truth of how it all started."

"Fair enough," she conceded. "But how did the transition initially happen? When exactly did the surface environment become so toxic to humans? Did anyone among the old leadership try to stop the escalation before the war? Who was it that unlocked immortality? None of our salvaged history logs mention a name. Who knew about the research? How did the Axis powers manage to synthesize the serum?"

"Those questions could take days to answer." Talus said, a tightening sensation forming in his chest. "and many of them have to do with things I cannot reveal until your arrival."

"You expect me to come on nothing but faith?"

A genuine, faint smile touched Talus' lips. "Yes. I do."

"Is there anything at all that you can tell me about yourself?"

That question was not any easier for him to answer. Talus stared down at his gloved hands, completely unsure how to summarize his own existence. Who was he anymore? Who was he then? Just a scientist trying to live up to expectations, just trying to be who his parents wanted and then he lost them both before he accomplished anything. Perhaps, he thought bitterly, it was a profound mercy that they never lived long enough to witness what his research had ultimately accomplished.

"I do not know what to say."

"Start at the beginning." she encouraged, her voice warming slightly. "Tell me about kid Talus, if you can remember that far back."

He laughed, the old jokes were definitely something he should have been expecting.

"I was orphaned at six. Things were…not as good as they used to be or so I was told. The orphanages were completely overwhelmed and critically low on basic food rations; the civic social services were crumbling under the weight of the resource war. I was living on the streets barely surviving. Then, the woman who I would eventually call my mother found me behind a warehouse and brought me home one afternoon."

"Did they love you?"

The question arrived with a sudden, piercing sharpness that caught him off guard. He thought back to the rigid, clinical architecture of his childhood home, remembering the profound debt of gratitude he had carried for his parents. His mother had been a matter-of-fact woman, always straightforward, always brutally honest about why she had chosen to pull him from the gutters; she believed it was the ethical duty of every citizen who possessed excess resources to do their part to alleviate the collective suffering. It was a noble, structural philosophy—but she had ultimately never viewed him as anything more than a necessary moral obligation.

His father, however, had been built from entirely different material.

"My father did," Talus murmured, his throat tightening as his eyes focused on the empty space of the room, visualizing his father's brilliant, wide smile. "He would tell me he loved me every single morning. He was always offering a warm hand or a strong hug to lift my spirits when things were bad—which was often for me. A stray child pulled from the lower street sectors didn't exactly belong in the high-tier prep academies they enrolled me in. To the rest of the class, I was always the street trash. Never the companion. Never the friend." His throat was constricting and his eyes were seeing nothing but his father's smile. That big smile he had when their project had been chosen to come to the most advanced base in the country.

He shook his head, trying to banish the images. He had given so little thought to his father over the past few decades. He had so many regrets that there were moments he wondered if there was even time to ponder the loss of his father in the grand scheme of it all.

"I could have used a father like that." Anya said quietly.

"Your parents were not there for you?"

"I thought they were," she replied, her voice dropping into a flat, detached register. "I spent my early childhood believing we were all perfectly happy, the four of us. I believed they loved me, that they desperately wanted me as part of the family. I was so completely content with my little family, with parents and an older brother who protected me. Then, a few weeks before my seventh birthday, I was processed for mandatory screening within the Phoenix base Ranger selection program, like every child born there. Two days after my birthday, the enforcers arrived with the transfer mandates. I was cleared for enlistment. Without so much as a final hug goodbye... my family simply signed the transfer logs and gave me away to the barracks."

Talus frowned, his scientific mind attempting to reconcile the logistics. "Why would you say goodbye? Were you not still operating within the same base?"

"At the Phoenix installation, natural family bonds are categorized as a distraction to military efficiency," Anya explained, the coldness of her training bleeding back into her voice. "Children who clear the screening metrics are immediately relocated to separate training sectors, and every single hour of their existence is dedicated to combat readiness and tactical optimization. It can take years before a recruit is granted a twenty-minute supervised visitation window with their biological family. My family was reassigned to a completely different southern base structure shortly after my transfer, so I never even received that chance."

"I am truly sorry, Anya," Talus said, the words heavy with a genuine, heavy sorrow.

"We do what we must to ensure the survival of the species, right?" she countered, a cynical edge returning to her tone. "The drill instructors trained me remarkably well. Because of that conditioning, I possessed the capability to drag civilians out of hot zones; I learned how to track and neutralize immortals. My deployment missions at Phoenix provided a sense of fulfillment. I suppose it is a fair trade to ruin a life or two if that sacrifice ensures the preservation of others, right?"

"You can keep telling yourself that if it helps. But an individual can be a great success and a great fighter, perhaps even a better one if you have people that you can count on. Were you not as capable at Tigris as you were at Phoenix?"

He was intrigued. There was only so much that he was able to learn from the pictures and videos. Maybe there was a reason why they had not seen rangers taken from other bases. Maybe the Others had realized the strength of Phoenix warriors too and wanted to use them.

"Tigris puts more value on life." Anya explained. "There were far fewer surface supply sweeps ordered by the Captain, which naturally meant fewer emergency rescue operations. The Rangers were almost never deployed into active immortal territory unless a critical structural resource was compromised. The only combat exposure I received was inside the training simulator wings. It wasn't the same."

"So being a ranger lacks value to your mind unless you get to hurt your adversary?" Talus asked, testing her boundaries.

"Being a Ranger has to mean something," she snapped back, her voice flashing with a sudden, bright intensity. "Every single thing I have sacrificed across my life has to mean something, accomplish something, Talus. I was happy once. My family was happy. I know we were. And then the entire world is stripped away from me just so I can wear a Ranger uniform. It has to amount to something more than just training simulations. I have been thrown away like garbage twice now in my life. I refuse to accept that all that hurt was for nothing."

There it was, Talus realized. That was the driving force propelling her across a continent into the unknown.

"You do mean something, Anya," he said with absolute, unyielding certainty. "And you will realize that worth when you arrive."

"Talus? What on earth are you doing at this console?"

Talus spun his chair around to find Elan standing behind him, rubbing the sleep from his eyes, his hair a disheveled mess from the bunks. The ambient lighting of the hub had shifted to a pale morning gray; their dialogue had consumed far more time than he had realized.

"I just thought I would get a look at…" Talus began, his voice trailing off as he realized with a jolt of panic that the outbound audio feed was still active. Anya could hear every syllable. He quickly leaned into the microphone.

"Get some rest Anya. Elan will be on comms if you need anything."

"Bye Talus." her voice came back, soft and clear.

"Goodbye, Anya."

Slowly, deliberately, he lifted the headset from his ears and set it down on the terminal desk, his eyes remaining fixed on the dark monitor screen as if he could see her face through the glass. He made a quiet, unyielding promise to his own conscience that he would find a way to make that girl feel worthwhile when she finally crossed his threshold.

"Sooooo," Elan droned, his voice dripping with an insufferable, theatrical amusement as he stepped forward to examine the logs. "You've gone and developed a little soft spot for the human soldier, have you?"

Elan's teasing words instantly shattered the fragile gravity of the moment, snapping Talus violently back into the stark reality of his position. He remembered exactly who he was—and what he had done. He was the architect of the end; she was the product of the ruins. He could never become an entity she could safely trust. Even if he managed to earn a fragment of her faith over the coming weeks, the absolute second she discovered the truth, she would never forgive him.

"Do not be ridiculous," Talus barked, his voice regaining its stiff, clinical coldness. "I was simply managing the comms as someone had seen fit to abandon his post."

"Some of us have to eat and sleep Talus. Even you sleep sometimes, out in the grass."

Talus shot Elan a dark, lethal glare that could have wilted a field of daisies.

"Or so I've heard through the grapevine!" Elan added hastily, raising his hands in retreat. "I mean, honestly, who in their right mind believes a single syllable that comes out of Cary's mouth anyway? Absolutely no one. That's who. Now, what can I actually do for you this morning, Talus?"

A slight nod at the apt change in subject and Talus got up to offer Elan back his seat.

"I am trying to find satellite images of other base attacks, images of right before the explosions."

Elan's demeanor instantly shifted into serious, professional focus. He nodded, his fingers moving across the keyboard with blinding speed as he entered a complex series of search parameters into his proprietary indexing program.

"You are trying to see if there were other rangers taken that we missed. It is worth a try."

He spent the rest of the morning with Elan going through the photos. They found absolutely nothing. The previous base attacks had been executed with too much speed, the smoke screens too dense to yield a clear look at the courtyard traffic. It had been a long shot from the start, but Talus was grateful for the tedious work; at the very least, it kept his mind from drifting back to the sound of Anya's voice for a few hours.

"Thank you for the assistance regardless, Elan," Talus said, standing up from the terminal as the morning shift technicians began filtering into the room. "Let me know if you hear from An- the humans and keep an eye on their departure. I will speak to the rest to make sure they are ready as well. I take it everyone knows that we are welcoming humans."

"Abso-fucking-lutely! But don't worry, I told them to be completely discreet."

He had no idea when Cary got here, but he was pretty sure that he had told Cary to keep the arrival of the humans on as need to know basis as possible.

"Cary, do you recall what happened the last time someone new arrived at the base after years of isolation?"

"Well yes but-"

"And they weren't even human." Talus cut him off, taking a step forward.

"I know but I told them-"

"When in our entire collective history has a single individual in this mountain ever demonstrated the capacity for discretion?" Talus interrupted, his hands flaring out in exasperation. "Our people are functionally incapable of it! They cannot even walk past a standard goldfish tank in the corridor without violently tapping their knuckles against the glass just to see what happens!"

He knew that one from experience because anytime someone entered his lab for the first time they felt compelled to tap on his glass fish tank. Luckily for his fish, everyone had visited his lab by now.

"Well think of it this way, at least they will get all those seriously boring introductions out of the way quickly."

"Or scare them off."

"Yes or that."

"Just make sure they are comfortable and try to keep them away from the rest of the group until they possess a baseline level of trust with us. Swarming two rangers is likely to lead to several people being shot."

Cary shrugged, pulling out a digital layout of the residential tiers. "What do you think, one room or two?"

Talus looked at Cary with confusion.

Cary let out a loud, theatrical sigh, shaking his head at the ceiling. "What? You might choose to live like a completely celibate, ancient king of loneliness over here in your dark lab, Talus, but think about the context. We have one male human who voluntarily chose to abandon everyone he knows just to stay behind and nurse one female human back to health in a dead base...seems a bit like a couple to me." Cary continued.

"Wait...are you suggesting that others in the base are not like I am? I have not seen any children wandering about...not even sure that it is possible or what would..." Talus said.

"You sound like a prude old maid. Talus, Kit's parents are not the only couples that remained here. And there are plenty who are single and well some still have needs. Elan and I have a close relationship in fact. And children are easily prevented in this day and age, even for us Talus."

He had to concede the point to Cary. He was so absorbed in his memories and his lab that he paid little attention to anyone else.

"I suppose the best place for them would be the quarters by you. Because your wing is the most isolated and we don't want to overwhelm them with too many people." Cary continued, his finger tapping a specific coordinate on the digital map.

Talus narrowed his eyes. "Of course you would think that."

"You said you wanted to work with them, now they won't have far to walk to get you."

"Anything to make me uncomfortable."

"Wouldn't have it any other way Tally."

"My payback has always been worse Carebear." Talus warned, though the edge had completely left his voice.

Cary delivered a heavy, affectionate slap to Talus' back as he turned toward the exit. "Yeah, yeah, keep threatening me, old man. But your game has been off as of late."

Cary walked off and headed toward wherever he was going. Talus really wondered if Cary just spent his days wandering around because he always seemed to be passing through anywhere Talus happened to be on his way to somewhere else.

"Need I remind you that you are nearly as old as I am?" Talus shouted down the corridor after his retreating form.

Cary didn't stop, simply hoisting a single arm in the air to deliver a parting gesture. "Key word right there is nearly, old man! You're still senior to me, Grandpa!"

Talus shook his head, a genuine, soft smile breaking through his stern composure for a brief fraction of a second before he consciously forced the expression back down into the dark. He turned his steps back toward the silent sanctuary of his laboratory.

If his midnight conversation with Anya had demonstrated

anything at all, it was the crushing magnitude of what he had to answer for in this life and what little right he had to feel even the fleeting comfort and happiness of normal existence.

11

Anya

"Are you completely sure you have everything packed and ready?" Anya asked, leaning forward to peer into the narrow cargo space in the back of the fuselage. It was packed so tightly she couldn't make out the shapes of the individual bags. "Should I do another quick pass for gear? If you missed something, or if you packed a bunch of food that's just going to spoil on us——"

"Anya, please stop worrying and second-guessing me," Ryan interrupted, not looking up from the navigation console. "I packed exactly what we need, enough of what we need, and honestly, that is all this plane can physically hold. We're good on rations for the entire trip, provided we don't eat like pigs. The only downside is that it's strictly tube food. Our space is too limited to waste on anything fresh."

She gave a reluctant nod, watching him shove the very last items into the remaining gaps: a heavy camouflage tarp and a compact two-person tent. Because of her injury, she hadn't been allowed to lift a single crate——a strict condition Ryan had set to even allow her to make the journey. Still, as she scanned the cargo, she noticed he had tucked an extra-large trauma kit into the corner, despite his constant reminders that he wouldn't know how to help if her new kidney started failing mid-flight.

"Are you still sure about this?" Ryan asked suddenly, his hands flying up as he began gesturing wildly. "I mean, what if this is all for nothing? What if they don't even have food up there? Do immortals even eat? What if we can't breathe the air in their sector, or our respirator masks fail? What if they just decide to kill us the second we touch down?"

His voice was climbing in pitch, his frantic scenarios proving just how terrified he actually was. In all honesty, Ryan wasn't the greatest Ranger to ever carry a rifle into the field, but he was exactly the guy you wanted back at base pushing the buttons. He could build, fix, or reprogram absolutely anything; he was just a little short on a backbone when it came to the unknown.

"Well, if they do kill us, then we will have had one last great adventure before we die," Anya said calmly. "What else is there left for us, Ryan? Do you really want to spend the rest of your life scurrying into the dark every time the lights come on? That just makes us the cockroaches and those monsters the superior beings. Personally, I'd like to flip the tables for once and have a real shot at being on top."

Ryan sighed, closing the main cargo hatch and stepping up beside her. They were standing on the ground floor of the Tigris hangar, surrounded by a dozen different heavy vehicles. Most of them had barely been used over the last decade, but Ryan and his engineering crew had spent thousands of hours keeping every single engine functional and operational. Even so, the subterranean tunnel transport system had always been the squad's preferred method for getting around. It took significantly less power and kept them entirely off the enemy's radar.

Anya leaned back against the smooth hull of the plane, trying to take in the sheer scale of the empty hangar. Her side pulled sharply at the motion. It was still incredibly sore and tender, considering she had only been disconnected from her medical tubes a few hours ago. She winced, accidentally drawing a sharp, warnings-laced look from Ryan.

She had only been stationed here a few years, yet Tigris was the only place that had ever genuinely felt like home. Phoenix base was where she had been born and raised, sure, but Tigris was where she had actually lived. It was the place where she finally figured out who she was and who she wanted to be. Standing here now, she felt a sudden, heavy guilt, like she was abandoning a teammate in the middle of a firefight, leaving the base behind to die. She had to forcefully remind herself that it was just concrete and steel now. Nothing more than empty rooms. Everyone she cared about was already gone and safe. At least, she desperately hoped they were.

"Are you 100% sure you know how to get where we're going?" she asked, breaking the silence.

"Not a clue," Ryan admitted, checking a terminal readout. "I've never flown this specific aircraft this far out. To be honest, I'm not even entirely certain it can make the distance. The Captain never authorized us for long-range missions. It was always just short reconnaissance flights."

Anya blinked, turning her head to stare at him. "Wait. You've actively wanted to fly this thing further away from the base? Into enemy territory?"

"Look, being able to push this plane to its absolute physical limits is half the reason I agreed to this crazy plan," Ryan said, a sudden spark entering his eyes. "There's just something about gliding up among the clouds that makes your spirit feel completely free. You get that feeling when you're fighting on the surface, Anya. I get it when I'm up in the sky."

It was time to move. The sun was just beginning to crest the jagged horizon, and the plane's battery banks were topped off with as much power the base's generators could give them. It was just enough juice to get them airborne until the morning sun could hit the wing panels and provide the continuous energy needed to stay aloft. Yet, neither of them moved. They just stood there, staring up at the vaulted ceilings of Tigris. They both knew it was highly likely they would never see this fortress again, and though neither wanted to say it out loud, it was just as unlikely they would ever lay eyes on any of her old inhabitants again either.

"Did you ever tell the Captain we weren't coming to Tressle?" Ryan asked quietly.

Anya cringed internally. She knew she should have, and it wasn't entirely her fault that she hadn't. Captain Tennant had checked in over the shortwave channel just yesterday, asking if they were still holding out until her vitals stabilized. But according to Elan, the enemy was steadily cracking the human encryption codes. She hadn't wanted to risk letting the primary immortal divisions know exactly which direction she was heading. For all she knew, Talus' rogue faction was exactly who the enemy commanders were actively hunting down. Besides, she knew the Captain would never, under any circumstances, approve of her marching straight into a nest of the monsters. It was better to let him know once they were safely inside the northern perimeter. He still had weeks of heavy foot travel ahead, and their long-range comms wouldn't be truly secure until they reached the Tressle relay station anyway.

"No," Anya said softly. "You know exactly how he would react. Why worry him while he's managing a massive civilian evacuation? We can ping his channel when we get there safely."

Ryan nodded, accepting the logic, and the pair settled back into a heavy silence.

"Well, I guess it's time to go then," Ryan muttered, reaching for the cockpit handle. "I'm really going to miss this place. Especially the way it was after you showed up."

"You mean after I was banished here?" Anya asked, a sudden flash of bitterness clipping her words. It surprised her; she genuinely thought she was past those old wounds. After all, hadn't she just taken a bullet to the torso to save children from Phoenix base? Hadn't one of their medics saved her life in return?

"I wouldn't call it a banishment, Anya. That certainly wasn't how the crew saw it here, especially not Captain Tennant," Ryan said, turning to look her dead in the eye. "He knew from the very first day you arrived that you were going to change the entire dynamic of our unit. You were a liability to the brass at Phoenix because you wouldn't blindly follow their archaic rules, but you were a savior to us. The Rangers here would have followed Captain Tennant to the literal ends of the earth if he had asked them to. But the thing is, he never would have asked. He was too cautious. Then you came along, and suddenly there was someone else the squad was willing to follow anywhere. And unlike the Captain, you were actually brave enough to lead them there.”

Anya frowned, her chest tightening. She wasn't entirely sure that was a compliment. Was she really the type of leader who would march her people directly into danger just for the fleeting chance of getting the upper hand for a day or a week? Wasn't that exactly what she was doing to Ryan right now?

Seeing her expression, Ryan quickly held up a hand. “That... came out completely wrong. What I mean is, you gave people something to fight for again. You made us think we might actually stand a chance in this war. Yeah, you take massive risks and you put people in danger, but it’s always because you genuinely believe there’s a greater reward waiting out there. Phoenix never understood that and yet it was what saved the lives of those children. Maybe this risk, this crazy chance of leading us right into the north, maybe it will end up saving everyone. Now come on, get in. If we treat this like a tragic goodbye, we’re going to lose our hope of ever seeing this place again. And who knows? We might just see it again yet.”

As she reached for the passenger frame, Anya found her mind drifting back to the day she had first arrived at Tigris. The culture at Phoenix base was incredibly rigid; they trained the absolute best Rangers in the world, and then they immediately shipped them off to secondary outposts like products on an assembly line. Technically, Anya had never even finished her formal training; the brass at Phoenix had shipped her out to the only installation willing to take her a full year before her final evaluations. Mamoru had been the only instructor who fought for her to stay, but he was barely out of the training barracks himself back then and possessed zero bureaucratic authority. She had no family left and very few friends because she simply couldn't force herself to live the way they demanded. She had arrived at Tigris broken and utterly defeated, fully expecting to be treated like the lowest tier on the totem pole. Instead, she had been met with open, welcoming arms. She had found true friends, trusted comrades, and maybe—in the Captain and Ryan—something resembling a family.

“I hope so,” she said quietly. She took one last, sweeping look at the concrete hangar before climbing into the cockpit seat next to him.

Ryan handed her a heavy headset that matched his own, then buckled himself into the pilot's harness. The cockpit was incredibly tight; the space was so confined that Ryan had to brush against her arm just to reach some of the primary environmental controls, and his knee would touch hers if he moved even an inch in her direction. Still, the claustrophobia was a small price to pay. They were finally getting away from the silent corridors and that horrible white room, and they were on their way to meet a completely unknown faction of immortals. Now that was exactly the sort of impossible adventure she had always dreamed about when she was a kid staring at the barracks ceiling.

"Alright, systems are green," Ryan said, throwing a series of master breakers. "Time to head up."

The heavy maintenance elevator beneath the plane's landing gear began to rumble and creak in the dark. The mechanism was old and it was rarely used for aircraft deployment anymore. But the massive hydraulic cylinders held, steadily pushing the plane upward toward the mountain's surface apex. When they finally reached the primary airlock platform, the heavy steel blast doors split apart in a perfect, overlapping sequence, allowing the nose of the plane to clear the vault while the internal seals prevented the contaminated surface atmosphere from rushing into the lower base levels. It never ceased to amaze Anya the sheer, desperate lengths the old world scientists had gone to all those generations ago just to engineer a way to survive after the planet broke.

"Hey," Ryan said, a teasing smirk pulling at the corner of his mouth as he gripped the throttle. "Have you ever actually flown before?"

Anya glared at him through her visor. He was joking, obviously. There were probably only a handful of humans left on the entire planet who had ever been inside an operational aircraft. The high-ranking command staff had always claimed it was far too dangerous to utilize the skies; for all they knew, the primary immortal divisions possessed automated anti-air arrays that could swat them out of the clouds in seconds. Not that it would take an advanced targeting computer to do it, experimental solar planes didn't exactly move very fast.

"Am I going to get horribly sick from this?" Anya fired back, her voice deadpan over the comm link. "Is there a window I can roll down, or are we going to be stuck sharing the contents of my stomach for the next three days? Is there a backup parachute in case I completely lose my mind and need to bail out over the ridge? What happens if the sun goes behind a thick storm cloud, Ryan? Are we just going to instantly fall out of the sky like a rock? What if—"

"Alright, alright, I get the point," Ryan laughed, cutting her off as he brought the electric motors up to a high-pitched whine. "You're hilarious. And just for that, I am going to intentionally hunt down some massive turbulence the second we hit those clouds."

She shot him a sharp look, her hands instantly reaching out to find a handle bar to hold onto. She was completely fine with heights, but only under the strict condition that her boots were still firmly anchored to the dirt.

With a quick sequence of button presses, Ryan jammed the throttle forward. The plane accelerated down the short launch ramp, the electric motors screaming as they gathered speed. Anya's hands clenched into white-knuckled fists and she squeezed her eyes tight as they rocketed out over the cliff face.

She felt her stomach instantly drop into her throat as the ground vanished beneath them, the entire vibration of the aircraft shifting from a harsh, mechanical rattle to a smooth, weightless drift. She kept her eyes locked tight, utterly unsure if her equilibrium could handle the visual input that went along with what her gut was currently experiencing.

"You know, I feel like I am witnessing something truly monumental right now: seeing the legendary Ranger Anya this incredibly nervous," Ryan's voice chuckled in her ears. "I always figured there had to be something that would get under your skin, but I never would have guessed it'd be something as simple as a little altitude. Open your eyes, Anya. It's really quite beautiful out here. Just make sure you look up, and not down."

She didn't want to listen to him. She honestly preferred the idea of keeping her world completely blacked out, picturing herself safely back on solid ground. In her mind, she tried to imagine she was just standing on the highest peak of the Tigris ridge, watching the sunrise. But then a sudden, minor pocket of air caused the cabin to dip, and that weightless, floating sensation in her stomach made her feel like she was actively falling off the edge of that same cliff. Realizing the mental gymnastics weren't working, she decided opening her eyes might actually be the lesser of two evils.

She cracked one eye open, then the other, squinting hard against the piercing brightness of the morning sun.

There, stretched out as far as the horizon could reach, was a brilliant, endless sky of deep blue, highlighted by wispy, glowing swirls of high-altitude clouds. Looking up at the sky from the muddy basin of the surface was absolutely nothing compared to being high enough to feel like you could reach out and touch the vapor.

"Why exactly can I not look down?" she asked, her curiosity finally overriding her panic.

"Two reasons," Ryan answered, his eyes scanning the primary battery readouts. "First, if you're already terrified of the height, staring at a three-thousand-foot drop isn't going to do your heart rate any favors. And second... it's not always a very pretty sight down there."

Naturally, that was all it took to completely spark her stubborn streak. Anya turned her head toward the passenger window, bracing her shoulder against the frame, and forced herself to look straight down.

Directly below their wingtips, the world was a jagged, monotonous expanse of gray rocks and the same pale, beige sand she had witnessed every single day of her life. Endless, dead plains of dust and stone. She found herself wondering if she would ever live long enough to see another color cover the ground, such as green grass or purple flowers. She knew from the navigation charts that they would have to cross over a massive body of dead water in order to reach the northern territory, so at least there might be some variation of blue in their future.

But as she continued to study the shifting landscape below, she finally realized what Ryan had meant about the view.

They were gliding directly over the skeletal remains of an ancient, pre-war town. From this altitude, the structural damage was almost beautiful; it was incredibly easy to see exactly where the grand grid of streets used to run, and how much of the crumbling brick and concrete buildings had been slowly, systematically reclaimed by the desert sands. She knew this was a sight that would only increase in frequency as they flew further north, especially when they began crossing over the massive, high-density ruins of the old world cities.

"There are so many stories buried down there," Anya murmured, her forehead pressing against the cool plexiglass. "I would love to just spend a week wandering through all of it."

She knew the history of these specific settlements; the towns scattered across the middle of this barren desert had mostly been constructed as support hubs for the military installations before the war reached its nuclear climax. They had been engineered to blend seamlessly into the beige terrain to avoid orbital targeting. She had never once in her life seen a real, functional city where ordinary people just lived normal, civilian lives. She knew from the archives that there were places where millions of humans had once walked the streets simultaneously—a number that her brain, raised in the quiet isolation of the underground, could barely even begin to comprehend.

"Our trip would take much longer that way." Ryan said, adjusting the trim of the aircraft to catch a steadier pocket of air. "It's going to take us a few days to reach their coordinates as it is. But don't worry, you'll get to see your big cities before the day is out."

Anya quieted down, her eyes still tracing the fading outlines of the dead settlement below. "Thank you, Ryan. For coming with me. Honestly, I'd probably be trying to walk the entire distance right now if it weren't for you, and I don't think the odds would have been in my favor."

Ryan turned his head toward her, a bright, incredibly warm grin breaking across his face. Anya smiled back, a sudden wave of absurdity hitting her so hard she nearly laughed out loud. It was completely crazy. Who would have ever thought some reject Ranger, kicked out of her own division, would be flying high above the clouds on her way to broker a deal with a hidden faction of immortals? Immortals who just might possess the structural capability to stop the entire world from burning.

Her mind wandered back to her origins. What would her old drill instructors at Phoenix base think if they could see her now? What would Captain Tennant think? Sometimes she felt that she was nothing more than a weapon born and bred, entirely stripped of a normal human identity. The only people whose opinions had ever truly mattered to her were her commanding officers and a few lucky Rangers she had been assigned with. No civilian friends, no biological family to speak of. What sort of life was that, really?

A sharp, static tone chimed through their headsets, shattering her thoughts.

"Ryan, this is Elan," the voice filtered smoothly through the tight-beam channel. "Are you currently underway?"

Ryan tapped his microphone arm. "Ryan to Elan, we are officially in the air. Clear skies so far. With good winds and a little bit of luck, we should be able to make the entire journey in three days."

"I will let the rest know. Keep in touch and if you need anything I will be here. Talus has ordered me to stay on comm to make sure you get in safely."

Anya leaned closer to her microphone, her curiosity piqued. She couldn't help but wonder what kind of individual this Talus actually was. It certainly wasn't a name she had ever encountered in the salvaged pre-war history logs or the Ranger databases. He was obviously the supreme commander of the hidden base, judging by the authoritative way he had spoken during their midnight transmission and the distinct tone of respect Elan used whenever he mentioned him. But his voice... it had sounded so profoundly pained, carrying an exhausting, heavy fatigue that she hadn't known how to process. Maybe he was just ancient. If he was an immortal from the first generation, he had to be well over 100 years old.

"Hey, Elan?" Anya interjected. "Who exactly is Talus? I mean, he's your Captain, right?"

There was a brief, low hum of static over the line before Elan answered, his tone thoroughly amused. "We do not operate as an army within these tunnels, Ranger, so no, he is not a captain. If your vocabulary requires you to label him as our leader, you may do so, though I can guarantee he would vehemently deny the title."

"Then what is it that you actually do down there?" she pushed, eager for any scrap of data.

"We simply try to live as best we know how," Elan explained softly. "Many of the individuals within this base are specialized scientists in their own right. They have merely continued their historical research projects here, buried in absolute privacy and silence. You will understand the layout much better when you arrive. In fact, Talus has personally granted you the vacant residential quarters directly adjacent to his own laboratory tier. That means you'll have the absolute best guide on the base to answer your questions when you want them, and plenty of privacy when you do not."

Elan's voice was light, carrying a vague, teasing edge, but he was speaking with a deliberate, slow caution—as if he were navigating a minefield of classified protocols, unsure of exactly how much truth he was allowed to give away.

"But who is he really?" Anya insisted. "Where does he come from?"

Ryan shot her a sharp, panicked look from the pilot's seat, his eyes practically screaming at her to drop it. She knew exactly what he was thinking: he desperately didn't want her wearing out their welcome or provoking their hosts before they even crossed the regional border. But the burning curiosity was eating her alive. This entire mountain facility was a massive, unprecedented mystery, intentionally hidden from the human race for a century until Talus had suddenly decided to reveal its existence to her.

Through the static of the earpieces, they heard Elan let out a rich, genuine laugh. Anya watched Ryan's shoulders visibly relax as the tension left the cockpit.

"Your relentless curiosity is going to serve you remarkably well within these walls, Anya," Elan said. "But Talus' story belongs strictly to him, and I am sorry to say it will not be an easy task to get him to tell it. However, speaking of curiosity, I currently have your transponder signal mapped on my terminal display, and you are about to pass directly over one of their primary surface camps. Perhaps that will keep your mind satiated until you reach us."

A small, clean click echoed over the channel, signaling that Elan had disconnected his microphone for the time being.

Anya didn't mind the sudden silence, because Elan's assumption was entirely accurate. She pressed her face against the window, her heart rate spiking. In all her years deployed with the Rangers, she had never come anywhere near an operational enemy outpost. Did this mean the main hostile divisions actually lived openly on the surface? No subterranean vaults or reinforced bunkers?

The encampment was impossible to miss. It loomed directly on the jagged edge of the northern coastline, a massive, dark scar against the pale sand.

Colossal, matte-black towers punched high into the atmosphere, belching thick, toxic plumes of greasy black smog into the clean blue sky. Long, brutalist concrete buildings stretched in a sprawling labyrinth along the deep-water channels, all of it enclosed by an immense, reinforced perimeter wall studded with automated sentry nests. The architectural style was terrifying. A grotesque, seamless mixture of a medieval fortress and an advanced industrial manufacturing factory.

"What could they possibly be doing down there?" Anya whispered, her eyes wide as she tracked the perimeter.

They were obviously manufacturing something on an unprecedented scale, but what? And more importantly, why? She found herself wishing Ryan could drop the plane's altitude just a few hundred feet, just close enough for her to see what was moving along the massive, uncovered conveyor belts snaking out of the central structures. She had encountered hostile immortals numerous times during supply skirmishes, but those raiders had always fought with basic infantry gear and salvaged human weapons. They had never displayed this level of high-tier industrial technology or heavy machinery. If they possessed this kind of manufacturing power, why weren't they using it on the front lines?

Elan had been completely wrong, she realized. Seeing this camp didn't satiate her curiosity at all. It fueled the fire until it burned her throat. Why had the command staff at Phoenix never shown them satellite reconnaissance of these facilities? Had the human radar networks simply never looked this far north, or had Captain Tennant intentionally classified the data to prevent a total collapse of military morale? Maybe this was the exact reason the Captain had operated with such a paralyzing, deeply entrenched fear. Maybe he craved so desperately to give the people of Tigris a shred of hope because he knew, with absolute certainty, that there was absolutely no real hope to be had against an industrial machine this massive.

"What do you think they're building down there?" Ryan's voice was barely a breath over the internal comms.

Anya swallowed hard, staring at the sprawling complex. She wasn't even sure her vocal cords would function well enough to formulate a coherent answer. The sheer structural scale of it was completely overwhelming to witness. The entire facility looked to span a mile or more along the ocean coast, and it cut at least a mile deep into the rocky trenches. If this was nothing more than a localized outpost—a mere camp as Elan had called it—how many more of them were hidden across the continent?

"I don't know," Anya said, her voice dropping into a tight, hard register. "But I really don't think it's anything good for the human race. I wonder if Talus or Elan actually know what's inside those foundries."

"If they do," Ryan muttered, his knuckles white against the control stick, "I have a distinct feeling they aren't going to tell us a single syllable until our boots are safely on their floorboards."

"Yeah..." Her voice trailed off, her eyes locked on the rhythmic, mechanical pulse of the black towers.

She was completely in awe, her mind in overdrive. A wild, reckless part of her brain desperately wanted to tell Ryan to drop the flaps, land the solar glider right there on the coastal flats, and let her infiltrate the perimeter walls. It was an incredibly strange paradox; she had been absolutely terrified of the weightless sensation of flying in a perfectly safe airplane, yet here she was, actively plotting a way to sneak into a heavily fortified industrial complex containing thousands of hostile immortals.

131

Ryan cut a glance toward her, a nervous, disbelieving chuckle escaping his lips. "You are practically salivating to get down there, aren't you? There is really something fundamentally wrong with you, Anya. Do me a favor: let me take you to the faction of immortals that has a slightly greater chance of not trying to murder us on sight. We can save the ones that I know will brutally kill us for another day. Deal?"

Anya nodded slowly, never taking her eyes off the coastline until the dark towers finally dipped below the trailing edge of the wing profile. They were off and away, flying out over the deep, dead water of the open sea.

But even as the sky cleared around them, her mind refused to rest, continuously conjuring up every terrifying, catastrophic possibility of what the enemy was engineering in the dark. Their odds of survival were significantly worse than she had ever allowed herself to believe.

12

Talus

"I want a satellite tracking that compound around the clock," Talus commanded, his voice tight as he stared at the terminal display. "Get the highest resolution sweeps you can pull. I want to see if any more transport trucks arrive, or if that tunnel network opens up again. And Elan? Do not breathe a single word of this to anyone else on the crew."

Elan nodded slowly, his fingers hesitating for a fraction of a second before hitting the command macro that cleared the display. The horrific imagery vanished into the black of the terminal—uncompressed satellite captures of bound human men and women being systematically offloaded from transport beds, marched down concrete ramps to possibly be transformed into immortal slaves.

A silent fury burned deep in Talus' chest. He felt a sudden, violent anger toward the Others, a crushing wave of self-loathing for sitting safely on the sidelines of this war for so long, and despair for the systemic failures had dragged their world down to this tragic state. This wasn't where the human race was supposed to end up. They were a species that had possessed such boundless, beautiful potential, and now they were being systematically extinguished like guttering candles. How much more damage could they possibly cause by finally entering the fray this time? Of course, he had asked himself that exact same question once before, right before the sky turned to soot.

"Are we actually going to tell them?"

Cary's voice broke the silence of the hub. Good old Cary—always asking the foundational questions that nobody had a clean, comfortable answer for. By the look Elan was giving him from the console, it was entirely obvious that both of his companions expected Talus to possess the necessary wisdom to navigate the fallout.

Anya and Ryan would likely be devastated and furious that such a thing was happening to their friends. It was one thing to be granted eternal life like the one Talus had, it was quite another to become one of the Others. That was the reason why they stopped all thoughts of turning the human race immortal because they saw the evil it could bring. Even if they knew what had happened, there was nothing they could do about it now. The photo had been taken several days ago and he doubted there was any chance that they had not been turned.

Turned. Talus thought bitterly. It was like they were talking about vampires. Although they were immortal and bloodthirsty, it would take more than a stake through the heart to kill them.

"To what end?" Talus answered, his tone shifting into a cold, clinical detachment to mask his own grief. "It is best we keep this to ourselves for the time being. This girl already ran a reckless, single-handed rescue operation at Phoenix base. If we show her these frames, she will instantly hijack that solar glider and fly straight into the teeth of that compound to try and save those Rangers."

There would be absolutely zero chance of her survival, and the Others would be more than happy to break a soldier as remarkably skilled as Anya, adding her lethal instincts to their own lines. Deep in his gut, Talus felt a heavy, sickening guilt. He was initiating their fragile new alliance with the human race through a profound act of betrayal by actively withholding the truth. Yet, he knew that absolutely no good would come from the revelation. When the time was right, if another human outpost came under direct threat, or if they managed to formulate a viable strike plan, then he would tell them everything. Not before.

"Do you think there is a chance those rangers are still alive?"

Cary asked softly.

"Alive? Definitely." Talus said, his voice dropping into a grim whisper "Anything resembling who they once were? No."

The thought of it turned his insides. The first time he saw an Other he realized that there just might be a fate worse than death. An eternity without feeling anything but hate and anger. Just cold calculating hatred for anything that wasn't what? Immortal? An equal? Dead inside? He never quite knew what the anger was directed at but he knew that it always spelled bad news for the humans and for him.

"We should have intervened sooner," Cary murmured, staring down at his boots. "Who knows how many bases we could have saved if we hadn't locked ourselves in these mountains."

"And do you happen to remember exactly how many people we lost the last time we made that choice?" Talus countered sharply, the ancient weight of his regrets pressing down on his chest. "We honestly believed that once the first nuclear exchange concluded, that was the absolute bottom. The global war we had all feared for a generation was finally upon us, and we thought, what else could happen if we entered the war? And yet there was something worse, something much worse to follow. I may be immortal Cary but I am just a man and I do not have all the answers. A long lifetime of catastrophic mistakes, and yet every single soul in this mountain still looks to me for guidance."

Unable to bear the deafening silence of the communications hub for another second, Talus turned on his heel and marched out. Instead of retreating to the familiar, sterile sanctuary of his laboratory vats, he directed his steps toward the surface access lifts. He needed to walk through the ruins of the town again.

With every hard choice he was forced to execute, with every single minute he felt himself being dragged back into the grinding machinery of the war raging across the continent, he could feel himself slipping further into the dark. He was constantly trying to remain unyielding, trying to calculate the specific choices that would save the most lives, all while carrying the absolute, exhausting knowledge that it was mathematically impossible to save everyone. Every single death, every horrific new revelation from the satellite arrays, simply left him feeling more profoundly tired and isolated. He desperately needed to touch something that reminded him of who he had been before the world broke.

Cary followed him but he did not care. Talus stepped out into the bright glare of the surface world, navigating the cracked pavement toward the skeletal section of the town where a few multi-story brick buildings still managed to defy gravity. He knew every single crevice, every cracked foundation, and every rusted iron beam of these structures; he had explored them thousands of times across the decades. These were buildings she had physically occupied. Walls her fingers had casually touched, faded hardwood floors her boots had walked upon. He had audited every square inch of the debris, trying desperately to salvage some physical trace of her existence left behind in the dirt—a lost button, a scrap of paper, a stray strand of hair—but the obstinate passage of time had left absolutely nothing.

He approached a rusted iron fire escape clinging to the side of an eviscerated apartment complex and began to climb. The architecture was remarkably similar to her old building in the high-tier district, though this specific structure had been built above an industrial grocer rather than a neighborhood bakery, and the crumbling brickwork was a washed-out, industrial gray rather than the warm, vibrant red of her home. But the height got him up into the open air, allowing him to feel the fierce bite of the mountain breeze and the heat of the sun against his skin.

There it was. The rushing wind and the blinding light. The raw beauty and violent turbulence of nature colliding in a flawless, indifferent harmony. Normally it would calm him. Normally he would stand here enveloped in the breeze and think of her. But not today. Not now. Now all he could feel was the anger and the fear that every decision he had ever made had been the wrong ones.

"Where is your God now, Lily?" Talus suddenly screamed into the empty expanse of the valley, his voice tearing raw against the wind. "Where is he? Why would he allow this absolute Hell to continue on the earth! Tell me, Lily! Talk to me! Do you still believe in his grace now, Lily? Wherever you are, do you?"

He had no idea what he was saying or even why he was saying it. He was tired, tired of everything, tired of war, of death, of never once knowing what the right answer was.

As the mountain wind rushed past his ears, the sound seemed to morph, echoing her voice in his mind. They were the exact words she had articulated on the final night they had spoken, a sequence that had repeated on a continuous loop inside his brain every single day since she left him.

"You have absolutely no idea what you have done, Talus. This biological blessing you think you've unlocked in your laboratory... It is a curse. You are closing your heart to God and his plan, and you are going to end up completely alone in the end, Talus. This is a path that I cannot and will not follow."

In his youth, he had absolutely hated her steadfast belief in that archaic theological mythology. The comforting concept of a supreme, benevolent entity in the sky who was supposedly guiding humanity toward righteous deeds, preserving those who deserved grace and punishing those who committed evil. Looking down at the scarred topography of the continent, it seemed blatantly obvious that there wasn't a single soul left on earth deserving of grace in God's eyes, because there was nothing but endless punishment for everyone. Including her. Lily had deserved every ounce of grace, beauty, and blessing a creator could possibly manifest, and instead, she had ended up tied to a monster like him, trapped in a war she could never survive.

He looked down from his high perch on the roof, his eyes scanning the rubble as he tried to mentally reconstruct the pre-war city from the ash. He wanted to revisit every place he had ever seen her. He wanted to violently drag back every single memory of her face that remained clear in his dreams, the beautiful moments and even the agonizing arguments. He needed anything at all to remind his cold heart what he was actually supposed to be fighting for, and exactly who he was trying to earn redemption from. There was no life after this, he still believed that. And yet he often felt as if her ghost were actively standing somewhere over his shoulder, watching his movements, patiently waiting for him to find a way to make the world better. She had always stubbornly believed he would figure out a way to set things right, and here he was, ages after her body had returned to the dust, and still the world burned because of him.

"Talus? Why are you screaming at the fucking imaginary man in the sky?" Talus stiffened, turning his head slightly as Cary finally dragged himself over the final lip of the fire escape. Cary was leaning against the rusted railing, catching his breath with a wry, exasperated expression. "Logic won that battle, remember? No one on the planet believes that old story anymore."

There was Cary always missing the point or rather missing the emotion. Talus could feel himself breaking apart at the seams, a systemic collapse of his inner walls, and there was absolutely nothing he could do to halt the progression because he knew with total certainty that things were only going to get worse.

"Coincidentally, Cary, most of the planet's population is also completely dead," Talus replied, his voice dropping into a dry, cynical murmur. "For all we know, we represent the ones who were intentionally left behind during the Second Coming."

He didn't actually believe that, of course. His mind would never truly accept a theological framework, and yet, a weak, irrational part of his soul almost wanted to believe it. If the myth were true, it would mean Lily had actually made it to her promised Heaven. It would mean she was currently resting with her God, and every beautiful, faithful dream she had ever harbored had come true. It would mean all those millions of human lives lost in the war weren't truly gone, but had simply transitioned onward to some paradise of peace. Just the fleeting thought of it caused a faint, painful smile to touch his lips. No wonder religion had caught on so intensely among human populations; it was an exceptional psychological coping mechanism for culling the overwhelming guilt and terror that permanent death brought.

Cary walked over, stepping up to the edge of the parapet to stand directly beside him. Talus felt his friend's heavy hand rest firmly against his shoulder. Cary was always there, his constant companion that knew him better than anyone else alive and yet, his presence did absolutely nothing to quell the profound, empty loneliness that carved out Talus' chest.

"You know, the entire time I was dragging myself up that fire escape, I kept thinking to myself: man, this feels incredibly familiar," Cary said, his voice bright as he stared out over the ruins. "I've been on this fire escape before."

Talus let out a soft scoff, shaking his head in mild disbelief. Cary was talking with the casual air of a man sitting in a lounge, completely unbothered by the fact that his oldest friend was having a total psychological breakdown right in front of him. But despite his exhaustion, Talus couldn't resist the bait. "You? On a fire escape? Before or after you became immortal?"

"It was before actually." Cary chuckled, a distinct spark of mischief returning to his eyes. "Which makes it all the more surprising I suppose."

"How have I never heard this story?" Talus asked, turning his head to look at him.

"Oh, you know me—saving the best material for a rainy day," Cary grinned. "Actually, I never really planned on sharing it with anyone. It was kind of the exact reason I was climbing down the fire escape in the first place. See, I was fucking this absolutely beautiful girl... totally forgot her name by now, it's been a minute, but she was incredibly smart and gorgeous. Sadly, I found out the hard way that she didn't exactly harbor the same deep, romantic feelings for me that I did for her. In fact, I discovered that when the husband I had absolutely zero knowledge existed came home through the front door at the exact same moment I was coming-."

Talus held up his hand to stop Cary. "I get the picture...unfortunately." Despite his annoyed tone, he smiled. Once again, Cary had proven exactly why he was such an invaluable companion, even if Talus was usually too consumed by his own dark thoughts to acknowledge it. Cary possessed a brilliant, almost supernatural radar for sensing when Talus' mind was spinning out of control, and he knew exactly what his friend truly needed was a distraction.

"I have been meaning to ask you a specific question for oh... about twenty years now, Carebear," Talus said, his tone softening as the

139

wind whipped around them. "What exactly happened to that poised, remarkably refined public intellectual who used to deliver flawless, elegant lectures to university rooms filled to the brim with high-tier scholars and politicians? Why does a crass, drunken sailor currently stand in his place?"

Cary shrugged casually, leaning his elbows against the concrete parapet. "Look, I figured if I'm forced to live forever, I might as well have a little fun with the logistics. I mean, think about it, how many conscious entities in the history of the universe get the chance to actively try out completely different personalities? To live an entire, full lifetime as one person, and then get to wipe the slate clean and do it all over again as someone else? Honestly, Tally, maybe it's the only way I manage to keep my humanity intact. Every generation or so, I'll just kill off my current personality and adopt a fresh one. Preferably one with a lot more fucking in it."

Talus raised an eyebrow.

"No, I'm totally serious," Cary laughed, matching his gaze. "Just watch. One of these years, I'm going to flip a psychological switch and turn into one of those absolute sex maniacs you used to see in those late-night documentaries on old television. Getting completely turned on by popping birthday balloons or making out with sports cars or some weird shit like that. Then you'll really be standing on this roof saying, 'Man, whatever happened to that brilliant guy who once received a formal nod from the Nobel Prize committee?'"

A sudden, booming roar of laughter rang out over the open rooftop.

Talus laughed long and hard, the sound tearing out of his chest for the first time in decades, maybe for the first time since the very first bomb fell. It was an incredible, weightless sensation; the sheer absurdity of Cary's mind forcefully pushed out a massive volume of the suffocating stress and grief that had been threatening to completely consume his sanity.

He knew the dark thoughts would inevitably return. He knew the horror of the war was still waiting for him down in the tunnels, and it would likely be infinitely worse when the reality of the human alliance finally collided with their hidden world. But for right now, in this single, fleeting moment of time, he could just be a man standing on a rooftop with his oldest friend, shooting the breeze and laughing over absolute nonsense.

Today, the world smoldered in rubble. In two days, the entire trajectory of their history would shift forever when humans and immortals took the field side by side once again. But right now, high above the ruins, there was nothing but the sound of laughter in the wind.

13

Anya

The solar plane's landing gear hadn't even finished settling into the dense, sand of the clearing before Anya ripped the cabin door open. She didn't wait for the electric props to spin down to a whisper. She didn't wait for Ryan to finish checking the post-flight telemetry.

If the stark white walls of the Tigris Medbay had been her personal version of hell, this cramped, aluminum-framed cockpit was an unmitigated purgatory. For fourteen hours straight, she had been strapped into a nylon harness, her knees nearly pressed against her chin, her lower back screaming from the rigid posture, and her legs weeping from a total lack of blood circulation. Fourteen hours. And she had done it two days in a row. It was, by her own internal metrics, the absolute definition of her psychological breaking point.

When she finally scrambled to her boots, she didn't just walk—she sprinted. She ran at breakneck speed in a wide, frantic circle around the perimeter of the clearing, her breath coming in ragged, desperate gasps as her joints groaned and creaked, protesting the sudden burst of violent movement.

"You really shouldn't do that," Ryan's voice drifted out of the open cockpit, carrying his signature dry, exasperated tone. He slowly climbed down from the cockpit, stretching his arms over his head until his spine popped. "First of all, you could have easily snapped an ankle in a hole out there. Then you'd really learn what it means to be immobilized for a few weeks. Second of all, if you think being trapped in a metal tube for fourteen hours is bad, just try to possess a shred of empathy for the poor bastard who was forced to sit next to you while you did it."

Anya finally skidded to a halt a few yards away, though she still couldn't bring herself to stand completely still. She kept pacing back and forth, shifting her weight from foot to foot, her chest heaving as she tried to catch her breath.

"I am serious, Ryan," she panted, rubbing a hand over her sore side where her surgical incisions were still knit together with thick medical thread. "If we don't make it to that hidden base tomorrow morning, I am going to lose my mind. I cannot handle a third full day in that cage. I just can't."

The first six hours of the flight had admittedly been spectacular. For a girl who had spent her entire existence navigating the barren, beige dust-bowls of the Phoenix perimeter and the jagged, lifeless stone valleys of Tigris, seeing the world transform beneath them had been breathtaking. She had stared open-mouthed at actual, living forests. There were vast expanses of deep emerald canopies that looked like a thick blanket draped over the ridges. She had seen wild, overgrown meadows and glittering, untamed rivers cutting through the valleys.

But by hour eight, the novelty of the geography had thoroughly worn off. The walls of the cabin had felt like they were actively closing in on her, and she had spent the final quarter of the journey practically clawing at the smooth, gray composite paneling of the fuselage, desperately searching for a non-existent emergency release lever.

"It was exactly like sharing a cockpit with a caged field rat," Ryan muttered, walking toward the tail section to check the solar panel alignment. "All I heard from the passenger side was this constant, rhythmic shuffling. Scritch, scratch, shuffle. Every time you made one of those sudden, jittery movements, my hand jumped on the flight stick. I was on the verge of a panic attack for the entire afternoon. So, mental note to self: never, under any circumstances, agree to an extended cross-country flight with Ranger Anya again. If we survive this little stunt, I am personally going to rebuild the pre-war commercial jetliners just so I can drag you from one side of the continent to the other in three hours flat."

Anya let out a weak, breathless laugh. "Please do. I would be eternally grateful if I ever found a need to fly that far again."

Forcing her body to be useful, Anya walked back to the rear cargo hatch to drag out their overnight gear. Ryan didn't offer to help; instead, he collapsed directly onto a thick patch of grass near the port wing, propping his back against a smooth boulder and watching her work.

She didn't mind the lack of assistance in the slightest. Ryan had been working the manual flight controls through three separate weather pockets, and his eyes were bloodshot from staring at the navigation arrays. Besides, she desperately needed a physical task to keep her racing mind from short-circuiting.

Still, as she hoisted the canvas bundle of the tent onto her shoulder, she couldn't help but look down at him. He was lying there so perfectly still, completely content to just exist in the silence after being confined for over half a day. It baffled her. What kind of brain did a person need to possess to go from total confinement to total stillness without wanting to tear their own skin off?

"You forget so easily." Ryan said softly, his eyes tracing the slow movement of the clouds in the night sky above.

Anya dragged the tent bundle across the clearing, dropping it with a heavy thud a few feet from his boots. She wiped a layer of sweat and grease from her forehead, turning back toward the plane to fetch the massive camouflage tarp.

"Forget what?"

Ryan shifted his gaze from the sky, his expression turning uncharacteristically serious. "In order for us to eventually get to Tressle... we're going to have to get right back inside that exact same cockpit. Unless, of course, your master strategic plan involves walking a thousand miles back through hostile territory with a freshly transplanted kidney."

Anya paused, the bundled tarp gripped tightly in her

white-knuckled hands.

The honest truth was that fourteen hours of solitary confinement in that passenger seat had given her far too much time to think. She had spent hours wondering if a return trip to the southern bases was even realistic. Tigris was the only place that had ever felt like a genuine home, but deep in her gut, she had a terrible, lingering premonition that the southern bases wouldn't be safe much longer. No matter what occurred when they finally met Talus and his hidden faction, she no longer possessed the blind confidence that their old companions would be waiting for them at the end of the line. The world was shifting too fast, and the margins of human survival were growing too thin.

"Yeah... well," Anya said, her voice dropping into a quieter, more subdued register. "If that day actually comes, I guess we'll just have to find a strong sedative, right? Knock me out cold before you clear the runway."

"Good idea." Ryan said, his tense posture relaxing as he leaned his head back against the stone, returning his gaze to the early evening stars.

Anya dragged the massive camo tarp over the frame of the solar glider. It was an awkward, irritating process; the high-tech fabric was specifically designed to distort light waves and mimic the surrounding foliage, but it was incredibly slick, constantly sliding off the smooth composite wings every time she managed to anchor one corner. By the time she finally had the aircraft completely concealed from potential satellite sweeps or passing drone scouts, her arms were aching from the effort. She stepped back, taking comfort in the fact that the plane was invisible in the dark. If she couldn't see it, she could temporarily pretend it didn't exist. She could pretend she wouldn't have to strap herself back into that purgatory in the morning.

Setting up the shelter proved to be an infinitely simpler task. The pre-war survival gear Ryan had salvaged from the lower engineering vaults was a marvel of ancient manufacturing. She cleared a patch of level ground, untwisted a heavy polymer locking ring at the center of the bundle, and watched as the tent literally snapped into place. Internal carbon-fiber ribs expanded with a series of sharp, pressurized clicks, erecting a sturdy, weather-resistant dome structure within a matter of seconds. It was spacious enough to comfortably house both of them, containing built-in insulation layers that would protect them if a mountain squall rolled down from the northern peaks.

She walked back to the edge of the tarp, reaching through the cockpit hatch to pull out a few heavy wool blankets, a couple of standard military nutrition tubes, and a small, low-intensity dome light.

Starting a fire was completely out of the question. Even a small, sheltered blaze could emit a thermal signature that could be tracked from miles away by an immortal reconnaissance patrol, or an operational satellite network. They had to settle for a cold camp, huddled beneath blankets to stave off the biting northern chill and relying on the dim, amber glow of the electronic dome light to navigate the dark. It was a sparse arrangement, but it had kept them hidden for forty-eight hours. Just one more night in the wilderness, she reminded herself. One more night, and the entire course of their lives would change.

Not that she minded the nights out under the stars. She used to beg or sneak her way out of the base in order to be under these stars. Now, she had the entire night stretching before her. Her legs were still demanding movement, so she began to slow-pace the perimeter of their camp, her boots crunching softly over wild roots and fallen pine needles.

It was still utterly astonishing to look at the sheer volume of organic life thriving out here. In the jagged, high-altitude trenches of Tigris, nothing grew except maybe an odd scrub-brush and pale lichen. She had spent her development years operating under the implicit assumption that the entire surface of the planet had been permanently sterilized by the atomic fire of the old war. But looking at these towering trees, their thick bark smelling of pine and damp earth, she realized a fundamental, terrifying truth: the planet wasn't dead at all. The earth was actively clawing its way back, reviving its ecosystems and healing its wounds. It was only humanity that was fading away into the dark.

"So, who exactly was he?"

Ryan's voice cut through the rustle of the wind. He had crawled closer to the shelter, wrapping a dark wool blanket tightly around his shoulders as he leaned against the tent's structural ribbing. "The guy you went back to Phoenix for. As soon as the long-range channels confirmed that Phoenix was experiencing a terminal sector breach, Captain Tennant explicitly pulled me into the coms deck. He told me to keep a continuous sweep on the emergency frequencies for any mention of a Ranger named Mamoru. He knew the absolute second you heard the news, you'd abandon your post to go after him."

Anya stopped her pacing, a familiar, heavy ache settling deep into her chest. She walked over to the shelter, accepting a blanket from Ryan, and slid down into the grass beside him. She popped the plastic seal on one of the nutrition tubes, staring down at the grey sludge inside. Ryan had obviously been waiting until the right time to bring up what he knew would be a sensitive subject.

"Phoenix is very different from Tigris. Over time it turned into a Ranger training camp, sending the best of the best to bases all over to help their Rangers. If you show any knack for fighting, or athleticism or intelligence they streamline you into the Ranger program. Then it's like you become nothing more than a soldier."

She took a slow, unenthusiastic sip from the tube. It tasted faintly like artificial strawberries mixed with wet clay, with just a bizarre, lingering hint of dried basil. Food tubes had never been designed for culinary enjoyment; they were strictly a delivery mechanism for quick, calorically dense macros and balanced electrolytes.

"Your parents write you off as someone that will either die or leave them. You're entirely cut off from civilian society. You live, eat, sleep, and bleed alongside the other recruits. Discipline, unquestionable order, and skill. That was all that mattered. And if I'm being entirely honest, I only possessed one of those three qualities. I had the skill, very little discipline and absolutely zero respect for the order. It made it nearly impossible for me to survive the social hierarchy."

She sighed, a cloud of condensation forming in the frosty air as she wrapped the heavy wool blanket tighter around her shoulders. Sensing the sudden drop in her emotional energy, Ryan shifted slightly, extending his arm over her shoulder and pulling her in close. Anya didn't resist. She leaned her head against his shoulder, allowing his steady warmth to wash over her, a faint, genuine smile touching her lips at the simple comfort of the gesture.

"Mamoru was the only soul in that entire base who would put up with my shit," she whispered. "He was the only one who didn't look at me like I was a broken cog in the machine. When I would talk back to senior instructors, or actively point out the flaws in their tactical parameters, or straight-up refuse to execute a brainless order, Mamoru was always the one stepping into the gap. He was constantly running interference, pulling extra night-watch duties just to keep my name off the disciplinary rosters."

She squeezed the plastic tube, her knuckles turning white. "He was older than me by a few years but he was always willing to stick his neck out to shield me from the officers. No one had ever done that for me before. Not my instructors, not my squadmates, not even my biological parents. That kind of selflessness is entirely unheard of in a place like Phoenix. Everyone is taught to look out for themselves. So, to this day, I have absolutely no idea what made him care about me."

Her voice cracked slightly, a heavy wave of unresolved grief spilling over. "Just once... just once, Ryan, I wanted to be the one who had his back. I wanted to be the legendary Ranger who came out of the dark to rescue him when his walls fell. But I failed. I arrived too late. The base was already a tomb. I guess, in the end, I just proved that the command staff at Phoenix had been entirely right about me from the very beginning. Always a liability. Never an asset."

The clearing lapsed into a heavy, thoughtful silence, save for the rhythmic, soft clicking of the cooling aircraft engines beneath the tarp.

Ryan remained quiet for a long time, his arm still securely anchored around her shoulder, his eyes fixed on the immense tapestry of the galaxy stretching across the black sky above them. The Milky Way was a brilliant, swirling river of violet, silver, and deep indigo light.

"Personally, Anya? I think things went perfectly with you." Ryan said, his voice unusually steady and devoid of his usual sarcastic edge. "Who knows? Maybe the rest of the human race has it completely wrong, and you're the very first person who managed to get it right. Look at Captain Tennant. He is an incredibly brilliant commander, he genuinely loves his personnel, and he would sacrifice his own life in a heartbeat to protect the civilians inside the Tigris perimeter. But the thing is... he would never, under any circumstances, possess the reckless imagination to authorize a mission like this. He's too busy managing our slow decline. You might just single-handedly execute the one choice that stops our species from fading out, Anya."

"Or," Anya countered softly, her eyes tracking a brilliant shooting star as it sliced a burning white line through the atmospheric vapor, "I might just be the person who gets us all killed."

She watched a shooting star dance across the sky. She would never get tired of this view, the bright stars and colorful clouds of the galaxy. There was a whole great wide universe above, telling tales of stars millions and billions of years old. Each with their own collection of planets with untold creatures living upon them. How small their lives seemed to her, looking up at them from across the galaxy and likely her struggle was just as small to them. It was so humbling to consider their place in the grand design of it all.

"You know, you are an absolute walking contradiction," Ryan chuckled, shaking his head against her hair. "It's honestly fascinating to watch. On the surface, you preach absolute hope and unyielding confidence. You can walk into a room of terrified, bleeding Rangers and inspire every single one of them to pick up a Fulgar and follow you anywhere. And yet, the second you're left alone with your own thoughts, you do nothing but doubt your own worth at every single turn."

He tightened his grip on her shoulder, his tone turning fierce. "Tomorrow morning, when we approach the perimeter of that immortal base. I am probably going to be shaking so hard my boots will rattle. I will be scared entirely out of my wits. But even if those immortals open the blast doors and shoot us dead before we can even clear our holsters, I will have absolutely zero regrets about getting into that plane with you. You were right, Anya. We can't just keep sitting safely in our mountain bunkers, circling the drain, watching every other human base slowly get pulled down into the dark, and stupidly pretending like our turn isn't eventually coming. We desperately need a drain plug. And these northern immortals might just be holding it. That is a variable worth risking my life for."

Anya blinked, processing the words, and then she couldn't help it. A sudden, violent burst of laughter tore out of her throat—a loud, ringing sound that echoed off the surrounding pine trees. She laughed so hard her sides ached, her hand pressing against her sore abdomen to protect her healing kidney.

Ryan stiffened, his face reddening in the dim amber light. "Hey! I was trying to deliver a profoundly moving, heroic monologue here. What part of that was funny?"

"I'm sorry, I'm sorry," Anya gasped, wiping a tear from her eye as her laughter finally subsided into a steady chuckle. "It's just... that is quite possibly the most mechanically accurate, yet ridiculous analogy I have ever heard in my entire life. A drain plug, Ryan? Really?"

"Hey, I'm an engineer," Ryan grumbled, though a small, infectious smile was breaking across his own face. "I view existential dread through a plumbing framework. Sue me."

Anya's smile softened, her gaze returning to the warmth of his face. She nudged her shoulder against his chest. "Well, I suppose if I am ultimately destined to lay down my life for a glorified piece of plumbing hardware, I couldn't have possibly selected better company to die with. I can never thank you enough, Ryan. For staying behind when the base evacuated. And for getting into that plane with me."

Ryan's expression turned soft, the humor fading into a quiet, unyielding loyalty. He leaned his head down, resting it gently against hers as the cold northern wind swept through the clearing.

"Anytime, Anya," he whispered into the dark. "Anytime."

14

Talus

The alarms did not merely ring; they lacerated the silence of the bunker in rhythmic, high-decibel shrieks. Above the screeching frequencies, a synthesized voice broadcasted a continuous, muffled loop of automated distress data just beyond the heavy blast doors.

"Warning. Structural perimeter compromise. Level Three airlock seals deteriorating. Evacuation protocols are non-viable."

With every concussive thud of the artillery hitting the surface town miles above, the reinforced concrete walls of the private quarters groaned, shedding a fine, gray mist of ancient mortar dust onto the floorboards.

Talus did not move. He sat rigidly on the edge of his cot, his shoulder blades pressed hard against the vibrating partition wall, his eyes clamped shut.

The war had finally tracked them down. It had hunted them into the deep fractures of the earth, ignoring the fact that the civilian population had abandoned the grid weeks ago and the remaining local militias had already been broken on the front lines. The violence was patient, systemic, and absolute.

In the quiet, clinical corners of his mind, Talus wondered if Cavalk had personally steered the war to their coordinates. Was his former colleague truly holding the leash of this entire global conflagration? Was Cavalk's desperate, deep-seated thirst for retribution so relentless that he would systematically crack open the planet just to ash the man who had built him?

Talus opened his eyes, the harsh, alternating pulse of the red emergency strobes painting the interior of his laboratory in bloody, stark intervals.

Through the reinforced glass partition of the adjacent clean-room, rows of amber-tinted glass vials sat cradled in sterile steel centrifuges. Inside those cylinders lay the culmination of his life's work, a synthetic cellular matrix which he now believed, with absolute empirical certainty, had fundamentally doomed the human race to an evolutionary nightmare. Yet, those exact same vials represented the solitary barrier between life and death for the five hundred terrified refugees currently huddled in the secondary reactor bays down the hall.

The logistics were cruel. The timeline required for a subject's primary blood supply to successfully synthesize with the active immortal cells was narrow. He had mere minutes to initiate the cellular bonding. It was barely enough time to ensure that the violent psychological deterioration that had consumed Cavalk was an isolated genetic anomaly, rather than a structural flaw inherent to the serum itself. A flaw that both he and Cary had somehow, through blind statistical luck, managed to bypass.

He leaned his head back against the concrete wall with a dull thud, closing his eyes once more against the crimson flashes.

Was he truly preparing to do this? Was he genuinely about to inflict his own permanent curse onto five hundred innocent souls? Would they even choose this existence if they truly understood it?

But then, his mind cataloged the bleak alternative. If the seals breached and the surface atmosphere flooded the lower decks, their colleagues and refugees left from the town would choke to death within ninety seconds. After that, it would be just him and Cary. Two immortal ghosts wandering the cavernous, pitch-black corridors of a dead mountain for the rest of time, waiting for the heat death of the universe, or praying for the day that humanity might one day engineer a weapon capable of killing them.

He could survive the isolation; he had always been a creature of text, formulas, and quiet observation. But Cary... Cary was a social organism. He was anchored to the presence of others, fueled by conversation, emotion, and connection. Cary would never survive a world containing only a single companion. The silence would break him.

"Talus!"

The automated warning track grew louder as the pneumatic seals on the laboratory door hissed open. Cary stumbled through the frame, his chest heaving under a sweat-stained engineering vest. His knuckles were bone-white as he gripped the steel jamb to anchor his trembling frame against a sudden, violent tremor that rolled through the floorboards.

"The primary airlock... it's failing, Talus," Cary panted, his voice cutting through the mechanical din of the alarms.

Talus didn't look up. He kept his head pressed back against the concrete, his gaze fixed on the ceiling. "I can hear the alarms from here, Cary."

"Talus, look at me!" Cary shouted, taking a frantic step into the room. "The gas they're dropping up there isn't just toxic—it's corrosive. If that air clears the secondary intake vents, they're dead. Every single person in this base is going to die."

Talus slowly opened his eyes, his gaze drifting back toward the amber vials glowing under the red emergency lights. He let out a long, ragged sigh that felt like it came from the soles of his boots. "I know, Cary."

"You have to do something." Cary pleaded.

"You know the only thing I can do Cary and if I recall you were not thrilled last time I "did something."" Talus said, his voice dropping into a dangerously quiet, level cadence.

The laboratory fell into a sudden, stifling silence, punctuated only by the distant, rhythmic thuds of heavy artillery pounding the mountain's crust. Somewhere deep within the lower residential tunnels, a muffled human scream echoed through the ventilation shafts, cut short by the low, industrial groan of shifting structural steel. The entire installation was weeping under the weight of the shelling. Talus found himself wondering if the old military generals had lied about the subterranean load-bearing metrics of the bunker, or if the weapons Cavalk was deploying had simply evolved past their defenses.

Cary's hands fell to his sides, every ounce of defiance draining from him. "You could give them a choice," he murmured, his voice barely carrying across the space between them.

"A choice?" Talus scoffed, a flash of bitter, cold cynicism sharpening his features as he finally stood up from the cot. "Under the immediate threat of agonizing chemical death? Is that a genuine choice, Cary? And if it goes wrong, what then? Does the horror become morally acceptable simply because they consented while their lungs were burning?"

Cary's shoulders slumped. He let his back slide slowly down the steel door frame until he was sitting flat on the dusty floorboards, his knees pulled tightly against his chest. "I can't just watch them all die, Tal."

"I thought the exact same thing once before," Talus said softly, staring down at his old friend.

"This isn't about me Talus!" Cary snapped, his head jerking up, his eyes wide with a mixture of terror and raw frustration. "We're running out of time."

"It is when you're asking me to do to them what you still haven't forgiven me for!" The sheer, unchecked ferocity of the words ripped out of Talus' chest with the force of a physical blow. The sudden exertion left him feeling entirely hollowed out, his lungs working hard as if he had just sprinted through a toxic wasteland. The accusation had been floating just beneath the surface of their conversations for decades; a silent, toxic current running beneath every shared meal, every research log, and every quiet night on the surface. He hadn't known if he would ever possess the strength to bring the unspoken conflict into the open, but now that the words were vibrating in the air, the silence that followed felt heavier than the mountain above them.

Cary froze. He refused to meet Talus' gaze, his eyes tracking a thin line of dust shifting across the floorboards.

For a terrible, prolonged moment, Talus genuinely believed he had broken the final fragile thread holding their companionship together. He imagined the grim, absurd reality of the aftermath: the two of them, the last remaining remnants of a dead era, giving each other the silent treatment across empty concrete rooms for the next ten thousand years.

"I wanted to hate you for it," Cary whispered. His voice was so quiet it was nearly swallowed by the low hum of the emergency generators. "For a long time, Talus, I tried to despise you for what you did to me. You knew I had accepted the diagnosis. You knew I had explicitly asked you to let me die naturally. And you went behind my back and pushed that needle into my arm anyway while I was unconscious."

Cary paused, letting out a shaky breath as he finally raised his head, forcing his eyes to lock onto Talus' gaze.

"But the absolute truth of the matter is that I was just so profoundly happy to be alive when I awoke. But knowing what the serum could do, knowing what Cavalk had turned into, and realizing that you had unilaterally made that decision for my entire existence without my consent; it took a piece out of me. I am glad to be breathing right now, Talus. I am. But I still needed time. This is forever. There is no moving on to a secondary stage. No peaceful resolution. No rest. I had spent months mentally preparing for my death, and it took everything I had to accept that conclusion. I am forced to figure out how to accept my life now."

Cary reached out, his hand wrapping around the steel rail of the nearby equipment console as he pulled himself back up to his feet.

"I have forgiven you, Talus. Truly. I understand the absolute terror you must have felt. I know how heavy that needle must have felt in your hand. But it was my life, and that choice should have belonged to me. Just like this choice belongs to those civilians down in the bay right now. Give them the choice, Talus. Please."

Talus stood entirely motionless, his throat tightening as he swallowed hard against a sudden, unfamiliar lump in his chest. He felt the outer corner of his left eye turn damp and warm. He quickly brushed it away with the back of his sleeve, mentally telling himself that it was merely a reaction to the concrete dust in the air, rather than the massive, overwhelming wave of relief currently flooding his system.

The ground beneath their boots shuddered violently as a secondary blast breached the outer mountain defenses.

The atmosphere inside the central medical bay was thick with the copper tang of blood and the sterile, sharp scent of vaporized antiseptic.

The conversion process was already underway. Four civilian volunteers, including two former maintenance mechanics and two security guards, lay strapped to the primary surgical tables along the eastern wall. Their bodies were locked in the initial, violent throes of the cellular rewrite, their muscles contracting in involuntary, rhythmic spasms as the immortal matrix began the brutal process of restructuring their genetic baseline.

Across the room, over one hundred sterile glass containers held blood samples collected from the other refugees, their dark crimson fluids currently mixing with the synthetic serum inside the automated thermal agitators, waiting for the precise chemical balance required for injection. Still others would join them as Cary assisted the medical staff with the remaining blood draws.

Talus stood over a central gurney, his fingers steady despite the chaos around him. Beside the bed stood a mother and a father, their clothes stained with soot, their fingers intertwined so tightly their knuckles were white. They were staring down at the youngest among them, their sixteen-year-old daughter, Kit.

The biological reality of the serum was uncompromising: whenever the cellular clock was arrested, it remained frozen permanently. Kit would never physically age past this specific year; her cellular matrix would exist in a perpetual state of mid-adolescence for the rest of eternity. But she would live. That was the desperate, heartbreaking choice she and her parents had faced.

"It's okay, sweetie," the mother whispered, her voice trembling as she stroked the girl's damp hair. "It's just a single injection. Then the bad air can't hurt you anymore. We'll be right behind you. We're going right after you."

Kit was terrified. Her wide, dark eyes were fixed on the rhythmic, aggressive pulsing of the red emergency strobes overhead. She was gripping her father's calloused hand with a desperate, white-knuckle strength as another low rumble vibrated through the metal frame of the gurney.

Talus reached down to the sterile tray, his gloved fingers selecting the heavy glass syringe containing Kit's synthesized blood-serum mixture. The fluid within the cylinder was a deep, iridescent crimson, swirling with a faint, unnatural violet hue under the warning lights.

"Keep her left arm perfectly steady," Talus commanded softly, his clinical tone acting as an anchor in the chaotic room.

The father nodded grimly, leaning his upper body weight across Kit's forearm to reinforce the heavy canvas restraints buckled across her wrist.

"Look at your mother, Kit," the father murmured, his voice cracking with a fierce, protective love. "Don't look at the tray. Just look at your mother's eyes."

The girl turned her face away, her entire body tensing into a rigid line as Talus expertly guided the thick bore needle through the skin, piercing the vein. Slowly, methodically, Talus depressed the plunger, forcing the immortal cells out of the chamber and directly into her circulatory system.

The sirens outside the medical bay wall rose to a deafening, piercing shriek as a secondary pressure valve blew somewhere in the primary corridor.

"The injection is complete," Talus announced, pulling the needle free and immediately applying a sterile gauze pad to the puncture site. He stepped back several paces, clearing the space to allow the parents to crowd close to the gurney to offer emotional comfort as the initial chemical reaction began its descent into her bone marrow.

The red lights continued their relentless, maddening pulse. Talus cut a sharp, irritated glance toward the environmental monitor on the wall. The visual and auditory static was making it nearly impossible to monitor vitals.

Suddenly, a sound tore through the room—a wet, guttural rattle that did not sound remotely human.

Kit's eyes snapped wide, the dark irises completely vanishing as her pupils dilated into massive, pitch-black circles. A violent, unnatural tremor seized her spine, her back arching so high off the mattress that the structural steel of the gurney groaned under the sudden kinetic force.

"Talus!" Cary shouted from across the clean station, his medical scanners spiking into the red zone. "Her neurological readings are destabilizing rapidly! The temporal lobe is overloading!"

"Kit? Kit, look at me!" the mother cried out, reaching out to grasp her daughter's shoulders.

With a terrifying, explosive burst of physical strength that defied the limitations of her adolescent frame, Kit snapped the heavy canvas restraints across her wrists like wet paper. The metal buckles sheared off the frame, rocketing across the room and shattering a glass display case.

Before anyone could react, Kit threw her weight forward, tumbling off the gurney and crashing hard onto the concrete floor.

Talus lunged forward, his hands reaching for a fast-acting sedative on the prep tray. From the periphery of the bay, Cary emerged from the shadow of the monitors, diving toward the girl to pin her shoulders to the deck.

But Kit was already on her feet. Her face was twisted into a horrific mask of complete hatred that Talus had only ever seen once before in his life.

Cavalk.

She didn't scream; she let out a low, predatory hiss as her hand snaked out toward the prep tray, her fingers wrapping around a long, heavy steel spinal needle.

"Kit, please!" her father begged, taking a step forward with his hands raised in a peaceful gesture. "It's us! It's your mom and dad!"

The girl didn't hesitate. Moving with the blinding, terrible velocity of a striking viper, she lunged inside her father's reach. She drove the heavy steel needle straight through his throat, completely ignoring the wild, frantic scream that tore out of her mother's lungs. The father staggered backward, his hands clutching his neck as blood sprayed across the white linen of the gurney.

Kit spun on her heel, her black pupils fixed on her mother's face, the bloodied steel needle raised once more in her trembling, hyper-oxygenated grip.

"Kit, no!" Talus roared, throwing his entire weight across the examination table to intercept her as the red lights flashed in a blinding, crimson wave.

✳ ✳ ✳

Talus shot upright, his spine snapping taut as his palms slammed against the cold, industrial tile floor. He blinked rapidly, looking around the stark, concrete confines of his quarters.

He had fallen asleep while reviewing... what, exactly? He couldn't even remember. His mind was a tangled knot of fragmented data and lingering shadows. Letting out a heavy, fluid sigh, he pulled himself to his boots and began the brief, groggy stumble into his laboratory. He tried to shake the residual cobwebs from his brain, but a bizarre sensory anomaly was making it difficult: every single time his left heel struck the ground, a loud, perfectly synthesized trombone blast blared into the room. *Wah-wah.*

He paused, lifting his foot in confusion. He took another step. *Waaaaah.* It was an incredibly odd, lingering side effect of a dream so vivid it had practically rewired his auditory cortex. Or so he assumed.

He placed a flat palm onto the brushed steel of a central work table to steady himself. Instantly, the trombone blast vanished, replaced by a massive, sweeping crescendo of a dramatic orchestral symphony that seemed to bounce directly off the concrete walls.

He ignored the music, knitting his brows as he raised his left hand toward a shelf of amber-tinted biological cultures. The moment his fingers drifted within two inches of the glass, a sharp, abrasive digital buzzer cut through the symphony. *BZZZZT.*

He flinched, pulling his hand back, and tried the shelf directly beneath it. The buzzer sounded again. *BZZZZT.*

Frowning, he slid his palm toward a solitary, dust-covered vial sitting at the far end of the rack. The moment his skin touched the glass, the room was rewarded with a cheerful, high-pitched elevator chime. *Ding!*

"Right," Talus muttered to himself, grabbing the vial.

He reached out his other hand toward a secondary storage locker containing specialized reagent fluids. He navigated the shelves, his movements met with a relentless barrage of tactical rejections—*BZZZZT, BZZZZT, BZZZZT*—until his fingers finally rested over a beaker filled with a viscous, glowing green chemical. He honestly couldn't remember what the compound's molecular structure was anymore; the label had long since faded into a smear of yellowed adhesive. He checked the container curiously, gave a slight, indifferent shrug, and tilted the contents of both vessels into a clean glass beaker.

The moment the liquids collided, a booming, pre-recorded voice erupted from the overhead intercom speakers, dripping with cheap, game-show enthusiasm: "You're a winner!"

The two substances swirled together, bubbling aggressively as they settled into a thoroughly unappetizing shade of brownish-purple.

"Chug! Chug! Chug!" a rhythmic, low-frequency chant began to loop through the lab's auxiliary audio monitors.

Talus stared at the beaker, his expression tightening into a hard line of scientific disapproval. "Absolutely not."

Instantly, a massive track of canned television studio audience laughter, followed by a synchronized, theatrical "Awwwww", echoed through the ventilation ducts.

Talus gripped the edges of the lab table with both hands, his knuckles turning white as he actively fought the urge to smile. He was determined not to give in to the absurdity today. He maintained a perfectly stoic, unreadable expression as he turned on his heel and began walking toward the chemical synthesis vats at the opposite end of the facility. As he walked the notes of a deeply familiar, menacing imperial march began to pipe softly through the ceiling grates.

That time, he couldn't help it. A short, breathless laugh escaped his lips before he quickly wiped the amusement from his features and forced his face back into a stern mask.

"I saw that," Cary's voice crackled through the speaker, sounding thoroughly delighted.

Talus stopped in front of the vats, looking up at a nearby security dome.

"Have you nothing better to do than rig my lab for sound effects."

There was a brief pause over the line, followed by the sound of a shirt rustling against a microphone. "Tally, I'm immortal. So, statistically speaking, no. I have absolutely nothing better to do."

Talus let out a defeated sigh. He couldn't argue with that.

A few moments later, the pneumatic door hissed open, and Cary sauntered into the laboratory frame. The sight of his friend instantly triggered a violent, unbidden playback of his nightmare, the image of Cary collapsed against a metal door frame, choking on toxic air while the bunker collapsed around them. Talus forced the memory back down into the dark corners of his brain, refocusing his attention on a manual glass regulator.

He carefully adjusted the dial, adjusting the precise drip of concentrated chloric acid into a boiling, iridescent vat below. A dense, pale plume of noxious gas began to curl over the rim of the container. Talus knew the chemical cloud was likely entirely benign against the robust cellular structure of the hostile immortals, but at this point in their research, every single variable was worth a trial run. Even if the gas couldn't permanently halt an Other's cellular regeneration, perhaps the sheer, blinding agony of the chemical burning through their lung tissue would be sufficient to buy the human defense lines a few extra minutes during a breach.

"So, what specific flavor of nightmare was it this time?" Cary asked, his voice losing its playful edge.

Talus looked to Cary in surprise. Cary gestured up to the ceiling. "I saw it on the cameras, thought you might need a little cheering up."

"It was when we decided to change everyone." Talus said softly, his fingers tightening on the acid dial.

"First off, every single civilian inside that reactor block made that decision for themselves. We didn't force a single syringe into an unwilling vein." Cary interjected, leaning his back against the steel door frame. This time, however, he didn't slide down; instead, he braced his boots against the opposite side of the narrow casing, effectively suspending his entire body a few inches off the floor like a climbing mechanic. "Who turned evil this time?"

"'Kit." Talus murmured.

Cary paused his wall-climbing maneuver, blinking down at him. "Well, honestly, if anyone in this facility was going to flip a switch and go completely homicidal, it would definitely be her. She plays the whole sweet, innocent teenager routine flawlessly, but I am telling you, that kid is terrifying when she's crossed. Have you ever tried to claim the last square of strawberry shortcake when she's around? She straight-up stabbed my hand with a metal dinner fork, Talus. A flippin' fork! I entirely blame the parental units. When I marched over to show them the hole their daughter had engineered in my skin, they just sat there laughing."

Talus smiled at that. "You must have run quickly to have anything to show before it healed."

"Hey! Just because I can heal the wound does not excuse the underlying sociopathic behavior!" Cary shouted back, gesturing wildly. "It is mother-flipping psychotic! Normal, well-adjusted human adolescents do not weaponize cutlery over baked goods!"

The pale, acidic gas was beginning to spill over the laboratory floorboards, hanging low like a morning fog. It made Talus' eyes sting slightly, watering at the margins, but when he drew the chemical deep into his lungs, his modified respiratory tissue processed the toxin without a single hitch. He frowned, deeply dissatisfied with the lack of systemic reaction.

Cary, meanwhile, looked down warily at the creeping fog, his eyes darting back and forth between the chemical cloud pooling around his boots and the clean, filtered air of the corridor behind him.

"'Mother-flipping'?" Talus repeated, raising an eyebrow as he adjusted the vat's ventilation hood. "I think it might finally be time for us to stage a formal intervention for you."

"I know, I know," Cary sighed, letting his feet slide back down to the floorboards with a dull thud. "I am hoping when the humans get here they will be able to revitalize my vocabulary. I need some fresh profanity."

The laboratory lapsed into a heavy, quiet stillness. The images from the dream flashed across Talus' vision once more, the visceral terror on Cary's face when they had argued over the morality of the serum. Talus squeezed his eyes shut, but the darkness did nothing to block out the memory of the spoken conflict.

He cleared his throat, his voice dropping into a low, vulnerable register that felt completely out of place beneath the red emergency lights.

"Have you come to terms with what I did to you yet? With all of this? Last we spoke about it…"

Cary froze. The residual humor drained from his features, replaced by an uncharacteristic, serious intensity that made him look every bit as ancient as he actually was.

"Last we spoke about it was nearly a century ago and I told you I forgave you. It's a subject you tend to avoid at all costs."

"Because I couldn't bear it if you hated me." Talus couldn't even look at him.

"I think we're far past that." Cary looked down at the ground. "The fact of the matter is this: given everything that has transpired across the planet, you needed an anchor down here, Talus. Whether or not I was ever turned, you would have had to face the collapse of the world anyway. Maybe the universe intended for me to be right here, the one person tasked with keeping your brilliant, neurotic mind sane long enough to actually fix this."

It wasn't the precise validation Talus had been searching for, but it was infinitely better than the lingering terror that his closest companion harbored a secret, burning malice toward him.

"Besides," Cary's mouth twitched upward into a small, familiar smirk, "if you hadn't pushed that needle into my arm while I was crashing, just think of all the premium entertainment I would have missed over the last century. I wouldn't have been around to watch Alton accidentally ground the main generator tier, electrocuting you until your entire skeleton practically lit up like a neon billboard. I wouldn't have been here to see you get tangled up in those bio-engineered vines in the greenhouse tier, hanging upside down like a bat until I brought the clippers. And the day you completely lost your temper and punched out the General? Man...I don't think I could have properly enjoyed the peaceful quiet of an afterlife knowing all the absolute fun you were having without me."

Talus swallowed hard, a wave of warmth loosening the knot in his chest. "Thanks, Cary."

"Anytime, Tal," Cary said softly. He took a short step back toward the corridor. "And thanks for saving my life."

Talus jerked his head up in genuine shock, his mouth opening slightly to speak, but Cary simply flashed a quiet, knowing smile, turned on his heel, and vanished down the concrete hallway before Talus could formulate a response. In all their years of shared isolation, Cary had never once offered a formal expression of gratitude. But now? Perhaps there was one less mistake to haunt his nightmares, even if Talus had never seen saving his friend as such.

Talus turned back to the diagnostic terminal, adjusting the flow control dial on the chloric acid line. The pale gas was turning a darker, more opaque shade of grey, causing his tear ducts to sting aggressively, but his respiration remained entirely unhindered. He let out a sharp grunt of frustration and leaned forward to enter the negative data into the master logging matrix.

He turned around to grab a fresh syringe—and immediately jumped backward against the edge of the workbench, his elbow clipping the glass container. The brownish-purple chemical splashed violently across the back of his gloved hand, sizzling against the steel table and causing the ambient smoke in the room to instantly curdle into a thick, foul-smelling black cloud.

"Kit!" Talus gasped, his heart rate spiking into overdrive.

The horrific image from his nightmare, the young girl savagely tearing through her parents' tissue with a clinical needle flooded his mind with terrifying clarity. But the entity standing in front of him wasn't a monster; it was just Kit, bouncing eagerly on the tips of her sneakers, her bright eyes wide with uncontainable energy.

"Is it true?" she practically squealed, completely ignoring the toxic black smoke rolling off the table. "Are the humans actually inside our perimeter coordinates? What do they look like? Are they tall? Can I talk to them? Do they know any games?"

Talus closed his eyes, exhaling a long, slow stream of air through his nose to force his blood pressure back down to a normal level. It was just normal, real-world Kit.

"Yes, Kit, the human representatives are currently en route," Talus said, his voice resuming its rigid, authoritative commander register. "But let's establish the ground rules immediately: this is not a social gathering. They are coming here to execute highly serious, collaborative military work. That means you are to grant them absolute physical space. Furthermore, they can die and take time to heal when wounded. So, under no circumstances are you to stab them with anything. No forks. No needles. Clear?"

Kit tilted her head to a sharp angle, her dark eyes narrowing into a calculating squint that made her look remarkably predatory for a split second. "Why on earth would I stab our guests, Talus? Mom is already prepping three full trays of strawberry shortcake for their arrival, so it's not like they're going to have any reason to steal mine. Are they?"

The strange, icy cadence she used to articulate those final two words sent a distinct, cold shiver directly down Talus' spine. He froze, realizing with a jolt that Cary's assessment might actually contain a grain of empirical truth. Kit could be deeply unsettling when she chose to be.

"No, Kit," Talus said carefully, taking a step around the chemical spill. "They aren't going to touch your cake. Just do me a favor." He paused, struggling to find the vocabulary to articulate exactly what he needed from her and from the rest of the base's eccentric population. The only thought running through his brain was don't terrify the humans, but if Anya and Ryan had managed to navigate a thousand miles of hostile terrain to get here, they likely weren't individuals who scared easily. "Just ensure they feel welcome. And please, do not pester them with an infinite series of questions the second they clear the main airlock doors."

Kit nodded. "You got it! I promise I won't ask a single question for at least 15 minutes! I'm going to start writing some down! I can't wait to tell mom you said I could talk to them!"

"That wasn't exactly what I was—"

Talus reached an arm out to correct her, but the girl was already a blur of motion, her sneakers squeaking loudly against the tiles as she sprinted down the corridor toward the residential quarters.

Talus stared at the empty doorway for a long moment, then slowly looked down at the ruined, smoking chemicals on his workbench. Well, he could only pray that Anya and Ryan possessed an immense amount of patience, because apparently, as the supreme, all-powerful commander of the most technologically advanced base left on the planet, his operational authority over a sixteen-year-old girl topped out at exactly fifteen minutes.

15

Anya

"Well? Are you actually ready for this?"

Ryan's voice carried over the internal cabin comms, his fingers flicking across the avionics array to prep the descent manifolds.

"Ready for what?" Anya shot back, her voice tight with a volatile mix of exhaustion and raw adrenaline. "Jumping out of the fuselage mid-flight? Absolutely. Let's go. Do I just twist this manual release lever right now or what?"

She reached her left hand toward the primary hatch locking mechanism, but Ryan immediately leaned across the center console and slapped her fingers away from the metal bracket.

"No, Bad Anya! You're worse than a toddler." he joked, his eyes fixed on the horizon.

She really was losing her mind from the confinement. Three days straight in the plane had reduced her minimal patience to a fine powder. All sense of time had been erased; there was no longer a structured morning or afternoon, only the shift between light and dark. The nights had been miraculous and wonderful; cool air, vast galaxies, and absolute stillness, while the daylight hours had transformed into pure torture.

"I would really like to keep this plane in one piece," Ryan muttered, resetting the flap trim. "Just in case we need to use it again, so please do not open the door. At least not until we are on the ground, which should be in about ten minutes."

Anya looked out the window and then she saw it. Emerging from the low-hanging morning mist was a massive, jagged mountain peak reaching like a stone finger toward the sky. Sprawled along the lower eastern terrace of the ridge were the vast ruins of an old-world surface town.

But unlike the hidden valleys surrounding Tigris, this town was massive. Dozens of towering, concrete-and-steel multi-story buildings still stood remarkably intact, their empty window frames catching the early light. And there was an incredible volume of vibrant green vegetation creeping over the architecture. Actual trees, thick ivy, and wild grasses. She was going to get the chance to walk through real grass and trees.

The landing zone was still a few miles ahead, requiring Ryan to execute a wide banking turn to locate their designated landing spot. Anya felt her stomach churn nauseatingly. Part of the nausea was undoubtedly the natural consequence of consuming nothing but synthetic, clay-flavored nutrition tubes for days, but there was also the feeling of utter dread. She had absolutely zero clue what they were stepping into.

It was the exact same sickening sensation that had hollowed out her chest the day the high command had shipped her off to the Tigris sector. Captain Tennant had been the only one willing to take her in, and she had tried so hard not to disappoint him. All she had ever wanted was to demonstrate her gratitude to him for granting her a home, and yet, here she was, executing a rogue mission that she knew with absolute certainty he would have explicitly forbidden.

Ryan reached down, switching the radio transceiver to their encrypted, low-frequency channel. "Elan, do you copy? We are on final approach. Can you confirm our landing coordinates?"

The radio hummed with a layer of static before Elan's calm, level voice came through the cabin speakers. "I have you on my screen. Direct your glide path toward the southern terrace of the mountain structure. The terrain is level dirt. We can manually transport your aircraft onto the primary vehicle maintenance pad from that position."

"Rodger that." Ryan said, adjusting the descent rudders.

"No one says Rodger that anymore Ryan. Just land the plane. I will send Cary up to meet you."

Anya could not help but feel a pang of disappointment. She wanted to meet the man in charge, not some lackey. Although Cary had always been there when Talus was. Perhaps Cary was the second in command.

"Cary?" Anya asked, leaning toward the mic cluster. "What about Talus? Isn't he meeting us?"

A short, weary chuckle drifted through the speaker. "Talus is likely cutting his hand off and setting it on fire. He had not left his lab since…well for about two days now. You will meet him in time. Though I would take Cary over Talus any day. Just don't tell him I said that."

"Alright Elan we will be on the ground in five minutes." Ryan said, a faint smile touching his mouth.

"Rodger that. I will send for Cary." Elan replied cheerfully.

"Hey I thought you said that-"

Ryan cut himself off, shaking his head with a quiet laugh as the comms channel went dead. Anya smiled too, the heavy tension in her shoulders easing a bit.

Whoever these immortals were, they really did not seem much different from the people who used to inhabit Tigris. What had allowed this particular group to preserve their humanity, while the factions they called the Others had turned into predatory monsters? The fragmented electronic histories stored in the Phoenix and Tigris archives contained almost zero data regarding the exact origins of the immortals. She supposed that she would find out soon enough because the plane was finally descending into the shadow of the mountain.

She held tight to the handle and braced for the landing. Since the solar plane was not very fast the actual landing wasn't awful, but the rattling of the light aluminum airframe still gave Anya a sharp case of the jitters. She expected it to crash and fall apart at any minute. Yet, she trusted Ryan's hands on the stick implicitly. It was a bit of a conflicted stream of emotions every time they landed the plane.

The plane skidded across the hard-packed dirt, coming to a final, shuddering halt inside a massive, roiling cloud of yellow dust and loose gravel. The second the plane stopped, Anya popped the latch and threw herself out into the open air. She was just about to expand her chest and draw a deep, triumphant breath of unfiltered air into her lungs when a heavy, rubberized filtration mask was forcefully pressed over her nose and mouth.

She blinked through the dust, seeing Ryan standing directly beside her, his eyes wide with a stern, professional caution as he pulled the elastic straps tight behind her ears.

"We best be cautious here Anya the North was hit much harder than the South." he warned, his voice muffled through his own integrated breather unit. "I do not have the ability to test if the air is safe to breathe here."

Anya let out a long, muffled groan of frustration. More stale, recycled air. It felt exactly like breathing through a wet wool blanket after it was processed through the plastic charcoal filters of the mask. She wanted nothing more than to claw the rubber straps off her skull.

"And Anya I know you are just bursting to find out everything there is to know about this place. But how about holding off on the questions just for a little while okay? We don't want to offend or upset our hosts with too many questions."

"But what else did we risk our lives to come here for, Ryan, if not to find out everything they know?"

Ryan let out an exasperated sigh, stepping closer to ensure his voice didn't carry across the clearing. "Listen for me huh? I'd like to minimize the chances that the people inside who cannot die are going to have reason to want to kill me."

Anya wrestled with the suggestion, her fingers twitching. He had a valid point, as irritating as it was to admit. She didn't want to offend the immortals and it was probably best to let them take the lead. But at the same time, the sooner she knew everything they did, the sooner they could work together to get a solution. But they undoubtedly had their own questions regarding the status of the human bases, and since they were the ones holding the keys to the kingdom...

"Fifteen minutes," she grumbled.

Ryan paused, adjusting his gear pack. "What?"

"I won't ask a single question for 15 minutes." Anya clarified, crossing her arms. "After that I make no promises."

Ryan groaned but nodded. He knew her well enough to know that she was not going to offer anything better.

Anya began to pace the immediate perimeter of the clearing, her eyes tracking upward to admire the massive, complex network of ancient solar arrays mounted along the face of the mountain. The sheer engineering scale of the collection grid was staggering; it was undoubtedly the primary power infrastructure supporting the entire subterranean base below.

Still, her eyes kept drifting back toward the abandoned surface town. She had never once in her life been inside a building that had stairs rising up toward the sky. Every structure she had ever occupied had been carved down into the safety of the dark earth.

"Welcome."

Anya spun around on her heel, her hand instinctively dropping toward the grip of her Fulgar before she caught herself. Standing at the edge of the tree line was a man dressed in an incredibly casual, crisp white linen shirt and faded blue denim trousers. He possessed bright, piercing blue eyes and a relaxed, distinctly cocky smirk.

He was the complete opposite of what she had expected. She had spent the better part of the last week mentally preparing herself to face a legion of cold, identical, uniform-wearing emotionless soldiers. She had assumed these immortals would look and act somewhat the same as the ones she had already encountered.

"Hello....are you Cary?" Anya said, her voice cautious as she took a slow step forward.

She extended her right hand toward him, her movements tentative. Did they shake hands? Did anyone still shake hands? They certainly did not do it back at Tigris but she remembered reading that humans once used the gesture to signal peaceful intent.

Cary took her hand with a smile and took it. He shook it gently before holding his hand out to Ryan.

Cary's smirk widened into a genuine, warm smile. He stepped forward without a hint of hesitation, his grip firm and steady as he took her hand and shook it with a gentle, practiced ease before immediately extending his palm toward Ryan.

"The one and only," Cary said, his voice bright. "Come on, let's get you inside. It is far too damn hot to be standing around out here. And I am certain you guys are eager to get a look at things anyway. And take off those masks you don't need them here, I promise you it's safe."

He turned, gesturing for them to follow as he led the way toward the left flank of the rock face. As they approached a seamless junction in the granite wall, a hidden hydraulic track groaned, and a massive section of the reinforced stone deck slid smoothly aside to reveal a steep, concrete staircase descending straight down into the subterranean dark.

Cary immediately began navigating the steps, his movements fluid and quick. Anya followed close behind his shoulder, but she stopped three steps down when she realized the heavy thud of Ryan's combat boots hadn't followed them into the hatch.

She turned her head back toward the surface glare. "Ryan? Are you coming or what?"

Ryan was still standing on the dirt terrace, his eyes fixed on the solar plane. "Of course I am coming. I did not come all the way here to stand in the sun. I was just worried about the plane, is all."

Cary paused on the landing below, turning back to look up at the young engineer with an amused expression.

"There hasn't been an operational base for the Others within a three-hundred-mile radius of this valley for nearly two decades, Ryan, so I would not worry too much. Elan already has a team coming to move it into the hangar"

Anya watched as Ryan cast one final, lingering look of parental anxiety at the glider before he finally let out a sigh and stepped down into the concrete stairwell with them. As soon as the hatch closed behind them, both Anya and Ryan removed their masks and clipped them to their belts.

Unlike Ryan's cautious descent, Anya practically bounded down the steps, her adrenaline surging. She could not wait to get to know these immortals and the life they led. But more importantly she wanted to know their weaknesses.

The concrete steps were aggressively steep, and by the fourth flight, a dull, lactic burn began to flare across her calves. She actually would have preferred a ladder but she did not complain as she maintained a steady pace behind Cary. She kept cutting glances over her shoulder to ensure Ryan was still behind her. Once again she was very glad for his company. It was one thing to decide to meet with the immortals, it was an entirely different reality to be completely alone when the blast doors finally closed behind you. Not that he would be able to do anything if they were walking into a trap.

Cary stopped at the base of the long descent, his hand resting on a massive, heavy hydraulic lever mounted to a brushed steel partition. He turned back to flash them another roguish, white-toothed grin.

"Well, here we are," Cary announced, throwing his weight against the manual override. "Welcome to our little secret as shit underground laboratory."

Anya raised an eyebrow at the swearing but stepped down the final set of stairs. Each time her foot descended her heart quivered and her lungs took a shaky breath. Her hands were ice cold and every molecule in her body seemed to be vibrating with anxious energy. She found the presence of mind to look around once she touched the final step. There was just a long hallway stretched out before them. A long, uniform corridor stretched out before them into the dim distance. It looked absolutely nothing like the underground bases she was familiar with.

"I know it doesn't look like much here. Cary said, his voice echoing off the smooth masonry as he ventured a few paces ahead of them down the hall. He reached out, his fingers casually wrapping around a heavy steel latch to swing open a bulkhead door that looked structurally identical to every other nondescript panel dotting the corridor. "But I promise you, just around this corner, the view becomes a little more impressive."

173

They followed him through the threshold. The secondary corridor didn't remain tight; it gradually expanded outward, the low concrete ceiling sloping radically upward until the walls fell away entirely to reveal a massive, cavernous atrium.

Anya froze in her tracks, her chest hitching as her eyes struggled to catalog the sheer scale of the space.

To her right lay a vast courtyard bathed in a warm light that perfectly mimicked a late-afternoon sun. Massive, thick tangles of deep green ivy and wild flowering vines stretched up the rock face for at least two full stories, clinging to engineered support lattices. And trees—actual, living, dwarf-pine and birch trees—were growing out of deep soil trenches cut directly along the perimeter walls.

But it wasn't the greenery that made her pulse race. It was the people.

In the center of the courtyard, dozens of people were scattered about. They were sitting at small, quaint wrought-iron tables, casually conversing or reading text files. Every single table was laden with platters of food that looked positively, beautifully delicious with vibrant colors, fresh textures, and actual steamed greens, and yet, virtually none of the occupants seemed particularly concerned with consuming it. Their focus was on their conversations, or simply sitting in unbothered silence.

Anya's eyes darted frantically from table to table, counting heads, her right hand instinctively drifting down to where her fulgar was secured. The cold, smooth cylinder beneath her fingertips offered a brief feeling of security.

Before her fingers could wrap around the grip, Ryan's hand shot out. He grasped her wrist, gently pulling her fingers away from the weapon. Anya cut a sharp glance at him; his own eyes were scanning the crowd with a rigid intensity, but his grip on her arm remained. Don't, his silent gesture warned. Not here.

Cary casually sauntered over to a nearby table where two men in mechanic jumpsuits were sitting. Anya could not hear what Cary was saying but the two men immediately shifted their gaze from Cary to briefly land on Anya and Ryan. They nodded to Cary, shoved their chairs back, and broke into a fast, purposeful jog, disappearing down a secondary transit tunnel off the western flank of the atrium.

"There. They will get your plane now like they should have been doing already. Sorry we do not really operate on a timeframe around here. Are you hungry? We have plenty of food and Dalia just made some fresh strawberry shortcake for your arrival. It is one of her specialties." Cary began leading them deeper into the seating grid, his words dropped in volume as he continued. "I will give you a word of advice. If Dalia is baking make sure you visit the courtyard to have some. If she is cooking, well let's just say you might want to wait until the normal chef is cooking. Don't tell her I said that though she'd throw boiling oil on me or send her crazy daughter after me. But the shortcake is good, you don't have to worry about that. Fuck Fuck Fuckity Fuck."

Cary's voice moved faster and faster, the final sequence of words degenerating into a string of casual nonsense as if his brain were trying to outrun his own internal pacing.

Anya's fingers still drifted toward her weapon causing Ryan to take her hand and hold it. She took breaths to steady herself and try to cease the adrenaline that was piping through her veins telling her that she needed to fight. Even in her current state her nose was twitching; the atmosphere of the courtyard smelled incredibly, potently sweet—the distinct, rich aroma of caramelized sugar and fresh fruit.

"Here, have a seat." Cary said, gesturing toward an empty iron table near the edge of the green lattice. "Kit will bring over the cake."

Anya remained standing, her boots glued to the tile. She kept reminding herself she could trust these people, at least for now. This was what she had wanted. She was the one who had convinced Ryan to come, what did she expect to find? She knew it was going to be filled with people who could kill her and that she would never be able to do the same to them. However, knowing something and experiencing it were two very different things, she was discovering.

Right now, Ryan was being the calmer one, the braver one, the stronger one and that was simply not something her pride was going to permit. Cary continued to gesture toward the empty chairs with an easy smile. Ryan gently guided her forward, pulling her toward the table until she finally relented and slid into the seat. Only then did he release his grip on her hand.

Cary left them alone at the table, walking across the floor toward a low-set service window cut into the kitchen partition.

Anya's eyes tracked his movement across the room, and as she did, she realized with a cold jolt that the noise in the atrium had vanished entirely. Every single conversation at the surrounding tables had ceased. Several pairs of ancient, unblinking immortal eyes were fixed squarely on Cary, and then, by extension, on her and Ryan.

The service window slid open with a metallic hiss, revealing the face of a girl who looked remarkably young, nothing more than a teenager. She flashed a soft, bright smile at Cary as he spoke to her. Anya watched as the girl's dark eyes scanned across the seating layout, tracking Cary's pointing finger until her gaze rested directly on the two human Rangers.

The girl's smile faltered for a fraction of a second before she immediately ducked back into the kitchen, returning a moment later hoisted up by a massive, tiered white platter.

It was a cake, but it was a structural marvel. The surface was garnished with fresh, vibrant red strawberries, more than Anya had ever seen at one time. A thick, snowy layer of whipped white cream completely enveloped a dense, golden-yellow base beneath. Anya had absolutely zero idea what any of the cake was other than the fruit, but she knew if nothing else, she was going to gorge her stomach on those beautiful, glistening strawberries. No matter what the cake was made of, it had to be infinitely superior to the grey, sludge-filled meat tubes she had been surviving on.

Cary hoisted the massive platter and brought it over to their table, setting it down with a dramatic flourish. The young girl, Kit, followed close behind his shoulder, deftly arranging polished ceramic plates and a heavy crystal pitcher filled with a dark, rich crimson liquid. Another woman, older with similar features to Kit, walked over from the counter, bearing a collection of polished metal utensils.

As the cake was systematically cut into sections, Anya couldn't shake the distinct, uncomfortable sensation that she and Ryan had been transformed into a pair of exotic circus animals performing for an audience. The older woman expertly sliced through the golden layers, sliding a massive, cream-heavy portion in front of both Rangers.

Cary and the girl remained standing at the edge of the table, staring down at them with an intense, unblinking curiosity. Anya wanted to grab her fork, the rich, buttery scent of the baked dough was calling to her, but she hesitated. She cut a glance at Ryan. He was sitting perfectly solemn, staring down at his own slice of cake as if it were an unexploded mortar shell.

"Eat, eat!" the older woman chided, clapping her hands together with a maternal sharpness that shattered the tension. "You two look like two starving children in front of a candy shop with no money in your pockets. You're allowed to eat."

Anya swallowed hard against her dry throat. Even if there was some specialized toxic agent laced within the food, there was practically nothing she could do in her situation. If she didn't eat the cake there were a hundred different ways a group of immortals could overpower them and kill them. Baking a poisonous cake was a very illogical way to go about it if they wanted to do something to her.

She picked up her fork, her fingers steadying as she pressed the prongs down into the yellow layer covered in cream. The metal slid through the sponge-like texture with absolute ease, a perfect, uniform bite remaining anchored to the shiny tines.

With one final, deep breath, she raised the fork to her lips and slid the food into her mouth.

Her lips closed around the fork and instead of chewing she just let the food melt upon her tongue. Her eyes closed and she moaned involuntarily. If she was destined to die inside this mountain, she decided right then and there that this was quite possibly worth it. The cake was unbelievably sweet and cloud-soft, and the fresh strawberries were the juiciest, most flavorful things her taste buds had ever experienced.

She raised her empty fork toward Cary and the woman in an appreciative gesture, her mouth still full. The shortcake was magnificent, and every cell in her body demanded she immediately harvest another bite, but as the initial rush of delightful flavors began to fade from her tongue, the harsh reality of the room locked back into focus. Dozens of silent, immortal eyes were still tracking her every chew.

Did she make a miscalculation? Had she really come all this way to be poisoned by strawberry shortcake? She still had no reference for what the yellow material actually was; it was spongy, airy, and intensely sweet, but it wasn't a sugar profile she recognized. The only sweet flavors she had ever experienced back at Phoenix base came from wild root berries or synthetic fructose syrup.

Besides her, Ryan had reached the same conclusion she did. After his initial, cautious bite, he appeared to completely lose all awareness of the crowd growing around the perimeter of the courtyard. Apparently, it was true that a way to a man's heart was through his stomach. Ryan showed no apprehension at all after trying the shortcake.

Anya's anxiety, however, only continued to mount under the weight of the silence until she could no longer tolerate the stares. She slammed her palms flat against the iron surface of the table, causing the dishes and utensils to clang loudly.

"Could someone please tell me why everyone is staring at us? Is this going to turn me into a green zebra or something?" she demanded, her eyes flashing through the crowd.

The words weren't exactly the most intimidating or tactically profound phrases her Ranger training had drilled into her, but her mind was going entirely haywire under the stress.

Her voice echoed through the high-vaulted atrium, sounding significantly louder than she had intended. At her outburst, the ambient rustle of the entire courtyard ground to a dead halt. The solitary exception was Ryan, who didn't even lift his eyes from his plate, his fork continuing to systematically excavate the final remnants of his whipped cream.

"They are staring at you because you are going to die," Cary said, his voice perfectly casual, a bright, friendly smile plastering his face

178

as if he were explaining the obvious. He waved a hand toward the surrounding tables, signaling for his people to return to their activities. "Go on, keep eating. Have another slice."

Cary's blunt, cheerful delivery caused Anya to slowly sink down into her chair, her breath catching. Beside her, Ryan's fork froze mid-air. He looked up from his empty plate, his gaze darting from Cary's smiling face to the silent line of Immortals, and then over to Anya. He set the metal utensil down onto the ceramic surface with a slow, deliberate caution.

Standing behind Cary, the young girl, Kit, immediately delivered a sharp, aggressive elbow directly into Cary's ribs.

Cary flinched, wincing as he rubbed his side and looked at the expressions on the two Rangers' faces. "Oh! Oh. Not now, of course. I didn't mean you're going to die right this second. But you will eventually die someday, and the rest of the individuals inhabiting this facility will not. It has been a very, very long time since anyone so afflicted has set foot inside these walls."

Ryan let out a loud, shuddering sigh of profound relief, though his fingers didn't move back toward his fork to reclaim his dessert.

"Affliction?" Anya repeated, her defensive posture returning as her voice sharpened. "It's part of the natural way of things, you are the ones with the affliction."

"Everyone has afflictions dear, just different kinds. Now eat up you must be starved after that long journey here and I promise you are safe here. Cary and Talus are the most dangerous ones that you will find here." the older woman said softly, leaning over the table to pour a measure of the dark crimson juice into Anya's cup.

"Hey!" Cary shouted, throwing his hands up in mock offense. "I am absolutely not the one they should be afraid of. I don't go around manually cutting my own damn hand off with laboratory hardware or attempting to freeze my appendages off in liquid nitrogen just to log the cellular recovery speed. Masochist that one is."

"Really, Cary?" the woman countered, crossing her arms and skewering him with a flat, unimpressed look. "At least he only hurts himself, there's a trail of broken hearts in your wake."

"Bringing that up again?" Cary groaned, rolling his eyes dramatically toward the ceiling. "That was over 100 years ago, I was a different fucking person then."

"Language, Cary!" Dalia snapped, her eyes narrowing. "And that is not what I've heard. Would you like a list of names?"

Anya sat frozen, her mind spinning as she struggled to decipher the bizarre, domestic nature of the exchange bouncing between Cary and the older baker. Beside her, Ryan's eyes were just as wide and thoroughly confused as her own. One thing she did know was that she wanted to meet this mysterious, self-mutilating scientist named Talus, now more than ever.

"Mom! Cary! Stop it!"

Kit stepped between the two older immortals, holding her hands up like a referee terminating a combat exercise.

"Right, right. Apologies to our guests," Cary said, smoothing down the front of his linen shirt as he regained his composure. "When you have completed your cake, we can officially commence the tour of the primary areas, and then I will personally escort you to your designated quarters."

Before Anya could respond, a sharp, rhythmic electronic beeping rang out from the tactical comms bracket secured to her left wrist.

The sound was piercing in the quiet courtyard. Every single immortal at the table immediately dropped their gaze to track the flashing green light on her arm.

"A bomb isn't about to go off is it?" Cary asked, his voice deadpan as he took a step back from the table. "Because I spent twenty minutes getting my hair to sit exactly the way I prefer it this morning."

Ryan shook his head, a faint, technical smile touching his lips as he read the data track on the interface. "No. Not a bomb, Cary. More like... the formal opening of the floodgates."

Anya smiled, her eyes flashing with a dangerous, triumphant light. Her fifteen-minute wait had officially been exhausted, and ironies of ironies, she had been far too terrified and overwhelmed by their surroundings to formulate any questions during the fifteen minutes anyway. But now, the clock was at zero. It was time to get the answers she had traveled across a continent to claim.

"I think we are done for now. I cannot wait to see the rest of this place." Anya said, sliding her chair back and standing up with a fluid, commanding grace. She shot a sharp, unyielding look at Ryan that left absolutely zero margin for counter-argument.

"Alright then." Cary said, turning to lead the way toward the northern archway "Well if you ever get hungry there is food here, either chef is cooking, this woman here is baking or there's just fresh fruit and vegetables for you to grab. Help yourself anytime."

They stepped out of the courtyard, their boots clicking in unison behind Cary as they descended deeper into the hidden world of the immortals.

"So, you guys actually eat real food, huh?" Anya started, her words rushing out the absolute second they cleared the archway. "What happens if you don't? I mean, you can't exactly starve to death, so why even bother with it at all? And does it still taste the same to you?"

Ryan simply smiled, casting a knowing side-glance her way. "Told you. The floodgates are officially open."

Cary let out a loud, easy laugh, matching their stride as they walked. "Look, I am more than happy to answer what I can, but some of the more complicated stuff I'm going to leave for Talus. As for the food, it's simple: we need energy to keep moving, and most of us choose to get a portion of that energy from eating because we genuinely enjoy it. But there's a practical reason as well. If we don't eat, our bodies will automatically start sucking the ambient energy out of absolutely anything close by."

"Talus rarely eats," Cary continued, rolling his eyes playfully. "And the man absorbs so much energy from his surroundings that there have been plenty of times where the engineering crew had to crank up the main generators just to keep the lights from flickering in his sector. As for the taste, if you had asked me fifty years ago, I might have given you an answer. But now? The memory of what things used to taste like back when I was a normal human has completely faded away."

How incredibly strange, Anya thought. The idea that their bodies could just absorb energy like a plant from the sun. It had to be a massive advantage to never feel the heavy, bone-deep exhaustion that followed a long day.

"So you don't need to sleep either then?" she pressed, leaning in closer. "Do you just stay awake at all hours of the night?"

"Oh no, we sleep. Trust me, some of us sleep way more than others," Cary said with a grin. "But sleep is incredibly good for us. It helps our bodies regenerate, fixes any systems that are lagging behind, and lets us store up a reserve of energy so we aren't constantly draining the facility's power grid during the day. Think of it like this: you get energy from food but your brain still needs sleep to reset. We get our energy from the world around us, but we still need that downtime to keep our minds screwed on straight."

Anya was practically buzzing with excitement. For the first time in her life, she was getting real answers. Even at Phoenix where they knew more about the immortals than any other base, there were things they did not quite understand, such as the immortals' relationship with food. She also was fascinated by Cary who seemed just as comfortable lecturing and explaining as he was being cocky and cursing in the courtyard.

"And here is our primary farm," Cary announced, stepping through a wide threshold and presenting the room with a proud sweep of his arm.

Anya's mouth fell open. It was probably a completely unflattering gape, but she couldn't help it. While Phoenix and Tigris both maintained hydroponic bays to keep their populations alive, their facilities were nothing like this. Human farms were sterile, depressing rows of plastic tubes and harsh UV lights, strictly conditioned to mimic a bare-minimum environment.

This place looked like a dense, towering jungle. Massive curtains of vibrant green leaves cascaded from the ceiling, looming stories above her head. If she squinted through the thick foliage, she could catch glimpses of different fruits and vegetables hanging in heavy clusters, but the growth was so wild and interconnected that it was nearly impossible to see where one plant ended and another began.

"We've been working on ways to increase our overall production and grow things in completely new ways," Cary explained, stepping up to a thick vine and pointing to a cluster of yellow fruit. "For example, we've re-engineered bananas, sugar cane, and even coffee to grow on climbing vines instead of traditional trees or stalks. It saves an immense amount of physical space and makes the harvesting process a breeze. Not to mention, we've made these strains robust enough to survive in practically any climate. That right there is easily one of my proudest achievements."

Anya looked down the endless, leafy rows, a sudden thought striking her. How many people actually lived down in these tunnels to justify consuming a food supply of this magnitude?

"We mostly keep it running for experimentation purposes right now," Cary said, his voice dropping into a softer, much more grounded tone. "But once the world outside is finally ready, and the timing is right, we will possess the knowledge and the capability to feed every surviving man, woman, and animal on the planet. We are just waiting for the surface conditions to stabilize. In the meantime, you two are welcome to come down here and pick whatever you want whenever you get hungry."

She could hear the deep, genuine pride vibrating in Cary's voice. He truly, completely believed that this room held the key to saving the biosphere, and looking at the sheer abundance of life dripping from the walls, she realized he might actually be right. The only real roadblock was finding a way to make the surface safe to inhabit again. But the more Cary talked, and the more she witnessed what this collective was capable of achieving, the more a single, heavy question began to drown out all the others rattling around in her brain.

She stopped walking. "Why are you guys so different?"

It was the one fundamental question that tied all her curiosity together. Her entire life, the word immortal had been synonymous with absolute evil. She had been raised on stories of the immortals; cruel, predatory monsters who wanted nothing more than to butcher her family and burn whatever scraps of humanity were left. Yet, here she was, standing next to an immortal who was using his limitless existence to figure out how to feed a dying world. So what was the explanation for it? Why were so many so evil and so few so good? And for that matter, if this base was so advanced, why hadn't they done anything to help the human resistance over all these years?

Cary let out a long, heavy sigh, his gaze dropping to his boots as they resumed walking.

They moved past a series of wide-open bays that looked like a cross between advanced chemistry labs and high-end engineering workshops. Inside, she could see various projects left mid-assembly on the counters, but Cary wasn't forthcoming with the details anymore. He seemed entirely lost in his own thoughts, his face clouded as if he were trying to figure out how to translate a century of history into words she could actually grasp.

Ryan caught her eye from across the corridor and gave a slight, helpless shrug of his shoulders.

They passed another room where a man was hunched over a workbench, connecting thick copper wires to what looked like a massive audio speaker. The terminals suddenly erupted in a violent cascade of vibrant green sparks. The man jumped back, reaching for a pair of heavy safety gloves, and offered them a cheerful, casual wave as they walked by.

But as they kept moving the signs of life began to fade. The silence of the mountain settled back in. The rooms they were passing now were empty, dark, and cold; just a wide, echoing corridor with identical metal doors appearing every once in a while. Anya looked back over her shoulder, suddenly wondering if she would ever be able to find her way back to the dining courtyard on her own; they had been walking for quite a while now.

"I am not sure how to answer your question because we do not have a clear answer. Talus has some idea but we have no way of knowing for sure. We believe that the Others have a way of ensuring anyone that they give the stem cells to will become like them. There was no such modification when those of us took the serum. It is a hard thing, this was never planned...we never thought...come let me take you to your quarters. After you've had a chance to rest, if you still want answers, you can speak directly with Talus. His story is completely intertwined with almost every question you have, so he is truly the best person to tell it."

Anya felt her posture straighten at the prospect. She was actually going to see the man behind the curtain. Talus seemed to be the central pillar of this entire base; his name was on the tip of everyone's tongue, a shadow that influenced everything they did.

"Is everyone here a scientist or an engineer?" she asked, trying to fill the quiet void of the hallway. "Is this place just entirely populated by geniuses?"

"If they weren't a genius when they were turned, they probably are by now," Cary said, a faint, weary chuckle coloring his words. "You have to understand, this facility was never originally constructed to be a sanctuary from the war. It was built as a top-secret government laboratory designed for high-risk experiments and cutting-edge technology. So, naturally, many of the people who sought shelter here have simply continued their life's work. Partly because they genuinely enjoy the research and they're incredibly good at it... and partly because, honestly, what else is there for us to do with all this time?"

She got a sense of fatigue and almost longing in Cary's voice. It caught Anya completely off guard. Did he actually resent his longevity? Did he not want to be immortal anymore?

Back at Tigris, she had always loudly declared to the other guards that she would rather face a firing squad than live an immortal life, but that was because her only reference point had been the vicious nature of the cruel monsters she knew. These people, on the other hand, had somehow managed to hold onto their humanity, and they got to exist without the constant, suffocating fear of death hanging over their heads. To her, that seemed like a pretty great arrangement. Was it possible for Talus to replicate their specific serum for the rest of the surviving human race? If he could turn the refugees into stable immortals, they would finally stand a real chance against the enemy factions.

But the more she thought about the idea the more she realized that it was not for her. It would take so much of the thrill and the beauty out of her life. There was something about the risk of death or the shortness of life that compelled her to do things that she might not do otherwise, like coming here.

They rounded a final bend and passed another laboratory, but this one was easily the largest, most chaotic module they had seen yet.

Endless rows of long worktables stretched across a massive, dimly lit room. The surfaces were entirely littered with a messy sea of glass vials, bubbling beakers, cluttered storage drawers, and specialized electronic equipment. It looked like absolute chaos. Strange, colored vapors were smoking out of several containers, but what caught Anya's eye was a glass cylinder sitting on a central tray. Inside the fluid, a pale, distinctly fleshy mass was slowly disintegrating into nothingness.

She stopped dead, her eyes widening as she pointed a trembling finger through the glass partition. "Is that... is that a human finger?"

Cary stopped beside her, his gaze tracking the direction of her hand. He let out a low, muttered curse under his breath and shook his head in absolute exasperation.

"Well," Cary sighed, rubbing the bridge of his nose. "That would depend on your definition of human."

"So that's..."

"My finger," a voice cut in from the shadows.

Anya jumped slightly, her hand dropping toward her fulgar. She hadn't heard a single footstep, but suddenly, there he was, stepping out from a dark corner of the laboratory.

He was holding up his right hand for them to inspect. The index finger was completely missing, leaving a blunt, raw gap. But as Anya watched in horrified fascination, a smooth, pale stump rapidly formed over the wound. The tissue stretched, lengthened, and reshaped itself with terrifying speed until a perfectly formed, brand-new finger materialized out of thin air. He wiggled the fresh digit at her with a faint, humorless twitch of his mouth.

"Ryan, Anya," Cary said, stepping forward to bridge the gap, though his tone had lost all of its casual warmth. "I would like you to meet Talus. Like I stated earlier, he is the one you genuinely need to be afraid of around here. He's the crazy one." Cary turned a sharp glare toward his colleague. "Why on earth did you chop off your finger this time, Talus?"

Talus ignored Cary entirely, his focus locked on the glass cylinder where the discarded flesh had just finished dissolving into a clear liquid.

"I was testing a specific biological theory," Talus said, his voice low, gravelly, and entirely stripped of emotion. "There is an underlying chemical messenger that allows the immortal stem cells to recognize whether they are still integrated into the larger body mass, or if they belong to a detached segment that no longer requires regeneration. I posited that if I submerged the severed digit in a highly concentrated acid compound I recently engineered, the intense localized trauma would trick the cells. I hoped they would focus entirely on preserving the detached finger rather than recognizing it as an unnecessary, discarded piece of mass." He let out a dry, clinical sigh. "Wrong again. Fascinating results, though."

Anya could only stare at the man, her mind struggling to process what she was seeing. She had absolutely no idea what she had been expecting from the leader of this facility. Ever since the first moment she had heard his voice through the radio comms, he had been such a complete enigma that her brain hadn't even been able to conjure a stable mental image of him.

And now, seeing him standing beneath the harsh laboratory lights, he looked entirely different from the cheerful citizens in the courtyard. He was wearing a dark, heavy lab coat that seemed to absorb the light. His dark hair was completely disheveled, sticking up in wild angles, and his skin was a stark, ghostly pale. Structurally, he looked far more like the cold, intimidating immortals from her nightmares than anyone else she had met in the base.

For the very first time since she had stepped off the plane, a cold wave of genuine fear washed over her, especially when his dark eyes settled their storm upon her.

16

Talus

Talus wasn't sure how this experiment was going to go. For decades, he had been trying to figure out the exact localized mechanics of their mutation: how did the modified stem cells know which part of the body was the "host" that needed to be saved, and which part was just discarded tissue left to die?

If he cut off his entire hand, his wrist would regenerate a new one in minutes. But the severed hand lying on the table didn't grow a new body. It just sat there, cold and decaying. Why? He wondered if the biological blueprint was anchored to his heart or his brain. Were the stem cells constantly receiving a cue from his vital organs? And the moment that signal was cut off, did the cells in the severed limb just assume they were unnecessary and choose to die?

He wondered if there was a way to actively confuse the stem cells. If he could block them from realizing they were no longer receiving signals from the host body, would they instinctively start building a brand-new torso? If he could prove that hypothesis, he might finally figure out how to do the opposite and trick an entire immortal's body into never regenerating again.

He didn't exactly like the ethical implications of creating a physical double of himself, but he could always drop the tissue into an incinerator before an entire new Talus actually formed. Besides, could a single severed finger truly recreate his entire consciousness, complete with all his memories, scars, and personality? That seemed scientifically impossible without a brain.

He needed to start with baby steps. What if the severed tissue was immediately suspended in a highly aggressive acid? If the cells were forced to endure a rapid chemical attack, perhaps the sheer panic of the localized trauma would override their programming. They might become so desperate to fight off the acid and preserve the tissue that they would start regenerating automatically, even without a green light from the host nervous system.

He gave a slight, indifferent shrug. It was a long shot, but it was at least an empirical puzzle he could play around with today. The human Rangers were supposed to be arriving at the perimeter any hour now, and he desperately needed to keep his mind occupied. He didn't want to dwell on the political reality of their arrival. He still had absolutely no idea what he was actually going to say or do when he finally had to look a mortal in the eye again.

He reached across the cluttered workbench and grabbed a glass container filled with the experimental acid he had formulated. It was a highly concentrated, corrosive compound, if it worked as efficiently on his modified tissue as it did on the organic matter he had tested yesterday, it would dissolve his flesh almost instantly. The liquid was a sickening, vibrant shade of orange, and it fizzed aggressively against the glass the moment he jostled the beaker.

He set the beaker down on the central tray and grimaced. He steeled his nerves for the next phase. Cellular regeneration was never a pleasant experience, and actively severing his own finger was even less so. But a distraction was a distraction.

He laid his hand flat against the cold steel of the lab table, spreading his fingers wide. He reached out his right, his fingers wrapping tightly around the grip of a heavy, sterilized bone-cutting knife.

Biting his lower lip, he drew a single, deep breath through his nose and slammed the heavy blade down into the joint.

The initial bite of the steel was white-hot, a familiar, agonizing flare of nerve pain that made his vision blur at the edges. But after surviving a century of devastating war and countless self-inflicted diagnostic trials, he was getting remarkably efficient at compartmentalizing pain. He panted heavily for a few moments, his chest heaving as he dropped the bloody knife onto the table.

Using a pair of medical tweezers, he carefully hoisted the severed index finger from the steel table and dropped it directly into the glass cylinder of fizzing orange acid.

He turned away from the tray, reaching into the small lab refrigerator to grab a cool, damp cloth to wrap around his right hand. The wound was bleeding heavily, the dark crimson fluid pooling on the table despite his fast regenerative qualities. He pressed the cloth firmly against the raw stump to manage the mess.

It was exactly then, through the heavy hum of the laboratory's ventilation hood, that he heard the distinct sound of footsteps approaching down the outer corridor.

There were voices. One was Cary's familiar, casual drawl, but the other was a lighter, sharper cadence that Talus didn't recognize at all. They were already outside the door.

The heavy hiss of the pneumatic door signaled Cary's entrance. Talus didn't look up, but he listened as two sets of unfamiliar boots followed Cary's casual stride into the room.

The boots suddenly stopped dead.

"Is that... is that a human finger?"

Talus looked through the gap in the equipment racks. The girl, Anya, was staring at the glass cylinder, her face pale and her finger trembling as she pointed at the melting fragments of tissue.

Cary stopped right beside her, tracking her gaze. He let out a low, muttered curse, rubbing the bridge of his nose in absolute exasperation. "Well," Cary sighed, his voice dripping with that familiar, weary sarcasm. "That would depend on your definition of human."

"So that's..."

"My finger," Talus said, stepping out from the dim corner.

The girl jumped slightly, her hand instinctively dropping toward a round cylinder at her hip. Talus noted the reflex, a soldier's instinct.

He kept his posture entirely non-threatening, raising his left hand so they could see it clearly. The index finger was missing, leaving a blunt, raw gap where the bone had been cleanly severed.

He waited, watching her expression shift from alarm to horrified fascination as his biology did what it always did. A smooth, pale stump rapidly bubbled over the wound. The tissue stretched, lengthened, and knit itself back together with terrifying speed, spinning new skin and a perfect nail until a brand-new finger materialized out of thin air. Talus wiggled the fresh digit at her, his mouth twitching into a faint, humorless smile.

"Ryan, Anya," Cary said, his casual warmth completely vanishing as he stepped between them to bridge the gap. "I would like you to meet Talus. Like I stated earlier, he is the one you genuinely need to be afraid of around here. He's the crazy one." Cary turned a sharp, annoyed glare in his direction. "Why on earth did you chop off your finger this time, Talus?"

Talus ignored Cary entirely. His focus drifted back to the glass cylinder, where the last microscopic traces of the discarded flesh had finally finished dissolving into nothingness. Another dead end.

"I was testing a specific biological theory," Talus rattled off his explanation, his voice sounding low and gravelly even to his own ears, entirely stripped of the emotion Cary wore so easily.

He let out a dry, clinical sigh, tapping the glass cylinder with his newly formed fingernail. "Wrong again. Fascinating results, though."

He finally turned his full attention to the newcomers, letting his heavy, tired gaze settle directly onto Anya. She was just staring at him, her mind clearly struggling to process the reality of who he was. He knew what he looked like—disheveled dark hair, a stained lab coat, and skin made ghostly pale by decades beneath the earth. He could see the sudden, cold wave of apprehension in her eyes, and he couldn't blame her. He didn't look like a savior; he looked exactly like the monsters they had been running from.

"You cut off your own finger?"

Talus turned his gaze back to the girl, studying her face. She was a strange creature in her own way. Her blue eyes were a striking, vibrant contrast against her short, reddish-brown hair. The color was a near-perfect match to Lily's long, flowing curls, but Lily had green eyes, and there had been significantly less fire in them.

Next to her stood a man who looked exactly as plain and ordinary as one would expect from a person. He possessed dark, non-descript features, short hair, and spirited blue eyes. He was the kind of person Talus wouldn't have looked twice at on a crowded street.

"Not the first time, nor will it be the last," Talus replied, his voice flat. "I have also cut off my hand, and my foot once. The hand is easier, logistically speaking."

He wrinkled his nose as a sudden, unpleasant memory surfaced of the sheer number of heavy blade swings it had taken to chop through his own leg bone. It was a massive hassle. A finger or a hand was much more efficient.

"But why would you do such a thing?"

The girl was walking closer to him now, slowly edging her way into the center of the laboratory. Talus shifted his weight, entirely unsure of his next move. He shot a glance at Cary and the other human male, but they were absolutely no help, choosing to just stand by the door like statues.

Yet, the girl persisted. She moved right through his personal workspace, pushing past him without a hint of hesitation to inspect the neatly arranged rows of glass vials on a neighboring table. Talus felt a faint, amused smile touch his lips as he watched her pace up and down the aisles, auditing his chaos.

"To find an answer," he said.

"An answer to what?"

Now it was the male human's turn to speak up. Talus shifted his attention between the two of them as the man walked right up to him. It was a physical maneuver Talus recognized as a standard military intimidation tactic.

"The exact same questions I have been asking for a century," Talus said, stepping closer. "And the exact same questions you currently have burning in your eyes. Well, maybe not so much you," he clarified, tilting his head toward the man, "but definitely her."

He pointed a finger at the girl. The way her intense, curious eyes bored into him was completely unsettling; it felt like she was trying to systematically extract every secret locked inside his brain. Her gaze hadn't left his face once. Cary had probably been right in his assumption that Talus would lack the social grace to talk to the humans. This was turning into a terrible first impression.

"Anya," she corrected sharply, her chin coming up. "I have a name, and I expect you to use it. But you're right. I want answers. You clearly haven't made any real progress on your own down here despite constantly maiming yourself, and I have lost far too many comrades on the surface with zero progress to show for it. So, whether you like it or not, we both need to find a way to work together."

Talus blinked, entirely caught off guard. That was unexpected. Here she was, stranded deep inside an unmapped mountain, surrounded by immortal beings she didn't know and completely defenseless against, yet her voice still carried an immense weight of strength and courage. There was so much raw passion and emotion vibrating in her tone.

Had he truly possessed that kind of fire once? His memories suggested he had, but he honestly couldn't remember the last time he had felt something so intense. Not even looking at the photographs in his office had elicited the kind of emotional response she had just expressed in a single breath.

"And we shall, Anya." Talus said, forcing his voice into a calmer, more deliberate register. "That is the precise reason you are here. You…and any others who wish to be. You are the first to come here since the war, the first to trust us and you must not think that I discount you in any way. I am glad you are here, both of you. But for now you must follow along with Cary and get settled into your quarters. I am sure your things will be brought over from the hangar."

Cary nodded, having remained uncharacteristically silent for the entire exchange. "It's already being taken care of," he said, stepping forward. "Come on, Anya, Ryan. I have the rooms ready for each of you."

Ryan was quick to turn and follow, but Anya was much slower

to move. Her eyes remained locked onto Talus, and he found himself staring right back, unable to break the circuit.

"Anya, just go to your fucking quarters with Ryan and get cleaned up," Talus muttered, waving a hand toward the exit. "When you're ready, return to this lab, and I will begin to answer any questions you may have."

Anya froze, her brow furrowing in deep confusion and shock. "My what?"

"Your fucking quarters," Talus repeated plainly. "Cary suggested to the engineering crew that the two of you were actively copulating and would therefore require some fucking quarters, as he so eloquently put it."

"Talus! You absolute arsebadger!" Cary yelled, his eyes narrowing into a furious glare as his face flushed. "You know damn well that's not what I meant when I—"

Talus couldn't help but let out a smug, satisfied smile at Cary's sudden panic.

Both Anya and the one called Ryan immediately held up their hands in perfect, synchronized horror.

"No!" Anya shouted, her face reddening as she gestured frantically between herself and her partner. "We will definitely be needing entirely separate quarters. There will be absolutely no... that going on here. We are just friends."

Talus nodded and sent a smug look toward Cary. He had been right to think that the humans were not involved in such a way. "Go on to your quarters then. And when you are ready you and I shall take a walk around."

He figured a walk would keep her away from the highly breakable, dangerous chemical equipment in his lab if their dialogue took a disastrous, angry turn. After all, he already knew the historical answers, and even now, they were often enough to incite his own rage and cause him to smash things.

"On the surface?" she asked.

The suggestion caught him completely off guard. He was almost always entirely alone in his desire to walk through the skeletal, ruined town above their heads. None of the other Immortals cared to look at the past.

"Yes," Talus said, nodding slowly as the idea took root. "If that is what you wish."

Anya nodded back. She slowly let go of the metal doorframe she had been leaning against, giving him one final, perplexed look over her shoulder as she turned and followed Cary down the corridor.

Talus watched her disappear around the bend. There was something so deeply odd about her, and it took him a moment to realize what it was: she was much like him. Hard, determined, fiercely strong, and brutally focused. They were the kind of qualities that sounded perfectly noble on paper, until they all came together inside a person and created a monster like him.

So far, those traits seemed to look a lot better on her. But then again, he remembered a time when they had looked pretty good on him, too.

Talus moved over to the eastern wing of the laboratory, a clean, organized space where he actually made tangible progress and spent the few hours he genuinely enjoyed. He tried to force his focus onto a new compound he was engineering, a refined serum designed to completely eradicate the common cold in humans without triggering immortality, but his thoughts refused to cooperate.

His mind kept drifting back down the dark corridor toward his personal quarters. Toward the small, framed photograph of Lily sitting on his desk.

The image was a constant, bitter reminder of the life he could have had. The life so many millions could have enjoyed if he had simply possessed the intelligence to listen to her warning. This ruined, dystopian wasteland would have remained nothing more than a work of science fiction if only he hadn't been so blinded by his own ambition and fear.

But even more pressing than the ghost of Lily was the living reality of Anya. Talus mentally calculated the inevitable barrage of questions she was bound to throw at him. What could he actually answer? How much could he tell her without inciting her hatred? He desperately needed her to at least tolerate his presence if they were ever going to successfully collaborate. Would she ever be able to look at him with anything other than pure disgust if she found out the absolute truth of who he was and what he had done?

He bent his newly regenerated index finger, testing the joint. The tissue was completely normal now; the sharp, white-hot distraction of the pain had vanished entirely. He hated how much he missed that distraction.

Since the acid experiment hadn't successfully fooled the stem cells, he needed a different theory. His previous test showed that extreme sub-zero temperatures drastically slowed down cellular communication. Perhaps if he froze a limb and then severed it, the internal messaging system would be delayed or completely scrambled by the frostbite, forcing the detached piece to attempt a full regeneration anyway. The scientific bonus to this theory was that he would only have to endure the agony of a single frozen finger, rather than the horrific recovery of freezing his entire hand again

It was infuriating. After living several lifetimes, he realized he still had absolutely no fundamental understanding of how these modified stem cells actually operated. He had foolishly assumed he knew everything the day he first synthesized the serum and merged it with his own blood. He thought he held all the answers, and now, years later, the data proved he knew absolutely nothing. Not even a genius of his caliber could have predicted the bizarre, terrifying nature of the immortality the cells would ultimately grant.

He leaned his back against the cold concrete wall, holding his hand up to inspect it under the fluorescent light. If he amputated the finger before freezing it, would there be enough of a chronological window for the cells to register that they had been disconnected from the host? If he froze the digit first, the signal would undoubtedly be delayed.

The more his brain turned the logic over, the more ridiculous it sounded to his own scientific mind. The absurd theory that their modified stem cells were organized enough to possess a localized "leader" that instructed individual cells whether they were part of a body to be saved or just useless, discarded tissue left to scrap. And then what? The cells in the severed limb just rolled over and chose to die? After thousands of experiments, his brain was spinning down some incredibly unhinged tangents. But then again, in a dead world, what else was left to occupy his time?

Rubbing his hands together he looked toward the cursed fridge that he had used to freeze his hand before. It was, without a doubt, one of the most agonizing physical experiences he had ever forced his body to endure. To test this new hypothesis, he would have to subject himself to that exact torture a second time... and then find a way to cleanly slice the frozen bone.

He was going to require physical assistance for this one. Last time, he barely possessed enough presence of mind to scream at Cary to cut his hand, let alone execute the cut himself. And Cary was going to be absolutely furious if he was asked to do it again and this time sever an entire finger.

He continued tossing options back and forth in his mind, pacing through his thoughts so intently that he had no idea how much time had passed or how long she had stood there watching him. It was only when he had reached the conclusion that he might as well try it and looked up that he noticed she was there. She had returned much earlier than he had expected.

Anya gave a slight, casual shrug of her shoulders. "You seemed busy and I did not want to disturb you."

Talus nodded slowly, trying to smooth over his sudden alarm. His efforts to distract his brain had succeeded a little too well; he didn't even know what time of day it was. Had she actually slept? Had night officially fallen over the mountain?

"I've spent the last several days crammed into the close quarters of a solar plane or trapped in a medical room," Anya said, crossing her arms. "Now that I'm finally here, I don't think my brain could sleep even if I were drugged. Ryan, on the other hand..." She shrugged again, a faint smile touching her lips. "He flew the entire flight path, so the trip took a lot more out of him than me, not to mention the stress I've put him through." She trailed off looking toward the shelves. "Honestly, during the trip, I would have given absolutely anything to jump out of that cockpit just to walk through half the ruined cities we flew over."

"So, you want a guided tour of a town from someone who actually lived there?"

Her eyes grew wide.

Anya's blue eyes snapped wide, her posture immediately straightening. "Wait. You mean you actually lived up there when it was a real, functioning town? You know what it was like before the collapse? I've spent my entire life wondering what a place like that could have even felt like. There's a small residential ruin near Tigris base that I used to explore because, for some reason, the concrete structures are still standing. It's nothing like the sector around Phoenix. That city was completely leveled during the final bombardment campaigns."

Talus felt a strange, genuine smile touch his face. It was fascinating to watch her get so visibly excited over something he considered so incredibly mundane.. Another time another place it would have been such a boring offer, especially his little town. But for her it was a trip to an amusement park.

"In a manner of speaking, yes," Talus said, gesturing for her to follow as he walked toward the rear exit. "I lived here. The town above us was as much my home as it was anyone else's, I suppose."

They began to walk in unison down the long, uniform corridor toward one of the primary surface access points. The facility maintained several operational shafts, but the logistics crew almost exclusively used the reinforced exit cut directly into the northern face of the mountain.

Talus kept his eyes tracking strictly forward, but even without looking, he could feel the weight of her intense gaze focused entirely on his profile.

"So, Ryan only agreed to fly this high-risk mission because you wanted to come," Talus noted, breaking the silence.

Anya nodded, her boots clicking against the concrete.

Talus stopped walking. He turned his body around, leaning his shoulder against the wall as he looked down at her. "So, tell me...what exactly makes you so different?"

She stopped at his words and looked at him with an expression that he could not place. "Excuse me? You immortals are the ones who are different down here, remember? I flew across a continent to ask you that exact question! What do you mean, what makes me different?"

There it was again. That overwhelming, volatile wave of human emotion and raw passion. It was deeply invigorating to witness, but Talus imagined it must be utterly exhausting to experience. Had it been that exhausting for him back when he still possessed those emotions? Had he ever allowed himself to be that passionate about anything other than his work and perhaps Lily?

"Allow me to explain." Talus said, his voice low and steady. "You are not the first humans I have contacted. Very few individuals in this facility are aware of this, actually only Elan and I know. But I have actively reached out to various human bases over the years. I was always listening, reaching out when I thought the time was right, trying to find a way for our groups to work together. But every single attempt failed."

He took a step closer, his dark eyes locking onto hers. "I wanted to speak with humans who had direct contact with the Others. But time and time again, my requests were completely rejected. Not a single human outpost was willing to offer me a modicum of trust. Eventually, Cary discovered that we were actively monitoring your military communication frequencies and demanded I make one final attempt. So, after completely giving up on the project, I broadcasted the transmission. Your Captain Tennant gave me the exact same hostile, dismissive response as every other commander before him."

Talus leaned in, his gaze unyielding. "But then, you came along. You overrode his protocols. You stole a solar glider and flew directly to an unmapped mountain. So, I ask you again, Anya: what makes you so different from the rest? Why did you choose to answer my call when every other human refused?"

17

Anya

"I'm not all that different," Anya said quietly, the words leaving her mouth before her filters could stop them. "Just desperate."

It was probably not the grand, heroic explanation he was expecting. There was no poetry about bravery, no noble speech about building trust, and certainly no display of military intellect. It was just the bare, ugly truth, but it was all she had left to offer.

"I am just so tired of running," Anya continued, her voice tightening as she stared past him. "Tired of the constant thought of death strangling not just me, but every single person I know. It isn't even that I'm terrified of the act of dying itself. I just hate the fact that we aren't able to actually live, because trying to do anything more than survive will get you killed. People are so afraid to love or get attached to anyone, because we are taught from childhood that at any given moment, everything can be ripped away from you. And there is absolutely nothing you can do to stop it."

She surprised herself by having a tear wet the corner of her eye. She was almost getting into hard territory. The reality of growing up inside the militaristic confines of Phoenix base, with a family that ended up being nothing like the families she had read about in books.

For a second, the cold, calculated distance in Talus' eyes slipped. A shadow passed over his face, a look so burdened and deeply exhausted it felt like looking at the mountain itself.

"That I can understand," he murmured, his gravelly voice dropping so low it was almost swallowed by the ambient hum of the corridor. He looked away from her, staring down at his own newly formed hand as if tracing the lines of a century of regrets. "Perhaps more than you will ever know. Desperation is what drove every single one of us down into this mountain in the first place."

Hearing those words from him, sent a strange chill through Anya's chest. There was no mockery in his tone, no ancient superiority. It was just a quiet, devastating admission that underneath the laboratory coats and the terrifying biology, they had all crawled into the dark for the exact same human reason her people had.

A dozen different questions immediately began racing through her mind, fighting to get out all at once. She wanted to know what had initialized this facility, why they had chosen this specific valley, but most of all, she wanted an empirical answer to the exact question she had asked Cary.

"Are you going to answer my questions now?" she pressed, stepping closer to him. "Like the one I wanted you to answer when we spoke on the comms? You explicitly promised you would answer it once we were in person."

"I did," Talus acknowledged, "And I have little doubt you will find out everything you want answers to. But you must understand... my story is not an easy one to tell, and it is wrapped up in so many of the answers you're looking for."

"Will I ever actually hear it?"

"Oh, I imagine so," he said, a faint, dry inflection coloring his voice. "Bits and pieces at first. But stick around, and someday you might know the whole story."

"Does anyone down here know it?"

"Probably not," he replied, adjusting his dark lab coat. "Cary comes remarkably close, though."

Anya nodded, absorbing that. He turned to a sleek interface panel set into the concrete wall and pressed a rapid sequence of buttons. Almost instantly, a heavy mechanical rumble echoed above them as the ceiling segments began to slide open, letting in a brilliant, cascading orange glow. The sun was just beginning its evening descent. Talus immediately began scaling the structural steel stairs, and Anya scrambled right up after him, her previous exhaustion completely forgotten, replaced by a sudden, electric surge of eagerness.

With a pressurized swish and a heavy metallic bang, the security doors sealed shut behind them, and Anya found herself standing back on the surface.

The mountain wind swept past them, carrying a crisp, unpolluted draft that made her chest expand. She took a deep breath, her nose twitching. The air smelled remarkably fresh, clean... and distinctly sweet. She froze, her eyes widening. Could that actually mean...?

"Flowers?" she asked, the word coming out as a hushed whisper.

Talus was already several paces ahead of her, his dark coat snapping in the wind as he navigated the gentle slope leading toward the valley floor. He stopped and turned around to look at her.

"Yes, a few have begun to grow here over the last decade. Mostly what many would have considered weeds during my time, but I suppose they are pretty enough."

Anya broke into a quick jog to catch up with him. As her boots hit the ground, she realized the terrain beneath her was completely foreign. It felt soft and remarkably squishy—a stark, jarring contrast to the jagged rocks, packed clay, and barren sand she had spent her entire life navigating. There were actual, vibrant blades of green grass reaching toward the sky, resiliently springing back into place even after the heavy soles of her combat boots flattened them into the dirt.

"So," she said, trying to sound casual despite the awe bubbling up in her chest. "When exactly do I get to learn this story of yours?"

They kept walking toward the ruins of the city, and with each step, Anya couldn't help but marvel at the sheer abundance of the grass and the various plants carpeting the ridge. But what truly made her feel almost dizzy with excitement was the thought of seeing the inside of those buildings. She looked up at the monolithic structures, concrete and steel towers that looked tall enough to scrape the underbelly of the clouds. It was hard to comprehend an era so densely populated that humanity required buildings of that size.

Talus kept his eyes forward, tracking their path. "What are you so curious about?"

Everything. But she knew throwing a blanket demand at him wouldn't work. He obviously was not going to tell the whole story. At least not at once and she doubted he would trust her enough to tell all of it anyway. She had a hunch that a specific question would get her at least something of an answer.

"I want you to tell me everything. Why are you different? Not just you, all of you. What is this place? Or what was it? Why are you here? How did you become... But right now mostly I want to know why aren't you like all the rest of them?"

His eyes turned away and his expression changed to match the dark and serious man she had seen down below with the missing finger. The ground beneath her became hard and almost jagged.

Suddenly, the soft, forgiving earth beneath Anya's boots abruptly vanished. Her stride caught on a rigid, jagged surface. She looked down, observing a dark, fractured expanse of ancient asphalt that had cracked and crumbled into pieces over a century of neglect. It was a road. They had officially breached the town perimeter. It was a bizarre visual boundary, the wild, encroaching greenery of the valley suddenly halting at a sharp line of human engineering.

"A park," Talus stated flatly, noticing her analytical stare. "One of a few municipal recreational zones that used to occupy this section of the town. The plants have started to actively reclaim it."

A park. Anya turned around to look back, taking in the massive square of grass and flora that stretched out in front of the facility. From this vantage point on the asphalt, the true nature of their sanctuary was completely exposed. The solar mountain loomed over the valley, a gargantuan, geometric monolith of dark, polished panels designed to drink in the sun.

It was a brutal, towering testament to old-world ambition, entirely undisguised and fiercely out of place. It hit her then that this mountain was completely different from the hidden power arrays at Phoenix and Tigris. Those had been explicitly engineered to blend into the natural topography of the land, acting as camouflaged hideouts. This one made absolutely no attempt to hide. It was never meant to be a sanctuary for the last remnants of a dying race.

"I know very little about why we are different," Talus said, his tone dropping into a quieter, more reflective register. "I have a few working hypotheses, mere feelings on the matter, really, but they are difficult to quantify. In the beginning, the project was initialized with a single objective: saving the human race by completely eliminating mortality. The first subject was an absolute success. The second, however... the second subject became what you would call an Other."

He trailed off, his voice flatlining as he stared down the empty street. Anya watched him lapse into the silence, realizing with a chill that this was precisely why his history remained secret. He couldn't articulate the story without getting completely ensnared by the ghosts of his past.

"So they kept trying and they kept making these Others?" She prodded.

He shook his head.

Talus shook his head, a grim, humorless smile twisting his lips. "No. Can you even begin to comprehend the risk of creating a creature that possesses absolutely no humanity, yet cannot be killed? How could anyone justify continuing the program when having just a single specimen was trouble enough?"

That made sense. Even now, modern human archives contain precious little data regarding the true origin of the immortals. Everything Anya had read about the final campaigns of the war simply stated that they had materialized one day, aligning themselves with one of the primary warring factions. Some historians believed the immortals had been pulling the strings behind the global conflict from the very start; others assumed they had simply picked a side at random to expedite the slaughter.

"So then what happened?" Anya asked, her voice tight with curiosity. "Where did they all come from? Where did the rest of you come from?"

Here she was in the town that she was so eager to explore. Walking beside buildings that she wanted to walk inside and see what was left. What was it like to sit at a coffee shop? Or to work in a cubicle? And yet her gaze remained locked on Talus. The moment he spoke of the past, his eyes became entirely detached, as if he were staring through a century of concrete.

"Well for a time there were just the two. They got separated. It was decided there would be no more until it could be understood what happened in the second test. Then later one of the scientists on the project was faced with the choice of saving a friend or letting him die...then there were three."

Anya felt a cold knot tighten in her stomach. It was a massive, terrifying gamble—one she couldn't imagine ever taking. To risk permanently trapping someone you loved inside a cold, emotionless, unchanging shell for the rest of eternity seemed less like medicine and more like a curse.

"What an awful choice to make," Anya said, her voice laced with a sudden sharpness. "I would never do that to someone I cared about."

Talus stopped dead in his tracks. He snapped his head toward her, his stormy eyes boring into hers with a sudden, volatile intensity that made her breath catch.

"You would never save their life?" he demanded, his voice dropping into a dangerous, guttural growl. His shoulders hunched forward, his chest heaving as his entire physical demeanor shifted into something predatory. He looked less like a scientist and more like a cornered beast ready to tear her apart. "You would just actively choose to let someone you care about die from some stupid disease like cancer?"

The sheer force of his anger radiated off him in waves, but Anya refused to step back. She squared her shoulders, matching his glare with the hard, uncompromising fire she had learned to cultivate at Phoenix base.

"It is a thousand times better to let them die than to force them to exist as an emotionless killing machine!" she shouted back, her voice ringing off the hollow concrete walls of the skyscrapers. "Have you ever actually looked into the eyes of one of those creatures on the surface? What sort of life is that, Talus? An eternity spent as a mindless monster, systematically destroying every single good, beautiful thing left on this planet? If you honestly believe that nightmare is a better fate than a peaceful death, then you are completely blind."

The words seemed to puncture his rage. The raw fury in his expression suddenly cratered, softening into something fragile and hollow, though his shoulders remained stiffly braced against the wind. He ran a trembling hand through his dark hair, shaking his upper body slightly as if physically trying to break free from the memory loop.

"That..." Talus whispered, his voice cracking slightly before he forced a brittle, shallow lightness back into his tone. "Well. I suppose we should be profoundly grateful that didn't happen, then."

His lightness had returned but only slightly and she knew that she had gotten her piece of the story for now. Maybe later she would get another bit. The strange thing was that he had not told her anything about how he became immortal or why he was different. But it was more about the origins of the immortals than she had ever known.

She fell into step beside him as he resumed walking down the center of the derelict street, her eyes finally drifting upward to map the architecture. Some of the municipal buildings were small, rising only a story or two above the sidewalk, while others towered so high she couldn't even finish counting the structural tiers before they had walked past the footprint. The entire grid was in a state of catastrophic disrepair. Massive, jagged craters tore through the upper concrete facings, clear evidence of missile strikes and heavy artillery fire from the collapse.

It was still infinitely more intact than anything she had ever witnessed on the surface, save for the fleeting glimpses she had caught from the cockpit of Ryan's solar glider. They pushed through one desolate city block, and then another, the sheer scale of the urban ruins beginning to weigh on her limbs. Her boots felt increasingly leaden against the merciless asphalt, and her muscles were just beginning to ache with fatigue when, up ahead through the canyon of concrete, she finally spotted a welcome flash of green.

"Look up there!" Anya pointed toward a large outdoor terrace that bridged the gap between two towering concrete office buildings.

Most of the glass panels along the railings had long since shattered, their jagged remains glinting like diamonds under the dying orange sun. Through the gaps in the framework, she could just make out the rusted, skeletal remains of old café tables. Thick, heavy vines crawled up the stone supporting columns, their dense green tangles dotted with tiny, vibrant bursts of red flowers. The growth had completely taken over the building, spilling out of the terrace floors to drape over windows and cover the outer walls. Even from a distance, it was breathtaking, a beautiful, quiet victory of life over concrete.

"It is nothing," Talus said, his voice dropping into a gruff, dismissive tone. "Just a communal area where office workers used to eat their midday meals. The local flora has simply become overgrown."

"I bet you can see the entire valley from up there," she murmured, her eyes tracing the vertical lines of the structure.

"You can."

Anya looked at him. She was having a hard time focusing on whatever they had been talking about. "You've been up there?"

Anya snapped her head toward him, her focus instantly shifting away from their previous conversation about the origins of the war. "You've actually been up there?"

Talus offered a stiff, reluctant nod. His gaze remained locked entirely straight ahead, deliberately tracing the cracked asphalt of the empty road instead of looking back at the terrace. "Yes. But not since..." He trailed off, inhaling sharply through his nose as his jaw tightened, "not since before the war."

"Then you are much overdue." Anya declared, a spark of stubborn energy cutting through her physical fatigue. "Let's go up."

She pivot-stepped, shifting her weight to march toward the primary glass-and-steel entryway of the building that grounded the terrace.

"No."

The word was a flat, uncompromising barrier. Anya stopped and looked back over her shoulder. Talus hadn't moved an inch, his body still rigid, his face pointed firmly away from the glass atrium.

"Come on," she prodded, turning to face him. "We can easily keep talking on the way up. It'll give us a change of scenery."

"No," he repeated, his voice sharpening. "You will remain on the ground. That building has been in a state of unmonitored ruin for a century. It is structurally unsafe."

"You don't know that for a fact," Anya countered, crossing her arms. "You aren't even looking at the building, and you just admitted you haven't set foot inside it since before the world burned. Now, come on."

Talus remained rooted to the spot, his head pivoting in the exact opposite direction of the terrace, an active, deliberate evasion. "We will continue this conversation on the ground. If it is a higher perch you seek then there are other options."

Anya's eyes snapped wide, a flash of white-hot irritation flaring in her chest. "A perch?! I am not some fragile little bird, Talus, nor am I some delicate human refugee you need to protect from the elements! I've spent my entire life taking care of myself in active combat zones. You arrogant jerk—how dare you assume you have any sort of control over what I do."

Shaking her head in sheer disbelief, she spun around and marched directly toward the heavy metal frame of the office building's entrance. She certainly didn't need a grumpy old scientist's permission to climb a few flights of stairs, and she was perfectly happy to leave him rotting on the pavement. At this point, it wasn't even about the flowering vines or the view anymore; she simply refused to be ordered around or treated like a helpless child by an immortal who thought he owned the world.

"If you cross that threshold and climb that building," Talus called out, his gravelly voice echoing off the concrete, "I will answer no more of your questions."

That caused her to freeze. Her fingers were a mere inch away from wrapping around the rusted handle of the door.

For one long second, the world hung in a balance as she just stared at the metal handle, her breathing tight. Then, she forced her hands into her pockets, turned on her heel, and marched back to where he stood. She stopped right in front of him, her arms crossed tightly over her chest, anger flashing in her blue eyes.

"I came all this way," she hissed, her voice vibrating with suppressed rage. "I defied direct military orders, I abandoned my outpost, I risked my life in a stolen glider, and you are honestly telling me you'll refuse to talk to me because I want to walk up a few flights of steps? It is utterly ridiculous."

"Up those specific steps to that specific terrace? Yes," Talus said, his dark eyes finally shifting to meet hers, cold and unmoving. "Feel free to scale any other skyscraper in this valley. Break as many bones as you like on crumbling stairwells and failing floorboards. But not that one."

Anya's eyes narrowed into dangerous slits as she studied his rigid expression. "Are you ever going to tell me what issue you have with this building, or is this just you flexing your muscles on a pathetic little power trip?"

"My reason is my own." Talus stated flatly, his chin coming up. "Now what is your decision?"

Anya let out a long sigh, the fight draining out of her as she realized she had been thoroughly backed into a corner. She couldn't risk him following through on his threat. She gave a sharp, resentful nod and gestured aggressively down the road, indicating for him to keep leading the way.

"Has anyone ever told you that you are infuriating?" she muttered as they fell back into step.

"Almost constantly," Talus replied, the rigid tension leaving his shoulders as he guided her back through the maze of streets toward the massive, darkened silhouette of the solar mountain looming in the distance. "But if it offers any comfort, you can get your revenge tomorrow morning."

Anya glanced at him, her brow furrowing. "I'm listening."

"I require your physical assistance," Talus said, his tone shifting back into that dry, clinical register. "I need you to cleanly amputate my index finger after I subject it to a localized cryogenic freeze."

Anya blinked, a startled, sudden laugh escaping her lips before she could catch it. "Well. It's definitely not the body part I would have picked at this moment, but I'll take it. And I have to say, that is officially the strangest thing anyone has ever asked me to do."

"Not the first time I have heard that either," Talus murmured, a faint, fleeting twitch of amusement touching the corner of his mouth.

Anya smiled, shaking her head as she looked out at the ruined city blocks passing them by. It was going to be an incredibly strange, hazardous friendship, but as they walked together into the shadow of the mountain, she realized she wouldn't have it any other way.

18

Talus

"So you are doing what now?"

The sheer skepticism in Anya's voice made Talus regret inviting her to help him in this. He stared at her, the heavy bone shears glinting under the harsh fluorescent lights of the laboratory's eastern wing, and wondered if he should just abort the entire plan. Maybe their time would be better spent cataloging her field data regarding the Others, and he could simply manipulate or bully Cary into swinging the blade for him later. But that path involved a completely different set of exhausting arguments he desperately wanted to avoid. He was already halfway into this endeavor with her. There was no sense in turning back now.

"For the absolute last time," Talus said, his gravelly voice tight with an edge of fraying patience, "I am going to plunge my hand into the cryogenic processor. The sub-zero exposure drastically forces the cellular mutation to stall, slowing down our regeneration curve. Once I remove my hand, you will immediately use those shears to sever the index finger before the tissue thaws."

Anya looked down at the heavy metal shears in her grip, her fingers tightening around the handles with unadulterated disgust. Talus found her squeamishness entirely illogical. They were just inanimate pieces of tool steel, they were not going to hurt her after all. They were however going to hurt him quite a bit.

"Why?" she demanded, her blue eyes snapping up to lock onto his. "Why subject yourself to that?"

"To determine if the detached finger initiates its own regeneration sequence," Talus snapped, turning his back to her to check the digital pressure gauges on the liquid nitrogen tank. "I must map out the exact parameters of how these modified stem cells compute their instructions. When a limb is cleanly amputated from my body, why does the discarded tissue simply decay instead of building a brand-new iteration of me? There is a centralized biological anchor. The head, the heart, the nervous system—something is actively broadcasting a master signal to tell the cells whether they are the host or the scrap. But isolating that variable is proving to be an empirical nightmare."

Anya didn't answer. She just went back to staring at the shears, her jaw set in a stubborn, immovable line.

Talus felt a hot surge of frustration prickling against his consciousness. He was ready to throw his hands up in the air and call the whole thing off. He reached out and violently tapped the digital display of the freezer, confirming the internal temperature was sitting at a stable minus-one-hundred-and-eighty degrees. He was dreading the pain of the next five minutes, and her hesitation was only stretching the tension out.

"What does it even matter?" she asked quietly.

Talus spun around, his boots clicking sharply against the tile floor. He was about two seconds away from calling Cary into the room to take over. This girl just needed to do what he said and stop asking so many questions. What happened to being angry with him, wanting to cut off one of his body parts?

"It matters," Talus said, his voice dropping into a dangerous, low rumble, "because if I can prove a signal is being actively broadcasted, it means the signal can be intercepted. We can disrupt it."

"Okay," Anya countered, her tone remarkably steady as she took a step toward his workbench. "But even if you disrupt it in a single finger, you still don't know where the broadcast is originating. You already know the regeneration happens, Talus. The micro-logistics of a severed digit don't mean a damn thing unless you are actively willing to decapitate yourself or carve out your own heart to find the source. Are we going to start systematically hacking away your vital organs until the lights turn off? Because I have a very strong feeling that the answer isn't hidden in your finger."

"For the last time –"

He was going to tell her that he was right. That the experiment was necessary and that this was something that was going to provide a wealth of information. He just did not have time to explain it in a way she would understand since all his current attempts fell on deaf ears.

And yet…she had a point. Something was controlling the regeneration. Proving that it was there was not going to help him figure out a way to stop it. The most he was trying to do now was confuse or make it regenerate a new him. What an awful thought that would be.

The silence stretched between them, heavy and suffocating. Slowly, Talus reached out and took the heavy bone shears from her hand, setting them down on the stainless steel tray with a hollow metallic clang. He let out a long, ragged sigh, watching the frost vapor curl off the open cryogenic tank. There went another useless hypothesis.

"You really don't know, do you?"

Anya's voice had lost all of its sharp defiance, softening into something quiet, heavy, and entirely uninvited. She took another step closer to him. Too close. Talus immediately felt his defensive instincts flare. What was it with women and this compulsive, suffocating drive to offer comfort? Lily had possessed that exact same trait, stepping into his personal space with that soft, maddening empathy long before they had ever been anything to one another.

"Know what?" Talus muttered, deliberately stepping back to break the circuit. He turned his face away from her, leaning his weight against the edge of the lab table, his hands resting on the steel deck in a posture of quiet, bitter defeat.

"Your own limitations," Anya said, her eyes tracking his movement. "You have absolutely no idea what will actually kill you."

Talus let out a sharp, mocking bark of a laugh. "If you want to

213

know if I've tried decapitation or pulling my own heart from my chest, well, I haven't resorted to that yet."

"Don't," Cary whispered. The word carried a ghost so heavy it stilled the entire room. "I've seen it. I know exactly how it ends."

The raw trauma bleeding through her tone struck him like a physical blow, making him pivot instantly to face her.

All the color had completely drained from Anya's face. Her expression was utterly grim, her blue eyes wide and fixed on the blank concrete of the lab floor, as if they were seeing something completely horrific. He then remembered her earlier mention of the Fulgar and how it could be used to temporarily paralyze the neural pathways of the Others. A dark, jagged realization began to piece itself together in his mind. She hadn't just fought the immortals from a distance.

"We always knew something had to be able to do it," Anya said, her voice trembling slightly, though she fiercely tried to lock it down. "Something had to be capable of killing them. At Phoenix base, we were raised to be soldiers. Nothing but cold, efficient soldiers, and the high command treated us exactly that way. Before the base was compromised, the rangers managed to capture an immortal. They brought him back into the lower levels. Kept him chained to a reinforced concrete pillar for months."

She swallowed hard, her gaze remaining locked on the floor as the memory took over.

"They did absolutely everything they could think of to try and break his biology. Every horrific thing you can imagine to see what would finally stop the healing. And then... the commanders turned it into a training exercise. They made the new recruits take turns. They made the adolescent soldiers take part in the executions to harden us. I..."

Anya choked on the words, her chest heaving as she gripped the edge of the table, her knuckles turning a stark, bloodless white. "I couldn't do it. I wouldn't..."

A visceral nausea coiled in Talus' stomach, threatening to make him retch. Looking at the starkness of Anya's face, he could tell she was fighting the exact same physical revulsion.

How could the humans have descended into such absolute depravity? To be pushed so far into the dark, feral corners of survival that they were willing to systematically, continuously torture a living, sentient being. Granted, it wasn't far off from the atrocities the Others committed on the surface daily. But Talus had always desperately clung to the belief that the humans were better than that. They still possessed their humanity. Didn't they?

So that was the real reason why she had been expelled from Phoenix. She wasn't just different; she possessed a moral code that her superior commanders had tried to violently grind away.

The implications of what Anya was telling him caused Talus to reevaluate his assumptions about the Others' behavior. If the high command at Phoenix had been running these bio-mechanical trials, were the soldiers currently being abducted across the continent being taken to create new, engineered battalions? Or was it pure vengeance? He did not want to even contemplate the fate of the poor soul who was trapped at Phoenix or how many more were currently chained up across the ruined hemisphere.

The thoughts consumed him so entirely that the laboratory grid seemed to fade. He barely registered the sudden, sharp rustle of fabric until Anya's knees buckled.

She slid down the front of the stainless steel workbench, sinking heavily onto the cold tile floor. Her trembling hand slapped over her mouth, her blue eyes wide and fractured with a profound, bleeding agony.

"How could anyone do that, Talus?" she whispered, her voice cracking as a breathless, ragged sob escaped her throat. "I watched them do it. I stood there and I watched as he screamed while they cut his actual heart out of his chest cavity. I watched them hold it up in front of his face while it was still pulsing. He fainted from the pain, but they just stood there... holding his dead heart in their hands, waiting for him to open his eyes again."

Her chest was heaving, her breath coming in sharp, hyperventilating gasps.

Talus froze, his own pulse hammering in his ears. Panic, cold and clumsy, seized his chest. He had absolutely no idea how to calm the girl. What would Lily do? What would Cary say? Anyone but him. He had spent a century isolating himself from the messy, volatile landscape of feelings; he was utterly ill-equipped for this. He didn't even know this girl, but her pain was so overwhelming it seemed to bloom within his own chest as well.

"Do you...do you want me to fetch someone?" Talus stammered, his hands hovering uselessly in the air. "That Ryan character. Where can I find him?"

They were obviously close so he would likely be much better at doing whatever it was she needed rather than him. He got up and was headed toward Ryan's quarters when a sudden, fierce tug snapped against his left forearm.

He stopped, looking down. Anya's small, pale hand had lashed out, her fingers wrapping with surprising, desperate strength around the dark fabric of his lab coat sleeve. She was still deathly pale, her expression utterly despondent, but the sheer panic in her eyes had hardened into a silent, pleading command.

"No," she choked out, her grip tightening on his arm, anchoring him to her spot on the floor. "Don't go. It's alright. I work very hard to keep those pictures out of my head. Most days I can do it. But when the memories start, I just have to force them to leave again. Which only makes me feel entirely worse, because I only had to watch it. He had to live it. Every single day."

Talus slowly turned back around. He didn't break her grip on his sleeve. Instead, he allowed the tension to pull him back to her side.

Her revelation was providing a terrifying, invaluable stream of biological data. It was horrifying for the entity who had been subjected to the blade, but for Talus the scientist, it was a profound revelation. Not even having his heart removed would kill him? That was an odd sort of science. Was there anything that his stem cells could not repair? But beneath the cold scientific math, a deeper, stranger current was shifting in his chest. Looking down at her shattered form, the science felt secondary.

"How did they manage to keep him contained?" he asked

quietly.

The words left his mouth, and he instantly wished he could tear them back out of the air. It was incredibly callous. Cary would have told him to shut his mouth, or more likely, slapped him across the jaw. For a man who liked to be loose with women and men, he was much better at the emotional side of things than he was.

Anxious to repair the blunder, Talus awkwardly, hesitantly eased his tall frame down onto the floor beside her. It was a clumsy, unpracticed movement. Every instinct screamed at him to stand up, to maintain his distance from her and her emotions. But looking at the way her shoulders shook, a strange, powerful gravity kept him rooted right there on the tile, their shoulders nearly brushing. He wanted the answers, yes—but a small, buried part of his old human heart simply didn't want her to be alone on the floor.

Anya didn't pull away from his sudden proximity. If anything, the taut line of her spine seemed to lean into his space, drawing a fragile sense of warmth from his bulk.

"The Fulgar at first," she whispered, her gaze still fixed on the dark spaces under the worktables. "That was how the rangers managed to capture him. After that. It was heavy titanium chains and conductive wire wrapped directly around the nerves in his neck. They kept the frequency live. They could send an electrical surge through his spine anytime he even tried to flex his muscles."

Talus' jaw tightened. A captured immortal had to be one of the most heavily guarded military secrets on the continent. He had listened to human communication frequencies for decades and had never heard a single syllable whispered about a test subject at Phoenix. Then again, given how aggressively both factions monitored the airwaves, absolute radio silence was standard operating procedure.

"Did the high command at Tigris have a specimen to train their soldiers on as well?" Talus asked, turning his head to look at her profile, his voice carrying a dark, dangerous edge of skepticism. "Is that how the human resistance has successfully been holding the frontline? By systematically capturing and torturing the Others?"

He was genuinely starting to question whether humanity

possessed a soul left worth salvaging. Of course there were always good and bad in people. Plenty of horrible things had happened long before the war ever did, in fact the history books were bloody with evidence that the cruelest individuals always enjoyed a longer, more successful evolutionary run than the righteous ones. Maybe that was the case now, maybe it was really the Others that he should feel sorry for and want to help.

But then he looked at Anya. His eyes traced the sharp, beautiful line of her jaw, the fierce, burning purity in her profile even while drowned in sorrow. She was the living variable that broke his cynical reasoning.

"No," Anya said softly, finally turning her head. Her blue eyes looked straight into his, so close he could see the amber flecks around her pupils. The sheer intensity of the connection sent a sudden, electric jolt straight down his spine. "Just Phoenix. They are different and they are brutal and they only live to breed and train soldiers. I think they found it too much trouble to keep the immortal entrapped, not to mention the amount of energy he must have sucked up trying to stay alive."

Maybe the energy was the key. If they could find a way to remove the energy in the area so the Others could not absorb it then they would not be able to regenerate either. So all they needed to do was turn off the sun and kill everything on Earth...easy. Or, alternatively, engineer a containment chamber that blocked all atmospheric energy, and then ask the thousands of bloodthirsty monsters roaming the surface if they wouldn't mind politely stepping inside. Maybe he could fill it with cake, everyone liked cake.

At the very least, a strange, quiet sense of relief washed over him as he looked down at Anya. If he ever found himself captured by a human outpost, it was comforting to know that most of them wouldn't immediately string him up like a macabre marionette and brutally harvest his internal organs.

"That is likely the exact reason why Phoenix base was completely destroyed," Talus murmured, his voice softening as he kept his eyes locked on hers, the initial awkwardness of sitting beside her on the floor beginning to melt away into a strange, shared gravity. "The Others must have detected the anomaly, or perhaps realized what was being learned. They struck to ensure that whatever data was extracted from those horrific experiments was permanently lost. Was that intelligence ever shared with the rest of the surface network?"

Anya shook her head, a stray strand of blonde hair brushing against her cheek. "Only bits and pieces. Usually when Phoenix would rotate their veteran soldiers out to reinforce the other outposts. We were explicitly commanded never to speak of it, likely because the high command knew the other base Captains would have panicked, or worried about a retaliation. If Captain Tennant at Tigris had known the truth, he would have been absolutely furious. But, I guess Phoenix got exactly what they deserved in the end. They stood by and let it happen. They traded their humanity for an edge."

What a bizarre, terrifying crucible that base must have been. Talus wondered how a human society could have evolved into something so utterly detached. A few radical ideologues in a position of absolute authority, spreading their ruthless doctrines over generations, could easily warp an entire society's moral compass. Yet, there had to be dissenters. There had to be individuals who still possessed a different moral compass. Were they all systematically purged or traded away like commodity scrap, just as Anya had been?

He could hear the sharp, cutting edge of bitterness vibrating in her voice, a profound resentment for the bunker that raised her. But that didn't align with her recent behavior. It didn't explain the glaring contradiction of her choices.

"If you hated them so deeply," Talus asked, his voice dropping into a quiet, intensely personal register as he leaned a fraction of an inch closer, "then why did you go back? Why risk your life for such people?"

For the first time since they had stepped into the cold laboratory, a faint, fragile smile touched Anya's lips. It was a beautiful, devastatingly sad expression. She looked down, her small fingers nervously twining and fiddling together in her lap.

"You have to believe that everyone deserves to be saved, right?"

she whispered, her voice barely carrying over the hum of the facility. She looked up, her blue eyes piercing right through his defensive layers. "Or that, at the very least... one single person there was worth dying for."

She swallowed hard, her chest hitching. "There was a ranger at Phoenix. He was probably the only person in that entire concrete hell who realized, just like I did, that no matter what the world did to us, it was absolutely no excuse for what we were doing to that creature. He tried to defend me when I refused to play their sick little training games. He stood between me and the instructors... but it didn't matter. They still broke my rank and threw me out into the wasteland."

She trailed off, the tight, military composure she carried like armor finally fracturing entirely. For the first time, hot, silent tears began to spill rapidly down her cheeks.

Talus felt a sudden, sharp ache bloom directly behind his ribs. Panic didn't seize him this time; instead, a profound, overwhelming urge to alleviate her suffering took its place. He wanted to reach out, to brush the tears from her skin, but his hands felt too large, too heavy, too inherently monstrous to offer real comfort. Where the hell was Cary? Where was the other human? Anyone else would know how to hold her, how to steady her through the storm.

With a sudden, fierce burst, she forced herself up off the floor. She aggressively wiped the tears away with the back of her sleeve, squaring her shoulders. It was a behavioral pattern Talus recognized with striking familiarity, the brutal suppression of internal pain solely to keep the body moving forward. What else could survivors do?

Talus rose smoothly to his feet alongside her, his towering frame casting a protective shadow over her smaller form. The distance between them felt entirely gone now, burned away by the raw exposure of her grief.

"I am sorry, Anya," Talus said. The words felt leaden, carrying a weight he hadn't anticipated. He reached out, his hand hovering near her shoulder before he finally let it rest there, a steady, solid warmth through the fabric of her jacket. "We will find a way to stop them. I promise you."

It was a promise he was pretty sure he could not fulfill. If he hadn't managed to crack the genetic code of the Others in a century of isolation, he had little reason to believe he ever would. But as he looked down into her tear-streaked face, it felt like the only absolute truth that mattered. If he completely abandoned hope now, what purpose did his eternal existence even serve? He could help Cary bring back the animals and vegetation that they could and rebuild upon the surface. But all that would just inevitably lead up to another war depending on what the Others were planning. And this war would have no end.

Anya looked up at his hand on her shoulder, a bittersweet shadow crossing her face. "No. The one good thing Phoenix successfully beat into my head was that getting emotionally attached in a world where we are actively fighting just to survive is entirely pointless. It was always going to end in tragedy for one of us. So, what is our next objective?"

Talus stared at her, Cary's prophetic words echoing in his mind. She is exactly like you. It was almost uncanny, a mirror image of his own cynical, fiercely guarded psychology wrapped in a human shell. He wasn't entirely certain yet if that mirrored nature was a blessing or a curse. But if she truly operated as he did, then he knew exactly what medicine she needed to process her grief: a directive. A mission.

"We start sharing information, like we planned." Talus said, his voice regaining its firm, authoritative resonance as he withdrew his hand. "We combine what we know, so we can hunt down answers for what we don't. Tell me about this Fulgar technology of yours. What are the specific mechanics of the neural paralysis?"

Anya reached deep into the tactical pocket of her combat pants. For a fleeting microsecond, Talus wondered if he should be concerned by how fluidly her hand moved, or how readily accessible her weaponry was. She pulled her fist out, revealing a compact, matte-black metallic cylinder. She held it tightly in her grip, her thumb resting deliberately against a recessed activation toggle on the base.

"It's remarkably elegant," Anya explained, her demeanor instantly shifting back into that of a cold, calculated field operative. "Each independent cylinder houses a single, high-density electrical charge. I simply depress this activation toggle to ready the payload, and then this terminal end..."

She seamlessly flipped the cylinder over in her palm, exposing two wicked, micro-machined titanium prongs that hissed as they extended from the casing.

"...goes directly into the exposed base of the neural stem. Like so."

"Like-?"

He should have seen it coming, especially considering the fact that he had promised her payback. But still having the cylinder jammed into his own neck came as a bit of a surprise.

A blinding, white-hot torrent of electricity exploded through his central nervous system. Every single nerve ending in Talus' body jumped to absolute, violent attention, firing in a chaotic symphony of agony before freezing completely solid in a state of rigid, paralyzed stasis. His muscles locked, his breath trapped in his chest, leaving him staring down at her with wide, entirely stunned eyes as the room tilted on its axis.

"See how it works now?" Anya's voice floated down to him, entirely conversational, as if she hadn't just completely hijacked his central nervous system. She leaned over his frozen periphery, a bright, dangerous spark returning to her blue eyes. "I am going to grab some breakfast. I'll be back shortly. Honestly, this was a much better alternative than cutting off a finger, because this way I don't even have to listen to you."

She flashed him a brilliant, wicked wink, her lips curving into a genuine smile that made her look entirely human, entirely alive, and entirely terrifying. Then, she turned on her heel and scurried out of the eastern wing.

Talus was profoundly dismayed to realize that not a single muscle fiber in his body would respond to his commands. His lungs were locked in a mid-breath expansion, his jaw was rigidly fixed, and his left knee was bent at an incredibly awkward, unnatural angle against the tile. This was definitely a compelling piece of engineering, and he was rapidly starting to regret inviting her into his inner sanctum. He also deeply kicked himself for not asking a vital diagnostic question before she vanished: how long does the payload last? Because he was currently in one of the most uncomfortable positions he had occupied in a century.

Yet, as the silence of the lab settled around him, the sensory deprivation offered an unexpected sanctuary. It was a good way to get entirely lost in his thoughts.

The time he had spent with Anya was acting as a mirror, showing him a reality he had spent decades avoiding. He was not nearly as human as he had stubbornly treated himself as being. So much of that raw, messy emotion had long since evaporated from his core. He was a completely different entity from the man he vaguely remembered being before the bombs fell. But as he stared helplessly at a speck of dust on the floor, a strange thought surfaced: Was that truly such a terrible thing? After all, the universe was filled with worse fates. Like having a heartbeat, but no life at all.

"Talus? Anya? How goes things?"

If Talus could have physically rolled his eyes, he would have. He recognized the melodic, slightly frantic cadence instantly. Cary. Oh, magnificent. This was bound to degenerate into an absolute theatrical panic. Talus remembered he had instructed Cary to give the other human, Ryan, an extensive tour of the lower mechanical hangars precisely so he wouldn't have to listen to Cary complain about severed body parts. What the hell were they doing back so early?

"Talus! Talus! Oh my god, what happened to you!"

Suddenly, Cary's face erupted into his limited field of vision, wide-eyed, pale, and thoroughly hysterical. Predictable. Exactly as modeled.

For a fleeting second, Talus was almost grateful the electrical current prevented him from speaking; it saved him the exhausting labor of formulating an explanation. But his silence was clearly a mistake. Cary was already gripping his rigid shoulders, hyperventilating, preparing to drag his dead-weight body down the corridor to the primary medical bay. It would be a completely fruitless endeavor, no one had calibrated the medical equipment in decades, and even if they had, Talus was the one they would have come to.

He was mercifully spared further handling by a loud, booming burst of human laughter emanating from the threshold of the lab.

"Man," Ryan's voice echoed, thick with amusement. "He must have pissed my girl off pretty damn good."

"What did she do to him?!" Cary shrieked, his face instantly vanishing from Talus' view. The frantic thud of Cary's boots indicated he had marched directly across the room to physically confront the pilot.

Talus internally groaned. He hated being slumped over on the floor like a discarded sack of rations while Cary and Ryan squabbled above him. He couldn't even blink to try and direct their movements, or signal them to shift his torso into a position that wouldn't ruin his lower spine. He might be paralyzed, but his nerve receptors were fully online. He could still feel the painful prickle of the current.

"Aw, calm down, look at him, he'll be completely fine," Ryan said, his tone dripping with casual, cocky assurance. Talus could practically see the smug, crooked grin on the pilot's face. "She just gave him a quick pop with the Fulgar device. Just a standard neuro-paralysis. Never lasts more than thirty minutes, tops. She's insanely quick with that thing, ain't she? Man, I tell you, she is the absolute worst sparring partner because you're flat on your back before you even realize the match has started."

Humans. They were all so infuriatingly arrogant, so foolishly flippant. There was scientific work to be done, a global threat to analyze, and instead, Talus was forced to play the part of a sprawled-out ragdoll while they swapped anecdotes.

"She paralyzed him?" Cary's voice dropped, the hysterical panic instantly transitioning into something calculating, dark, and deeply concerning. "Thirty minutes, you say? Is there any chance I could acquire one of those things?"

Oh, brilliant, Talus thought, a cold dread spiking through his locked nervous system. Just what he needed, Cary with the ability to paralyze him. He would never get a word in edgewise then. Granted, Cary barely listened to him now but at least he still got his way most of the time.

"You want to paralyze him?" Ryan asked, a chuckle vibrating in his chest. "So he pisses people off a lot then?"

"Oh yeah, you will never run out of orders for these around here."

Great that really sounded like Ryan handed over one of the cursed things. This was definitely going to come back to hurt him in the future. He was going to have a long talk with Anya before he allowed her back in his lab again. If this was what she was capable of he really did not want her loose in his lab where she could cause real damage.

"So...he'll be perfectly functional when whatever the flub she did to him runs its course?" Cary asked, his voice moving closer again.

"As far as I know. I have never really stuck around to find out, but Anya has. I assume she would not do anything that would cause permanent damage. She likes him enough."

If only you knew, Talus thought bitterly. Anya was a fascinating, multi-layered anomaly. For all her lethal efficiency and sudden strikes, she was fundamentally incapable of causing him real, malicious damage. Her visceral, weeping reaction to the dark phantoms of Phoenix base proved that.

"You up for breakfast then? I think we might be able to get some pancakes with strawberry syrup." Cary's tone shifted with a dizzying, lighthearted velocity that made Talus want to scream. The absolute depth of Cary's worry had completely ebbed, entirely replaced by the primal thought of breakfast.

"You guys actually have eggs down here?" Ryan asked, his footsteps already migrating toward the exit corridor.

"Well, not from chickens, obviously, but we have bio-reconstituted proteins that remarkably resemble eggs if you cover them in enough pepper." Cary's voice faded slightly, before halting. "You know...we really shouldn't leave him like that. It looks a bit undignified."

Finally, a shred of decency between them. Talus prepared himself for them to carefully lift his heavy frame and place him onto his bed.

Talus heard the rustle of a nearby storage cabinet opening. A second later, Cary's face didn't reappear; instead, a heavy, scratchy wool emergency blanket was unceremoniously dropped directly over Talus' head, cascading down his rigid torso and draping over his bent legs.

Talus was trapped in absolute, pitch-black darkness, the heavy wool smelling faintly of old ozone and storage grease. He couldn't even see his tormentors anymore.

"Still missing something," Ryan's voice boomed from the dark.

A split second later, Talus felt a hefty, metallic weight being carefully, deliberately balanced right on top of his paralyzed head.

"Perfect," Cary giggled, his footsteps finally retreating down the hall alongside Ryan's heavy combat boots. "Let's go get those pancakes before they run out of fresh syrup."

The security door slid shut with a definitive click, leaving Talus alone in the dark, waiting for his body to belong to him again.

19

Anya

She managed to find her way back to the facility's communal hub with only a few wrong turns. The sprawling layout of the lower mountain was a dizzying maze of reinforced concrete and sleek, old-world geometry, but she was a tracker by trade; she possessed an innate compass for navigating the dark. Luckily, whenever her mental map faltered, she found a resident to point her in the right direction. But only after they had thoroughly processed the sheer shock of seeing a fresh, unfamiliar human face wandering their subterranean sanctuary.

Now, sitting alone at a small metal table in the corner of the mess hall, Anya stared down at the plate. It was a stack of something flat, round, and fluffy, completely drowning in a thick, viscous pool of deep red liquid. But looking at it, she had lost her appetite entirely. The deep red dripping off her fork did little to push away her memories from Phoenix. The brutal systematic torture of that chained immortal was the exact architecture of her nightmares. And now, her memories were pulling a fresh set of ghosts into its wake.

A smiling, sun-darkened face. A strong, calloused embrace in the shadows of the bunker corridors. Quiet, fiercely whispered assurances of a future that had never belonged to them.

All of it was completely lost to her now. She would never get those moments back.

227

Mamoru. He had been the one beautiful, uncorrupted reality she had ever discovered inside the militaristic hell of Phoenix, and she had left him behind to rot. No matter how warmly she had been welcomed by the rangers at Tigris, no matter how many genuine friendships she forged or how many times her new comrades offered her shelter and safety, it was still his face her soul desperately pined for in the quiet hours of the night. It was still his voice echoing through the empty chambers of her mind.

He hadn't been perfect, even if her grief consistently painted him that way. The reality was that she had fled the base with barely a word of goodbye because she hadn't known if she could forgive him for his compliance with the high command. And now, because the Others had scrubbed Phoenix from the face of the earth, she would never get the chance to tell him anything.

She stared blankly at the plate. What even *was* this red substance? It smelled intensely sweet, almost intoxicatingly so, but it looked utterly sickening.

"We saw the results of your handiwork..."

Ryan's voice cut through the fog of her thoughts. She looked up to see the pilot striding toward her table, a broad, cocky smile plastered across his face. But the moment his eyes locked onto hers, his grin immediately withered into a look of deep concern. Great. Apparently, her internal turmoil was completely painted across her features.

Ryan dropped his pace, sliding into the metal seat right beside her. "Anya, hey. Are you alright? What happened in there?"

"What did Talus do?" Cary asked, appearing right behind him, his tone sharp with a strange, protective edge.

Anya forced a weak, fragile smile onto her face, looking between the two of them. Ryan was an inherently good man and her best friend. Cary, meanwhile, was acting like a worried older brother trying to protect her from the facility's resident monster, though she had a strong suspicion he was just as protective of Talus. There were simply too many demons to go around the table.

"No, Talus didn't do anything," Anya said softly, her voice flat. "We were just discussing an experiment, and... I just started thinking about Phoenix. It brought up some bad memories. That's all."

Cary studied her face for a long, silent beat. He gave a slow, understanding nod and turned toward the food counter to gather their breakfast.

The moment Cary was out of earshot, Ryan reached out and placed his heavy arm around her shoulders, pulling her slightly against his side. It was meant to be comforting. But to Anya, the contact felt like nothing more than a dead weight. While she could normally draw comfort from her friend, this time she felt nothing.

She stared down at her hands, a cold realization settling in her chest. Maybe this specific flavor of trauma was simply too massive to be comforted so easily. Or maybe Ryan wasn't the one she needed right now. The only person she truly needed to hear from was a ghost she would never lay eyes on again.

But as she sat there, the image of a tall, rigid scientist slumped helplessly on the floor flashed through her mind. Talus had the right idea: work. That was the only thing capable of dragging her consciousness out of the graveyard and placing it back where it could do some actual good. Wallowing in the past only served to preserve the ghosts; actively working toward a solution for the future was the only way to save the living.

Cary returned and took his seat next to Ryan, placing a massive, steaming plate of fresh pancakes in front of each of them

"I should probably head back down to the lab, once the paralysis wears off," Anya said, gently shifting her shoulder to let Ryan's arm slide off her back. "We do have work to do after all. The sooner we figure out the weakness of the Others the sooner we save the world right?"

She knew her voice sounded brittle, that she wasn't fooling a single person at the table, but she still felt the need to try. Ryan and Cary both nodded at her. She glanced at her flat round things and decided to take them back with her. Eventually she would need to eat something.

"So... that one over there?" Ryan suddenly broke the silence, casually gesturing with his fork toward a striking, dark-haired woman sitting a few tables away in the mess hall.

Cary looked up from his plate, his synthetic eyes whirring faintly as he tracked Ryan's gaze. "Ah, yes. Her too. About forty-five years ago, if I recall correctly."

"What about him?"

Ryan shifted his focus, pointing toward a burly technician working near the hydroponic filters. "What about him?"

Cary glanced over, chewing thoughtfully. "Yeah. A very long time ago. Just a once, though. The man talked entirely too much."

Anya listened to the exchange in absolute, unmitigated confusion. She blinked, her dark thoughts momentarily derailed as she looked between her friend and the ancient immortal.

"You really do get around, don't you?" Ryan remarked, a mix of awe and amusement coloring his voice.

"Well when you have my kind of time there is only so long you can plant strawberries and read poetry."

"Poetry? I prefer novels myself, much more story and I don't have to spend an hour trying to decipher the hidden existential meaning behind two lines of prose." Ryan said.

Cary offered a dry, superior smile. "As I stated, Ryan: nothing but time."

"What on earth are you two talking about?" Anya finally demanded, her curiosity overriding her melancholy. She looked at them, completely baffled.

"Oh, Cary was just providing me with every single person in this base he has had sex with," Ryan explained matter-of-factly.

Anya's jaw dropped slightly. "Excuse me?"

"He started it." Ryan explained. "I just asked how relationships work here, and he volunteered the information."

She shook her head. Men and their need to show off their prowess.

She raised an eyebrow, looking directly at Ryan. "So, what, are you jealous of his numbers now?"

"Not in the slightest. I may not have the numbers but I guarantee that my approval ratings are through the roof." Ryan shot back smoothly, leaning forward with a confident wink.

Anya felt her stomach twist again, though this time it was accompanied by a wave of theatrical exasperation. "Well, if I didn't completely lack an appetite before this conversation, I certainly do now." She aggressively pushed the plate of syrup away from her.

"Don't vanish just yet," Ryan said, his eyes lighting up with that signature, boyish enthusiasm she had grown so accustomed to during their long flight. "Cary was going to show me some of the other research around here. Apparently there is someone that is working on a much faster plane and then there is a new communications system that Cary tells me is beyond anything I've ever seen."

The more the pilot spoke, the more his entire demeanor radiated energy. Ryan was a creature of mechanics; he lived to understand how complex machinery operated, breaking components down just for the pure satisfaction of putting them back together.

"Oh, and there's also a senior researcher named Alton," Ryan continued, leaning in conspiratorially. "The guy literally invented a machine that shoots concentrated bolts of blue lightning across the laboratory floor."

Anya turned her head, fixing Cary with a deeply skeptical stare. "You have an eternity to solve the secrets of the universe or halt the collapse of humanity, and someone chooses to manufacture a machine that shoots blue lightning bolts?"

"Well, technically, that isn't the device's specific purpose, no," Cary admitted, a wide, wicked grin breaking across his handsome face. "But frankly, who cares what else the machine is programmed to do? Anya, it shoots *blue lightning*."

Ryan laughed, looking at her expectantly. "Want to come with us? It beats sitting in a dusty lab."

For a brief second, looking at the two of them, Anya felt a profound, warm pull toward the simplicity of their companionship. It would be so easy to go with them, to lose herself in the loud, fascinating gadgets of the research wings and pretend the world outside didn't exist. But then, the distinct image of Talus' intense, stormy eyes flashed in her mind. She remembered the raw, exposed vulnerability they had shared on the laboratory floor right before she paralyzed him. There was a strange, powerful gravity drawing her back to him, a realization that beneath his cold, arrogant exterior, he was carrying a weight that matched her own. They were locked into the same mission now.

"As incredibly fun as a lightning machine sounds," Anya said, her voice stabilizing as she picked up her plate and slid out of the booth, "I think I better go check on Talus.

She paused, looking down at the syrup-drenched food. She figured she should probably bring something back for him. She likely needed a peace offering to get back in his good graces after electrocuting him.

"What does Talus have for breakfast? He is probably going to be a bit woozy after that shock, some food might do him good." Anya asked, looking toward Cary.

"Your guess is as good as mine." Cary had replied with a dismissive wave of his fork. "I can't remember the last time I saw the bastard eat. Kit swore he ate popcorn when we were on comms one day but I didn't see it."

Anya let out a quiet sigh. So much for her peace offering. She took her plate of pancakes and made her way back through the winding hallways. She stopped only once, pausing briefly to peer through the thick observation window of a research lab that was currently violently emitting massive, brilliant blue sparks. She thought to ask what was happening but the man was sealed inside of a tube with only a window so she thought it best to give the lab a wide berth.

When she finally reached the heavy bulkhead of Talus' eastern wing, she froze. The massive steel doors had been slid completely, tightly closed.

That was certainly not a good sign. Throughout her brief time in the facility, none of the other labs had their doors closed and this was the first time that she had seen Talus close the doors to his lab. She saw two options here, the first and most appealing was to run away and wait for him to cool off for a while, and the second was to just knock and fess up.

Although to be fair he did want to know how it worked and what better way to find out than trying it himself? And no matter how you looked at it, it had to be better than having your finger cut off.

Steeling her spine, Anya stepped forward. The sliding door wasn't completely locked; it had been left unlatched by a mere three inches. She stepped in front of the gap, raising the plate of pancakes up to her forehead like a white flag of surrender, hoping the aroma of caramelized sugar would entice him.

'Flat cake things topped with red stuff?" she ventured, her voice echoing softly into the room. The pancakes still smelled good, but as they had cooled the red liquid was thickening and looking even more like blood than it had before.

Talus was hunched aggressively over a primary computer terminal, his massive frame casting a long shadow across the desk. His left hand was slowly, deliberately rubbing the base of his neck. Anya flinched slightly at the sight. She had very little recollection of how much her own fulgar strike had hurt because she was kept on some very nice pain medications afterward due to the bullet wound.

Talus struck a final key on his terminal, the mechanical clack ringing out like a gunshot, before turning his head to look in her direction. His dark eyes narrowed as they inspected her plate. "You mean pancakes with strawberry syrup?"

She looked down at the soft, golden cakes and offered a casual shrug. So the red stuff was strawberries. She did love the shortcake yesterday, suddenly the red gloop looked more appetizing.

'If that's what they're called. I've never seen them before."

An odd, unreadable expression crossed his features, before he let out a short breath and motioned with his hand for her to cross the threshold.

"You know there was a time when it would have been quite strange to meet someone who had never had pancakes." he murmured, his tone losing some of its rigid edge. "Used to be a breakfast staple around here."

Anya stepped fully into the lab, looking down at the plate with a sudden, quiet melancholy. "I wish I could know what it was like back then. Watching the old videos and walking through the ruins, it all just seems like a story."

She walked over to his primary workbench, carefully setting the plate down on the stainless steel surface between them. Talus looked at her curiously for a momentary beat, his gaze drifting from the tight, guarded line of her shoulders down to the drowning strawberries, before a faint, genuine smile broke through his stern expression.

"I take it you forgot the fork?"

Anya snapped her fingers, a bright, embarrassed laugh escaping her throat. "Oops."

Talus' smile widened just a fraction as he stood up, navigating to a nearby sterilization cabinet to retrieve a clean metal utensil. He rubbed the base of his neck once more as he walked back, handing it to her with a slight tilt of his head.

"Sorry about that." Anya said, her voice dropping into a softer register as she took the utensil. "I didn't really think about what I was doing or how much it might actually hurt you."

"I have done far worse to myself so do not trouble yourself about it. Just still not sure how they work, it shouldn't be as effective as it is." Talus replied smoothly.

She took a bit of the pancake on her prong, glad that Talus had acknowledged what she had thought as well. Getting electrocuted was far from the worst thing he had experienced.

Anya speared a piece of the pancake, coating it in the vibrant red syrup. "I could easily teach you how to avoid getting caught off guard like that in the future."

"You operate under the false assumption that I possess any martial training or desire any," Talus noted dryly, leaning his weight against the desk. "I am a scientist, Anya. Not a soldier."

Anya set the fork down with a sharp metallic clink. She immediately stepped back into the open space of the lab floor, her boots sliding into a perfectly balanced, wide stance, her hands rising instinctively to protect her vitals.

"Well, it's the apocalypse, everyone should be able to at least defend themselves." she declared, her eyes locking onto his with absolute seriousness. "Come on. Get up. I'll teach you a few tricks so that it will at least be harder for someone to sneak up on your blind spot with a fulgar."

Talus didn't move. "In my defense, I made the mistake of trusting you."

"Ouch, but deserved." Anya grinned, undeterred by the guilt trip. "Now get in a fighting stance like this."

"No."

"Yes."

"I have no desire to learn to fight."

"Isn't that what I am here for?" Anya countered, her brow raising. "To teach you things and for you to teach me? Well, one of the primary things I know is how to fight."

"I have no desire to fight," Talus repeated stubbornly, crossing his massive arms over his chest. "A simple punch is not going to neutralize an Other on the surface."

"Luckily, a punch is not the only tool in your arsenal, but it is an excellent foundation to build muscle memory from. Now—guard stance."

"No."

He was being as entirely stubborn as a toddler, but Anya had been raised by ruthless drill instructors at Phoenix base, which meant she knew precisely how to handle an uncooperative asset.

"Get into a guard stance or I'll give Kit a Fulgar. A teenager running around with a device that can stun everyone in the place, what could go wrong?"

Talus glared at her, his jaw locking into a stern, impassive mask. For a second, she thought she had genuinely crossed a line. But then, she watched the icy exterior of his eyes thaw. A sudden, radiant spark of genuine amusement lit up his pupils, slowly melting the rigid tension in his face.

"I'll remind you Kit has lived more years than you, though you're right about the havoc she would wreck."

With a heavy, theatrical sigh of defeat, he dragged himself away from the desk and stepped onto the floor. He assumed a limp, thoroughly tragic approximation of a guard stance, his shoulders hunched forward like a broken gargoyle, his arms weakly held up in two loose, unthreatening fists. His long legs looked as though they might completely collapse under his own weight because he had distributed his weight unevenly.

"Is the right your dominant side?" Anya asked, a wide smile breaking across her face. The moment she stepped into the role of an instructor, the lingering phantoms of her grief completely vanished. This was her element; even just the familiar feel of a fighting stance was a balm for her frayed nerves. This was the one domain where she felt she could take on the entire world, even if history had proven otherwise. "Switch your legs. Put your non-dominant foot forward to anchor your weight."

"This feels entirely idiotic," Talus grumbled, reluctantly shifting his boots against the tile. "And I look ridiculous."

"You do look ridiculous," Anya agreed cheerfully, circling him like a hawk evaluating a target. "And it only feels stupid because you have no idea what you are doing."

To demonstrate the contrast, Anya instantly dropped into a flawless, low-center guard stance. The warmth in her face instantly hardened into a cold, terrifyingly focused intensity. She advanced with explosive fluidity, her hips pivoting as she launched a flawless, blindingly fast roundhouse kick. The top of her combat boot stopped a mere millimeter away from his jaw, the displaced air rushing past his ear before she smoothly snapped her leg back to the floor.

"If you actually know what you are doing," she whispered, her eyes holding his, "it looks exceptionally impressive. And it feels incredibly powerful."

Talus rolled his eyes, though it was visibly a defense mechanism to hide how startled he was by her speed. He firmed up his loose fists slightly, squaring his broad chest. He was obviously not going to make this easy on her.

"Good," Anya noted, stepping back into his guard radius. "Now, your primary focus as a non-combatant should be entirely on dodging and evasion. Those long, unconditioned arms are not going to best a seasoned fighter, unless you've got some hidden immortal super-strength in there I don't know about."

Talus shook his head, a silky lock of his dark hair tumbling down over his forehead from the movement. He quickly brushed it away with the back of his wrist. Anya's breath caught slightly in her throat as his face was revealed. Without the shadow of his hair, she was suddenly forced to look directly into the full, piercing depth of his eyes. They were intensely striking, filled with a sharp, ancient intelligence that momentarily unnerved her, sending a strange, unfamiliar flutter through her chest.

She quickly forced her focus back to the lesson. "Alright. You need to constantly scan your opponent's frame for any physical indication of an impending attack that you can actively block or avoid. Novice fighters always possess distinct 'tells', they'll subconsciously cast their gaze toward the specific body part they plan to strike, or execute a micro-punch that looks like a nervous flinch. But against a trained soldier, you have to be purely perceptive and incredibly fast. To execute a proper dodge, you are either going to step back with your trailing foot to slide sideways, allowing the trajectory of the punch to pass harmlessly in front of your chest, or you lean your torso out of the alignment track. Let me demonstrate. Punch me."

Talus immediately shook his head, his fists dropping. "I am not going to punch you."

She let out a bright, challenging laugh. "I guarantee you won't land a punch, just try."

With visible reluctance, Talus threw a slow, incredibly floppy, telegraphed right hook. Anya didn't even have to break a sweat; she smoothly dipped her shoulder, exaggerating her evasive lean so he could visually map out how her body displaced itself around the blow.

"Again. Use the left hand this time."

She had him repeat the motion several times, forcing him to utilize different hands and varying angles so he could comprehend the sheer number of spatial avenues available to evade a kinetic strike.

"The key to survival is constant situational awareness," Anya lectured, her voice falling into a rhythmic, steady cadence as they moved together across the floor. "You must always be aware of your surroundings and exactly who you are sharing space with. The second you let your guard down, you become susceptible to attack." She paused, offering him a sharp, wicked wink. "Now, back into your guard stance. Try to actively block my incoming blows. Don't look at my hands, look directly into my eyes, my elbows, and my knees for mechanical cues. Those joints are where the strike initiates; they will always tell you an attack is coming."

She started off at a deliberately slow pace, lightly tapping his forearms with her open palms, but as she noticed his reflexes adjusting, she steadily increased the speed of her strikes. She began to actively glide around his massive frame, forcing him to pivot his weight, practicing the vital skill of noticing and blocking a blind-side punch that might manifest from behind.

"See?" Anya asked, a breathless smile breaking through her focus as he successfully managed to swat away three consecutive taps. "Want to learn how to truly fight now?"

"Fight? I am not going to fight you Anya." Talus said, his voice straining slightly.

Anya didn't answer with words. She flashed a wicked grin and threw a sudden, crisp punch straight toward his left shoulder. Talus' instincts fired cleanly; his forearm snapped up and successfully deflected the blow.

Anya's smile widened. Before he could celebrate the victory, she instantly converted the momentum, dropping her level and driving a lightning-fast secondary punch straight into his exposed abdomen. Her fist landed with a soft, solid thud against his core.

She stepped back, tilting her head up to meet his gaze. "How about now?"

Talus stood perfectly still, taking a slow, deep breath as he processed the impact. "I have no desire for retaliation."

Anya let her hands drop to her sides, her intense combat posture instantly evaporating into a relaxed, easy stance. "Fair enough. You're an odd sort of duck to be a pacifist but if you do need to know how to defend yourself. A few strikes can be part of a good defense if they are done in a way that disrupts my concentration, the attack I am planning or trips me up, literally. During a kick is a good time to duck down to dodge and do a trip against the other leg."

Talus smoothly reverted back to his typical posture, leaning his tall frame back against the edge of the lab table, his dark eyes studying her face with quiet intensity. "Why do you find it odd that I am a pacifist?"

Anya walked over to the workbench, picking up the metal prong and taking another bite of the pancakes. Even though they were now cold, they were delicious.

"Because you look like you're constantly angry at the entire world," Anya said softly, her blue eyes holding his with unblinking candor. "Or just angry at yourself. Most men I've encountered like that are men who look for any excuse to fight."

Talus stared at her for a long, silent beat. The faint hum of the laboratory machinery seemed to fade into absolute insignificance against the weight of her observation. Slowly, he offered a single, solemn nod of agreement.

"I am many flawed things, Anya," he murmured, his voice carrying a quiet, resonant gravity. "But I am not such a man."

Anya put down the metal prong and stood in front of Talus again. "Then let's just keep working on defense, but sometimes a good defense requires some offense."

She raised her fists, her chin tucking instinctively behind her lead shoulder. To her quiet satisfaction, Talus mirrored the motion. The tragic, limp posture from before was gone; his tall frame was beginning to subconsciously follow her stance. If nothing else, Anya was determined to break his stubborn pacifism and force him to throw a real punch at her. He would never actually land it against her reflexes, of course, but she wanted him to try.

She began to circle him, her weight shifting invisibly from heel to toe. Without warning, she zipped forward and tossed a quick jab toward his right side. Talus reacted with surprising fluidity, dipping his torso to let the strike pass through empty air. Capitalizing on his movement, Anya instantly pivoted on her back foot, throwing a fast secondary punch toward his exposed left rib cage.

The blow landed with a dull thud against his dense muscular frame. He flinched slightly, a sharp breath escaping his nose, but his hands stayed up. He refused to counter.

Anya didn't give him time to rest. She pulled a series of rapid, rhythmic punches before spinning into a low, snapping kick. Talus managed to clumsily parry the hand strikes, but the kick was too high. The toe of her combat boot hitting his ribs.

"Why won't you actually come at me?" Anya demanded, her breathing completely steady as she danced back out of his reach.

"I already told you that I have little need for fighting," Talus rumbled, his stormy eyes tracking her movements with a strange, exhausting patience. "And I have no wish to inflict harm upon you."

Anya let her fists drop, stepping entirely inside his guard radius until she was standing a mere foot away from his massive chest. The intense, competitive heat of the sparring match gave way to a sudden, highly charged proximity.

"Come on, Talus. Take a real shot," she prodded softly, her blue eyes locking onto his with an intensity that made the air in the lab feel thick. "If you are genuinely terrified of breaking me, then I give you my word as a ranger: I won't let your fist actually touch my skin. Trust me."

Talus let out a long, heavy breath, his shoulders sagging slightly. "Anya, I feel that this is a waste of time."

"Then show me you've learned about fighting and maybe I will do whatever you like." she countered, a wicked, brilliant smile flashing across her face.

"I have no desire to learn to fight, I simply agreed to this so that I would not have to worry about Kit with a Fulgar."

"I knew that would be excellent motivation," Anya laughed, leaning in closer.

Talus closed his eyes for a fraction of a second, letting out a defeated sigh that sounded like rushing wind. When his eyelids snapped back open, the passive, intellectual detachment was entirely gone, replaced by a sudden, volatile focus.

He advanced on her.

He threw a heavy, slow, halfhearted right jab. It was an obvious feint, completely lacking in velocity, and Anya easily slid her head to the left to let it glide past. But she had miscalculated his reach and his intent.

Before she could capitalize on the opening to sweep his lead leg, Talus' left hand lashed out. His strong, soft fingers wrapped with absolute, unbreakable force around her right wrist.

Using her own forward momentum against her, he executed a sharp, fluid jerk, pulling her smaller body violently forward. Anya gasped as her chest slammed directly against the solid wall of his torso. The sheer force of the maneuver left her completely pinned, her trapped arm pressed against his chest, her face drawn upward.

He was so incredibly close. His nose was nearly brushing against her own, his hot, rapid breath fanning across her lips. Up close, the deep, piercing amber rings within his dark eyes were mesmerizing, radiating a power that made her heart hammer violently against her ribs, not from fear, but from a sudden, dizzying rush of raw electricity.

"I have absolutely no desire to fight you, Anya," Talus whispered, his voice dropping into a dangerously low, gravelly timbre that resonated straight through her bones. His grip on her wrist was forceful, yet remarkably careful, ensuring the pressure didn't bruise her skin. "If it takes Kit having a Fulgar to stop this then you are free to give her one of your toys. I will prefer those consequences over fighting you."

Anya's breath was trapped in her throat, her pulse racing in the heat of his proximity. She swallowed hard, fiercely fighting to keep her composure from cracking under his gaze. "What's the matter? Afraid of a strong woman?"

"Quite the contrary," Talus murmured, his eyes dropping to her lips momentarily, before snapping back to her gaze. "I profoundly admire a strong woman. But I have no desire to engage in physical violence with you, or anyone else on this planet. I do not believe in it. I have already witnessed more than enough slaughter to last me several consecutive lifetimes. I realize that it may be necessary to use violence against the Others for the benefit of humanity, but I will not use it against you."

Slowly, deliberately, he released her wrist.

Anya remained frozen on the spot, her arm hovering in the air as he smoothly stepped around her. The sudden loss of his physical warmth left her feeling strangely cold, her mind spinning in absolute silence. She had no idea how to respond to him. She could only stand there and watch as he ran a hand through his dark hair, sweeping the stray locks back from his eyes with a motion that she was starting to find familiar before returning to his primary workstation.

The defensive walls she had spent years cultivating at Phoenix base suddenly felt entirely irrelevant. Dropping her guard completely, she walked over to the desk, her boots silent this time as she leaned over the edge of his console to look at the complex cascading lines of code and genetic sequencing strings filling his monitors.

"Well, then," she said softly, her tone entirely stripped of its sarcastic armor. "Tell me what you are working on right now. Is there anything I can help with?"

Talus shook his head, though his fingers hesitated over the keyboard. "It is merely a secondary, long-term experiment I initialized decades ago. It tests the evolutionary limitations of highly volatile pre-war viruses when they are introduced to immortal stem cell cultures. I cannot get the viral pathogen to affect immortal cells at all."

Anya watched him closely as he spoke. A fascinating shift occurred the absolute second his mind re-engaged with the science. The stern, grumpy facade he used to keep the world at bay completely evaporated. His voice became lighter, infused with a vibrant, unforced enthusiasm, and his posture straightened with a clean, dynamic energy. He looked remarkably alive. She realized with a sudden, quiet warmth that she desperately wanted to see more of *this* Talus, the brilliant, passionate soul buried beneath years of isolation and grief.

"Explain the science to me," Anya said, pulling up a nearby metal stool and sitting down right beside his primary terminal. "Talk it through everything you've done. Back at Tigris, we used to try explaining a problem out loud to someone else. Sometimes it can help you realize what it's missing or we can brainstorm together…once I understand it all."

Talus looked away from the monitor, his dark eyes studying her face for a long, quiet beat, evaluating the sincerity in her expression.

"I suppose it is worth a try," he admitted softly.

Together in the quiet sanctuary of the lab, the distance between them vanished entirely. Talus began to systematically talk through the complex equations of his current experiment, his hands gesturing through the air as he mapped out the molecular structures. Anya listened with rapt attention. She couldn't contribute to the high-level genetic algorithms, but she offered a few raw, practical suggestions from her field experience, different angles of looking at structural adaptation, and how surface mutations behaved under environmental stress. Mostly, though, she just let him speak, providing a steady presence.

When he finally finished breaking down the viral metrics, Anya didn't let the momentum falter. She pointed to a secondary window on his screen, asking him about another old project, and then another, and another.

Before either of them possessed any idea of the time, the pancakes on the workbench had grown completely cold, the vibrant strawberry syrup congealing into a forgotten dark mass. But for just a while neither the ancient scientist nor the exiled soldier seemed even remotely bothered by the passage of the hours, entirely content to let the world burn outside their door as long as they were charting the dark together.

20

Talus

He sat at his heavy metal desk, staring down at the framed picture of Lily.

For the past several days, he had done nothing but work with Anya. They had gone over centuries of experiments, talking for hours while she listened patiently to every granular detail. As he stared at the faded ink of Lily's smile, a sudden, jarring realization hit him. He had barely given a thought to Lily in all the time he had spent with Anya.

He had never really talked about his work with Lily. He had always been too terrified of what she would think of him if she discovered the true, grim nature of his research. Anya was different. She might not know the whole truth yet, but he could talk to her about his projects without filtering himself. She was smart, too. Not in the sense of memorizing chemical compounds or running complex lab equipment, but once he explained the core parameters of a problem, she would offer an entirely different way of looking at it. Her practical perspective was actually helpful. She might be exactly what he needed to solve his greatest challenge yet.

But as he stared at Lily's picture he wondered if there was something else. He not only hadn't faced a nightmare last night, but he hadn't dreamed of Lily either. That was a milestone that hadn't occurred since the day she had walked out of his life.

"Dreams again?"

Cary was standing in the entrance, leaning awkwardly against the metal doorframe. If he put too much weight on it, the automated sensor would trigger and the door would slide away, but Cary stubbornly insisted on using it as a prop anyway.

Talus shook his head, keeping his eyes on the desk. "No. I've been too busy. I barely gave a thought to her."

Cary's eyes widened before quickly smoothing back into an impassive expression. "So you thought you would wallow by her picture now just to make up for lost time?"

Talus did not want to admit how right his old friend was, but then he did not have to. Cary knew the truth well enough. He pushed himself against the desk to stand up from his chair to turn away from the picture.

"You don't have to completely forget her, Talus," Cary said, his tone softening into something genuinely human. "But you do have to finally let her go. You don't have to marry anyone else, you don't have to fall in love with anyone else, and you don't have to go rolling around in the hay with a new partner. But gee willikers, Talus, you need to just let her go."

Talus paused, blinking. "Gee willikers?"

"An old-fashioned euphemism for taking the Lord's name in vain," Cary explained without missing a beat, crossing his arms. "But don't think you can successfully change the subject, Talus."

"I have never heard that particular phrase before," Talus muttered, genuinely curious. "What historical period is it from?"

"It originated from a Southern regional dialect, and it was exceptionally common in—hey, don't think I don't know exactly what you are trying to do right now."

Talus offered a ghost of a smile. "It is not my fault you are so easily distracted by linguistics."

Cary let out a long, dramatic sigh. "Just think about what I said, Tal. Okay?"

"Yes, Cary. I will think about it, I promise," Talus replied, his voice heavy with routine. "Just like I have promised every other time in the last one hundred years that you have repeated that exact speech to me."

"Good things can come if you are simply willing to open up to someone new, Tal," Cary said, stepping fully into the room. "Ryan and Anya, they make this entire place feel fresh. They bring a sense of newness that breaks the gray melancholy that has hung over this base for far too long. Personally, I have laughed more with Ryan in three days than I have in decades. There is finally someone here who truly understands my unique humor."

Talus raised a skeptical eyebrow at the terrifying thought of there being a second person alive who could comprehend Cary's erratic sense of humor.

"Thank you for that profound psychological insight, Cary," Talus said, adjusting his lab coat. "Now, if you do not mind, I have specific plans for the day. Have you seen Anya? I would like to get an early start."

Cary's eyes narrowed instantly. His arms locked tight across his chest, and he squinted closely at Talus, examining his face in much the exact same manner he used to inspect root rot on one of his beloved greenhouse hybrids. The intense scrutiny made Talus significantly more uncomfortable than the romantic conversation they had just been having.

"So," Cary said, his voice dripping with accusation, "you were planning on spending the entire day with her, and you just let me stand here talking without saying a single word?"

Talus gave a calm, deliberate nod. "You never know what valuable things you can learn when you simply let people talk. You are certainly no exception to the rule."

Cary sighed, rolling his eyes toward the ceiling. "She was in the central dining hall when I left. I think she was coordinating a meeting with some of the female technicians to talk about their projects. It seems she possesses a pretty intense curiosity about all the different operations running around here."

"Yes," Talus agreed, his mind already drifting back to the day before. "She does seem to have an insatiable curiosity. And yesterday, she actually helped me make a minor breakthrough with my viral research."

Cary leaped backward, leaning his full weight against the doorframe in mock, theatrical surprise.

The physical calculation failed instantly. The sensor triggered, and the metal door slid away into the wall significantly faster than Cary was anticipating. Talus' lips parted into a genuine smile as Cary lost his balance entirely, flailing his arms in a desperate, clumsy attempt to maintain his dignity as he crashed directly onto the hard corridor floor.

Cary quickly scrambled to his feet, fiercely brushing off his trousers and trying to piece his composure back together. He glared into the office, his cheeks slightly flushed. "Oh, really? What specific experiment did she help you with?"

"I was able to get one of the immortal cells sick with a cold," Talus said, his tone entirely matter-of-fact. "I have never been able to achieve that specific metric before. She thought of a way around the issue I was facing, something I simply had not previously considered. It must have just been a matter of a fresh perspective, or perhaps the benefit of having someone in the room who is not wired to think like a scientist. Now, if you will excuse me."

Talus moved past Cary, but stopped at the threshold of the door and turned back. "And keep your communicator on. I may require some assistance later. See if you can rustle up something resembling what the old coffee shops used to serve."

Talus could not help but notice the strange, thoughtful look his old friend was giving him. It was likely just a byproduct of the limp Cary was trying to hide after his sudden fall, but for a fleeting moment, Talus wished he could know exactly what was behind Cary's eyes. His friend sometimes possessed a far better insight into Talus' own mind than he ever did.

Making his way through the familiar concrete halls, Talus mentally formulated a list of the different experiments he was hoping to execute with Anya today. Perhaps they could make more substantial progress with the viral mutation. If nothing else, he thought with a dry swell of amusement, he might find a way to surprise Cary with a mild head cold for a week. But on a serious track, they might actually discover a real answer if he could find a methodology to keep the host cell infected for longer than a few fleeting seconds.

When he reached the cafeteria entrance, he stopped. He leaned his tall frame against the concrete archway and scanned the crowded tables until he located her. It was not a difficult task. She was completely surrounded by several of his colleagues, male and female alike. The residents were clearly just as curious about her as she apparently was about them. Ryan was sitting right beside her, and they both appeared perfectly happy to field the endless questions. Ryan was currently making his best effort to make the others laugh with some of his signature, animated antics. It was a significantly happier, louder picture than Talus had witnessed in this base in years.

"Talus! Over here, Talus!"

He pushed on a smile that was fake compared to the genuine one that had graced his features only a moment ago and walked over to where Anya was calling and waving to him.

As he approached the table, he noticed that she made a conscious, deliberate effort to clear the empty seat directly beside her so there would be a dedicated place for him. It was a kind, protective gesture. Yet he could not help but notice that the bright smile on her face did not fully reach her blue eyes. She was pretending, of course. Pretending to be entirely happier and more at ease than she actually was. A quiet ache formed in his chest; he did not want her to feel like she had to wear a mask just to be welcomed inside his home.

"Have a seat, Talus," Anya said, her voice carrying a slight strain. "We were all just talking. Everyone seems *very* curious about how Ryan and I have been living."

So that was the root cause of the weariness in her eyes. His former colleagues were treating her more like a fascinating science experiment than an actual human being.

"Actually," Talus said, his deep voice cutting through the chatter as he looked directly at her, "I was hoping you would take a walk with me. I have some things that I would like to show you and perhaps we can make more progress on what we were working on yesterday."

She looked from him to Ryan, who was currently busy telling an incredibly loud story about how he had once consumed ten full rations of survival pie because the compound's pantry was going bad. Talus shook his head slightly. Before the world had changed, he never would have expected a team of some of the most brilliant scientific minds on the planet to be completely enraptured by a story about a basic stomachache.

He held out his hand toward her. Anya looked at it for a brief second, and then slowly, softly slid her fingers into his palm. She offered a quick wave to Ryan, who simply waved back with a grin and continued his theatrical story. But Talus did not miss the flash of protective seriousness that entered the man's eyes the moment they walked away.

They walked in absolute silence as they left the crowded dining hall, but they did not head toward the eastern laboratory wing. Instead, Talus steered them toward a different corridor entirely. It had come to him after she went to bed the night prior that he wanted to do something special for her. They had been so far focused on his interests, so now he wanted to do something for her that he knew she would appreciate.

"Where exactly are we going?" she finally asked as they traversed the final deep passageways leading back to the main surface entrance.

"I thought maybe you could use a break from being the main attraction and as I could not guarantee you would not be disturbed at the base, the city seemed a better option." Talus explained.

He threw the heavy manual release lever, opening the reinforced hatch to reveal the brilliant, blinding sunlight. The sun's glare illuminated the pale, dusty color of the dirt and sand surrounding the mountain. Talus motioned for her to ascend the concrete steps, following closely right behind her.

The moment Anya reached the top of the stairs and stepped into the open air, she stopped dead in her tracks. She just stood there, looking around at the vast expanse. Talus waited on the top step for a moment, but growing slightly impatient, he smoothly squeezed past her smaller frame to stand on the parched earth.

"Have you ever gotten used to it?" she whispered.

Her body was completely motionless, but her eyes were scanning back and forth across the horizon with an intense, quiet reverence. Talus stopped and looked around the barren landscape, trying to perceive what she was referring to.

"Used to what, exactly?"

"Being outside."

Talus shifted his weight, moving closer to her side. He stood close enough that the fabric of their sleeves brushed, close enough that he could have easily held her hand if he chose to. He opened his mouth to speak but realized he had no idea how to respond. How could he explain to a child of the bunkers that the sky was both entirely new and ancient to him? He had once spent so much of his early life under the sun that he grew to actively hate the heat, and then spent so much consecutive time below the ground that his soul had pined for the simple warmth and light the sun brought.

"I have found that the things we miss and the things we take for granted are only differentiated by the time we spend among them." Talus said softly. "Come on."

He deliberately moved his hand down, brushing his knuckles against hers in a subtle, quiet offer for her to hold it. He was not entirely certain if he wanted her to accept the gesture or reject it, but it felt like the polite, human thing to do. Anya looked down at his large hand, staring at it for a long, silent beat before she slowly closed her smaller, warm fingers tightly around his.

"Where are we going?" she asked again, her voice lighter now.

"To take a walk," he replied.

He began leading her away from the reinforced entrance and down toward a wide, open asphalt space that had once functioned as a commercial parking lot. It was little more than weathered gravel now. The remnants of the old world crumbled and crunched rhythmically beneath their boots as they walked side by side. He led her directly toward a cluster of structures that were themselves slowly bowing to the passage of time and a total lack of human care.

As they approached the perimeter of the first ruined building, Talus noticed how Anya reached out her free hand to gently stroke the rough, exposed cinderblock wall. Her fingertips slid reverently along the cracked stone, brushing past a rotted wooden window frame and a faded, metal sign that retained only a few visible, rusted letters.

"It was a post office," Talus said quietly.

There were rows of small, metallic mailboxes built into the walls, and yellowed envelopes scattered across the floor like dead leaves. Old posters displaying pictures of colorful stamps were badly stained, turning to literal dust against the drywall. To Talus, the space was nothing more than desolate, useless rubble. But as he looked at Anya, he saw that her blue eyes were wide open, filled with an absolute, unmitigated wonder.

She slowly let go of his hand, stepping behind the rusted iron counter where dozens of parcels and letters lay scattered about the floor. She knelt down, picking up a single, faded package. Her thumb gently traced the delicate, elegant cursive writing that still clearly told of its desired destination, a place that no longer existed.

"Stand over here," Talus said, pointing a finger toward a patch of sunlit dust on the opposite side of the counter.

Anya blinked, a little amused, but obliged. She stepped back into the designated spot while Talus smoothly took her place behind the counter. He cleared his throat, stood up a bit straighter, and made a grand show of shuffling through the crumbling remnants of old packages and letters scattered on the desk.

"What exactly are you doing?" Anya asked, holding her faded package against her chest and looking at him with a quirked brow.

"I will be with you in just a moment, Miss." Talus kept his eyes down, shifting a piece of decayed cardboard from his left to his right. He had no real idea what he was doing. He felt utterly foolish, but a quiet, pulsing need to see her smile again pushed him forward. He wanted to give her whatever little taste he could of the world before the war.

"Talus, what is going on?" Her voice was softer now, a little laugh bubbling just beneath the surface.

"Ma'am, I understand that you would like to mail your parcel," Talus said, his voice dropping into a flat, practiced monotone. He motioned with his hand toward the empty space around her, indicating a long, entirely imaginary queue. "But as you can clearly see, I have a substantial line of customers ahead of you, and you will simply have to wait your turn."

He attempted to offer her a smooth, reassuring wink, but his unpracticed facial muscles failed him, resulting in a dual-eye blink that looked more like a sudden neurological spasm.

Anya raised an eyebrow, her breath catching before she broke out into a wide, brilliant grin. It was the first time he had seen her eyes completely light up with happiness. She played along instantly, making an elaborate show of looking over her shoulder at the imaginary crowd, turning back to the counter, and letting out a heavily exaggerated, dramatic sigh.

Talus hid a smile, deliberately moving even slower as he rearranged a stack of dust. Finally, he looked up, his dark eyes locking onto hers. "Miss? Are you ready?"

Anya stepped up to the counter, her boots clicking softly on the tile. She carefully placed her faded package in front of him, leaning her forearms against the wood. The proximity was sudden, her blue eyes bright and fixed entirely on his face. "I'd like to mail this, please."

"Very well. Let me just check the weight." Talus took the box and set it down on the counter, checking the imaginary readout of the scale. "Any perishables, hazardous materials, or explosives housed in this package?"

She leaned in closer, her smile softening. "No."

"Alright, then. Have you properly filled out your customs declaration form?"

Anya paused, her lips parting. "My... what?"

"Next time, please attempt to arrive at the service counter prepared, ma'am," Talus lectured dryly, though the corners of his eyes crinkled. "Here. Fill out this form."

"Oh, my. I am terribly sorry," Anya said, her voice dropping into a theatrical, breathless mock-apology that made Talus' chest tighten in a strange, entirely new way. "I had absolutely no idea I required a...what was it? A customs form?"

Talus couldn't help but smile, the warmth of it completely altering his usually stern features. He handed her a blank piece of scrap paper. Unfortunately, there was no working pen to be found, largely because the city's paperwork had gone fully digital a decade before the war. Anya didn't mind. She took the invisible pen from his fingers, her hand brushing against his smooth skin for a lingering second, sending a quiet spark through his veins. She made a graceful show of writing out her name and address in the air, before sliding the paper back to him.

"Alright," Talus murmured, his voice dropping a register as he took the paper, his eyes lingering on her face. "You are all set. This should reach its desired destination in ten to fourteen business days."

He tossed the old box into a half-dilapidated sorting bin behind him and stepped out from the counter, returning to her side of the room. Anya laughed, a clear, musical sound that echoed beautifully in the dead building, and he found himself chuckling along with her, the weight of his years of heartbreak and isolation melting away.

'So," Talus said, gesturing toward the sunlit exit. "Lunch?"

Anya blinked up at him. "Lunch? But I've only just had breakfast!"

"That was before you visited the post office, remember?" Talus countered smoothly, stepping close enough that his shoulder brushed hers as they walked out into the open air. "You spent the entire morning waiting in an incredibly slow line, and all that frustration was bound to work up an appetite. Lucky for you, I happen to know just the establishment."

He led her down the cracking asphalt of the main street, turning down a familiar, narrow avenue until they reached a small, weathered storefront. It was a strange sense of nostalgia, once Talus had met Lily all those decades ago, he had lost all desire to eat anywhere else in the city. His life back then had been a binary loop: the laboratory or this coffee shop.

Near the front window, a small metal table and two chairs sat in the exact coordinates where his usual table used to be.

"Welcome to The Daily Grind," Talus said, stepping ahead to pull out a chair for her. "Where we specialize in artisanal coffee, fresh sandwiches, and exceptionally bad puns."

Anya slid into the chair, looking up at him with the same soft, radiant smile she had worn since the post office. She watched him closely as he stood beside her.

"Now, what would you prefer for lunch, Miss?" Talus asked, slipping easily back into the rhythm of the game. "We have a delightful club sandwich, or an avocado chicken option that is highly popular with the locals. Also, if this is your first time visiting, I highly recommend the cinnamon pastries and the house blend coffee."

Anya rested her chin in her hand, her eyes locked onto his, a teasing warmth dancing in her gaze. "You are really going all out with this performance, aren't you?"

Talus gave a slow nod, his voice dropping. "Now, what would you like, Miss?"

"For you to stop calling me 'Miss', for starters," Anya said softly, though there was no real bite to her words. "Was that really a thing? Because I find it incredibly irritating."

Talus laughed. "Well it is supposed to be a sign of respect and a way of addressing someone when you do not know their name."

Anya tilted her head, her gaze dropping to his lips for a fraction of a second before meeting his eyes again. "Can I just get two coffees?"

"Two?" Talus asked, a faint twinge of something like jealousy sparking in his chest before he could stop it.

"Yes," she whispered, her smile turning entirely gentle, entirely private. "I am waiting for someone special."

"Very well then I shall be right back with those coffees."

Talus felt his breath hitch. He cleared his throat, nodding quickly. "Very well, then. I shall be right back with those beverages."

He turned and disappeared into the shadowed interior of the building. Waiting just inside the kitchen doorway was Cary, holding two steaming ceramic mugs, a pair of synthetic sandwiches, and two fresh pastries. Cary was wearing an intensely amused, almost manic expression.

"This was the best I could scare up in the fifteen minutes of notice you gave me." Cary handed over one coffee but then held the other back.

He squinted at Talus. "You...look strange."

Talus reached aggressively for the second coffee. "Strange? I just want my coffee."

"You're happy," Cary stated plainly, a triumphant grin breaking across his face. "Admit it, Tal. You are absofrickinlutely happy right now."

"I admit that I am having a bit of fun showing her life in the past but after coffee it is back to work." Talus muttered, his cheeks growing warm as he grabbed the food tray. "I appreciate her help over the past few days and considering I am the reason she will never get to experience this life; I owe at least this much to her."

"Ah, magnificent," Cary groaned, rolling his eyes. "It had been at least twelve hours since that God complex of yours reared its oversized head. Here is your coffee, Tal. But do not rush back to the lab. Having fun looks exceptionally good on you."

"Well I do not want to keep you from your work otherwise you might not have a new swear word of the day for tomorrow." Talus shot back dryly, stepping toward the exit.

"Dadgumit Tal, I already got one."

"Somedays I really do wonder how you managed to get a Ph.D." Talus murmured.

"And I wonder how you managed to get a girl to fall in love with you." Cary countered softly, his voice losing its teasing edge as he looked past Talus' shoulder.

"Not very well obviously." Talus paused, the words hitting him with unexpected weight. "Thanks for the help Cary."

He stepped back out of the shaded doorway into the warm afternoon sun. Anya had stood up from the metal table. She was walking slowly along the edge of the cracked concrete sidewalk, her head tilted back as she eyed the sweeping architectural lines of the decaying buildings above. The sunlight caught the scarlet strands of her hair, casting a soft, ethereal glow around her shoulders.

Talus stood by the door for a long, silent moment, the tray heavy in his hands, simply watching her exist in his world. She looked entirely beautiful, a living, breathing piece of hope standing amidst the ashes of his past. He took a deep breath, his heart hammering a rhythmic, steady beat against his ribs, and walked back out to meet her.

'Sorry for the delay," Talus said, breaking the quiet spell as he approached the table. "It seems our barista is a bit chatty today."

Anya returned to her seat, a soft smile returning to her lips as she immediately wrapped her hands around the warm ceramic mug he placed in front of her. Talus carefully set the other coffee across from her, along with the pastries, before sliding his own massive frame into the metal chair opposite hers.

"The buildings are so incredibly tall," Anya murmured, her eyes drifting back up to the decaying concrete structures towering over the narrow street. "There must have been so many people who lived here."

"About ten thousand, one hundred, if I recall the census data," Talus replied, taking a slow, cautious sip of the dark liquid. "Not nearly as many as you would think. People simply had significantly more living space back then."

Anya cradled her mug, absorbing the information before looking at him across the table. "Is this where you used to eat? Back before everything?"

"Yes. As often as I could spare the time."

"Was it for the food," she asked, her voice dropping into a gentle, teasing lilt, "or was it strictly for the coffee?"

Talus ran a large, blunt finger up and down the rough ceramic side of his coffee cup. He froze, his brow furrowing as his mind began to dangerously wander backward in time. Back to the vibrant, laughing person who used to occupy the exact chair where Anya was sitting right now.

"I came for the coffee," Talus said quietly, his voice losing its mechanical edge. "I stayed for the company."

Anya's gaze softened, her blue eyes locked onto his with an intuitive, quiet understanding. "For her? The girl whose picture you keep on your desk?"

He gave a single, slow nod. "Lily."

He immediately looked away from Anya then, his eyes tracking a piece of windblown debris across the asphalt. That was definitively not something he wanted to discuss right now and certainly not with Anya sitting across from him, looking at him with a raw, searching vulnerability that made his chest ache.

"It must have been so beautiful here back then," she said, gracefully steering the conversation away from his grief.

"Few people back then would have appreciated the environment as you do," Talus noted, looking back at her.

She nodded, a faint, melancholy smile touching her lips. "They take for granted the things they see every single day."

"It is a bit of that but there were also plenty of distractions. The street would be filled with cars and people would be walking along the sidewalks. There would be noise and chaotic movement everywhere, so the buildings simply faded into the background. Sitting here at a coffee shop was merely a way to people-watch."

He watched her features carefully as she finally took a substantial sip of her coffee. Instantly, her face twisted into a sharp, comical grimace.

"That is absolutely terrible," she gasped, staring down at the brown liquid.

"Tried to be as historically accurate to the original recipe as possible," Talus explained, a rare, genuine chuckle vibrating in his chest.

Anya shook her head, a soft, beautiful laugh escaping her lips as she looked back up at him, her eyes dancing in the sunlight. "Well, then it must have been truly spectacular company to force you to put up with this coffee."

Talus' laughter faded into a quiet, intense stillness. His eyes locked onto hers, held captive by the sudden, profound warmth radiating between them. "She was."

They sat in silence for a moment. Talus felt a deep wave of gratitude that Anya did not press him further about Lily. Even now, as he looked down at the dark fluid in his cup, a phantom limb of his old life tried to manifest; he could almost believe that if he turned his head,

Lily would come bounding down the concrete steps to wrap her arms around his shoulders. But as he looked across the table at the sunlight catching Anya's red hair, the memory faded, replaced by a very real, very vital presence.

'So, what exactly did you do?" Anya asked softly, leaning forward over her mug. "Before you were completely dead-set on stopping the Others. What was your research?"

The sudden question made Talus stiffen. His fingers tightened around his cup. "My work prior to the war was highly complicated, and exceptionally difficult to explain. I do not wish for you to misunderstand and get the wrong idea about me."

The bright smile that had been permanently painted on Anya's face since they left the hatch instantly withered into a hurt, guarded frown. She pulled her hands back from the warm mug.

'You think I wouldn't be capable of understanding it?"

'No! Anya, what I did back then was something that was supposed to completely revolutionize the human condition," Talus fumbled, his words tripping over each other in a sudden, panicked rush. More than anything else in the world at this exact moment, he did not want Anya to look at him with hatred. When he claimed he did not want her to get the *wrong* idea about him, what his cowardly soul was truly terrified of was that she would get the absolute *right* idea about him. She would see the horrible, arrogant monster he had been, and perhaps still was. "Few people could even begin to comprehend the evolutionary implications. I simply want to tell you when I am certain you would not get the wrong impression of my character."

Anya's eyes narrowed, a cold, familiar wall sliding back into her expression. "So you do think I'm stupid. The past few days in your lab... I actually thought I was helping you. Apparently, you were just sitting there thinking about how stupid I was."

'No! That is not it at all!"

He had to tell her something and even if his own motivations in the immortality project were not exactly pure, he knew someone whose motivations were. His father had possessed only the highest, most honorable intentions for their research. Talus rapidly decided he would borrow them. He would wrap himself in his father's noble ambitions, because he knew with complete certainty that the unvarnished truth would prevent Anya from ever seeing him as anything but a monster.

She took another slow, guarded sip of her terrible coffee, her blue eyes unblinking. "Then what is the truth, Talus?"

He swallowed hard, his fingers gently stroking the rough sides of his ceramic cup as he searched for the words. "I was a core component of the original immortality project. I believed we could permanently cure cancer, or cellular degradation, or even the common cold. We had already made substantial progress in making terminal diseases a thing of the past, so we were merely attempting to expand the safety net. But there was a new discovery and the project got entirely away from us. Individuals in high positions of power took control and mutated the research into something far beyond what I had ever imagined."

It was all entirely true. But it was not *his* truth. It was his father's tragedy. It completely omitted the reality of how Talus had taken his father's noble ambitions and aggressively bastardized them, believing that total immortality was a far greater, more godlike achievement than merely curing human sickness.

Anya's breath hitched, her eyes widening as she processed the news. "You were there? You mean...it happened right here? The literal beginning of the end of the world was engineered here, and you were in the room. Wow."

Talus felt a cold chill wash over his neck. That was definitely not how he had ever imagined his life's monumentally historic work being categorized, and yet, "the beginning of the end" was likely a far kinder, more merciful title than he actually deserved.

"How did you" Anya paused, her voice dropping as she struggled to find the words. "I mean, well how did you personally become like this?"

Talus knew exactly what she was trying to tactfully ask.

"I was terrified," he confessed, his voice dropping into a low, raw whisper that he had never shared with another living soul. "I was profoundly afraid of death. Of the final end. Of losing absolutely

259

everything that mattered to my existence." He paused, looking wistfully past her shoulder toward the dry, empty basin of the old park where he had once held Lily in his arms.

Now, he was sitting in their sacred spot with someone entirely new. Someone who knew absolutely nothing of the real horrors he had committed in the dark. A heavy, familiar dread settled in his stomach; she would likely flee the perimeter of his life the second she discovered the truth, just as Lily had.

"I lost everything anyway," he added softly.

Anya leaned in closer, the space between them shrinking as she looked into his eyes. "Why isn't Lily here with you, then? If you possessed the capability to make people immortal and with everyone else in the base being fine there must have found a way to do it safely, so didn't you give it to her?"

"Because," Talus murmured, a bitter, tragic smile touching his lips, "her devotion to her faith ultimately ended up making her the smartest individual among us all."

Anya tilted her head. "So what happened?"

She wasn't letting it go this time. The old expression *curiosity killed the cat* was obviously not a tactical maxim she was familiar with.

"When I finally revealed to her what I had achieved in the laboratory, when I explicitly offered the treatment to her, she did not see salvation," Talus said, his dark eyes holding hers with absolute intensity. "She called it a curse. I truly believed I was offering her the greatest, most magnificent gift in human history, and she only perceived it as a mechanism preventing her from ever reaching her heaven. She left me. She packed her life, left the city limits, and I never laid eyes on her again."

They finished the remainder of their bitter coffee in absolute silence. Anya seemed entirely content to leave him undisturbed within the darkness of his own thoughts, and Talus was profoundly grateful for the quiet sanctuary of her presence. Cary would never have permitted such a raw admission to pass without forcing a prolonged, exhausting conversation to try and "fix" his emotional state. But looking at Anya, Talus realized that sometimes the most profound comfort did not come from the conversation at all, but simply from the shared company.

Anya slowly set her empty mug down, her blue eyes soft and entirely warm as she looked across the table at him. "Thank you for doing this, by the way. I know your objective was to provide me with a normal afternoon. It was really fun."

Talus gave a slow, deliberate nod, his chest expanding with a sudden, powerful emotion he couldn't quite define. "It was fun. Significantly more fun than I have permitted myself to experience in a very long time. This was merely my way of thanking you for your assistance in the laboratory. I found a majority of your suggestions to be incredibly insightful and useful to the project. So please.never again, even for a single fleeting moment, think that I find your mind to be lacking. We are simply intelligent in entirely different ways, you and I."

She nodded and she seemed to accept his answer. He was glad but he really did find her remarkable and intelligent.

Anya nodded slowly, the residual tension completely leaving her shoulders as she accepted his answer. Talus felt a quiet wave of relief wash over him; he truly did find her to be a remarkable, extraordinarily intelligent creature.

"I should probably return to the base," Anya said, gently sliding her chair back as she looked toward the mountain. "Ryan and I were planning to check if the Captain has reached Tressle yet. I've yet to actually tell him that Ryan and I are here, we told him we were on our way but soon enough he'll realize the truth when we don't show up."

Talus nodded, masking a sudden pang of disappointment that their time had reached its conclusion. He stood up, his tall frame towering over the small table. He extended his hand toward her across the metal surface.

Anya looked up at him, a beautiful, genuine smile breaking across her face as she reached out and smoothly slipped her hand into his. Their fingers locked together, warm and secure.

Together, holding hands in the quiet light of the dying world, they turned and began the slow walk back toward the base. As Talus cast a final glance back toward the crumbling city, to the post office and the little coffee shop, his lips curved into a quiet, peaceful smile. For the first time in years, the future felt entirely brighter than the past.

21

Anya

"This is Ranger Anya, verification code 466090 under encryption code 670. Do you come in?"

Anya gripped the edges of the console, staring intensely at the main monitor. She knew that calling the Tressle from an entirely unknown number and location would be incredibly difficult to explain. Technically, no one outside the inner circle was even supposed to possess the capability to patch into this specific network, but Elan had simply shrugged and agreed to her request anyway. She had initially suggested transmitting directly from the cockpit of their plane, which would at least provide a recognizable Phoenix-issue signature, but their actual geographic coordinates would still remain completely unexplainable. Elan had told her with blunt, practical logic that if she was going to have that much explaining to do, she might as well go all out, utilize the base's massive signal booster, and sit in comfort while she did it.

"This is Ranger Benson," a sharp, automated voice cracked through the static. "I have verified your security credentials, Ranger, but your signal is originating from an unrecognizable, non-standard source. Explain your parameters immediately."

Anya glanced over her shoulder at Cary and Ryan, both of whom simply offered an identical, helpless shrug. She knew Elan would be of absolutely no assistance here. She looked around the room, a sudden pang of longing hitting her. Where was Talus? Perhaps his brilliant mind would be better at creating a believable lie on the fly; he was the architect who had engineered these exact encrypted communication protocols, after all.

"We received a faint, automated distress beacon from an unmapped sector," Anya lied, forcing her voice to remain smooth and authoritative. "We chose to deviate from our flight path to investigate the perimeter before meeting up for the scheduled rendezvous at Tressle. The facility..." She paused, looking at Cary again. The old soldier shook his head sharply, silently warning her not to reveal anything specific. "The facility is entirely abandoned, or appears to be. However, we were able to successfully hotwire their archaic communications array to establish contact."

"Understood. Give me a moment to confer with my commanding officer."

"Affirmative."

The line fell into a heavy, crackling silence, and Anya slumped back into the leather chair, letting out a long breath. A dark cloud of anxiety began to settle over her. What if they weren't even going to relay her message? What if the command chose to withhold the message out of sheer bureaucracy, never letting her real Captain know about the call? He would never know what had truly happened to her or Ryan, not until they arrived at Tressle. If they ever made it there at all.

Suddenly, the audio static hissed loudly, cutting through her thoughts. A different voice broke over the line, dripping with a cold, smooth arrogance that made the hairs on the back of her neck stand straight up.

"Ranger Anya. You will need to provide additional verification data to prove your identity before we process this transmission. Tell me: why exactly were you expelled from Phoenix?"

She squirmed uncomfortably in her chair, her fingers tightening into fists. The real reason behind her exile had always been hidden deep in the dark recesses of her mind. Her time with Talus was the first time in years she had allowed those memories to come to the surface. Not even Ryan or Captain Tennant knew everything about what happened.

At the time of her banishment, she had been informed that the exact details of her disciplinary records would be kept permanently classified under maximum security, strictly to protect Phoenix's darkest systemic secrets.

"Failure to follow direct orders, sir," she stated, her voice tight.

"What specific order, Ranger?"

Anya's throat went entirely dry. How was she supposed to answer that? She had never been provided a cover story to tell. She had simply been violently pushed out of Phoenix's doors with little more than a cold wave, and the command had fully expected her to perish in the wastes, never anticipating that any other regional bunker would be desperate enough to take her in. Her exit debrief had been completely non-existent. But with Phoenix's command currently reduced to rubble, could she finally tell the truth? Who would even believe her?

"What order did you fail to execute, Ranger? Respond."

"That data is permanently classified, sir."

A low, cruel chuckle vibrated through the speakers. "At least you still retain some pathetic sense of institutional loyalty in that worthless, broken body of yours."

Anya stiffened instantly, her entire frame locking up as the words sliced cleanly to her core. Her chest heaved. She would recognize that horrific, smooth voice anywhere. It was that exact voice that had coldly commanded her parents to turn her over to the training programs when she was a frightened child. It was his voice that had endlessly insulted and degraded her during brutal hours of solitary punishment and extra physical conditioning for one perceived flaw or another. It was his voice that had urged her to plunge a combat blade into a defenseless man as he begged for mercy on the cold floor. It was his voice that had forced her to stand in front of the entire assembly at Phoenix base, broadcasting to everyone just how worthless he found her existence, how worthless *anyone* would find her.

"Captain," Anya whispered, her military posture fracturing as a wave of raw fury and old terror collided in her chest. "I see you survived the raid on Phoenix."

"I was unfortunately deployed away from the base when the enemy attacked," the voice sneered. "I was unable to stand alongside true, loyal soldiers. Individuals who actually deserved to live far more than you ever did, girl."

Anya closed her eyes, fighting a sudden, dizzying wave of nausea. This was going to go absolutely nowhere. He would never provide her with the information she needed. He would happily keep her completely in the dark out of sheer, childish spite. But then, a cold spark of her stubbornness flared back to life. She remembered why Captain Tennant had been able to take her into Tigris base in the first place, how her real Captain had boldly interjected himself into the sentence of banishment and death that Phoenix high command had planned for her.

"I am not calling to converse with you, Captain," Anya snapped, her voice turning into a dangerous, sharp blade. "I am calling to establish immediate contact with my actual superior, Captain Tennant. I am certain he would hate to inform the High Council that you are actively withholding critical operational data from him out of petty, childish spite. Phoenix command and all of her precious secrets are gone. Tigris is completely abandoned. If you ever want to be granted a new base to command, you will want to stay in the Council's good graces."

It wasn't until she felt Ryan's warm, solid hand rest gently on her trembling shoulder that she realized just how incredibly tense her body had become. Her breath was completely trapped within her lungs, her heart hammering wildly. It felt entirely possible that this monstrous man possessed the supernatural potential to kill her using nothing but the sheer malice of his voice over a comm system.

The speaker let out another low, dismissive hiss. "Your precious Captain Tennant is not present at this facility, Anya. He and the rest of the fools following his command were forced to execute a drastically longer route after their envoy was trailed by a detachment of the enemy. They are currently spending long, exhausting days hidden away in regional safe rooms, seeking strategic assistance to find an acceptable path to Tressle. We do not expect their arrival for another week or more."

Anya held her breath, her eyes locking onto the frequency waves on the screen.

"When they finally arrive," the voice continued, dropping into a low, venomous purr, "I shall be sure to tell him to contact his favorite little pet project. But you are fooling absolutely no one with that pathetic cover story of yours, Anya. I know exactly where that signal is originating from. I only hope the Captain you have so much blind faith in will be expecting you to be there when he arrives."

The audio connection abruptly cut off into flat, dead static.

The screen blinked back into a standard diagnostic menu, and Anya could do absolutely nothing but stare blankly at the glass, her vision blurring. Finally, her trapped breath broke free, coming out in a series of jagged, strangled gasps. Captain Tennant wasn't at Tressle yet, but he was alive, and he was safe.

But as the realization settled, a cold, dark truth crystallized in her mind. Now, she had even less of a reason to fly to Tressle. There was absolutely nothing on this earth that would ever make her want to look upon her former captain's face again. But if her real Captain needed her she would follow his orders to the literal end of the world. She owed him that debt.

"Anya," Ryan's voice was incredibly soft beside her ear. "Are you okay?"

She gave a tight, rapid nod, fighting to stabilize her breathing. "At least we know that he's okay, and why we haven't been able to get through to his comm yet. And he knows exactly how to establish contact with us when he arrives."

Without a word, Ryan wrapped his arms tightly around her shoulders, pulling her smaller frame into his chest. Anya leaned into him, finally letting her guard drop completely as she returned the fierce embrace. A few silent, unbidden tears slipped down her cheeks, hot against her skin.

"He is absolutely nothing, Anya," Ryan whispered intensely into her hair, his hand gently rubbing her back. "I know who you are. I know your character. You remain one of the most remarkably amazing people I have ever had the good fortune to meet in this life. If you believe even a single word that asshole just said over that radio, I will never forgive you. Do you hear me?"

Anya offered a faint, watery smile against his jacket. Ryan always knew the exact, perfect words she needed to hear to piece her armor back together.

"I'll be fine," she said softly, gently pulling away from the embrace and wiping her face. "I just...I think I need some fresh air right now."

"I'll come up to the surface with you," Ryan offered immediately, his eyes filled with concern.

She shook her head, forcing a lighter tone into her voice. "No, it's okay. I just want to be alone for a few minutes. Besides, I wouldn't want to interrupt whatever chaotic plotting you and Cary are currently up to. You're exceptionally lucky Talus didn't overhear your little decoration plans earlier."

It was an incredibly weak, transparent excuse, and she knew Ryan could see right through it. But it was the only one she had right now, and he was kind enough to let her use it.

She turned away from the pair, leaving the communications center behind as she navigated the quiet, concrete corridors toward the hidden mountain exit Talus had demonstrated to her just the day before. It was a secluded, narrow shaft housing a long iron ladder that led straight up through the rock, opening onto a high, reinforced structural platform that directly overlooked the ruined city below.

As her boots rhythmically hit the floor, her thoughts drifted entirely to the one horrific realization that she couldn't shake. The one person in the entire world who absolutely did not deserve to survive the brutal raid on Phoenix base was still breathing.

He was alive. That stupid, cruel bastard had survived the attack when Mamoru did not. It felt like a sickening cosmic joke; there remained absolutely no justice or punishment for the wicked in this world.

Her feet automatically carried her out of the shadows and into the blinding, open air of the upper ledge. Her hands clasped tightly around the cool, solid metal of the ladder running up the side of the shining mountain.

Wisps of grey smoke were the first thing she saw, drifting lazily into the cold air before his dark coat and pale skin came into view. Talus remained perfectly silent as she climbed the final steps onto the mountain platform. She took a slow seat next to him, leaning her back against the hard, jagged rock wall. The smoke wafting from the thin white stick between his fingers smelled slightly sweet, but mostly bitter.

They sat together in peaceful silence. He seemed just as unwilling to initiate a conversation as she was. She couldn't help but wonder what was passing through his brilliant mind that had driven him up here, away from his beloved laboratory. Had he figured something out? Had his trials failed yet again? And if he wasn't working anyway, why hadn't he been down in the communications room with her?

"What is that?" she finally asked, her voice quiet against the wind.

Talus looked down at the burning tip, his features drawn and unusually exhausted. "A cigarette. At one time, they were colloquially referred to as death sticks. Yet, millions of individuals still consumed them daily. Apparently, they derived more psychological comfort from smoking them than the value of what it took from their lifespan." He gave a slow, heavy shrug.

'So now you smoke them, knowing they won't actually kill you?"

He gave a single, somber nod.

"Figure out the real draw to them yet?"

He shook his head, staring out at the ruined skyline. "No. But I have been executing the habit for so long that there is a sense of familiarity to them. A comfort in the routine." He paused, his dark eyes shifting toward her, shadowed by an intensity that made her breath catch. "How did the transmission go?"

She desperately wanted to tell him exactly who had answered the comms array. She wanted to tell him about the monster from her past. Talus was smart; he would instantly understand why that man's voice had chilled her straight to the bone. He would know the horrific memories that had been brought back to life by the gruff, arrogant baritone that had tormented her for years.

Instead, she just looked at him. "Why are you up here breathing in death sticks, Talus?"

He didn't answer right away. He stared at the cigarette, his jaw clenching so hard the muscles jumped beneath his pale skin. When he finally spoke, his deep voice was laced with a profound, aching reluctance.

"I want to ask something of you," he murmured, his eyes refusing to meet hers. "But after your emotional reaction in my laboratory... I am entirely unsure how to do so without breaking what we have built."

Anya instantly knew what he was talking about. He wanted to talk about the one thing she wanted to avoid at all costs. "The person who answered the transmission was my old Captain from Phoenix," she confessed bluntly, trying to shield herself. "The one who- well, it is safe to say he does not think highly of my existence. Just hearing his voice again brought the past back clearer than it has ever been."

"I'm sorry."

He said the words, but there was almost no emotion behind the delivery. It sounded incredibly awkward, forced, and entirely flat.

Anya let out a dry, bitter laugh. "What is it you want to ask me, Talus? The memories are already swirling around in my head anyway. We might as well get some use out of the damage."

Talus closed his eyes, a pained, deeply sorrowful expression crossing his face. The rigid, clinical mask he usually wore was gone, revealing a raw sadness that shocked her. He looked truly miserable, his broad shoulders bowing as if carrying an impossible weight.

"I want to know more about what you saw. What they did, how it may have affected him. I want you to relive those memories in detail so that I might be able to get some small bit of information from them."

He stopped, his breath hitching as he looked at her, his amber-flecked eyes filled with a desperate, pleading reluctance. "But to

270

ask that of you, to force you back into that dark room, I have to force myself to put the science first. I have to suppress my feelings, and I..."

He trailed off, unable to finish the sentence. He took another long, ragged drag from his cigarette, keeping his face turned toward the sky. Anya understood now why his tone had sounded so flat and devoid of emotion. He wasn't being heartless; he was desperately trying to numb his own conscience so he could force himself to ask her to do something he knew would cause her immense emotional pain.

"You want to use me," she said, her voice turning hoarse and thick with emotion as the realization settled. "You want to intentionally torture me by dragging up all the horrific memories I have spent years trying to forget, just on the hope that you might find some variable you've missed over the last century."

"No," Talus whispered, his voice cracking completely. He turned his head to look at her, his expression utterly devastated, entirely stripped of his god-complex. "I do not *want* to ask this, Anya. It makes me sick to my core. But I have to. We are running out of time, and I need to."

He took another long, desperate draw from his cigarette, and as he raised the white stick to his lips, Anya noticed the tremble in his hand.

She stared at his shaking hand, her heart aching in a strange, bittersweet rhythm. "Okay."

Talus snapped his head toward her, his dark eyes widening in complete, stunned disbelief. "You will do it? Are you sure?"

"This is the reason I am here, is it not?" Anya said, her voice softening as she looked at him. Then, a small, dangerous spark entered her gaze. "But if I am going to suffer through my past, Talus, you are going to suffer right along with me."

He froze, his hand stopping mid-air just before inhaling from the cigarette again. "What do you mean by that?"

"A trade," she replied, her tone leaving no room for negotiation. "For every question you force me to answer, I get to ask you one in return and you *will* answer it truthfully."

Talus' brow furrowed, a defensive wall trying to slide back into

271

his eyes. "So you acknowledge that my scientific request is entirely reasonable, and yet you wish to force me to relive my dark past simply because I am asking you to navigate yours?" His eyes bore directly into hers, intense and burning, as if the sheer weight of his stare would be enough to make her back down.

If that was his intention, he was going to be very disappointed. Anya didn't flinch. She held his stormy gaze, her chin lifting defiantly.

"It is only fair, after all," she countered. "A mutual exchange of information."

"But my questions serve a greater, global purpose," Talus reasoned, his voice tightening with a mix of sadness and frustration. "Whereas your inquiries do absolutely nothing but settle your own personal curiosity regarding my life."

Anya looked at him for a long, silent moment, the wind whipping her short hair around her face. Her voice dropped into a soft, piercing whisper that cut straight through his remaining armor.

"Perhaps," she murmured. "Or maybe the real reason your research can't move forward, Talus, is because you are far too afraid to let go of your own past."

He finished the cigarette and threw the butt of it into a container that she now noticed was somewhat concealed into the wall behind them. He opened the case and she saw the glint of a familiar face before he closed it again without taking another of white rolls. He fiddled with the case for a few moments before looking out over the horizon. "I doubt your ambition is quite so lofty but I concede the point. I agree to your terms, Anya. I only hope that you can accept the answers you seek and understand them for what they are."

Part of her wanted to ask about his cryptic answer but she didn't want to waste a question on something he could talk his way out of. They sat in silence for a few moments. While Anya was eager to finally get answers she had been promised, she was terrified of what Talus' first question to her might be. Already the wide eyes and choked screams were coming unwelcome to the forefront of her mind.

"Would you like to go back down to the lab to talk?" Talus asked softly.

Anya shook her head, her eyes fixed on the darkening sky. "No. I want to stay up here and see the stars come out."

She needed the escape that only the twinkling stars and swirling nebulas could provide. Staring into the endless void allowed her to think of a different planet, one far away from her cruel past and from people who cared so little for other living beings. Perhaps her ancestors had been right all along, and leaving Earth behind was the only true answer. But as the cool desert wind swept over the sands and rustled through her short hair, she couldn't imagine a sweeter smell or a softer caress. Would another planet ever feel as beautifully alive as Earth did, even as she struggled to survive against the harsh punishments that had been inflicted upon her?

Talus cleared his throat but said nothing. The sun began its final descent, and a warm, golden haze blanketed them both. Anya idly toyed with the buttons of her pockets to keep her hands busy. Her dark Ranger suit was still fully stocked with a Fulgar and a few tactical items she could use to get out of trouble in a pinch. She traveled lighter these days, but she still could not step outside without the familiar, reassuring weight of the Fulgar against her hip.

She took a breath and steeled herself. "Well? The sooner we get started with this, the sooner we can figure this out."

He nodded slowly. "You mentioned they removed the heart. How exactly was it done? With what?" He turned to look at her, his amber eyes unreadable, his mouth pressed into a tight, strained frown. "Be as specific as possible, please. I am sorry to make such a request of you, Anya, but it is necessary. Any small bit of information could help us."

She closed her eyes for just a moment, pulling the buried memories from the hidden, locked spaces of her mind. In the dark of her thoughts, she saw the victim hanging there, his eyes wide with pure terror, his bare chest heaving, and his knees bent under his own weight.

"He was chained," she whispered. She raised her hands above her head to demonstrate, showing how the man's wrists were kept shoulder-width apart but pulled slightly behind his back to forcefully push his chest forward. "Arms up. His feet could barely touch the ground. He could stand if he forced himself, but he often just sagged. His chest was entirely bare." Anya swallowed hard, her throat tight, and purposely avoided Talus' gaze.

She dropped her arms and glanced back toward the fading light of the sun. "They used a dagger at first. It was hard, black metal and incredibly sharp. It could cut through just about anything. They were completely ruthless, Talus. They started by cutting a perfect circle." She extended a shaky finger and gently traced a large, slow circle over Talus' own chest. "They never cared how much he screamed. Then, they would use a heavy bone saw to get through the ribs, or a particularly brutal recruit might just choose to smash through the bone with a blunt tool."

The trembling in her hands grew violent, and she took several deep, ragged breaths to steady herself. Suddenly, she felt Talus' large, warm hands wrap securely around her fingers, chasing away the icy chill that was pooling in her mind.

"Many of those soldiers at Phoenix were just so angry," she continued, her voice cracking. "So completely full of rage. They thought absolutely nothing of just reaching into the chest cavity, grabbing the muscle, and ripping it out with their bare hands. A few of the senior officers would use a specialized knife—a scraper that allowed them to scoop the heart out as if it were ice cream. The screams would finally be over by then. His eyes would be completely glazed over, staring at nothing. He would turn so pale. Whiter than any living person I'd ever seen. His breathing would be barely noticeable, and the blood would completely drench his chest and the floor."

Her stomach churned, and she fought the sudden urge to retch. The imagery was just as vivid in her mind now as it was all those years ago.

"The heart would keep beating," she whispered, staring at their joined hands. "It would keep pulsing even after it was completely removed from the body. But then, as we watched, the bleeding would suddenly stop. A brand-new heart would start to visibly grow in the cavity. The old heart that had been cut out would finally stop beating, and the broken ribs would slide back together, locking into place to form the cage again. Finally, the flesh on the chest would close up entirely. The color would return to his skin, and his eyes would start to focus. He wouldn't talk or scream or anything after it was over. He would just sit there and stare at us with such anger and hatred." Anya looked up, her eyes bright with unshed tears. "When I was ordered to perform that experiment... I was the only person in the entire room who refused."

The hands wrapped around hers tightened significantly, but Talus' arms remained completely still, and he kept his gaze fixed on the horizon. The slight, rhythmic quiver in his deep breathing was the only sign that he had been affected by what she had just told him.

She turned her head to look directly into his eyes. "Why was I the only one, Talus?"

He let out a long, heavy sigh. "I lived through the great war, Anya. I saw it begin, I saw it claim millions of innocent lives, and I saw it end with barely a whimper. Even before the world broke, I watched people do terrible, unspeakable things to one another. I saw individuals who simply didn't care who died or who suffered, so long as they survived. Fear and anger can cause people to completely lose their humanity. It strips away their ability to feel for another living soul. Sometimes that loss is temporary... and sometimes it is permanent."

He turned his head, his eyes locking onto hers with a fierce, quiet intensity. "Even with all that this dark, broken world has taken from you, Anya, you haven't lost your humanity. Losing it would be easier, certainly. It would be far less painful to feel nothing at all. But your empathy is your greatest asset, and your compassion is your greatest strength, if only you learn how to utilize it. Never lose it, Anya. Never. Now, I believe that would make it your turn to ask a question?"

Anya smiled softly, a wave of relief washing over her, and gave a slight nod. Her hands slowly fell away from his, but the profound comfort his touch had given her remained. She opened her mouth to speak, ready to demand her answer, when they were suddenly interrupted by the metallic scraping sound of someone climbing the iron ladder.

Talus' brow furrowed. "What is it, Cary?"

But as a small, slender hand gripped the top rung and came into view, it became very clear that it was not Cary climbing up to the platform.

"I see I am not the first person to realize what a gorgeous night it is," a cheerful voice called out. "Wine, anyone?"

Kit scrambled over the edge of the mountain platform, offering them a bright grin. She reached into the canvas bag slung over her shoulder and pulled out a dark glass bottle. "I didn't bring any glasses, though," she added with a loose shrug.

Kit paused, suddenly registering the heavy, loaded silence between the two of them. "Uh...should I go?"

Anya was just about to ask Kit to give them some privacy when Talus abruptly stood up, beating her to the punch.

"No, stay," Talus said, his clinical voice slipping back into place. "I was just leaving, anyway. Perhaps you would do me the honor of keeping Anya company for a while?"

"But—Talus," Anya protested, her eyes narrowing.

Kit didn't wait for permission. She settled herself right down on the rock next to them and popped the top off the wine container. She took a quick, healthy swig and then extended the bottle directly toward Anya. "Here. You look like you could seriously use a drink."

"Wine?" Anya asked, taking the bottle automatically. She was still entirely caught off guard by the abrupt, frustrating change in her evening plans.

"Are you familiar with it?" Talus asked, looking down at her.

"I've heard of it, yes," Anya answered, her tone clipping. "But strangely enough, fermenting grapes is not something we tended to trouble ourselves with."

As Talus stepped away, Anya felt his physical warmth entirely leave her, and the desert night instantly grew colder. She glared up at him, her eyes sending a silent, furious warning that this cowardly exit was no way to get out of his end of their deal. He still owed her a completely honest answer to a personal question, and if he didn't deliver, there would be severe consequences the next time he tried to get information from her.

"I have not forgotten my obligation to you," Talus said, noting her fierce glare and offering a small, respectful nod. "And you shall have your proper chance to question me in the morning. But for now, a drink and some lighter conversation may do your mind some good. I have a few things I want to look into in the lab after what you've just told me."

With that, he turned and made his way toward the ladder.

Kit slid over into the warm spot on the rock that Talus had just abandoned. She reached into her bag again, pulling out a small portable light and a large, heavy silver thermal blanket. Anya was intensely grateful when Kit unrolled the blanket and spread it over both of their laps, as the thin desert air was quickly turning freezing.

Talus' head was already disappearing below the lip of the platform when a sudden, terrifying thought struck Anya's mind. She leaned over the edge.

"You're not planning on cutting your own heart out down there, are you?" she called out, her voice sharp with sudden panic.

"Not without help," his deep voice echoed back up the shaft.

"Talus!" Anya snapped, instantly throwing off the thermal blanket to go after him.

"I have absolutely no intention of removing my heart... without a good night's sleep first," Talus called up, a faint hint of dry amusement in his tone. "Tomorrow might be a completely different story, but for tonight, I have enough."

"Enough of what, Talus? Talus!"

This time, there was no answer from the dark shaft. Anya let out a frustrated breath and finally turned to properly acknowledge Kit's presence. The young girl seemed completely unphased by the bizarre, morbid conversation that had just taken place and was casually taking another long drink from her own supply.

Anya silently studied the girl. Kit looked just like any other newly minted teenager she might have seen back at Tigris base. She had long, straight blonde hair, bright eyes, and a face that looked incredibly young, though she was exceptionally tall for her age. Kit finished her swallow and handed the bottle back to Anya.

"Here, seriously, have some," Kit said, wiping her mouth. "It's actually pretty good. They're hand-pressed grapes from Cary's hanging greenhouse vineyard. Making wine has recently become something of a dedicated hobby for Frederick, and since he has a massive, totally obvious crush on me, I get all the free wine I can physically drink. Personally, I think that's a pretty solid foundation for a long-term relationship, but he seems to have some weird reservations about the age gap."

Anya laughed, the sound surprisingly light in her chest, and leaned her head back against the cool, solid mountain rock. She took the bottle of wine from Kit's extended hand, looking down at the dark crimson liquid with a mix of curiosity and lingering hesitation. Wine was something she had heard mentioned in old stories, but she had never actually tried it. Back at Tigris, a few of the younger Rangers had once tried to blow off steam by clandestinely fermenting a portion of their moldy fruit rations in a hidden drainage pipe. Anya hadn't partaken, and the brutal, public disciplinary punishment those offending Rangers had received from the Captain had permanently turned her off from ever trying it.

But out here, under the open sky, those rigid military protocols felt millions of miles away. Eager for a distraction, she lifted the bottle and took a deep, brave swig.

The harsh, dry taste instantly caught her completely off guard. Anya sputtered slightly, her eyes watering as the alcohol burned its way down her throat. It was strong, fiercely bitter, and easily one of the oddest, most complex flavors she had ever experienced.

"It's an acquired taste," Kit volunteered with a knowing, mischievous grin, nudging Anya's shoulder with her own. "And by the end of the night, I can personally guarantee you'll have acquired it."

Anya laughed again, the burning in her throat fading into a pleasant, blooming warmth. She took a second, much smaller sip, letting the flavor settle before handing the bottle back to the younger girl.

She turned her face toward the sky, gazing out at the endless blanket of stars. Kit had been completely right about the skyscape; the sheer majesty of the universe was actively helping to push those horrific memories of Phoenix base back into the dark recesses of her mind where they belonged. A soft, clean breeze tousled her red hair and tickled her cheek. It smelled deeply of pine trees, wild mountain flowers, and damp grass from Cary's lower agricultural sectors.

It was a beautiful scent, but unlike at Tigris, there was not a single hint of ocean air. Anya felt a quiet pang of homesickness. She deeply missed the sharp, salty tinge in the wind that had always spoken to her soul of freedom, wild waves, and upcoming adventure. Now that she technically possessed both freedom and adventure, she found she still missed the raw anticipation and excitement that the mere smell of the sea used to bring to her mornings.

Kit pulled her legs up to her chest, wrapping her arms around her knees as she stared out at the dark horizon. "What is it really like out there, Anya? Beyond the mountains? Is there actually anything left to see or do? Are there real cities?"

Anya took the wine back from Kit, taking another sip that tasted noticeably smoother than the first. "Haven't you ever gone out there to explore? After all, it is not like you have much to physically worry about. No one out there is capable of killing you."

Kit let out a long, quiet sigh, her gaze dropping to the silver thermal blanket draped over their laps. "I could have. My parents always said I was allowed to, and Cary even offered to come with me as a scout. A few of the others did, too. But I am the only person in this entire facility who doesn't possess a single memory of what it was actually like out there before the world broke. I have never lived a single day beyond the perimeter of this hidden city, my parents took shelter here when the war started to get bad and before that I was pretty young. I was born in that city there. Mom says they had a little apartment somewhere. Everyone here talks about the past like it was this grand, amazing thing. The way the world used to be. I guess I'm just terrified of losing the beautiful pictures I've built up in my head by seeing the brutal reality of what it is now."

Anya listened quietly, a deep wave of empathy washing over her. She shifted closer to the girl, ensuring the thermal blanket covered them both tightly against the dropping desert temperature. "If it makes you feel any better, I had never seen a real, standing city myself until we flew the plane over this valley. The world out there is a completely different world from the one in your parents' stories, Kit. It's scarred, and it's dangerous. But it is still our world. And we can't ever hope to fix it if we aren't willing to look it in the eye."

"My parents, and everyone else, they all just stay burrowed in this mountain, thinking this isolation is the absolute best they can do," Kit murmured, her voice laced with a rare touch of bitterness. "They believe that until Talus finds a definitive way to stop the Others, it isn't worth the risk to leave. So they all work their isolated little projects, convinced they are preparing to rebuild and improve civilization when the perfect time comes. No one ever talks about what happens if that time never actually comes."

"We rangers always assume it won't," Anya said openly, her voice steady. "I spent my entire life being lectured that the absolute maximum I could hope for out of existence was to survive until the next sunrise. But just surviving... that was never enough for me."

Kit turned her head, her dark eyes shining with sudden appreciation for the older girl's grit. "Well, when you put it like that, it's pretty depressing. Here, you clearly need more of this." She handed the wine back to Anya, motioning dramatically with her hand for her to take a massive drink.

Anya gladly obliged, swallowing a substantial gulp. "I always thought our existence was depressing. At least, until I met Talus. That man is nothing but a walking soap opera."

Kit blinked, tilting her head. "A soap opera? What's that?"

"Oh, it's an ancient term Ryan told me about," Anya explained with a grin. "It's one of those old-world broadcast shows where absolutely everything goes wrong, every scenario is a crisis, and the main characters are perpetually, dramatically miserable."

Kit burst into a loud, bright fit of laughter, the sound echoing beautifully off the stone walls. "Oh my god, yes! He has been exactly like that for as long as I've been alive. But the way Alton and Cary tell it, even before the bombs fell, he was always naturally mopey and dopey."

"The least desired of all the seven dwarves," Anya countered seamlessly, taking another drink before passing the bottle back.

"Hey! As I recall from that old fairytale, Dopey is at least supposed to be sweet and cute," Kit pointed out, wagging a finger in the air. "The problem with Talus is that he skipped the sweet part entirely and went straight to dopey."

Loud, shared laughter rang out over the mountaintop, the sound cutting through the heavy, oppressive atmosphere that constantly threatened to drag them both down. For a few beautiful moments, they weren't a displaced surface soldier and an immortal anomaly; they were just two young women sharing a drink in the dark.

"Cary seems genuinely fun, though," Anya noted, wiping a tear of laughter from her eye. "I haven't gotten to spend much time with Alton or Elan yet. Elan doesn't seem to talk much."

Kit nodded sagely, taking a small sip of the wine. "Elan is currently harboring about one hundred years of severe social anxiety that has unfortunately not improved with age. You would think a guy who has spent a literal century trapped in a bunker with the exact same women would be capable of talking to them without constantly tripping over his own tongue. But at least he is equally as awkward around me as he is around anyone else. Honestly, him and Talus are the only ones in this place who don't treat me differently."

Kit's playful demeanor suddenly faltered. She looked down at the bottle, idly twirling it between her hands. On the inside, the crimson liquid swirled into a dark, vengeful whirlpool before the frustrated teen finally set the glass down on the stone.

"I am technically old enough to have died of old age by now," Kit whispered, her voice dropping into a vulnerable, quiet register. "But I still look like...this." She shrugged helplessly, gesturing to her petite frame.

Anya's smirk turned into a soft, understanding expression. She reached out, gently bumping her shoulder against Kit's. "Yeah, you would think after a hundred years of it, they would finally get used to the reality that you aren't actually fourteen years old. Although... if I'm being completely honest, Kit, I can't say I don't understand why they do it."

Kit looked up. "Why?"

"A world entirely devoid of children—even teenagers—must feel incredibly bleak to them," Anya said softly, her eyes reflecting the starlight. "It may not be fair to your personal development, but children are the ultimate, universal embodiment of hope. They look at you, and they see the future they're fighting to rebuild. They are desperately looking for that hope in you."

Kit stared at her for a long moment, the heavy tension leaving her face as a brilliant, genuine smile broke across her features. "Well, when you put it in those specific terms, I suppose I can successfully suffer through a mandatory eleven o'clock curfew if it means being the living embodiment of human hope."

"Exactly," Anya cheered, raising her eyebrows playfully. "And at the very least, they allow the living embodiment of hope to drink Frederick's wine stash."

"Absolute truth." Kit laughed, instantly brightening back up. She raised the bottle high in a silent toast to their new friendship, tilted her head back, and took a long, triumphant swig.

22

Talus

Talus was profoundly grateful for Kit's abrupt interruption on the mountaintop. His carefully cultivated composure was fraying at the edges, his stomach twisting into a sickening knot that had become terrifyingly unfamiliar to him.

When he finally reached the sanctity of his lab, he leaned heavily against a metal workbench, breathing deeply through his nose to try and ease his tumultuous insides. For once in his miserable life, he was lucky that he hadn't consumed a single scrap of food all day; if he had, he was entirely certain it would have ended up pooled on the concrete floor.

"You are looking particularly green around the gills this evening, Tal. Might I inquire as to the momentous occasion?"

Cary's sarcastic voice was, for once, an incredibly welcome distraction. But as had often been the case as of late, the old soldier didn't travel alone. He stepped into the lab with his own modern mortal in tow.

"Did Anya get the absolute best of you again?" Ryan asked with a smug, knowing smirk, leaning his back against the doorframe.

Talus shook his head weakly, running a trembling hand over his face. "No. It is simply an unwelcome side effect of listening to her relate exactly what occurs when a human aggressively rips out the beating heart of an immortal."

Cary audibly gulped, his sarcastic smile vanishing instantly, while Ryan's smug expression hardened. The young ranger stepped forward, his eyes locking onto Talus with a cold, intense stare.

"Anya told you that?" Ryan's jaw clenched, a grimace breaking across his features. "No. No way. She may be incredibly cold, angry, and really fucking brutal if you piss her off, but she wouldn't do something like that. Not even to a monster."

Talus snapped his head up, his dark eyes flashing sharply at Ryan. Out of the corner of his eye, he noticed a dark, haunted expression cross Cary's weathered face as well.

Ryan quickly held up his hands, realizing the weight of the word. "Not that you two are monsters, obviously. Look, I'll admit I was completely terrified to fly out to this valley because the only immortals the rangers have ever documented are bloodthirsty killing machines. But now that I'm here, it actually feels like home."

Talus did not miss the brief, emotional way Ryan's gaze rested on Cary as he uttered those words.

'She did not do it," Talus clarified, his voice dropping into a low, gravelly register as the queasiness in his stomach finally eased enough for his scientific mind to take control. "She merely witnessed it as an observer."

He began to pace the narrow aisle of the lab, his thoughts rapidly firing. "She stated that the severed heart explicitly continued to beat on the floor until the brand-new heart completely regrew within the thoracic cavity—or at least, until it initiated its own pulse. Think about the cellular biology, Cary. Perhaps the mutated cells function on a magnetic frequency. The larger cluster of cells remaining in the body acts as a beacon, pulling at the displaced cells, drawing the residual electrical charge back to regenerate the mass. The cells feed entirely off raw energy, meaning it is possible that—"

Talus trailed off into silence. His thoughts were moving at a speed far too rapid to vocalize to his less-than-interested audience. *Energy.* It was the key to the lock. He knew it had to be. The cells thrived on energy, but if that data held true, then another targeted form of energy could theoretically disrupt their internal communication array.

"Talus, I thought the laws of physics dictated that energy cannot be created or destroyed," Cary reasoned, his voice unusually quiet and serious. "If these cells are pure, mutable energy, and they actively control what physical form they take, how do you logically hope to destroy them?"

Talus looked back at Cary and Ryan, a slow, dangerously sharp smile breaking across his pale face. "Rules can always be broken, Cary. And science is merely the magic of change and evolution. I *will* find a way to break them."

Talus barely acknowledged the sound of the blast doors sliding shut when Cary and Ryan finally left him alone. For the first time in a century, he possessed a real direction. He had a concrete theory, a viable idea, and a completely new variable to test. He worked through the dead of night and well into the bright morning, completely oblivious to the passage of time, the exhaustion in his muscles, or anything else in the world.

He was currently utilizing a high-frequency diagnostic device to monitor the microscopic electrical waves traveling between his once-again severed index finger and his main hand when a sharp voice interrupted him from the doorway.

"I knew that I was going to walk in here and find you literally cut into pieces," Anya said, crossing her arms as she strode into the lab. "Couldn't you at least execute your mad science experiments on your goldfish for once?"

"That would be highly unethical," Talus replied smoothly without looking up. He held up his left hand to demonstrate. "Besides, I am in one piece. That's old."

Anya scoffed, stepping closer to look at the cold, dead finger. "I think you passed the line of ethics and went straight to full-blown mad scientist a long time ago, Talus. What are you actually doing?"

Talus broke into a wide, uncharacteristic grin, his eyes bright with scientific fervor. "I spent the night analyzing exactly what you told me on the mountain. You stated the severed heart continued to pulse until the new one was capable of maintaining a beat. I realized these cells communicate across a localized energy spectrum. I calculated that if I can engineer a device to violently disrupt that specific signal, I can permanently halt cellular regeneration or perhaps even send my own operational message to the cells."

Anya tilted her head, her expression deeply skeptical. "You mean, like, politely ask the cells to just self-destruct? What living organism on this earth would willingly choose to die?"

"It wouldn't necessarily be self-destruction, but rather a forced mutation of form," Talus explained, his voice rising with excitement. "These cells are almost entirely composed of pure, compressed energy. For an organism of that nature, it wouldn't be death. It would simply be transitioning into an entirely different state of matter."

"If you say so," Anya murmured, her blue eyes scanning his schematics. "But I am far from convinced by your theory."

Talus was desperate to convince her, but he needed far more data to even convince himself of his own theory. He knew that if he could cross-reference her real-world observations with his own physical experimentation, he might reach a breakthrough.

He stepped into her immediate space, his eyes locking onto hers. "I wanted to ask you about your time with the other immortal. Did they ever—"

"Not so fast, bud," Anya interrupted sharply, a small, guarded smirk touching her lips as she stepped back. "You owe me a question first. Our deal was a question for a question. I am not about to drag up another vivid nightmare for your scientific entertainment without receiving my proper due."

Talus opened his mouth to point out that analyzing human slaughter was far from *entertaining* for him, and that forcing her to dredge up her trauma served a massive, global purpose. But he desperately wanted that information. And as much as his soul dreaded whatever deeply personal question was about to pass her lips, it was worth the cost.

"Of course," he said, forcing his voice to sound perfectly calm, collected, and detached..

But beneath his mask, his insides were churning. His mind instantly conjured the absolute worst demons of his long past. He was terrified of what brutal question she was about to demand, and how she would react to the truth of what he really was.

Anya fell silent. Her piercing blue eyes simply bored directly into him for several long, breathless seconds. Then, she slowly looked around the room, her gaze drifting over the cold metal tables, the whirring computers, and the archaic filing cabinets, as if she were looking for a specific, hidden truth.

"I want to know," she paused, her voice dropping into a quiet, dangerous register. "I want to know how it all started."

Talus stiffened. "I told you-"

"No," Anya interrupted, shaking her head sharply. "I mean this base. This specific facility where all of you brilliant minds locked yourselves away to work on your hidden little projects. The laboratory where you worked side by side with your father."

Talus felt his entire muscular frame lock into iron at the explicit mention of his father.

"Was this operation always fundamentally about saving yourselves?" Anya asked, her voice cutting through the silence of the lab like a blade. "Was this project always destined to end with millions of innocent people dying in the streets? Is that what this mountain facility was truly engineered for, Talus? Finding more efficient ways to kill human beings?"

He wanted to lie to her. He wanted to desperately paint a beautiful picture of his father's sweeping altruism and scientific nobility, but even his father had not been that hopelessly naive. They had both known from the very first day the military funding cleared that any cutting-edge research conducted within these walls would inevitably be weaponized. But humanity had always found innovative ways to murder one another, and his father had blindly hoped they could still manage to save a few lives in the crossfire.

"Yes," Talus whispered softly, the confession tearing at his throat. He kept his eyes locked on the floor, knowing she would demand more blood. "This base was always funded by the military, so while we all had hopes our work would be used to benefit everyone. It always belonged to the military and whatever they deemed to do with it to benefit their own ends."

Anya nodded slowly, her expression turning into one of disgust.

"So all of this...all of you came to this hidden sector just so you could efficiently kill other people? So you could initiate a global war and slaughter everyone outside your borders? Even you, Talus. Even your precious biological research. What was your grand plan? Were you going to infect the entire enemy population and withhold the cure strictly for yourselves?"

"No!" Talus shouted, his voice slamming against the concrete walls, louder and more furious than it had been in years. He would never allow his father's memory to be remembered as a clinical genocide, yet he knew with absolute certainty that he could not have put such a scheme past the General.

He stepped toward her, his breathing ragged. "The war was coming, Anya! It was always coming, long before we ever initialized a single experiment! Millions of people were already dying in the gutters. Poverty and disease were running rampant while the elite class ruthlessly exploited every single civilian ration. The world was completely suffocating on a daily diet of raw fear and systemic hatred! As long as the population remained angry and terrified, the politicians didn't have to actually solve the systemic collapse. It all just festered and grew in the dark. Global annihilation was merely a matter of time. We truly believed we could save human lives!"

"By slaughtering the other side?" Anya spat back, her eyes flashing with a dangerous fire. "Because your side was automatically 'right,' and their side was 'wrong'?"

"Everyone views war through the simplistic lens of right and wrong when they are the ones commanding the chessboard!" Talus roared, his control slipping entirely. "But the vast majority of normal people...they simply want to live, Anya! And very often, they desperately want the people they care about to live, too! They want to protect their loved ones, their countrymen, their innocent children. But rarely is that achieved without death, because someone else is always running the show! Someone else is deliberately sowing that hatred and fear from a throne, and the rest of the civilian population just has to violently claw their way out of the meat grinder!"

Anya didn't flinch at his shouting. Instead, she began to slowly circle him like a predator, her boots clicking softly against the floor. She walked over to the diagnostic console where the electrodes were actively flashing against his preserved, severed finger. She stared at his swimming goldfish for a moment, and then turned her cold gaze back to his face.

'So the high command wanted a compliant, immortal army," she said, her voice dropping into a chillingly calm whisper. "Do you honestly think they would have ever stopped, Talus? If the enemy population completely surrendered and your 'right' side won the conflict. Do you honestly believe the monsters running the show would have stopped the killing?"

Talus felt a sudden, violent urge to lie. He desperately wanted to believe that he had been a critical part of something better, something noble. But as he looked back across a century of isolation, he could only remember the toxic radiation of hate and fear. It was his own cowardice, his own paralyzing fear of mortality, that had driven him to conduct experiments he knew deep down in his soul were fundamentally wrong. Would the deployment of immortality have ever led to global peace and acceptance? Or was it always destined to become just another terrifying weapon of subjugation? What had it achieved now, other than a broken wasteland?

'I do not know," Talus whispered, his broad shoulders sagging as the anger completely drained out of him, leaving him hollow. "I truly do not know the answer to that, Anya. But back then, we all desperately wanted to try. Every major war in human history ended the exact millisecond one side successfully developed an unbeatable weapon. We blindly believed this project could achieve the same."

"Yeah, and we all know exactly how that scenario turned out," Anya said, her voice dripping with venomous contempt. She stepped directly into his personal space, her face inches from his. "You were perfectly willing to be a part of the machine. You sat in this pristine lab and worked side-by-side with the literal monsters who engineered this curse, because you arrogantly believed you could cure a few sick civilians at the absolute cost of the rest of the human race. You were willing to do absolutely anything just to secure your military funding."

She spat the words directly at his face like a physical insult.

It was the complete truth of his past, except for one crucial variable. She still did not know the true depth of how horrible a monster he actually was. She didn't know that the global collapse was entirely his fault.

Talus gave a slow, painful nod, trying desperately to swallow the lump in his throat. His eyes burned.

"The military was the only institutional body left with the capital required to fund the more expensive biological research," he whispered, his voice trembling with a raw, bleeding sorrow. "Any scientist who genuinely desired to pursue their projects had to prove its tactical worth to the General. Not even the major universities possessed the funding to back large-scale chemistry anymore... and half of my research was officially deemed highly unethical unless the military chain of command explicitly authorized the parameters. If any of us had known how it would truly escalate... that was the exact reason I tried to put restrictions into the data... to prevent my specific research from ever getting out into the world..."

Talus abruptly stopped speaking. The toxic wave of memories was crashing over him again. The blinding panic. The self-hatred. The absolute terror he had felt the exact second it became clear what had happened with his research.

Talus couldn't look at her anymore. He couldn't face the judgment in her blue eyes. He was so close to telling her the final truth, but if he confessed that he was the architect of the apocalypse, would she ever be able to look at him again? Could they ever work together in this lab? Could she *ever* forgive his existence?

"I was so incredibly stupid," Talus choked out, a single, bitter tear finally slipping down his pale cheek. He gripped the edge of the metal table until his knuckles turned stark white. "I was so utterly naive to believe I could sit in my comfortable chair and make high-minded demands to generals, expecting them to listen when I possessed absolutely no way to enforce my restrictions. I was nothing but a cocky, arrogant son of a bitch who genuinely believed the world would just play out perfectly according to my own brilliant designs. I thought I was a god. But instead, I lost absolutely everything, and learned exactly how young and stupid I truly was."

He closed his eyes tightly as the vivid imagery of the fall played on a continuous loop behind his eyelids. The frantic news bulletins detailing one fallen city after another, the burning skyscrapers, and the screams of a world dying in agony because of his brilliant mind.

They stayed frozen in a heavy, breathing silence for several long minutes, the air in the lab thick with a profound, crushing sorrow. Finally, Anya let out a long, slow sigh. She stepped forward and gently tapped her knuckles against the metal lab table right beside his hand.

"Well," she said softly, her voice completely stripped of its previous venom. "I guess you have officially earned your question. Ask away."

Talus forced his eyes open, swallowing the remaining emotion as his clinical focus returned, sharp and desperate. No matter what he had done, the only thing he could do now was fix it. "The head. Did the Phoenix soldiers ever successfully sever the immortal's head? What occurred to the biological systems?"

Anya offered a faint, incredibly somber smile. "You mean, did they behead him like some sort of ancient vampire?" She gave a slow nod, sucking her bottom lip into her mouth and raking her teeth against it before continuing. "Yes. They did. The severed head did just like the heart, blinking until slowly but surely, a brand-new head emerged from the neck cavity until things returned to exactly how they were before. At the very least, there was significantly less screaming during that specific trial. The brain functions stopped working entirely upon bisection, so it seemed far less painful than the other things they did to his chest."

She looked away toward the flashing monitors for a brief moment, and when she locked her gaze back onto him, her blue eyes were unusually bright, filled with a sudden, driving intensity.

"But when I witnessed the procedure, it wasn't the first time they had executed it. I heard rumors from the older guards—individuals who claimed to have known the immortal before his first decapitation. They said that originally, he talked constantly. He would loudly insult the staff, taunt the generals, and tell them that a rescue force was actively coming for him because he had successfully transmitted his coordinates. But after they cut off his head the first time and his body grew a completely new brain, he barely ever spoke again. He just hung from the chains and screamed when they cut him, he seemed more docile, even as he stared at us with hatred. The commanders always believed that cutting off the head made him unable to think, but I don't believe that. I still saw intelligence in his eyes. He was still in there."

The cells could perfectly replicate the physical electrical connections of the neurological pathways. But perhaps there was an intangible element, a piece of memory, of core identity, of true consciousness, that the cells were incapable of regenerating once the brain was completely separated from the central nervous system.

He spun around to face his goldfish, his mind racing with wild, frantic calculations, wondering if just maybe...but then he shook his head sharply, discarding the thought. There would be absolutely no way of determining whether or not a common goldfish had suffered a decrease in high-level brain function, and it was still highly unethical to mutilate the creature. If only his test monkey hadn't escaped the facility decades ago, but then again, would he have ever truly been strong enough to enforce such a horrific procedure on a primate either? Perhaps under heavy sedation, ensuring the poor beast felt absolutely zero physical pain...

"You care so deeply about that fish," Anya's voice softly cut through his spiral, her tone laced with a profound, searching curiosity. "You are so utterly obsessed with remaining ethical and preventing pain for a common pet. So tell me the truth, Talus, why did you do it? Why did you choose to force immortality onto Cary when he explicitly did not want to receive it?"

Talus froze mid-step, his breath trapping in his lungs. He snapped his head toward her, his eyes wide with a sudden, defensive shock. "Did Cary tell you that?"

"I asked him how he became immortal, and he said you saved his life even when he was too scared to make that choice himself."

Talus stood entirely paralyzed in the center of his lab. There was no possible way he could even begin to explain the crushing weight of that choice, and he hated himself for it. He would always hate his own soul for what he had done to his best friend, even as a dark, terrifying part of his mind knew with absolute certainty that he would make the exact same choice all over again if given the opportunity.

He looked at her, his voice dropping into a desperate whisper. "What exactly do you fear about the concept of death, Anya?"

"Answer my question first, Talus," she demanded softly, though her eyes were filled with a striking vulnerability. "That was our explicit agreement. You have to answer me honestly."

Talus gave a slow, defeated nod, but he found he could no longer look her in the eye. Everything on his cold, metal laboratory table suddenly seemed like a much more sympathetic audience than he imagined she would ever be once he spoke the truth of his selfishness.

"I will answer your question, I promise," he murmured, his voice thick. "But please... just humor me first."

There was a soft rustling of fabric, and Talus couldn't help but look back her way. Anya had crossed her arms and legs, leaning her back heavily against the concrete wall. Her gaze was cast downward, her features drawn into deep, agonizing thought.

"I don't know," she finally whispered into the quiet room. "I guess, the absolute unknown. Everyone is inherently afraid of that, right? People are terrified of being entirely alone in the dark. Of having absolutely no one there to catch them... just like I have no one left out here. But mostly, I think I am terrified of dying before I ever get the chance to actually *live*. To possess people in my life whom I can deeply love, who love me back in return, and whom I can completely trust and count on. Because even the people I think I have... the people I desperately want to believe in... it just never lasts."

Talus let out a ragged breath. "When I was a child, my mother used to tell me that the exact second you died, you were simply gone," Talus whispered, his voice cracking as the raw terror of his youth surfaced. "She insisted there was absolutely nothing waiting on the other side of the veil. That everything you ever were just turns to dust and blows away into the dirt. I never could logically wrap my head around that concept, Anya. Sure, I understood that my physical flesh would eventually wither away and die. But what happens to *me*? What happens to the actual person living inside this skull? To my thoughts, my memories, my dreams... to the 'me'! What the hell happens to me!"

He stepped closer to her, his chest heaving, his eyes burning with an intense, agonizing fright.

"What happens to everything I am? Do I just wander in an endless darkness for eternity? Do I simply cease to exist entirely? What does that concept even mean! It absolutely terrified me as a child, Anya, and it continued to paralyze me with fear as an adult. So the very second I was handed a mathematical opportunity to escape that terrifying fate. I took it. I took it without hesitation, and as a direct result, I eventually ended up losing Lily. I had known that could be a possibility and had accepted it. But losing Cary, that was never something I could have-"

Talus closed his eyes, his voice breaking completely as the memory of the war surfaced.

"He was actively dying right in front of me, Anya. His body was withering away to nothing on a cot, and I realized that I was going to be left entirely alone in this mountain. I was nothing but a clinical science project to the military, an anomaly to be poked, prodded, and dissected on a daily basis. I desperately needed him to stay. He is my best friend. He is my brother. He was the only human being on this miserable planet whom I knew, without a single shadow of a doubt, I could always count on to protect my soul. I wasn't strong enough to just sit there and let him die. I wasn't strong enough to be alone in the dark, to watch his chest stop moving."

He opened his eyes, staring directly into her soul, completely bare and vulnerable. "It was easily one of the most disgustingly selfish things I have ever done in my life, Anya. And even though he stands in this facility and tells me he has fully forgiven me. I can never, ever forgive myself."

Anya stared at him, her breath catching at the raw, shattering honesty of his confession. "Why not?" she asked, her voice barely a whisper.

"Because," Talus choked out, a fierce, dark intensity filling his eyes as he took a final step toward her, his hand reaching out to hover just inches from her face. "Because if I had the chance to do it over, knowing everything I know now. I'd do it again, I'd save him. Knowing everything we'd have to face and knowing exactly how he felt when he realized what I'd done."

She was silent and he knew she would be. He was a monster, even more of one than she saw him as now. Part of him wondered what was worse, the fact that he had created immortality in the first place or the fact that he had been so willing to subject someone he truly cared about to the same fate just so he wouldn't be alone.

"Well with friends like you..." She said softly.

His breath hitched and he closed his eyes as if blocking out the sight of the lab would take him away from her accusing eyes. Would they even be able to work together now?

"I get it though. I do. We've lived different lives, you and I, we have very different views on what immortality means. You risked Cary in more ways than one out of the fear of being alone. I can understand that I guess. But that you'd do it again? Would you do it to me? Why didn't you do it to Lily? If you were so willing to do it to Cary against his will, why not her?"

Her question was valid. A point he had barely considered. It seemed worse to do it against the will of someone who was healthy and alive, but he'd been given another chance. Another moment when he could have, when he knew what her fate would be if he didn't. And yet the desire and desperation to turn her had never arose through him and consumed him in the way that it had for Cary.

"I wasn't faced with watching her die and until we truly understood how to make sure we didn't create another Other, I couldn't do it to her. She left before we figured things out and I never took the time to try and find her. But it doesn't make me less of a monster simply because I was able to spare one person."

"I don't think what you did to Cary makes you a monster. I think it makes you human, you cared so deeply about someone and you made a choice to save them. A monster wouldn't care at all but you care Talus."

He nodded and looked at her. Her eyes were soft and gentle, but that fight and determination was there. It was always there. But this time the red lips were curled into a little smile and instead of looking like she was fighting against something, he couldn't help thinking she was fighting with something. Fighting with him.

"So you're still in?"

"All in. Let's work on this new theory of yours."

23

Anya

"So, zombie or vampire?" Anya asked, a slow smirk spreading across her face.

After several consecutive days of intense interrogation and very little sleep, her ability to formulate deeply profound, intelligent questions was officially waning. Talus, on the other hand, seemed to not require sleep at all—a fact she was finding increasingly unfair.

Talus paused his steps. He blinked at her, his expression entirely blank. "I am afraid I do not understand the question, Anya. What are you referring to?"

"You."

"Me?" Talus' brow furrowed in genuine offense. "I neither compulsively drink human blood nor do I consume raw brain matter. I am also demonstrably not a rotting corpse, and I do not burst into a cloud of dramatic flames when the sun comes out. Therefore, I fail to see how either of those references would suit my current state."

"Yeah, but you *do* actively suck energy from the grid, and you don't age," Anya countered, pointing a finger at him. "So, maybe you're an energy vampire. Still a vamp, you know? Just... less gory, more nerdy."

Talus let out a sharp, sudden sound that vaguely resembled a laugh. It was still a somewhat forced, strangled noise, but she noticed it was happening much more frequently lately. Without realizing it, she was becoming increasingly comfortable in his presence.

"Very well," Talus conceded, a glint of dry amusement in his dark eyes. "I suppose that would make it my turn to query you. If I am an energy vampire, what does that make you?"

"Merely human," Anya shrugged, entirely unbothered. "What else would I be? There is absolutely nothing remarkable about me, unless you count a deeply crappy childhood and years of round-the-clock military training designed to turn me into an emotionless battlebot."

She punctuated the statement by taking another massive bite from the warm, chewy pastry in her hand. She had been told the exact name of the baked good about an hour ago, but the technical term had completely slipped her mind. All she knew was that it was incredibly sweet, filled with a vibrant fruit jam she didn't recognize, and wrapped in a flaky, buttery dough that was entirely new to her palate.

She had already eaten four of them today and was currently standing there, deeply pondering whether she should just turn around to go back for a fifth. They were walking down the corridor back to Talus' lab after yet another abrupt detour to the cafeteria for what Anya called a "little snack." Talus had dryly commented earlier on how modern humans seemed to consume far more caloric mass than he remembered from the old world. Anya hadn't felt the need to correct him, mostly because the fresh food in the mountain facility was seemingly endless, and all the immortals in the base did not seem to eat nearly as much as Kit's mother baked.

"I have known a great many humans in my time, Anya," Talus said, his tone shifting into something quieter, his gaze locking onto hers. "And I can assure you, there is absolutely nothing mere about them. Furthermore, there is nothing ordinary about you. I believe I explicitly communicated that to you when we first met. You are certainly a bit rough around the edges, but there is definitely something intriguing about you. And a little terrifying."

Anya swallowed her pastry and grinned mischievously. "Terrifying? Like how if you end up betraying me, I will personally gut

298

you and tie you up with your own entrails?"

Talus didn't even flinch. "That is not exactly the context I intended when I said the word 'terrifying,' but the point is taken. Although, I am forced to wonder if that specific threat is more or less terrifying since you are fully aware it will not actually kill me. It is undeniably gruesome to consider, but my intestines will simply regrow within a matter of hours. At that point, I am merely tied to a chair with several feet of rapidly rotting meat."

Anya stopped walking, staring at him. "Wow. That does paint quite the vivid picture."

"Perhaps we should conduct some physical experimentation regarding the regenerative timeline of the lower GI tract," Talus suggested, his face entirely deadpan as he gestured toward his own stomach. "How would you like to personally remove a few feet of my intestine for science?"

"I'll pass, thanks," Anya said with a shudder, though a genuine smile broke across her face.

It was bizarre how easy their conversations had become over the past few days. She had somehow gotten completely used to their morbid banter, not to mention Talus' absolute, casual willingness to rip himself to pieces just to check his own cellular math.

As they approached the doors of Talus' beloved laboratory, a faint, rhythmic sound began to echo down the corridor. As they got closer, the sound grew louder, resolving into some incredibly strange, chaotic iteration of music. Or at least, someone in the facility might have technically classified it as music.

It was violently happy, aggressively upbeat, and insanely fast. The lyrics were entirely nonsensical, and the vocals singing them were far too high-pitched, digitized, and grating to even be considered human. It sounded like music specifically synthesized for hyperactive sewer rats to dance to in a strobe light.

Talus froze a foot from the entrance, his mouth slightly agape. He stood completely paralyzed, one hand slowly coming up to rest on his head as he stared into the room. Anya peeked over his broad shoulder, her eyes widening.

The sterile, perfectly organized laboratory was a disaster zone. High-frequency wires were draped like party streamers, and a tiny, automated medical rover was currently spinning in frantic circles on a lab table, timed perfectly to the obnoxious beat.

Talus' stoic composure vanished instantly. He took a deep, outraged breath and screamed into the room.

"Cary!! What have you done to my laboratory?!"

Anya couldn't help but stifle a laugh as her eyes scanned the room. Someone had meticulously taped vibrant, multicolored plastic films over the harsh fluorescent ceiling lights, transforming the usually sterile, blindingly white workspace into a chaotic, pulsing disco. Streams of stark white toilet paper hung like festive vines from every overhead pipe and conduit. Remarkably, her initial assumption regarding the music was entirely correct: dozens of crudely hand-drawn pictures of cartoon rodents executing various theatrical dance moves were taped across every available surface.

He aggressively slapped the intercom button on the wall, his voice shaking with absolute betrayal. "I leave my station for exactly ten minutes, and you execute this? I thought I explicitly changed the encryption passwords on all my secure lab protocols!"

"Correction," Cary's voice suddenly broke cleanly through the frantic music, broadcasting over the laboratory intercom with a distinct, self-satisfied smirk. "Alton changed the encryption locks for you. And as it turns out, he is easily bribed with dark chocolate."

Furious, Talus marched into the room and began aggressively tearing down the hanging strings of paper. He ripped the annoying cartoon rodents off his high-definition monitors, grumbling and muttering colorful curses under his breath as he worked.

At Cary's blatant declaration, Anya's ability to hold in her amusement failed entirely. A loud, bright laugh escaped her, causing Talus to spin around on his heel to face her.

"He was never this unhinged until you arrived," Talus muttered, his dark eyes flashing as he gestured wildly toward the technicolor ceiling with a large handful of crumpled toilet paper. "Ryan must be actively encouraging this juvenile behavior."

"Guilty as charged. Someone had to break up the stuffiness of this place. The creative genius of Cary will be stifled no longer." This time it was Ryan's cheerful voice breaking over the intercom system, followed by the distinct sound of Cary cheering in the background.

Anya shook her head, trying to suppress her grin. "Don't look at me. I had absolutely nothing to do with this." Though her continuous laughter probably made her look entirely guilty.

Talus stopped his aggressive cleaning, his broad shoulders relaxing slightly as he looked at her. A soft, half-smile broke through his stern mask, the kind of expression he only ever seemed to show when they were alone. He walked slowly toward her across the colorful room, his hands completely full of cartoon rodents.

"Are you at least going to assist me with the cleanup?" he asked, standing just a few feet away.

She crossed her arms, teasingly scanning the festive laboratory. "I don't know, Talus. I think I might actually prefer the room this way. It adds character."

He stepped into her immediate space, until they were standing face to face. "You cannot be serious, Anya. The music alone is mathematically configured to drive a person insane."

"Oh if the music choice is a problem I think I know just how to fix that." Ryan's voice boomed over the speakers again.

The high-pitched squeaking abruptly cut out into total silence. A brief, indistinguishable wave of arguing and laughing between Cary and Ryan could be heard muffled near the microphone before a brand-new audio track initialized.

The new music was slow, deep, and remarkably soft. It wasn't familiar to her, but it was infinitely better than the chaos from before. A gentle acoustic melody began to drift through the room, accompanied by a low, rhythmic bass.

"This song goes out to all you lovebirds out there," Cary announced over the comms, dropping his voice into a low, sultry register that sounded completely ridiculous coming from him.

Anya shook her head, a deep blush creeping onto her cheeks. She leaned her back against the edge of a heavy workbench to watch, while Talus turned back around to continue clearing the debris.

"So you really are not going to help me?" he asked, his back still turned to her as he cleared a workstation.

"I told you I like it this way."

"We won't get any work done." Talus reasoned, though his voice lacked any real irritation now. He pulled down a long strand of toilet paper dangling from a secondary light fixture. "I cannot even access half of my diagnostic tools. They are currently trapped behind rats doing the twist."

Anya rocked back and forth to the gentle melody filling the room, watching as the technicolor lights changed to a soft amber glow. "I think the point is that you are supposed to dance."

The music surrounding them was incredibly sweet, a slow ballad designed for bodies to sway to, though the lyrics were unashamedly sappy. Anya had to roll her eyes a few times at how the old-world songwriters went completely over the top with promises of endless, eternal love.

"Dance like this?" Talus asked, turning around to hold up a drawing of a rat bending over and aggressively shaking its tail

"Yes, exactly like that," Anya laughed, the sound warm and easy. "Although it doesn't quite fit for this incredibly cheesy song."

"Cheesy? I will have you know that this song is a classic." Cary's voice broke in over the intercom, sounding deeply offended. "In my era, they played this at weddings. Couples would dance to it in the earnest hope of remaining in love forever."

Talus let out a short breath, stuffing another handful of cartoon paper into a synthetic disposal bag. "I hope you will at least help me dispose of this into Cary and Ryan's beds."

"That much I will help you do." Anya promised, her smile softening as her mind drifted over Cary's words.

Weddings. A love that lasted forever. She wondered quietly about those ancient, forgotten traditions. The mere concept of a dance or a formal ceremony signifying a bond that outlasted time itself felt like ancient mythology. Now human pairings were practical, swift, and dangerous. There was no room for formality, just brief romances and families formed in the shadows of survival, without the luxury of celebration. Who possessed the time for such trivial things when the world was ending? And yet, looking at the soft lights, she felt a profound wave of nostalgia for the idea of a relationship built entirely on raw emotion rather than clinical survival.

"Did it actually work?" she asked quietly, looking up at him. "The song, I mean. Did it make things last forever?"

Talus paused his hands, staring down at a piece of tattered paper. "I would not know. I never got the opportunity to dance to it at my own wedding. But I suppose for some individuals, the sentiment held true. For others, it was simply another fictional story engineered to sell music."

Anya looked at him closely, the space between them suddenly feeling very fragile. "Som you and Lily?"

He stopped cleaning entirely. He let out a long, heavy sigh, his large shoulders dropping as he leaned against the table. "Never quite made it that far."

She gave a slow, understanding nod. "Well then that is something you have on me. I never learned to dance."

Talus turned around completely, discarding the trash bag. A soft, beautiful smile spread across his face, completely erasing his usual brooding expression, and for the first time, the warmth reached the absolute depths of his eyes. "I assure you, Anya, dancing is a much more useful survival skill than fighting."

"How so?" she laughed, leaning back against the bench. There was no logical way that dancing could ever be classified as more useful than combat, especially not in the brutal world they occupied.

"Well," Talus murmured, his voice dropping into a low, resonant register as he began to step slowly toward her. "Dancing brings people together. It creates happiness. It forges a connection between two souls. Physical fighting achieves none of that."

Anya's breath hitched as he stopped just inches away from her. A strange, intense look had taken hold of his eyes.

"Fighting keeps you alive, though," she whispered, her heart starting to beat a frantic rhythm against her ribs.

Talus stood face to face with her. His features shifted through a dozen unreadable expressions, and she desperately wanted to break through his skull just to know the exact thoughts racing through his brilliant mind.

"Yes," he said softly, his blue-gray eyes locked entirely onto hers. "But it does not help you to *live*."

He stared at her for another long, breathless moment, his chest rising and falling. He swallowed hard, as if steeling his courage for a dangerous trial. "Let me show you. Take my hand."

He slowly raised his left hand, holding it open at about the height of her shoulder.

Anya reached out, her fingers trembling slightly as she slid her smaller hand into his broad palm. His skin was warm, his grip steady and reassuring. Talus looked at her a bit awkwardly, a faint flush rising on his neck.

"Now... my other hand," he murmured, his eyes locking onto hers, silently pleading for permission. "My other hand is required to go around your waist."

He hovered his right hand just an inch away from her hip, waiting. Anya felt the heat radiating from his palm through her clothes, and she gave a slow, deliberate nod. She had no idea what was happening here but a part of her realized that this was translating into something far more significant than a simple dance lesson.

His hand finally made contact, sliding smoothly around the curve of her waist. His touch was firm, protective, and filled with an incredible warmth that made her entire body tingle. It felt entirely right. As if his hand belonged there, like she had spent her whole life waiting to be held in that exact space.

Anya swallowed hard, her eyes never breaking contact with his. "And where does my hand go? Here?" She tentatively placed her free hand down near his hip.

"No," Talus whispered, a small, encouraging smile touching his lips. "Up here, on my shoulder."

Slowly, deliberately, she slid her hand up the smooth fabric of his lab coat, letting her palm rest against the solid, muscular breadth of his shoulder. The physical position was agonizingly intimate, structurally designed to force two people to look directly into each other's eyes. It was a fate she found she didn't mind in the slightest. His dark eyes were filled with swirling, beautiful clouds of deep blue and smoky gray. There was an ocean of hidden depth within them, a quiet darkness that she was entirely happy to get lost in, because she knew with absolute certainty that deep within him was a light just waiting to be uncovered.

"Now what do we do?" she asked, entirely unaware that her voice had faded into a breathless, soft huff of air.

"We dance. Follow me. If I retreat you follow, if I advance, you retreat."

He executed a slow, rhythmic step backward with his left foot. Anya moved her right foot forward to follow. Her eyes never left his face as they began to glide slowly up and down the narrow, concrete aisle between his laboratory tables. The soft music washed over them, creating a private world amidst the now flickering amber lights.

Talus shook his head slightly as he looked up at the lights, a small chuckle escaping his lips. "That son of a bitch" he whispered.

Anya laughed softly, the sound radiating warmth against his chest. As she did, Talus smoothly executed a tight turn to navigate around a workbench. She wasn't expecting the sudden shift in momentum; her boot caught slightly, and she was pulled sharply forward, her body flushing directly against him.

Their chests pressed tightly together. The contact was electric. They were so close she could feel the rapid, hot flutter of his breath brushing against her cheek, and the steady, powerful thud of his heart echoing against her own ribs.

Talus stopped moving the exact millisecond her body met his. He didn't step back. He didn't release his grip on her waist. He just stood there in the dim light, holding her tight against him, looking down into her face as if he were seeing her for the absolute first time in his life.

Anya wanted to say something clever. She wanted to formulate some quick, witty remark to shatter the sudden tension that had gripped the small space between them, except it wasn't the hostile, defensive tension she was used to managing. This was infinitely more consuming. An unspoken expectation of something more from a man who occupied her every thought.

She wanted to get even closer to him, close enough that the frantic, shallow breaths escaping her lips would brush against his. She slowly tilted her head back, her gaze dropping to his mouth before rising back to meet his dark, conflicted eyes. Shifting her weight forward, she closed the final remaining distance between them, eliminating the safety of her personal space. She closed her eyes and held her breath, the lights and music of the laboratory fading as she became acutely aware of the warmth radiating from his skin. Every single nerve in her body felt alive, tingling in a sharp, nervous anticipation that made her fingers twitch against her sides.

She pressed her lips softly, desperately against his.

Though her eyes were tightly closed, the vivid imagery of his rare, beautiful smile and his stormy, impossibly deep eyes remained perfectly clear. Her entire body felt remarkably a sudden, desperate rush of adrenaline, but instead of being fueled by the cold terror of combat, this was entirely born of love, excitement, and a desire to be known. Her heart hammered against her ribs, a wild pulse that she was certain he could feel.

It was a singular, suspended moment that felt like it lasted a beautiful eternity, but instead of pulling away, the stillness between them broke.

Talus let out a low, ragged breath against her mouth, a sound of pure surrender that vibrated straight through her. The rigid, clinical restraint he had maintained for a hundred years dissolved in an instant. His hands, typically so precise and calculated, came up to frame her face, his long fingers tangling into her short red hair with a sudden, desperate hunger. He returned the kiss, deepening it with a fierce intensity that caught her completely off guard.

Anya gasped against his lips, a sudden intake of air that he instantly claimed as an invitation, his mouth covering hers fully. The soft, lingering sweetness of their initial contact vanished in a heartbeat, replaced by a consuming, heavy passion that seemed to ignite the very air between them. She wrapped her arms tightly around his neck, pulling her smaller frame flush against his broad chest. The hard, rapid pounding of his heart matched her own frantic rhythm perfectly. The electric sensation in her veins flared into a raging fire, burning away the cold walls of the laboratory, the shadow of the looming war, and the crushing weight of their pasts.

He guided her backward, gently lifting her with one hand so that she was sitting on the edge of the metal workbench, her legs parted around his waist. His other hand slid down from her hair, fingers tracing the burning line of her throat before gripping her waist to pull her even tighter against him. His length pressed against her through their clothes, hard and demanding, an unyielding heat that urged her on. Anya tightened her grip on his shoulders, burying her fingers into his shirt, pulling him closer, desperate to feel more of him, to be as close to him as possible.

"Told you I could get them to kiss!"

"Ryan, you blithering idiot, you pushed the button!"

"What button?"

"The one that activates the intercom!"

"Oh."

Anya felt her cheeks instantly flush white-hot as the sharp, digitized voices of Ryan and Cary echoed with terrifying clarity through the laboratory speakers. The realization hit her like a kick to the stomach: she had completely forgotten they were being watched by their friends.

Her eyes snapped open, her breath catching in her throat. Talus was still towering over her, his dark gaze burning directly into her soul. But the turbulent gray clouds that usually swirled in his eyes had turned into a torrent of lighting. The fleeting, beautiful smile she had managed to coax from him earlier was entirely gone. He abruptly pulled away from her, his chest heaving as his eyes widened in a mix of shock and dawning realization. He ran a trembling hand through his dark hair, stepping back until a cold expanse of air separated them.

She shook her head slightly, a sudden wave of sheer panic

crashing through her chest as the fog of passion evaporated. What had she been thinking? Why had she kissed him? Hadn't he made it abundantly clear over the last few days that he loved another woman? That his heart was permanently taken by a phantom from his past? It was entirely obvious by the tragic, reverent way he still spoke about Lily, by the framed photograph resting prominently on his desk, and by the fact that he had cut his heart off from the rest of civilization for a literal century. She had just thrown herself at a man who was essentially a living monument to a dead woman.

"Talus, have you seen—what in the world happened here? It looks like a colony of sewer rats threw a rave in your laboratory," Elan said, his voice suddenly cutting through the heavy silence as he materialized in the open doorway.

Talus kept his dark eyes anchored firmly on Anya's face. He did not even turn his head to acknowledge Elan's physical presence, standing entirely rigid as he spoke. "Really? I had not noticed."

"How could you not notice? You can't even get into your—oh. You were... never mind." Elan cleared his throat awkwardly, his face turning a shade of pink as he shifted his weight from foot to foot. "I came here looking for you, Anya. There is a representative from Tressle on the comms network requesting your immediate presence."

Anya finally managed to break her intense, suffocating eye contact with Talus. Without saying a single word to him, she spun on her heel and walked away, her boots clicking sharply against the floor as she crossed the threshold to follow Elan down the concrete corridor.

On the inside, she was profoundly grateful for the sudden, bureaucratic escape from the laboratory. This kiss was an anomaly, a horrible lapse in judgment that she never, ever wanted to discuss out loud with anyone. Yet, as she walked, the burning heat in her cheeks refused to fade, and the sheer weight of the lingering emotion made her feel incredibly weak, exposed, and vulnerable.

She absolutely hated it.

24

Talus

They sat together at their usual table outside the coffee shop. Even after all these years, it was still their favorite place to spend the mornings. It was their ritual to drink overpriced, not-so-great coffee and simply watch the world pass by in a blur of motion. One of his hands was wrapped securely around his warm mug, and with the other, he held her hand.

It was so incredibly peaceful. He would never get used to the soft, familiar feel of her skin in his, or the simple comfort of just enjoying the silence together. They did not even need to speak to communicate. To be perfectly content with her, trapped in a loop of a beautiful morning, was all that he could ever hope for.

"Look at that one over there," Lily whispered, pointing a slender finger toward the sidewalk. "She is looking a bit dark. She should really try smiling a bit."

Talus shifted his gaze to where his beloved was pointing. Lily was right. The woman was dressed in tight-fitting, utilitarian dark clothes with an oddly shaped belt secured around her waist. It was almost like a military tactical belt, loaded with numerous round cylinders.

They looked terribly familiar.

It was only when he looked up at her face and locked onto onto those sharp blue eyes and short red hair that a cold spike of adrenaline hit him. He knew exactly who it was. But what was she doing here?

"Anya?" he muttered, his grip tightening on Lily's hand. "What could she possibly be doing here? No one has ever...Lily, this is our space!"

"This is *your* space, darling," Lily said softly, turning her head to look at him. "I am only here because you want me to be."

He frowned over at Lily, a sudden, dark knot forming in his stomach. There were times that she talked so strangely in his dreams. As if there would ever be a time when he would not want her there. She was the only anchor that kept him sane in a broken world. She was the only one he could truly talk to.

"Well, I certainly do not want her here," Talus said, his voice tightening with a sudden, sharp panic. "Come on, how about we go to the park? You are finished with your coffee?"

He felt a wave of relief when she nodded and allowed herself to be pulled up from her metal chair. He wrapped his arm around her waist, and he could not help but smile wildly when she laid her head upon his shoulder. Years of this exact routine, and he still never got used to the perfect feel of her body against him. He wanted nothing more than this, for all of eternity, and he could have it. He could have it if only she—

He forcefully stopped his thoughts. Thoughts like that were dangerous. They were not welcome in their space.

They reached the edge of the park and found their usual spot on the vibrant grass. It was near the edge of the pond, tucked beneath two large, ancient oak trees. The thick leaves shaded them perfectly from the hot sun, and the pond allowed them to watch the sparkling, clear waters, the white lilies, and the little brown ducks that swam in endless circles.

She rested her head upon his chest, her fingers reaching between the buttons of his shirt to touch his bare skin. He shivered a bit at her warm touch. He moved one arm around her shoulders to hold her close, placing his other hand beneath his head as he stared up at the sky. Could anything possibly be more perfect than this?

"Have you thought about our future, Talus?" Lily asked, her voice a soft murmur against his chest. "What is to become of us together? We both seem so busy lately."

She was right, of course. In the real world, he was always down in his dark lab, aggressively trying to solve the mysteries of life, and she was always off trying to save the world in her own way. One person at a time. Not to mention her paintings; she was an amazing artist, and while she did not make much, it was enough to allow her to pursue her true passion of helping others.

"The only thing I know for sure in this world, Lily, is that we will be together," Talus said, his voice thick with a sudden, heavy emotion. "You and I against the world, for all eternity. I suppose one day we will have to slow down a bit and get that nice house. Maybe something on the beach, wouldn't that be nice? We could have a few kids, maybe a dog, and just live our lives out breathing in the salty sea air and playing in the waves. Then, one day, we will watch our grandkids and maybe our great-grandkids play in the same sand and the same water that our children did."

She sighed happily into his chest, her body relaxing completely. "That sounds perfectly lovely, Talus. Great-grandkids, hey? Planning on living for a long time, are you?"

He smiled down into her hair, his chest aching with a sudden, suffocating weight. That was exactly what he was planning. "When I have a life with you to look forward to? I plan on living as long as I can."

He raised his head to kiss the top of her head, closing his eyes to breathe in the familiar, sweet scent of her hair.

"Hey," Lily whispered, her body shifting slightly. "There's that woman again. How do you know her, Talus?"

Talus' eyes snapped open. His jaw locked.

Anya was standing at the edge of the pond, just twenty feet away. How was she here? No one came here. She was part of a harsh, brutal life that he did not want to be a part of, a reality that he did not want to remember.

"She is just a woman I know," Talus said quickly, the words tumbling out in a panicked defense. "She kissed me, but it meant absolutely nothing to me, Lily. There is no one who can ever take your place in my heart. It is for you, and you alone."

He smiled down at her, desperately hoping the words would soothe the growing chill in the air, but his declaration did not have the effect he was expecting. Lily didn't smile.

"If it meant nothing to you, Talus, then why is she here?" Lily asked, her voice losing its warmth, sounding distant and thin. "No one has ever come to our place before. You must find her special, too."

"Lily, I do not really want to talk about her right now," Talus pleaded, his chest heaving as a terrifying dark shadow began to creep over the edges of the park. "Let us just enjoy this beautiful day. You and me. The way it should be."

He tried to settle down with her again. He ran his hand along her shoulder and pulled her tighter against his chest, squeezing his eyes shut. He knew what was happening. He knew what was coming, and no matter how tight he held her, the dark reality was breaking through just the same.

"You should not be afraid of her, Talus," Lily's voice whispered, but it didn't sound like it was coming from his chest anymore. It echoed from everywhere. "She will help you. Let her help you, Talus."

"Lily! No! Not yet!"

But she was already fading. The warmth of her body was evaporating into cold air, her fingers slipping away from his chest. And Anya was still standing there in the silence, staring down at him with those sad, haunted blue eyes.

✳ ✳ ✳

"Talus! Wake up! I would electrocute you right now if I did not desperately need you to move!"

He dragged himself out of the depths of sleep with a low, loud groan. Why did Cary always have to rudely interrupt his sleep? Talus blinked against the dim light, looking around his quarters, and realized with a mild jolt of surprise that he had fallen asleep in his actual bed for once. That was an exceedingly rare occurence. He remembered dragging himself here after taking a freezing shower, desperately trying to wash away the phantom sensation of Anya's skin, right after she had left to receive her message from Tressle.

He must have fallen asleep before she had returned.

"What the hell did you do? I swear you are the biggest damn moron in this entire base, and I'll tell you what—you thoroughly deserve another shot to the neck!"

Talus sat up in his cot, his chest aching with a raw, empty tightness. For a century, every time he had closed his eyes, his mind had automatically conjured the torturous, elusive sensation of Lily in his arms. It had been his lifeline, his self-imposed penance. But as he sat there breathing in the dim light, a terrifying realization struck him with devastating force: over the past few weeks, he had barely given a single thought to Lily. Except in those increasingly rare moments when he allowed his body to collapse into actual sleep, her memory was fading.

Anya had crowded her out. Anya's sharp wit, her fierce, unapologetic life force, and the electric heat of her lips against his in the lab had completely colonized his mind. She was pulling him back into the land of the living, tearing down his comfortable walls of grief, and it absolutely terrified him.

"Talus! Look at me!"

"What is it, Cary?" Talus muttered, his voice thick and gravelly.

By the fierce, wild look on Cary's face, that was entirely the wrong choice of words. How long had he been asleep anyway? He had purposefully stayed in his lab after their disastrous, beautiful moment against the workbench, reasoning that she would want absolute privacy to speak with her Captain via the long-range array. He had crawled into his quarters afterward, seeking asylum from his own racing heart.

"They are currently packing their gear to leave, Talus! Leave!" Cary pointed behind him, in the direction of the hangar bay, his finger trembling for emphasis. The gesture did nothing to distract from the furious shades of crimson coloring his weathered face. "They fly all the way to this valley, and you just can't resist pushing them away!"

The world seemed to stop spinning. Talus' breath trapped in his lungs, a sudden, blinding spike of pure panic hitting his system. "You are mistaken. She would not just leave. She knows that I-that we need her to have any sort of chance in this war."

"Really? She knows that? She damn well knows that?!" Cary roared, stepping directly into his personal space. "When did you explicitly tell her that, Talus? What did you say to her that let her know she is actually important to you?"

"She knows I find her important! She knows she has been a great help in the lab!" Talus shouted back, his heart hammering violently against his ribs.

Cary narrowed his eyes, his voice dropping into a lethal, quiet register. "Did you say anything to her after you kissed her? Anything at all?"

"No."

"You know, I really have to wonder what Lily ever saw in you," Cary muttered, shaking his head. "You get your ass down to that hangar and you make sure her feet stay firmly on the ground. If you do not I will jam a Fulgar rod so hard into your neck you won't be able to pull it out! Then none of us will have to deal with your miserable self anymore!"

Cary's booming voice echoed off the concrete walls of the tiny room. But then, just as it always did, Cary's explosive anger suddenly fizzled down, collapsing under the weight of a century of shared sorrow. When he spoke again, it was softer, almost entirely resigned.

"Your fear and your anger are powerful things, Talus. You must stop letting them control you. You must be willing to let go of her... because this world needs you, Talus. All of you."

Never, Talus thought, a dark, primal desperation clawing at his throat. *This world could fall into the sun before I give her up.* He had been willing to sacrifice the entire human race to secure an eternity with Lily, and Cary knew that all too well. But the terrifying truth he couldn't admit out loud was that the "her" his soul was currently screaming for wasn't Lily anymore. It was Anya.

"Go, Talus."

He let out a ragged sigh and lunged past his old friend, his boots hitting the concrete corridor in a frantic sprint toward the hangar. Yes, he had fully intended to push her away, ignoring what happened between them. Being alone in the dark was so much easier, but as the distance to the hangar closed, his chest tightened so hard he could barely breathe. If he lost her too. If her fierce spirit vanished because of his arrogance, he knew he wouldn't survive it this time. He needed her. Hell help him, he loved the way she dragged him back into the light.

When he burst through the heavy doors of the hangar, his worst fears were realized. They were actively loading up their plane.

The sight hit him with devastating force. He truly hadn't believed she would just pick up and leave him behind. He had genuinely believed she possessed more fight than that, that she understood this was their absolute best chance at engineering a future together. The thought of her flying away, leaving him alone in his prison, sparked a terrifying, frantic desperation in his soul.

"I told you we would see Tigris again," Ryan's tone was light, completely casual as he shoved one tactical bag after another into the cargo hold. "But you didn't believe me. I saw it in your eyes, Anya. You completely expected that we would come back to nothing but ashes if we ever did return."

"Yeah, well, this wasn't exactly the game plan," Anya replied, her back to Talus as she checked the plane's wing flaps. "And it might still be ashes by the time we get there."

Tigris. Talus' mind reeled. That coastal base was a death trap. Why on Earth would they risk going back there? The tightness in his chest bubbled over into sheer panic. He couldn't let her get on that plane. He couldn't let the monsters out there take her from him.

"Anya!" Talus cried out, the sound tearing from his throat, raw and fractured. He stumbled to a halt just a few feet from the aircraft, his chest heaving as if he had run miles instead of corridors. His hands were trembling at his sides, his usual clinical armor completely shattered.

"What are you doing?!" he begged, his dark eyes wide with a frantic, unvarnished panic. Anya turned to him with a look of confusion on her face. "If this is about what happened before... if this is about what happened in the lab, look... I... It's just..."

He stepped closer, closing the distance between them as if he could physically secure her to the hangar floor. He felt the entire room spinning, his mind completely failing him as the chaotic storm in his heart finally breached the surface.

"You are special to me," he choked out, his voice dropping into an agonizingly desperate register. "There is something completely, undeniably extraordinary about you, Anya. I'm sorry I didn't say anything yesterday, I just... this feeling... I haven't felt a single spark of life like this in so long. I've loved before, you know that, but Lily never truly *saw* me. She never accepted all of me, the dark and the monstrous parts, the way you have."

316

He reached out toward her, his fingers twitching in the empty air between them, desperate to touch her but too terrified of what he might find.

"I just... I don't know how to do this anymore," he confessed, a bitter tear finally slipping down his pale cheek. "I don't know if I even *can*. I'm a broken, unraveled mess, and I know I am making absolutely no sense right now... but I think..., Anya, I want to try."

He paused, his jaw working silently as he stared into her piercing blue eyes. The admission left him entirely exposed. He was terrified of hurting her, terrified of failing her, and even more terrified of his own emotions. But beneath all the confusion and the fear, one singular, absolute truth remained: he could not let her fly away, at least not without him beside her.

"Just... please, stay with me, Anya," he whispered, his voice cracking into a ragged, breathless plea.

An absolute, dead silence fell over the hangar bay, the heavy hum of the aircraft's idling engines suddenly feeling miles away. Ryan froze in mid-motion, a heavy tactical bag clutched in his hands and his mouth slightly agape as he stared at the completely unraveled, bleeding heart of the desperate immortal standing before them. The stoic leader of the base had just stripped his soul bare.

Then, Anya, who was leaning her hip against the fuselage of the plane, slowly shifted her weight. She crossed her arms over her chest, but the rigid defiance in her posture was entirely gone, replaced by a smug, delightfully cocky grin that broke beautifully across her features.

"I knew it was a mistake to send Cary to wake you up," she said, her voice rich with a warm, sudden amusement that made her blue eyes dance. "Because he didn't actually bother to give you the real context, did he, Talus? Relax. We aren't abandoning the mountain. We are coming back."

Talus froze, the frantic, ragged breathing in his chest hitching as his brain scrambled to process her words. "What?"

"It will take a few days, but we will be back as soon as we can," Anya explained, her tone softening just a fraction, though her smirk remained firmly intact. "Our Captain went back to Tigris. Tressle said he showed up with the others from the base but then immediately left before they could even mention that Ryan and I had checked in. He must have gone back to look for us. It is entirely my fault that he is out there, and I have to go get him back."

Ryan silently went back to throwing bags into the plane, shaking his head, while Anya just kept giving Talus that beautifully arrogant, knowing look, the exact one that told him he had just made an absolute fool out of himself and she was enjoying it.

Talus stood frozen. He cleared his throat awkwardly, his stoic mask slamming back into place as he glared at the cargo hold.

"Ryan," Talus said calmly, trying desperately to salvage his remaining dignity. "Stop loading the aircraft immediately. Take it all back off."

Anya stood straight up and flashed an angry glare at him. From the rear cargo bay, Ryan moved toward him with an equally defensive expression. That was humans for you, all raw emotion and zero patience. Talus realized he really needed to work on his delivery.

"I am going after my Captain, Talus," Anya stated firmly, her jaw set. "I said I would be back."

Talus shook his head. They stood face-to-face, two unyielding, solemn expressions staring each other down. Talus knew his dark blue eyes were projecting an aura of calculated calm, but her green ones were swirling with a fiery, orange-tinged anger.

"I never said I was going to stop you," he countered quietly. "I was merely going to suggest a vastly superior method of transport. An upgrade, if you will."

He turned on his heel and strode toward a massive section of the hangar that remained shrouded in darkness.

"Upgrade?" Ryan asked, quickly trailing along beside him.

With a definitive push of a button against the concrete wall, a sequence of overhead floodlights hummed to life. The illumination revealed an advanced aircraft. It was structurally similar to the relic they had arrived in, but it possessed several major engineering overhauls. The engines were not only significantly more powerful, but they were also highly energy-efficient. The solar panel tracking systems were optimized to capture maximum solar radiation, and the battery banks were heavily upgraded to store that energy.

The result was simple: the aircraft was fully capable of sustained night flight at a significantly faster speed than the plane they arrived in.

"You want to reach your Captain, Anya? This is the way to do it," Talus said, crossing his arms with a thoroughly satisfied smirk. That would teach her to doubt him. "Your current plane took you two and a half days to get here. This plane will get you there by morning."

The defensive anger vanished from her face. Before he could even register her movement, Anya leapt forward and threw herself into his arms. The sudden momentum shoved him back directly into a startled Ryan as her arms wrapped tightly around his neck.

"Thank you," she whispered against his ear.

The unexpected proximity set his nerves on fire. Catching himself, he gently but firmly pulled her hands from his neck to create space. "Well, I do owe you one. This Captain., he means a great deal to you, then?"

She nodded sharply and immediately raced back to their old plane. Now, she was the one quickly unloading the heavy gear while Ryan stood idly by, watching the exchange.

"So, you've had this plane functional the whole time?" Ryan asked, his eyes narrowing as he stepped up beside the immortal.

Talus nodded once. Beside him, Ryan pursed his lips, nodding slowly in tandem.

"And yet," Ryan muttered, a hint of dry irritation in his voice, "you had us fly all the way here in our old piece of junk and take three whole days. Three days stuck in an enclosed space with her. You could have cut that time drastically."

He turned to Ryan. The thought had occurred to him to send a plane but he knew he had to read carefully over the whole situation. He thought by letting them make their own way there would be less chance of them changing their minds at the finish line. Not to mention he liked the idea of seeing one of the old relics again.

"Would you have gotten on?" Talus countered.

Ryan paused, shrugging. "Fair point."

Talus turned his attention back to the sleek vessel. It had been the absolute best of the best when the first prototypes were built, and it had been painstakingly improved and tinkered with over the decades by Alton and the other engineers. Talus was deeply enamored with the machine, having taken it out on several flights himself. He had been planning to pilot it over the Others' designated territory to gather better intelligence, but he hadn't wanted to risk them detecting the advanced thermal signature.

"Now, take good care of her," Talus murmured.

"I will," Ryan replied, his eyes on Anya as she hauled a crate.

Talus' eyes remained locked on the sleek hull. "I meant the plane, Ryan." He paused, the memory of her warmth against his chest in the lab flashing through his mind. He swallowed hard, adding quietly, "And her."

Ryan's expression shifted, becoming surprisingly grounded. "I know."

"Keep in mind, her flight mechanics are a little different from yours," Talus lectured, stepping toward the cockpit ladder. "She is a lot more touchy on the landing sequencing, and you will need to focus on keeping her stabilization active. She is incredibly fast, but completely unforgiving, especially in high-altitude crosswinds. We are still actively working on optimizing that. It features advanced satellite tracking; we will be actively masking your outgoing signal, but your map display will calculate the absolute best flight path and adjust in mid-air."

Ryan kept nodding as he spoke, but Talus noticed his eyes continuously darting between Anya's frantic loading and the overly complex cockpit interface. It was visually obvious that Ryan was not exactly thrilled about flying an experimental supersonic aircraft halfway across the planet as a maiden test flight.

Talus let out a heavy sigh. That left him with only one logical option.

"Ryan, are you going to stand there, or are you actually going to help me load up the cargo bay?" Anya called out, her voice echoing across the metal rafters. "Come on! The sooner we get in the air, the sooner we reach the Captain. And the sooner you get to try out a whole new aircraft."

She was almost childlike in her fierce eagerness to depart. Talus found himself smiling faintly at the sight of her rushing about, ensuring every single piece of survival gear was cleared from the old vessel.

"You two finish packing," Talus announced. "I will grab a few essential items from my quarters, and we will be on our way."

Anya froze, a heavy crate in her arms. "*We?*"

"Yes, Anya. You did not honestly think I would leave you two alone with a prototype of this caliber, did you? The head engineer would flay me alive if you managed to crash it into a mountainside. If you truly wish to pilot it on your own, I will instruct you on the flight mechanics while we are en route."

"Ryan is an excellent flyer, Talus," Anya defended, tossing the crate into the new hold. "He got us here in one piece."

Talus was highly tempted to agree with her and stay behind, mostly because this was a venture he felt entirely ill-equipped to handle emotionally. From the way Ryan spoke, staying in such incredibly close quarters with Anya for hours was likely to end in total disaster.

"Anya, do you want to get there quickly or not?" Ryan interjected, his voice laced with a tense pragmatism. "Talus actually knows the intricacies of this plane, and it's his tech. I am reasonably sure he can get us to the Captain faster than I could."

Well, that definitely proved his suspicion: Ryan was anxious about the experimental controls. Talus resigned himself to his fate; if he was forcing himself into this mess, at least it would get Cary off his back. He mentally resolved to focus entirely on the mechanics of the flight paths during the trip, hoping it would help him bite his tongue whenever other currently unwelcome and heated thoughts about Anya and her lips came to his mind.

"I already packed your bag," a dry voice rasped from the shadows behind him.

Talus sighed heavily. Cary was either psychic or entirely psychotic; most days, he wasn't sure the answer. His old friend must have calculated this exact outcome the moment he realized Anya wasn't leaving permanently. Cary had likely deduced that accompanying them was the only tangible way Talus would allow Anya to make the trip, and Talus had just proven him correct.

"Packed it with what, exactly?" Talus asked, turning around.

Cary shot him a flat, deadpan look that clearly stated he knew every single item of importance in Talus' life.

"Clean clothes, your primary data recorder, the high-resolution camera, and that portable field scientist kit you keep safely stored in the bottom drawer of the left laboratory table. Really, I am not entirely sure why I even bother, because we both know you probably won't even open the kit. Just make sure you actually eat something, or stick your head out the cockpit window so you do not crash the aircraft this time."

Anya and Ryan, who had been actively securing the final storage straps inside the new bay, stopped completely upon hearing Cary's parting words.

"*What?*" Anya's high-pitched screech echoed violently through the hangar.

Talus closed his eyes, seriously wondering if he could use this sudden breach of trust to gracefully back out of the entire trip.

"Are you telling me," Ryan said, stepping down from the wing with a horrified look, "that we are actively trusting our lives to someone who has already crashed this exact aircraft? Listen, Anya, I think I may just sit this entire mission out on the tarmac."

"Ryan! Don't you dare!" Anya snapped, pointing a grease-stained finger at him. "You are coming with me!"

"He is going to get us killed! He already weakened the structural integrity of the frame once!" Ryan shouted.

Talus turned slowly to face the pair, who were now standing precariously on the maintenance ladder leading up to the cockpit door. "If you have not noticed, the aircraft is currently perfectly intact. It descended rapidly, yes, but I managed to utilize the thermal updrafts to glide it down in mostly one piece."

"*Mostly?!*" Both Ryan and Anya echoed in a unified chorus of disbelief.

"He completely sheared the left wing off. That specific one right there, actually. But the structural welds are all better now. At least,

I am fairly certain someone ran a diagnostic flight since the rebuild. Very few of our people will even volunteer to pilot the thing because it is notoriously difficult to keep stable in the upper atmosphere. It has been taken completely apart and put back together more times than I care to count." Cary explained.

Cary was proving to be absolutely unhelpful at this juncture.

Talus threw his hands up in the air, his calm facade cracking. What was he even doing? If his subconscious goal was to talk them out of utilizing his technology, he was executing the strategy perfectly. The only tangible thing he was going to accomplish would be convincing them to abandon his superior vessel and return to their slow, dangerous relic. If they did that, it would take an entire week before Anya could possibly return..

"Maybe we should just stick to our original flight plan and take our own plane, Anya." Ryan muttered, backing down a rung on the ladder.

And there it was. Talus rolled his eyes toward the ceiling. At the very least, it meant he could return to the quiet safety of his laboratory.

"Not a single chance," Anya snapped, her voice leaving no room for negotiation as she climbed past Ryan. "You can stay here and rot if you want, Ryan, but I am taking *this* plane. Talus, get in the cockpit."

So much for a logical retreat. Now, he was going to be trapped in a pressurized cabin with a male pilot who was going to be visibly terrified for the entire duration of the flight, and a woman who possessed an open disdain for confined spaces and who had managed to send him into a complete panic only moments ago. This was not going to be his definition of a good time.

He made his way over to the base of the ladder where Ryan was still lingering, his boots planted firmly on the concrete as he contemplated mutiny. Anya had already disappeared into the plane, entirely done waiting on anyone else.

As Talus reached the ladder, he placed a firm, steadying hand on Ryan's shoulder.

"Come now, Ryan. Historically speaking, every single individual who has ever crashed this specific aircraft has lived to tell the tale. I give you my word of honor that you will return to this hangar safely."

Ryan let out a long, defeated sigh, his knuckles turning white as he gripped the metal sides of the ladder. "You know, Talus, that statement would be a whole lot more reassuring if I didn't already know that everyone who has flown this thing is an immortal who *can't* physically die. Can you at least promise me no one has lost any vital body parts in the process?"

Talus offered a small shrug. "Not permanently."

"*Not helping, Talus.*" Anya scolded.

Talus found a genuine, unbidden smile tugging at the corners of his lips despite himself. He was, against his better scientific judgment, starting to actually like Ryan. But as he looked up toward the cockpit where Anya had disappeared, any thoughts of casual camaraderie vanished, replaced by a quiet ache in his chest.

He was entirely done trying to analyze his thoughts on her. He didn't just admire her fierce composition anymore, he was completely consumed by it. For years, he had used his grief as a shield, but Anya had utterly shattered it, dragging him kicking and screaming back into the land of the living. The volatile, stubborn parts of her spirit that had once deeply frustrated his senses were the exact things he now realized he didn't want to live without. She was a beautiful, chaotic fire, and for the first time in a hundred years, he didn't want to hide in the dark—he wanted to burn right along with her.

"You should not be afraid of her Talus."

Lily's words from his dream echoed in his mind. He wasn't just afraid, he was terrified, but not of Anya, never Anya. He was terrified that the past would repeat itself and he did not believe he could survive it this time.

25

Anya

Anya smiled as Ryan finally strapped himself into the copilot's seat. She had known there was no way he would stay behind. Even if Cary had guaranteed that the aircraft was going to disintegrate on takeoff, Ryan still would have climbed aboard. He had already risked his life twice for her; there was no doubt he would do it a third time. One day, she would have to find a real way to repay that kind of loyalty.

'So, how exactly do we get out of the mountain?" Ryan asked, his eyes darting across the dizzying array of monitors. "I don't see a clear runway to drive out of, plus this thing won't even hold a proper charge until it's out in the sun."

He was trying to sound like a seasoned tech expert, but Anya rolled her eyes slightly. Given how quickly he had surrendered the controls, she knew he was just masking his anxiety. Talus likely deduced that variable, too, though Anya got the distinct impression that the immortal's mind was occupied by something else entirely.

"Your base scales downward—one big, deep subterranean bunker with multiple structural tiers," Talus explained, his voice smooth and steady as his long fingers flicked a standby toggle. "Our facility utilizes a single-level horizontal expanse, meaning it lacks depth. Which allows me to do this."

Talus signaled to Cary through the glass. The man below gave a mock salute and slammed a master breaker on the wall.

Suddenly, the shadowy hangar was flooded with brilliant, natural light. Far above them, the massive reinforced roof was splitting down the center, sliding back to reveal a pristine patch of blue sky and blinding sunlight. The true scale of the hangar finally became clear. Bathed in the sun, rows of highly advanced vehicles lined the floor—some Anya recognized as pre-war military assets, others from the height of the conflict, and a few that looked entirely alien to her.

The moment the ceiling fully retracted, Talus flipped the primary ignition.

The console flared to life with dozens of brightly lit buttons and dials. This vessel clearly possessed a complexity that made Ryan's plane look like a toy. However, as the anti-grav thrusters engaged and the ship began to lift, it became violently unstable. The airframe rocked sharply from left to right, swaying so dramatically that Anya braced for the sound of a wing shearing off against the hangar walls.

"Talus!" Ryan yelled, his hands white-knuckled as he gripped his armrests. "You literally just promised me you could fly this thing!"

"For some pilots, landing is the difficult part. For me, it is the initial ascent," Talus fired back, his own grip tightening on the yoke as he fought the manual stabilization loops. "Just allow me to get the craft into open airspace."

Anya was deeply grateful for the heavy-duty tactical harness crossing her chest; otherwise, she would have been thrown across the cockpit. The ship rose higher and higher, fighting the turbulent ground eddies until they finally cleared the threshold of the mountain. Peering down through the reinforced deck glass, Anya watched the massive hangar doors slide shut beneath them. Within seconds, the advanced active camouflage on the roof engaged, completely melting the facility back into the rugged mountain terrain.

It was a flawless piece of engineering. Yet, Talus had mentioned earlier that this place was never intended to be a sanctuary from the war. Rather it was meant to hide the weapons of war.

The higher they climbed, the more the violent wobbling subsided. Once the trees and outcroppings below thinned into unrecognizable specks, the flight turned remarkably smooth. A slight rhythmic rocking remained, but it was gentle enough for her to relax her posture.

"Well, that did absolutely nothing for my confidence," Ryan muttered, exhaling a breath he'd been holding since the ground. "Tell me you didn't actually expect Anya or me to pilot this piece of hardware. You can barely keep it straight."

"I was highly optimistic regarding your capabilities," Talus replied dryly, "until I witnessed the sheer panic on your face. Then I realized your flight experience is limited to a glorified, low-altitude glider. Allow me to demonstrate what a true aerospace vessel can do, Ryan."

With a precise flick of three sequential switches, the hum of the engines deepened into a terrifying, throat-rattling roar. A diagnostic screen illuminated the cockpit, showing the main thrusters firing at full capacity and the solar cells rapidly gorging on the clean sunlight.

Anya leaned forward from her seat behind Talus, gripping the headrest of his chair to look over his shoulder. She was struck by the expression on his face as he adjusted the throttles. He looked genuinely happy. The bitter sorrow that usually defined him had entirely vanished. It was a foreign expression on his sharp features, but it made her chest tighten with that same unbidden warmth from the lab.

"Talus! Talus, do you read me? Establishing communication link with SunStar."

Talus flipped a comm switch, and a high-definition video overlay projected directly onto the front wind-screen. Elan's face appeared, adjusting his headset. Anya leaned closer, wondering if Elan's chronic shyness translated to digital screens.

"I have you on visual, Elan," Talus said. "Do you have our telemetry?"

"Yeah, I've got your tracking, Talus," Elan replied, his expression uncharacteristically grim. "I would significantly accelerate your vector if I were you. I haven't picked up a precise coordinate yet, but the long-range arrays are flooded with encrypted chatter from the Others. They are actively hunting for something near your destination."

Anya's brow furrowed. Everything of tactical value at Tigris had been systematically sabotaged or destroyed before they evacuated. If the Others descended on the ruins while the Captain was there, he wouldn't stand a chance against an army of immortals.

Anya interjected, her voice tight over Talus' shoulder.

"No," Elan said, turning his head toward a secondary monitor. "They are tracking a specific asset, but they lack the precise coordinates. They are hitting the abandoned outposts to find something, maybe a data log, a map, or a hard copy manifest that will point them to it? I will patch through any further intercepts, but you need to move, Talus."

Talus nodded firmly to the screen. "Understood. Out."

The projection dissolved, and Talus turned his dark head slightly to look back at Anya. "I believe it is time to retrieve your Captain."

He shoved the twin throttles forward. The *SunStar* didn't just accelerate; it leaped into the stratosphere with a spine-compressing surge. The world outside instantly blurred into long, white speed trails of cloud cover. The ground below stretched out into a seamless, featureless ribbon of blended color, completely stripped of geography.

"What's our updated ETA, Talus?" Anya asked, her stomach still catching up to the speed.

Talus' eyes were locked onto the guidance arrays, his brief moment of joy replaced by absolute, razor-sharp concentration. "That variable depends entirely on how much you trust my calculations, and how much I trust Alton's structural modifications."

Ryan glanced back at Anya, vigorously shaking his head in a silent *absolutely not*. Anya's instincts were screaming the same thing. Whatever extreme performance mode Talus was hinting at was undoubtedly the exact reason this prototype had a history of dropping out of the sky. Yet, as she watched Talus' hand move flawlessly across the dials, adjusting the fuel-to-air ratios and bypassing safety governors, she felt a profound wave of reassurance. She wanted to believe he was remarkable. She had wanted to believe it from the very first moment she heard his voice echo over the radio weeks ago.

He had been a deeply frustrating, arrogant, and closed-off

monument to the past since they met in person. But looking at him now and knowing what he had risked just to stop her from leaving, she realized that maybe all it took for him to be the hero they needed was for her to keep believing in him.

"Well," Anya said, a reckless smile breaking through her fear. "What is the point of being mortal if you don't live a little? Get me to my Captain, Talus."

Talus raised a sharp eyebrow, casting a side-glance at Ryan, whose frantic head-shaking was slowly losing momentum.

"You stated that this ship could reach Tigris by morning," Ryan questioned, his voice straining against the g-force. "Was that estimation calculated with or without utilizing this maximum power threshold?"

Anya dismissed the question entirely. The logistics didn't matter anymore; speed did. If the Captain died because she hesitated or chose the safe route just to avoid a rough ride, she would never forgive herself. What kind of leader or inspiration would she be then? Just a coward who cut contact with her commanding officer, got cold feet, and let him get slaughtered by immortals.

"Flying at our current cruising velocity, we will breach Tigris airspace before dawn," Talus explained, his fingers hovering over a shielded red toggle on the overhead console. "If I force the engines to maximum output, override the solar absorption limits, and completely remove the power consumption governors...we will arrive significantly faster. Or..." He offered a slight, dark shrug.

He didn't know the exact math of what would happen if the engines redlined, but Anya could tell by the desperate, alive look in his eyes that he wanted to find out. He wanted to do it for her.

"I am not letting him die because of my oversight," Anya said fiercely. "If the Others are hunting for an asset, the Captain might be the only one who knows what it is. If we get there first, we can secure him and ensure whatever they're looking for stays buried."

Before the final words could fully leave her mouth, Talus slammed the overhead toggle.

The *SunStar* gave a terrifying, mechanical shriek as the secondary thrusters ignited. Anya's stomach twisted as the extreme velocity pinned her flat against her seat, her vision narrowing at the edges as the jet tore through the atmosphere like a bullet.

"Elan!" Talus roared over the deafening scream of the engines, his hands perfectly steady on the yoke. "If you intercept so much as a whisper from the Tigris sector, patch it directly into my cockpit!"

"Got it," Elan's voice crackled through the static over the intercom. "Alton is in the comms booth now and wants to know how she's flying. He also wanted me to relay that if you do not bring it back in one piece, he is going to make you fix it this time."

Ryan's eyes darted nervously toward the cockpit ceiling. "Just how often has this exact aircraft crashed? It's starting to sound like a known death trap, yet no one on your base seems particularly bothered by that metric."

Anya leaned back against her seat, a dry humor settling over her. She knew exactly why the base technicians treated a catastrophic crash like a running joke. For people who couldn't die, an experimental atmospheric vessel pancaking into a ridge was just an inconvenient afternoon of manual labor. They had nothing to fear from the sky.

"There are always test flights and minor variables when engineering something truly original," Talus replied calmly. His long hands remained loose, though precise, on the heavy controls. "It has admittedly become the butt of several uninspired jokes on base, but I give you my word: I will get you to Tigris and back safely."

It was infuriatingly easy for him to project that level of absolute, unbothered confidence. Ryan, however, looked like he was about to lose his lunch. The world beyond the reinforced canopy had dissolved into a blurred streak of brilliant white clouds and deep atmospheric blue. Talus was aggressively working the yoke, throwing the heavy ship into sharp, banking turns. To Anya, it seemed entirely unnecessary; it wasn't like they were going to collide with a mountain range at this altitude.

"The jet stream winds are exceptionally volatile at this tier," Talus explained, sensing their unspoken tension. "Because we utilize an expanded wing surface to accommodate the high-yield solar arrays, the airframe acts like a massive sail. At this velocity, manually maintaining a true heading is demanding."

"Why on earth don't you just let the onboard flight computer handle everything?" Anya asked. She was constantly baffled by the contradictions of these immortals. On one hand, they possessed localized technology that bordered on science fiction; on the other, they lacked basic short-range communication and chose to fly supersonic prototypes by hand.

Talus offered a faint, remarkably handsome tilt of his jaw. "Oh, the automated systems are perfectly functional. It is simply more entertaining to execute the corrections myself."

"Talus!" Ryan's shout came out as a strangled, terrified gasp.

Anya couldn't help but let out a genuine giggle, the sound echoing through the cockpit. The absolute contrast between Ryan's panic and Talus' dry, eccentric arrogance was deeply amusing. Despite the immortal's initial coldness, his secretive nature, and the walls he built around his past, Anya realized with a quiet jolt that she trusted him explicitly. She trusted the steady weight of his hands on the controls, and she trusted the fiercely protective instinct he had shown in the hangar.

Talus shifted his gaze from Ryan's pale face to Anya's smiling reflection in the glass, his dark eyebrows lifting slightly. The subtle, intense connection they shared flashed between them again. Then, he turned back to the console and pushed a flush toggle on the main array.

Instantly, the rattling ceased. The *SunStar* smoothed out seamlessly as the flight computer began processing the wind data, making micro-adjustments to the flaps. Talus relaxed his posture, keeping his eyes anchored on the digital GPS maps and diagnostic dials.

With the sudden tranquility of the ride, Anya watched Ryan's shoulders drop as he sank back into his seat. Her own internal jitters began to settle, the raw adrenaline of their departure fading into a quiet curiosity.

'So what is it actually like?" Ryan asked suddenly.

Talus was deep in his own thoughts, his attention consumed by the navigation monitors. Anya got the distinct impression that he lived mostly behind his own eyes, using the instruments as a convenient shield to avoid human interaction. He was a constant riddle to her; she spent hours studying his small mannerisms, trying to decode the ancient mind beneath the clinical exterior. It was as if they were only ever permitted to see fleeting glimpses of the man who wanted to be human, before the dark, isolated version of him pulled the curtain back down.

"Talus?" Anya prodded gently, leaning forward.

"Hm?" He didn't turn his head.

"What is it like?" Ryan repeated, louder this time, his voice cutting through the dull roar of the engines.

"Flying?" Talus asked monotonously.

"No. Being able to exist forever," Ryan said, his tone turning surprisingly philosophical. "Being able to do whatever you want, whenever you want, without a single care. Cary and the rest of the team seem to make the absolute best of it—they explore, they travel, they lose themselves in their research. But according to all of them, you just sit holed up in your laboratory like some sort of modern-day Tantalus. Always reaching for something just out of your grasp, never succeeding, but never giving up. You have the freedom to just walk away from the world. So, what is immortality actually like for you?"

Anya's eyes widened slightly at Ryan's bluntness. She realized then that while she had spent the last few weeks permanently attached to Talus' side in the lab, Ryan had been observing the broader community, gathering data from Cary and the other survivors. Yet, Ryan had just perfectly articulated the exact fascination that had been consuming her. Talus was a prisoner of his own eternity.

Talus' hands stopped adjusting the switches. He went entirely still, his gaze fixed out on the endless, open sky stretching before the nose of the plane. When he finally spoke, his voice was soft, devoid of any scientific coldness.

"It is everything I thought it would be and absolutely nothing I had hoped it would be."

Anya felt a chill go down her spine. The answer was a heavy, tragic confession wrapped in a single sentence.

"So is everything the same? Emotions, senses? Do you have any heightened abilities? Some of the others at the base seem to think there are differences, and they mentioned the obvious differences that occurred with The Others."

Anya suppressed a slight smile; Ryan was treating the immortal like a specimen from a pre-war comic book. Still, she shared his underlying curiosity. There were no intact historical databases detailing how the original immortality serum had been synthesized. The common rumor was that it had been a highly classified military project until civilian hacktivists leaked the data right before the war started. Anya hadn't put much faith in it, but it was starting to fit what she knew now and Talus and Cary would have been at the base when it happened.

Talus stated, his voice returning to a smooth, flat monotone. "You simply learn to forcefully manage or entirely suppress them as the decades accumulate. Senses are marginally sharper, and they appear to naturally optimize over long periods of time, based on our internal data. Aside from cellular regeneration and the cessation of biological aging, there is nothing extraordinary about our composition. We are merely ordinary people who discovered a method to cheat death while desperately trying to retain our humanity."

Talus' voice was monotone as he spoke. She knew why he decided to make the choice to become immortal, but she wondered about all the others. Fear could be the only motivation that she could see, and yet to escape death they all risked eternal Hell. The Others were not only the stuff of nightmares for the people they hunted down but they had to be the stuff of nightmares for the people who lived it as well. At one time they were all people just like her and Ryan, with families and jobs, just trying to live their lives and then they turned into that.

"Do you ever worry?" Anya asked, the question slipping from her lips before she could stop it. It was a fear that had been plaguing her since she first stepped foot into the hidden valley. "Do you ever worry that one day you will become just like the Others?"

Ryan turned his head back to look at her, the gravity of the question hanging heavily in the pressurized cabin. If these entities lived forever, and their humanity was a choice, what happened when they simply grew tired of choosing it?

Talus didn't answer immediately. He slowly turned his head, his dark blue eyes locking directly onto Anya's green ones. The raw vulnerability in his expression was staggering, stripping away a century of pride.

When he spoke, it was in a hushed, desperate whisper that chilled her to the bone, revealing that he carried the exact same terrifying nightmare in his chest every single day.

"Yes," Talus murmured, his dark blue eyes locking onto hers through the glass reflection with an intense, unyielding certainty. "But I had her, I have Cary... and now, I have you."

The confession hung suspended in the quiet cockpit, heavier than the g-force pinning them to their seats. Anya's breath caught sharply in her throat as a small, involuntary gasp escaped her lips. The words weren't analytical or clinical; they were raw and deeply protective. He had just placed her alongside the two most defining anchors of his entire life—the woman he had lost, and the best friend who kept him sane.

Beside him, Ryan turned his head back to look at Anya, his eyes wide with surprise. Anya felt a sudden, fierce heat rush to her cheeks, her mind racing as she stared at the back of Talus' head, utterly stunned by the depth of what he had just admitted.

"You may want to eat or sleep, since who knows what we will find when we reach Tigris," Talus said flatly, his voice instantly retreating into a shield of cool, professional detachment. "We may not get another chance for a while, and you will both need to be at your peak physical performance."

And there it was. The rigid, stoic mask had slammed back into place. The clear signal that any further discussion on the matter was strictly over. At least for now.

26
Talus

Talus had never once let the onboard computer fly this aircraft before. In truth, his stubborn refusal to relinquish control was the exact reason he had such a notorious track record with it. He knew Alton was thoroughly displeased with that fact, but to Talus, allowing an automated sequence to do the work was an absolute waste. Flying high above the clouds, aggressively whipping through the crosswinds, was one of the few visceral experiences that helped him feel genuinely alive anymore.

Yet, as his gaze flicked to the reflection of the two humans behind him, he knew the thrill was not worth risking their lives. It was incredibly boring with the computer handling the controls, but he kept his eyes glued on the gauges and the open sky ahead. They were making phenomenal time. The *SunStar* had been nothing more than a theoretical fantasy when the war began, and now he was piloting it faster than the historic Concorde without burning a single gallon of fuel.

He was also glad the conversation had stopped. He rarely talked of Lily with Cary and Cary had known her. Hard to believe that it was still too hard after over a century without her.

His knuckles tightened slightly on the arms of his chair. The question about the Others had bypassed his carefully constructed defenses, forcing an admission out of him that he was already desperately trying to claw back. He didn't want to need her. He was an immortal who had built an empire of isolation, yet the mere presence of Anya was actively threatening to dismantle it all. He was fighting the foreign warmth in his chest with everything he had, trying to force his mind back into cold, sterile science.

Beside him, Ryan began to snore softly, his head lalling to the side. A moment later, a bizarre, grinding racket shattered the quiet of the cabin.

Anya had begun loudly chewing something.

Talus winced. What on earth had they packed that made a sound reminiscent of razor blades trapped in a blender? He glanced back over his shoulder to investigate the source of the sound, only to discover she was simply making her way through a container of carrots. *Carrots?* He had to watch her for several seconds to truly believe someone was capable of producing that much noise with a root vegetable. But she was.

"What?" Anya asked around a mouthful of food. As she spoke, Talus was treated to a vivid visual of obliterated carrot shards migrating toward the back of her throat.

There went any desire he had to consume sustenance for the next fifteen years.

"I had determined that the tail section of the aircraft was being torn to shreds by atmospheric friction," Talus stated, his voice laced with a sharp, defensive edge to mask his internal turmoil. "But now I see it is merely your chewing. I found it improbable at first, but I can still see the evidence in your gaping mouth. Do you mind?"

Anya closed her mouth and swallowed. Exceptionally loudly. She didn't look offended by his hostility; instead, a soft, perceptive glimmer lit up her green eyes. She could see right through his sudden prickliness.

"Want some?" She asked holding out her partially gnawed carrot stick.

Talus stared at it, utterly horrified. No matter how many centuries he existed, he would strictly maintain a baseline standard of decency—namely, not consuming food that had already been slobbered upon by another.

Anya chuckled softly at his disgusted expression. Instead of tossing it in the bin, she carefully set the container aside, her smile softening into something entirely genuine, completely unbothered by his sharp edges. It was a quiet shift, but the way she looked at him held an openness she didn't bother to hide. She didn't push him about his confession; she just let him be.

It was a pity he refused the food, because his cells truly did require sustenance. If he didn't eat soon, his cells would begin siphoning electrical energy directly from the plane's backup grids, which would be highly detrimental to their flight. He could draw energy from the sun but that would only work as long as it was high in the sky.

He leaned back in his pilot's chair, staring out at the endless horizon of white vapor. With the automated systems in control, there was nothing left for him to do, and the boredom was excruciating. He detested sitting still; even when his body was paralyzed in a dream state, his mind was always moving, calculating, searching. The whole wide world stretched out before him, and he was stuck letting a machine tow him in a straight line.

"You look much happier when you are actually flying," Anya murmured, her voice close behind his ear. "Do you take it out often?"

"No," Talus replied flatly, still actively trying to purge the graphic image of the chewed carrot from his memory. Her proximity was not helping, nor was the faint, sweet scent of her breath drifting past his shoulder. It was making his chest ache with that same dangerous, unbidden warmth.

"Why not?" she asked softly.

Talus kept his eyes strictly on the blue sky. He had no intention of giving her the real answer to that question. It would only open a floodgate of reasons he wasn't prepared to analyze. He didn't fly because he didn't believe he deserved the luxury of flight. It was too much joy, too much unadulterated freedom for a man carrying his failures. His existence belonged to the laboratory. He had far too much to atone for to spend his eternity idly playing in the clouds.

"I am far too busy for such trivialities," Talus said, his tone dropping into a rigid, defensive monotone as he fought to suppress the urge to turn and look at her. "I still require answers. There are far too many questions regarding our biology, the regression of the Others and then, there is you. I am currently spending my days trying to ensure the survival of humanity."

Anya didn't retreat. Instead, she reached forward and gently placed a hand on his shoulder, the warmth of her palm bleeding through the cold material.

"You don't always have to be the savior of the world, Talus," she whispered, her voice laced with an affectionate, fierce protectiveness that caught him entirely off guard. "Sometimes, you're allowed to just enjoy the sky."

Talus went completely rigid under her touch, his heart hammering violently against his ribs as he fiercely fought the desperate urge to lean into her hand.

"Do you want something to eat?" Anya asked. "Cary said you should eat, and since I really do not want this plane falling out of the sky, I must insist."

Normally, Talus found eating to be an absolute waste of time. Over the decades, everything had begun to taste the same to him. At first, he had questioned whether his regenerated taste buds were simply dulled by the years, but after watching the others on base consume meals with reckless abandon, he realized he was entirely alone. His lack of appetite was a solitary, numbing affliction.

He didn't turn around, but his voice softened. "Just... anything but carrots."

"You don't like carrots?"

"Not anymore."

There was a frantic rustling behind him, though it was hard to distinguish what she was doing over the rhythmic, engine-rattling snores echoing from Ryan. Talus genuinely couldn't decide which of the two was the worse cabinmate. Ryan snored louder than a jet pulsar, and Anya seemed to be going completely stir-crazy after just a few hours.

Then, a slender, pale arm appeared to his right. Anya leaned in close over his shoulder, holding out a containment bowl filled with fresh strawberries, blueberries, and a thick slice of cake. Talus froze, his senses instantly overwhelmed by the clean, sweet scent of the fruit mixed with the intoxicating closeness of her skin. Up close, he could see the faint, golden flecks in her eyes.

"Thank you," he murmured, his throat suddenly dry. Desperate to create a microscopic bit of distance between them before his chest caved in, he added, "Would you like to fly while I partake?"

Anya let out a soft, breathy laugh, her shoulder brushing against his arm as she leaned against the console. "While you *partake*? Did people really talk like that before the war?"

"No," he said, his lips twitching slightly as he took the bowl from her. "Just me."

His mother had always had a very refined vocabulary and Talus found it still to be a habit. For an immortal, old habits died hard. He lamented the distinct lack of utensils; he was going to have blue and red juice staining his fingers by the time they reached Tigris.

"Now," he repeated, his eyes locking onto hers, the proximity making his pulse thrum. "Do you want to fly?"

"That is what the computer is for," she countered playfully, though she didn't step back.

Talus nodded, forcing his gaze back to the horizon. Yes, the autopilot would ensure they stayed aloft, but he didn't trust it entirely. He felt an intense, irrational itch to disengage the autopilot and seize the yoke, if only to channel the chaotic, terrifying energy Anya was stirring up inside him into something he could control.

"Let me join you," Talus said, unbuckling his shoulder harness and sliding out of the pilot's chair. "I have flown this region before, there is little to see." In truth, Talus much preferred the view inside the cockpit.

He moved to the secondary row of seats in the narrow cockpit where Anya sat. The quarters were exceptionally cramped; as he sank into the cushion beside her, his thigh pressed firmly against hers, the heat of her body instantly bleeding through the fabric of his pants. Talus stilled as his pulse took a sudden, erratic leap. He deliberately focused on the bowl in her lap, selecting a handful of fresh fruit.

The sharp burst of flavor on his tongue caught him completely off guard. "I had entirely forgotten how sweet berries are," he murmured. His voice had dropped into a low, velvety register, and his eyes never left hers. The physical proximity was overwhelming; with every breath she took, her shoulder brushed against his arm, sending a quiet tremor straight down his spine.

Anya's gaze darted to the front of the cabin.. "Are you sure we're okay with no one flying the plane?"

He offered a rare, remarkably handsome half-smile, his eyes locking onto hers with an intensity that made her chest tighten. "Anya, the computer is flying the plane. If you reach over and flip that autopilot switch to the left, *then* we have permission to panic."

His stomach protested the food slightly, a stark reminder of his own negligence. He wondered when the last time was that he had actually consumed more than a mouthful or two of anything. It was dangerously easy to forget basic biological requirements when time stretched out infinitely and your cells required no regular schedule of meals or sleep to survive.

Anya shifted slightly in her seat, turning her body toward him. Her eyes softened, filled with a deep, aching curiosity. "Why do you spend so much of your life in hiding, Talus? You live forever. You cannot physically die, and yet you stay locked away in your little laboratory box. Why don't you fly around the world if you love the open sky so much? You can work from anywhere and perhaps you'd learn something on the journey, meeting other people who could help."

Always with the questions. Her fierce, relentless curiosity refused to be satiated for even a moment. Talus found it increasingly exhausting to balance what information to give her and what dark secrets to protect. More than that, her presence was forcing him into a level of raw introspection he hadn't allowed himself in over a century.

"You saw what humans can do if they possess the tactical capability to trap an immortal," Talus said, his tone dropping into a solemn, guarded register. He leaned a fraction closer, his breath brushing the stray hairs near her temple. "We stay hidden until we know we can stop them because we have to stop them. If the Others manage to take control of our base, there will never be any way to stop them." It was true enough, but it wasn't the real reason. He didn't deserve the happiness that flying brought him.

Anya went quiet, the grim reality of his words settling over her.

"Did they ever teach you what truly occurred that day?" Talus asked softly, his fingers tightly interlaced between his knees. "The day the old world officially ended? Do humans even retain that knowledge anymore?"

"I read the surviving histories we have left," Anya answered, her voice dropping to a whisper as she stared at his sharp profile, completely captivated by him. "The immortals just appeared one day, fighting in standard battles. It quickly became apparent what they were. There were so many of them that the conflict escalated exponentially. Weapons that nations didn't even know existed were deployed. Tactics like detonating nuclear reactors or fuel refineries... anything to stop the regeneration. But the immortals just kept coming. By then, the civilian population was already underground, and information was scarce. Then, it just stopped. The records assume there was simply nothing left on the surface to destroy."

There was a massive, catastrophic piece of that story missing. His small group of scientists hadn't stood idly by during the final days; they had been called upon by world leaders to engineer a final solution. And how they had tried. They had come so close. Until the rules of the game changed and it was gone. Flashes of agonizing memories flooded his mind—panicked, screaming conversations in blood-splattered labs, watching glorious cities crumble into barren wastelands, feeling the global temperature plunge into a nuclear winter.

The memories were so vivid it physically choked him. Pressing his hands hard into his knees, Talus forced himself to sit up straight, desperate to shatter the painful memories. He looked at Anya, whose wide eyes were swirling with an intense, fierce empathy that made his heart ache violently.

"So," he said, his voice straining for a lighter tone as he looked down at her lips. "How about we teach you how to fly?"

Changing the conversation was what he did best. It would be highly useful if more than one person comprehended the flight controls. If something happened to him or the autopilot, Anya and Ryan would still have a chance of survival. But deep down, beneath his calculations, he simply wanted to share this joy with her. He wanted her to feel the freedom he felt.

"Me?" Anya blinked, startled by the sudden shift. "Ryan is the one you should instruct. He has at least piloted a plane before."

Talus tilted his chin toward the copilot seat. "That is accurate. But he is completely unconscious. And you are not. If you have no intention of resting, perhaps we should utilize the time wisely." He reached forward, gently patting the headrest of the empty pilot's seat in front of them.

"You mean you are just going to explain what the console buttons do, correct?" she asked, a nervous, beautiful smile tugging at her lips. "You aren't planning on turning the automated system off, are you?"

She stood up, keeping her head slightly bent beneath the low cockpit ceiling. As she brushed past him in the narrow aisle, her hip dragged slowly across his chest. The friction was dizzying. Talus looked up, his face mere inches from hers in the cramped quarters, the sweet scent of her skin completely invading his senses.

A half-smile broke through his rigid expression. "Well, not until you sit down, anyway."

Anya gasped softly, her eyes wide with a mixture of shock and exhilaration as she dropped into the pilot's chair. She threw her hands out toward his, instinctively trying to block him from reaching the console. "Don't you dare touch that autopilot button!"

Talus let out a low, incredibly rich chuckle that sent a shiver straight down her spine. He stepped up right behind her chair, leaning over her shoulder so closely that his chest was pressed against her back. He reached around her, his long arms flanking her sides as he pointed a finger toward the primary yoke.

"Come now, grab hold. Keep your grip loose, and I will guide you through the manual controls."

"Considering your track record with this plane," Anya quipped, "that is not remarkably reassuring."

"I will not allow you to crash, Anya. I promise you that," Talus whispered, his voice suddenly thick with an intense, fierce devotion. He leaned closer, his jaw brushing against the soft skin of her neck as he reached around her to point at a glowing red switch. "If anything goes wrong, simply flip this switch, and the autopilot will retake control."

Anya's fingers hovered over the switch, trembling slightly before she gripped the primary yoke. "If it is truly that simple, why have you crashed this prototype multiple times?"

Talus went quiet for a beat, his gaze softening as he looked down at her profile. "Because not every crash was an accident."

Anya's head snapped up to look at him. Flying wasn't always pure joy for him; there were dark, painful flights where the open sky did nothing but remind him of everyone he had failed. In those moments, he had occasionally craved the temporary nothingness that came with physical trauma. He would deliberately force a crash, knowing his immortality would piece his body back together, just to experience a single, fleeting second where the memories finally stopped.

Looking into her vibrant eyes now, however, Talus realized with a terrifying jolt that he didn't want the nothingness anymore. For the first time in countless years, he wanted to stay entirely present. He wanted to live, not just avoid death.

"Now, hold tight," Talus murmured, his hand gently sliding

over hers on the yoke to steady her trembling fingers. The sparks of electricity from their skin contact felt like lightning in the small cockpit. "You need to feel the wind. When I disengage the computer, I want you to simply feel the atmospheric resistance for one minute. Then, execute a counter-turn opposite the draft. Keep the craft straight. The ambient readings are perfectly calm right now, so despite our velocity, you will have no difficulty maintaining a true heading."

He was over-explaining, flooding her with technical data because he knew information was the ultimate shield against panic. He could feel her white-knuckled grip beneath his palm. She was terrified, but he knew the strength of her spirit.

"Are you ready?" he asked softly, his face inches from her ear.

Anya swallowed hard, staring at the blurred sky ahead, and shook her head.

"I am turning off the computer now," Talus whispered, his hand sliding off hers to grip the master toggle. "You are going to fly all on your own. If something happens to me down the line, someone needs to know how to command this plane."

"Good thing it's impossible for anything to happen to you, then," she retorted, though her voice was shaky as she tried to regulate her breathing. She was fighting her fear, bracing her shoulders, refusing to back down.

A profound wave of pride washed over Talus. He looked into her eyes, nodding once. She caught his gaze, her expression turning fierce as she nodded back.

He flipped the switch.

The *SunStar* instantly wobbled, tilting sharply to the right as the raw jet-stream winds slammed into the massive wings. Anya's elbows immediately locked, her shoulders tensing violently as the manual feedback rattled the yoke.

"Compensate for the draft," Talus instructed, his voice dropping into a perfectly calm, hypnotic rhythm right beside her ear. "Do not fight it with force; simply feel the resistance and glide into it. Think of it like guiding a leaf through a rushing stream. Keep the leaf moving precisely where you dictate."

His soothing, steady tone acted like a lifeline for her scattered nerves. Slowly, Anya began to ease her rigid grip. The aircraft began to settle as she mirrored the wind's movements. Bit by bit, her elbows bent, her shoulders dropped, and the sheer panic in her eyes softened into pure, exhilarating wonder. She was still breathing heavily, her rapid, shallow breaths echoing softly through the cockpit.

"Are you alright, Anya?" Talus asked, his voice incredibly gentle.

She nodded slowly, a breathless, radiant smile breaking across her face. "Yeah... I think so. You are not going to force me to execute a landing, are you?"

"Well, considering my track record..." Talus trailed off, purposely looking out the side window so she wouldn't see the massive, unbidden smile stretching across his own face.

"Talus..." she warned, cutting a sharp glare back at him, her eyes wide.

"The automated systems can execute the landing entirely on their own," he reassured her, his voice warm with an affection he could no longer fully suppress. "We can reserve that particular lesson for another day. Just relax. You are flying."

He leaned back against the bulkhead directly behind her, letting her immerse herself in the experience. Watching her navigate the clouds, he felt a strange, beautiful shift in his eternal existence. Usually, the sky was his lonely escape from the world. Prior to the war, humanity had been on the precipice of traveling among the stars—planning colonial missions to distant planets, sending advanced probes to foreign solar systems. The conflict had ripped all of that away, trapping them back in the dirt. But looking at Anya now, her face illuminated by the bright solar glare of the console, he realized he didn't care about the stars anymore. The center of his universe was right here in this cockpit.

They flew in a charged, intimate silence for nearly an hour. Ryan's snores continued to rumble from the copilot seat, completely oblivious to the quiet revolution happening beside him. Talus briefly contemplated if he could plug Ryan's nose to stop the noise, but he knew the open mouth was the primary source of the noise. Since he had been the one to command Ryan to rest, he could only blame himself. He forced his thoughts to remain focused entirely on Anya, monitoring her movements just in case the plane encountered unexpected turbulence. He wasn't quite ready to leave her in absolute, unassisted control of Alton's beloved prototype.

"How much longer until we reach the Tigris sector?" Anya asked, her knuckles still a bit white, though she was managing the micro-corrections with much better efficiency.

Talus glanced up at the main telemetry array over her shoulder. "An hour at most. With the jet stream backing our vector, we are maintaining absolute maximum velocity. You are currently flying at nearly one thousand miles per hour."

Anya's head snapped back, her eyes wide with disbelief. "That's impossible! This plane is running entirely on solar power. How can a battery bank push a plane that fast?"

"If you consider that our engineers have been developing high-yield solar atmospheric vessels for nearly two centuries," Talus explained, leaning in closer again, "and that over two hundred years ago, baseline humans built combustion aircraft that could cross the sound barrier, it is mathematically very plausible. Imagine what our species could have accomplished by this era if the war had never occurred."

Again, his thoughts drifted to the painful idea of deep space. They could have been exploring foreign galaxies by now, perhaps even establishing a colony on an agrarian planet. He had heard whispers of such blueprints before the collapse, and yet it was all turned to dust.

"If there had never been an immortal race, humanity would still be thriving," Anya said, her tone dipping into a sudden bitterness. "Whoever created that original serum is responsible for all this destruction."

Talus swallowed hard, a cold knot tightening in his chest. Why did conversations with her always spiral back to the one topic he spent his entire life trying to run from? He was constantly losing his footing around her, his defenses crumbling until he was backed right into the corner of his own identity.

"Someone who possessed a desperate, misguided belief that humanity could progress further if our most brilliant minds weren't constantly struck down by age and disease," Talus said, his voice dropping into a strained whisper. "Someone who wanted us to touch the heavens and survive the journey to the deep cosmos without aging a single day. Without the foresight of what would occur, many truly believed immortality was a gift, Anya."

Anya turned her head, her green eyes piercing directly into his soul. The sheer gravity of his tone sparked a sudden, shattering realization in her mind. "You speak as if you know him. As if you know the exact person who started it all. Have you met him, Talus?"

Talus' heart hammered violently against his ribs. He looked at her beautiful, expectant face, the urge to confess everything fighting savagely against his conviction that she would absolutely hate him for it.

"Yes," Talus whispered, his gaze locking onto hers with terrifying intensity. "And I hope that when you finally meet him, you will possess a greater understanding of how none of this was his intention."

Anya nodded. "The road to Hell is paved with the best of intentions."

Talus nodded slowly, his voice completely raw. "That it is."

The heavy, suffocating weight of his past seemed to lift slightly, replaced by a sudden, profound quiet. The silence returned, but it wasn't the cold, empty distance from before. It was deeply peaceful, and yet an unspoken, electric tension hovered between them.

"I can see why you love flying," she said softly, her eyes tracing the vast expanse ahead. "This really is incredible."

Talus nodded, though he knew she couldn't see him from her position at the yoke. The sun was slowly beginning its descent, painting the endless sky in brilliant, bleeding hues of deep pink, violet, and molten orange. Talus couldn't help but stare as the vibrant colors caught Anya's profile, lighting up her face in pure, unadulterated wonder. The way she saw the world, the raw capacity she had to appreciate a single fleeting moment despite the ruin below, was completely contagious. For the first time in over a century, he saw the sunset differently. It wasn't just a marker of passing time anymore. It was beautiful, radiating a hope that defied the dead world outside just as she did.

The sheer, overwhelming pull toward her snapped the final threads of his restraint. Without taking a single moment to think, he reached over her shoulder, his arm brushing firmly against her skin as he engaged the autopilot, locking the cockpit controls into a steady, automated cruise.

Before she could even gasp, Talus gripped her waist and pulled her cleanly out of the pilot's seat.

Anya spun around, her hands instinctively catching his broad shoulders for balance as he drew her flush into his embrace. The sudden impact of her body against his sent a violent jolt of adrenaline through his veins. He wrapped his powerful arms tightly around her, wanting nothing more than to simply hold her, to shield her, and to watch the horizon bleed into twilight together. He desperately needed to relish the impossible warmth and comfort she brought to his cold, infinite existence. Guiding her gently backward, he pulled her into the row of seats behind the main console, fully intending to do nothing more than quietly enjoy the fading sunset in her presence.

But as he looked down at her flushed face, his gaze tracing the inviting curve of her parted lips, logic shattered. The years he had spent building walls of clinical detachment evaporated, leaving him entirely at the mercy of a profound, primal hunger.

He leaned down, and what was intended as a soft, questioning brush of his lips against hers instantly detonated into a fierce, unbridled passion. Anya didn't pull back; she let out a breathless, soft whimper against his mouth and returned the kiss with a desperate intensity that completely destroyed his remaining control.

Talus groaned deep in his throat, a low, animalistic sound of pure surrender to a desire that was rapidly driving him mindless. Every refined, civilized instinct he possessed was swallowed by the urgent need to have her closer. His hands slid down to grip her waist, his touch frantic yet possessive as he pulled her down to lay across the wide leather seat, crowding over her until his heavy frame completely dominated her space.

The kiss became savage, starved, and utterly unyielding, a chaotic, beautiful collision of fear, ancient longing, and desire. He was drowning in her, his mind spinning into a dark, intoxicating haze where the only reality was the woman beneath him.

Anya tangled her fingers into the dark hair at the nape of his neck, pulling him down harder against her, mooring him to her lips. She responded to the demanding pressure of his mouth with soft, ragged moans that drove him even further to the edge. Her hand slid beneath the hem of his shirt, her bare palm searing against the skin of his chest, while her eyes bore into his with the exact same untamed fire he had witnessed in his laboratory the day before.

He was completely consumed, his thoughts entirely blanked out by the sheer, dizzying sensation of her. He tilted her chin up, guiding her mouth to meet his as his lips slid possessively over hers, his tongue deepening the kiss with a reckless, breathtaking urgency that left them both breathless. He cupped her face with one hand, his thumb softly stroking the smooth skin of her cheek before his fingers slid backward, tangling fiercely in the silken strands of her hair to pull her even closer.

The raw heat of her skin, the wild racing of her pulse against his chest, and the sweet, mesmerizing taste of her mouth tethered him completely to the land of the living. For that suspended, infinite moment, the aircraft, the war, the threat of the Others, and the ticking clock of the post-apocalyptic world completely ceased to exist. There was no past, no years of grief, and no terrifying future. There was only the low, rhythmic roar of the engines beneath their feet, the fading crimson light of the sunset painting their skin, and the violent, beautiful fire burning fiercely between them.

Suddenly, a sharp, piercingly urgent tone shattered the quiet of the cockpit, breaking the spell. Elan's voice burst harshly over the long-range comms speaker right above their heads, shattering the breathless spell that held them.

"Talus! Talus, do you copy? We have a problem. The Others have flooded the sector. You are going to have an exceptionally difficult time landing the *SunStar* without being spotted."

They pulled apart sharply, both of them flushed, their breathing ragged as they stared at each other in a daze of lingering shock. The transition from mindless passion back to the brink of war was dizzying.

"How far out is their perimeter?" Talus demanded into the cabin receiver. His voice was rough, as he forced his professional mask back into place. He pulled himself up from the seat, though his hands were trembling slightly with residual adrenaline as he reached for the main console.

"They are spread in a loose mile radius around the Tigris facility, but the highest concentration is clustered right at the primary hangar threshold," Elan reported grimly over the static. "I haven't observed any breaches into the subterranean levels yet, but they are actively searching for an entry point."

"Understood, Elan. Keep the satellite array locked on their positions and feed it directly to my terminal," Talus ordered, his gaze fixing on the primary tactical map.

Before sliding completely back into the pilot's chair, Talus paused. He turned back to Anya, his dark blue eyes dark with an intense, unshielded emotion. Leaning down, he pressed one last soft, lingering kiss to her lips before settling himself at the controls.

Anya was just as fast to switch back to being a soldier as she sat upright and nudged Ryan sharply in the shoulder.

The rough jostle finally woke the co-pilot, who, by some miracle, had slept through the entire encounter. Ryan groaned, running a hand through his hair as his eyes blinked open. His groggy expression vanished instantly, his muscles tensing as he registered the flashing red hostile icons lighting up the main monitor.

"We have to utilize the access tunnels," Anya stated, her voice remarkably tight as she forced her focus back to the mission parameters. "But the further away we ground the aircraft, the more exposed we are on the approach."

"Are there any localized access points close enough for a rapid entry that also provide cover for the plane?" Talus asked.

Ryan stretched, his soldier instincts taking over as he studied the map, though his eyes darted suspiciously between Talus' rigid posture and Anya's flushed cheeks. "It's a flat desert basin. We can move through the auxiliary tunnels quickly, but there is zero natural cover for a plane of this scale. The absolute best we can hope for is dropping her behind a high ridge dune and hoping the sand conceals the heat signature."

Talus nodded, his fingers flying across the console as he pulled back on the primary throttles. The *SunStar* was incredibly fast, which meant its atmospheric displacement was deafening. Even though they were still roughly ten minutes out, he couldn't risk encroaching on the sector without a definitive plan. He brought the vessel into a wide, silent glide pattern just outside their radar range.

"This is incredibly high-risk," Talus muttered, his jaw set as he fought to keep his mind clear of the intoxicating memory of her lips. "If we execute a rescue, we must ensure your Captain is actually alive inside that base, and that he is uncompromised. I will not risk your lives unnecessarily."

"Elan, patch me through to the Tigris internal mainframe," Anya ordered, leaning over Talus' shoulder to speak directly into the comm array, her chest brushing his back. "I need a localized broadcast across their entire communication loop."

A brief pause ensued over the static. "You can execute that broadcast directly from your console, Anya," Elan's voice returned, laced with a hint of dry amusement. "You just key in the auxiliary frequency—wait, Talus, you still haven't memorized the advanced communication protocols, have you?"

Talus let out a low groan, shifting his weight uncomfortably beneath Anya's close proximity. "Why should I expend my energy attempting to decipher communication arrays built for humans who want nothing to do with me? That is precisely why I tolerate your existence, Elan. Just execute the patch."

"We haven't utilized the term 'patch' since the turn of the century, Talus, but fine, the link is live."

A sharp click echoed through the cockpit speakers, followed by a low hum of audio feedback confirming an open, multi-channel connection to the abandoned base below. Talus looked up at Anya, their faces mere inches apart once more, the ghost of their kiss lingering heavily in the air. The unwavering determination in her eyes sent a sudden jolt straight to his heart.

"The frequency is yours, Anya," Talus said, his voice dropping into a quiet, intensely supportive register. "If he responds, we get him out. No matter what."

27

Anya

It felt a little bit impossible, but somehow, even within his stark and serious tone, Talus was giving her the exact confidence she needed. Against all logic, she genuinely believed they would get in and out with her Captain. All she had to do was make sure Captain Tennant was actually down there. That he had really come after her, proving he cared more for her than the man who was supposed to be her father.

'Captain? Captain, are you there?" Anya leaned closer to the console, her voice tight. "It's me. Please answer on the comms."

The cockpit was small, but she had the distinct impression that Talus wanted to pace. He sat rigidly in his chair, arms crossed tightly over his chest, his knees mindlessly bouncing up and down with restless energy. The ensuing silence lasted far too long, or maybe it wasn't long at all; it just felt that way because there were too many thoughts racing through her head. Namely, what she would do if her Captain was dead because of her stupidity, how they would ever manage to pull off a rescue, and what sort of dark secrets Talus was still keeping from her. The last thought was entirely unwelcome given the circumstances, but it forced its way into her mind just the same.

"Anya? Anya, where the hell are you?"

She sank back into her chair, letting out the breath she had been holding in a silent, relieved laugh. Talus, however, seemed far less pleased when the voice crackled through the speaker. He tilted his head back against the headrest and ran a frustrated hand through his dark hair, a gesture she was beginning to realize rarely signaled good news.

"It is a long story, Captain," Anya replied, flashing a brief smile. "Stay right where you are. I am coming to meet you."

She glanced at Ryan, who was smiling just as widely. It was good to know that there was a chance, a small one, but a chance nonetheless. There was still a chance her selfishness hadn't cost her Captain his life.

Suddenly, a sharp click cut the audio. Looking down at the interface, she realized Talus had reached over and switched off the comm link.

"What did you do that for?" she snapped, turning on him. "He's there! We need to talk to him! What if something happens and he can't get back through to us?"

The words raced out of her mouth in a panicked blur. She wasn't even sure if she was making sense, but she had just fought to get her Captain back, and she wasn't about to let Talus take that connection away. Her anger only intensified when he rolled his head toward her, treating her to a look of profound impatience.

"If the Others get to him in the next five minutes, there is absolutely nothing we can do from here; we are miles away, flying through the upper atmosphere," Talus explained calmly. "I merely turned off our outbound transmission so we can still monitor his audio, just quieter. Because right now, you both need to listen to me more than him."

Why, that arrogant son of a bitch. She genuinely hated the way he talked down to her. She wasn't stupid; it was just incredibly difficult to think critically with a storm of raw emotion flooding her system. Maybe that was the one thing Phoenix had actually gotten right: emotions were a dangerous distraction for a soldier. Even if Talus was making a sliver of sense, she still glared at him with pure venom.

"Now, first things first," Talus said, ignoring her look. "How do I physically access the base?"

Ryan was quick to answer Talus' question. "The base is on

lockdown so the tunnels can only be opened from inside Tigris."

"If the base is locked down how did your Captain get in?"

"There's a legacy handprint scanner at one of the emergency tunnel thresholds," Ryan explained. "He must have overridden it. Anya and I are still logged in the primary database, so we can use the exact same door to get in."

Anya watched the exchange for a moment. Like always, Ryan was missing the broader, more critical point because he was too busy enjoying the technical aspects of the conversation. She let them talk just until her patience completely evaporated, which didn't take long at all. It wasn't easy being patient when the person speaking was about to say something remarkably stupid.

"What do you mean, 'How do *I* get into the base'?" Anya interrupted, stepping between them. "If you think for one second that I am staying up here while you go down there, you are completely and utterly... well, you're just... I am going."

She knew she wasn't making a brilliant rhetorical argument, but the mere suggestion that she should stay behind and babysit the aircraft was infuriating. That was the job you gave to the incompetent person you just wanted out of your hair. She had vastly more field experience dealing with the Others than a lab-bound immortal; she was the one who belonged on the ground.

Once again, Talus executed that infuriating tilt of his head, giving her a look that screamed he knew better than her. In that moment, she wanted to snap his neck, and she really could have, taking a twisted comfort in knowing it would just pop right back into place afterward.

"Alright, you can come," Talus said, his tone dripping with mock compliance. "We will go down together, just as soon as you develop the ability to not die when a high-caliber bullet hits you. Right now, that entire sector is crawling with immortals who either want to execute you or, well, they just want to kill you. As you well know, a single operative gaining entry is much easier than three. Furthermore, a person who cannot die has a drastically higher probability of returning to this plane than someone who can. You two are staying here. I am

going. Remain on the audio feed with your Captain and tell him only
what he needs to know to trust me. If you need to omit the part where
I am immortal, do so."

His face carried a calm, smug certainty. He clearly knew he was
right, that his logic was ironclad, and it maddened her. She had a feeling
he was entirely used to being the smartest person in the room and
having people blindly follow his directives. He *was* right, but that didn't
mean she had to like it.

"You don't know the layout," she countered, trying a different
angle. "You have never set foot inside Tigris before. You need me."

"What I need is a digital map," Talus countered smoothly,
turning his back to her. "Ryan, I assume you possess the schematics?
Upload them directly to my communicator."

Anya raised an eyebrow, a triumphant smirk breaking through
her anger. "Aha! You told me you didn't have communicators! I knew
your people couldn't survive out here without tech." Comms were
everything in the Rangers, the way you gathered intel, shared data, and
navigated. There was no way a technologically advanced base like Talus'
didn't use them.

"I never stated we didn't possess them," Talus corrected,
looking back over his shoulder. "I merely said we have legs and prefer
to communicate in person. When away from each other we use these."

He pulled back his sleeve to reveal a thin, sleek black band
wrapped around his wrist. With a light touch, his entire forearm
illuminated, projecting a crisp, high-definition user interface directly
onto his skin. With a swift swipe, he detached the screen from his arm,
casting a flawless holographic display into the empty air before him,
before snapping it back down and turning the screen off.

Show-off.

"Alright, you had your fun," Anya muttered, crossing her arms.
"Now it's time to pay the price. I expect one of those exact models
when we return." Her own Ranger-issue communicator was a bulky,
primitive brick with a physical screen that swallowed half her forearm.
It was heavy, and when she started to sweat in the desert heat, it
became incredibly uncomfortable. Alright, fine—she was desperately

jealous of his tech.

"Deal. Assuming you remain in this chair," Talus replied. "Now that I have the schematics, how do I clear the physical doors?"

Ryan turned toward the main console where Captain Tennant's voice was fading in and out, still trying to regain their attention. Anya moved to answer him, but Ryan and Talus were blocking the primary terminal. She mentally cursed herself for not having Elan connect her personal wrist-comm to the plane's main transmitter earlier.

"The Captain can manually override the seals from the primary communications hub," Ryan explained, tapping at the keys. "I can walk him through the sequence from here. There are also closed-circuit cameras mapping those specific tunnels, so he'll be able to see if you're being followed. I might be able to intercept the visual feed and route it to our monitor so we can help watch your back. We won't exactly have anything else to do."

There was a distinct edge of petulance in Ryan's voice. Anya felt a minor surge of satisfaction knowing she wasn't the only one upset about being benched. It was utterly ridiculous; she was being treated like a child. Even when she *was* a literal child in the training camps, she hadn't been handled with such kid gloves.

"Excellent," Talus said. "All we require now is a clear drop zone for my insertion, and you can keep the plane in the air. That eliminates the need to camouflage it on the ground. I will maintain an active link via the communicator, and you can track my location on the map." He pointed to the primary display, which currently tracked the plane's trajectory alongside a cluster of hostile red dots moving along the desert floor.

Talus pinched the screen, expanding the holographic image until the Tigris facility and the surrounding enemy formations were sharply defined.

"This might work," Talus mused, pointing to a specific coordinate. "The tunnel entry located near the base of the mountain ridge. It will require a prolonged trek on foot, but it offers a secure, unexposed route in and out. I would prefer to avoid a direct engagement entirely if possible."

"Brilliant. We can avoid it completely if *you* stay behind in the plane and *I* go," Anya muttered. She knew she was being stubborn, but she truly couldn't help it. A few hours ago, she and Ryan were heading out on this mission alone, and they might have succeeded. Now, Talus was acting like they were completely incapable of doing anything more complicated than staring at a computer screen.

Talus paused, turning around slowly. "Remind me, Anya, how did your very last encounter with the Others unfold? The one where you simply marched into a base entirely populated by them?"

She went completely quiet, her jaw tightening. He was throwing her absolute worst day right back in her face. She had been completely outnumbered, and yes, she had successfully escorted three children to safety, but of course, he was going to focus exclusively on the fact that she got shot.

Talus let out a soft sigh, his rigid posture melting slightly as he leaned closer to her. He placed his large, warm hands on her shoulders, his gaze locking onto hers with a sudden, grounding intensity.

"I know you are not pleased with this plan," he said softly, his voice dropping into a gentle register that made her heart skip a beat. "But if you die under my watch, Cary will never forgive me. If I anger you, all I have to do is wait for you to die of old age and the argument is over. If I anger Cary, I am forced to hear about it for the rest of eternity. You are not going to win this debate, Anya. Now, please, try to cooperate."

Oh, she absolutely hated him. He was just so completely, effortlessly arrogant, as if the entire universe revolved around how things affected him.

Yet, as she stared into the intense, gray-blue of his eyes, a strange idea pierced through her anger. That elaborate, logical speech about satisfying Cary and avoiding an eternity of complaints was a shield. Maybe he wasn't just doing this to keep Cary from being angry; maybe he was doing this because he wanted to keep *her* safe. He was willingly putting his own body between her and a bullet.

The thought sent a sudden, complicated ache through her chest. It forced an even bigger question into her mind: could Talus ever truly care for her the way he had cared for Lily? Lily had been his soulmate, a monumental love that had defined his infinite existence. Did he have room in that cold, scarred heart to care for someone else like that? More frustratingly, she had to wonder if she even wanted him to.

Well, if he wanted her to be a team player, she would play along—for now, if only to stop the current train of thought going through her head. Leaning down to finally break the connection of his gaze, she reached into one of the tactical bags Ryan had packed, rummaging through the spare Fulgar charges, backup gear, and extra structural clips until she found what she was looking for.

'Shoes. Give them to me," she commanded. Her voice came out much more forceful than she had anticipated as she thrust her open hand toward him. Apparently, she was holding onto a lot more anger than she thought, and she was entirely ready to rip those boots off his feet herself if he didn't comply immediately.

Talus blinked, thoroughly taken aback. "What?"

The utterly flabbergasted look on his sharp face was deeply satisfying, almost making up for how intensely he had been annoying her.

'Give her the boots," Ryan interjected from the console, not looking up. "She needs to attach the guide clips for the tunnel lines. You have your advanced innovations, and we have ours. Just hand over the shoes."

Grumbling under his breath, Talus unlaced his sleek, specialized boots and handed them over. They were black and deceptively plain, but at least the outsoles were perfectly flat. That would make mounting the hardware easy, though it wouldn't offer him much traction if he had to sprint across loose sand. The life of a laboratory recluse was clearly not optimized for a high-intensity ranger deployment. There was absolutely no way she was letting him handle this entirely on his own.

She took the thin, metallic circles and pressed one firmly into the center of each sole, securing the locking pins. The internal magnets would activate the exact second he stepped over a live tunnel guide line, and he wouldn't know what hit him. It was a minor bit of revenge, and she relished it. She grabbed the simple safety strap designed to clip around the upper guide pole to help stabilize a runner at high velocities.

"Here," Anya said, handing the boots back along with the rig. "This is your primary handle. It wraps around the upper pole and snaps into place like this. Just hold on tight. Your boots, which were clearly not engineered for running, will magnetically lock onto the bottom guide rail."

Talus took the footwear, inspecting the modifications before slowly sliding his feet back into them. "And then what happens?"

"Hold on," she repeated with a tight smile.

Talus looked from her to Ryan, no doubt sensing the trap. Anya knew she probably had a slightly manic grin on her face as she pictured how he would react to his very first high-speed tunnel launch. Ryan merely nodded in reassuring solidarity. She still couldn't help but feel a bit betrayed at how easily Ryan was going along with Talus' plan, but she realized the two men in her life seemed to have the same idea, protect the poor female at all costs.

"Just... hold on?" Talus questioned skeptically.

"Yep."

"Hello? Anya! Anya, why the hell aren't you answering? Where are you?"

Anya shot a warning glance at Talus and Ryan, daring either of them to block her from reclaiming the comms. She motioned for Talus to vacate the space and take her seat at the back; if he intended to drop out of the cargo hatch on a tactical line, he couldn't be the one piloting the aircraft anyway. He quickly moved aside, allowing her to step up to the front.

"We are in the sector, Captain," Anya said, keying the mic. "We are on our way to pull you out. We need you to manually unseal the tunnel doors from your end. Ryan is going to walk you through the data override."

"What the hell are you talking about? Why do I need someone to pull me out of anywhere?" Tennant's voice barked back. "Just use your handprint override at the threshold! Where are you two? What is going on down there?"

Anya could perfectly visualize the look of absolute frustration wrinkling her Captain's face. She had seen that exact expression dozens of times, usually whenever she lied about where she had been scouting or what she had been doing. He always knew when she was withholding information, even if he rarely deduced the exact truth. At least, she liked to think he didn't.

'Like I said, Captain, it's a long story, and one better told when you are out of Tigris. We are currently tracking large groups of immortals in and around the base." Anya said. "An ally of ours is inserting to retrieve you. He will be able to guide you to our location and avoid the immortals as much as possible. His name is Tal. He'll be wearing a black coat, he has incredibly messy dark hair, and—" She gave Talus' nickname knowing that his full name would likely raise alarm bells seeing as the Captain had already spoken to Talus over comms. But then she hesitated, realizing she had no idea how to properly describe Talus. He looked just like one the Others, at least he did at first glance but now Anya knew better. His eyes were a bit more grey than the bright blue of the Others, his lips were not quite as pale, his hair was far less tamed than theirs, always falling over his eyes, and his personality was—well, it was going to be an explosive introduction. The Captain would likely figure out his nature the second they crossed paths. "Just trust him, Captain. I do."

'So do I," Ryan chimed in from the side, adding his own vote of confidence.

Despite the verbal unity, Anya still had a sinking feeling that once the two men came face-to-face, the interaction was going to go terribly wrong.

'Why is this friend of yours executing the extraction and not you, Anya?" Tennant demanded.

'Because, as he so eloquently reminded me, I got shot the last time I tried this," she replied dryly.

'Fair point," the Captain grunted. "Alright, Ryan, how do I open these damn tunnels for this 'friend' of yours?"

Anya could tell from the sharp emphasis on the word *friend* that the Captain already suspected something. He had likely deduced from the lack of Ranger in front of Talus' name that their friend was someone they had met while directly defying his orders, and that made him a bad influence at best and an enemy at worst. Not to mention the nickname was not likely to fool him for long.

As Ryan began detailing the tunnel mechanics and surveillance routing to the Captain, Talus moved to the rear of the cabin to prepare the extraction line. He secured the heavy tactical rope to a structural load hook mounted right beside the plane's lower deployment hatch. The placement provided an extra two feet of clearance, but looking across the space, the line still appeared dangerously short to Anya. She wondered exactly how deep of a drop she was going to have to navigate when her turn came. The rope was thick, woven from an advanced black synthetic fiber that seemed to glisten under the light inside the plane.

"The computer indicates we have reached your designated drop vector, Talus," Ryan called out, checking the diagnostics. "The tunnel threshold is located inside the ruins of the old church. Push aside the central altar pew, the one with the inscription carved into the wood."

"An inscription of what?" Talus asked, adjusting his gear.

It was a carving Anya had only encountered once before, during an extended long-range scouting operation with the Phoenix rangers. They believed in mapping every single tunnel so they would never be trapped without a fallback route.

"It's written in an ancient language from long before the collapse," Anya said quietly. "But I was told the translation reads: *'With the death of God, comes the death of humanity.'*" The phrase had burned itself into her memory because it felt remarkably prophetic—and more than a little terrifying for a twelve-year-old girl lost in the dark.

Talus paused, his hand resting on the hatch lever. "I always maintained the philosophy that humanity could not truly thrive until God died. But there were always those who violently disagreed with that."

That was the final thing he said before slamming the release lever. The lower hatch dropped open with a metallic roar, and the violent vacuum of the slipstream ripped through the cockpit, rendering speech completely impossible. Anya watched through the opening as

Talus swung himself out, disappearing down the glistening black line and dropping straight through the massive structural hole in the church's collapsed roof below.

From their high altitude, Anya had a clearer, more panoramic view of the abandoned town than she had ever experienced from the ground. Even as a nervous child on her first deployment, she hadn't been able to process the sheer scale of the ruins; she had only stayed on the surface long enough to mark the entrance before retreating back into the safety of the dark. Back then, it had been entirely about survival, never about actually living. She hadn't even had Mamoru with her in those days.

She focused on the primary monitor, watching the lone digital signature that represented Talus as it decoupled from the plane's tracking array and began moving rapidly away from the structural ruins.

"He's down," Anya reported, tapping Ryan on the shoulder. "Reel in the line."

She waited while Ryan quickly cranked the winch, hauling the black rope back into the cabin before sealing the heavy hatch. The deafening roar of the wind vanished instantly, returning the cockpit to a tense quiet. With nothing to distract her, her anger flared back to life once more.

"Why did you just agree to everything he said?" she demanded, turning on her co-pilot. "Why didn't you fight him on this? We should be down there retrieving the Captain ourselves! It's our fundamental duty as his rangers!"

Ryan dropped heavily back into his flight chair, letting out a weary sigh. "I didn't protest because his reasoning is right, Anya. If anyone belongs down there, it's him, because the risk to his life is zero. If something happens to you on this drop and Captain Tennant actually makes it out of that base alive, he will murder me. Likely with something exceptionally sharp and poorly maintained. Not to mention what Talus would do."

What was it with men? All they ever processed was how a situation directly impacted their own immediate survival or standing. How their choices affected everyone else was seemingly irrelevant.

Whatever weird dynamic was developing between them all had just gotten significantly more complicated, because she absolutely loathed that Ryan thought upsetting her was an acceptable trade-off to avoid Talus' *potential* wrath.

"He is *our* Captain, Ryan!"

"Yeah, he is," Ryan agreed quietly, his eyes fixed on the console. "And I trust that Talus possesses the means to get him out safely. More importantly, I know this cockpit is the safest place on the planet for you right now."

Ryan returned his full attention to the screen, keeping a watchful eye on the hostile red signatures to ensure none of them drifted close enough to the tunnel networks to suggest the perimeter had been breached.

"I don't like it," Anya muttered, pacing the narrow aisle. "The absolute first sign of trouble, and I am dropping down there myself."

"I know," Ryan replied without looking up. "Why do you think I didn't waste my energy fighting Talus? You always end up doing whatever you want anyway."

She blew out a sharp breath, her air ruffling the stray hairs that draped over her forehead. Apparently, her refusal to listen to anyone but herself was entirely predictable.

"Cary, Anya, I just wanted to assure you that there is zero surface activity from the Others directly above the primary hangar," Elan's voice cut through the cabin, smooth and clear. "My satellite arrays cannot penetrate the reinforced subterranean tunnels, however. They must know that an auxiliary entrance exists near the mountain ridge, and yet their forces are completely avoiding the coordinate."

Elan. She had completely forgotten he was still patched into their network. Had he been silently monitoring their entire argument? Not that it changed anything, but it was a little unsettling to realize he just sat in his distant communications room, silently absorbing their personal squabbles.

"Do you think they discovered an alternate entry point into the system?" Anya asked, leaning over the terminal.

"It is highly probable," Elan answered. "Our surveillance

records indicate they regularly utilize the deep tunnel networks to fall back to their primary compound following a base assault."

Anya's eyes went wide as she stared at the monitor, as if looking closer at the digital map would somehow explain Elan's words. How could the Others possibly be utilizing the ranger tunnels? It wasn't as if the monsters had engineered the subterranean network to connect to their own facility, and if they had spliced into an existing line, the human command would have flagged the change, right? All this time, the rangers had operated under the strict assumption that while the Others knew the tunnels existed, they lacked the means to map or navigate them. It was the single tactical advantage keeping humanity alive, or so they had foolishly believed.

"How do you possess data that they use our tunnels, Elan?" Anya pressed, her voice rising. "How is that even possible? Our lines don't even run in the direction of their territory."

"There are vastly more tunnel systems beneath the crust than just your localized ranger routes, Anya," Elan explained patiently. "Some were excavated before the war even began. We know they utilize them because our satellites have visually tracked their transport vehicles emerging from an underground threshold directly within their central compound."

Vehicles? None of this was making sense. In all her years on the surface, she had never once witnessed the Others utilizing mechanized transports of any kind. But then again, how else would they coordinate troop movements across long distances? It was terrifying to realize that while she thought she knew more about the enemy because she actually fought them on the front lines, Talus and his scientists had been collecting a completely different level of intelligence. They hadn't just been hiding away in a quiet box; they were operating like an apex predator, quietly stalking their prey from the shadows and waiting for the perfect time to strike.

"I have breached the church perimeter," Talus' voice suddenly rang through the cockpit, loud and perfectly clear. Figures the man would have the technology to automatically optimize his communicator's volume for the cabin speakers. "How do I activate the tunnel mechanism? The altar pew will not yield to physical force alone."

"Beneath the inscription, there is a concealed wooden square with a slightly lighter grain than the surrounding material," Ryan answered immediately, stepping smoothly into his role as mission control. "Depress it firmly, and a secondary mechanical panel will slide out from the base. Wait until the indicator light on the interface transitions to green, and then move the structure."

Ryan was always remarkably efficient at taking command whenever technology or data was involved. He could manage entire logistical chains, crack encrypted military codes, and coordinate operations without breaking a sweat. However, the moment he was thrown into a raw, fluid combat scenario where he had to physically fight or improvise on instinct, his usefulness rapidly degraded.

A brief pause ensued over the audio link, filled only by the distant, hollow echo of scraping stone from the surface.

"I have entered the tunnel shaft," Talus' voice returned, a hint of genuine confusion cutting through his usual calm composure. "Now, how exactly does this contraption of yours work?"

A wide, genuinely amused grin spread across Anya's face as she leaned toward the microphone. At least she was going to get to watch him struggle with a bit of human ingenuity.

28

Talus

Once the stone pew slid open, Talus found himself staring down into a subterranean shaft that immediately flickered to life, its guide tracks pulsing with a stark, cold luminescence. It was a remarkable piece of engineering if he was being completely honest. Heavy metal ribbing climbed the curved walls and scaled across the vaulted ceiling in an unbroken ribcage of polished silver. It was an oppressive, blindingly metallic corridor and not the most inviting entry point for a rescue mission.

He gripped the edge of the opening, apprehension sinking into his chest. He really should have stayed behind. But as he monitored the energy spikes on his wrist map, he knew he would never make another choice. These tunnels were not empty. And as much as he hated the idea of being captured by his own monstrous creations, he loathed the thought of Anya being slaughtered by them infinitely more.

Running along both sides of the corridor were thick, pressurized pneumatic tubes, their surfaces faintly stamped with directional arrows. Along the ceiling ran a parallel guide rail, glistening with grease. This was rapidly deteriorating into an exceptionally bad idea.

Leaning toward his transmitter, he called out, "I have entered the tunnel shaft. How exactly does this contraption of yours work?"

A muffled, distinctly amused laugh filtered through the receiver, a universal sign that his dignity was about to be severely compromised. He tapped his forearm, lighting up the holographic display to activate a localized proximity sweep. He needed a warning system before he ran into whatever was lurking in the dark ahead.

"The Captain has initialized the launch grid from the hub," Anya's voice crackled back, dripping with suppressed glee. "Take the safety strap and snap it securely around the upper guide rail. Then plant your boots directly onto the lower tube."

Talus fished the thick fabric strap from his coat pocket, throwing it over the overhead rail and clicking the load-buckle shut. He took a sharp, steadying breath. *If humans can survive this madness, so can I.*

Slowly, he extended his right foot toward the lower pressurized pipe. The moment his sole made contact, the newly installed metallic clip detected the guide line. The internal magnets activated with a loud CLANG, locking his boot to the rail with crushing force. He repeated the motion with his left foot, the second magnet slamming home, securing him completely. He took another breath, trying to discern the basic physics of what was about to happen. Yet, he couldn't shake the feeling that he was missing a very critical piece of information.

"Alright," Talus muttered, his knuckles turning white as he gripped the overhead strap. "Now what?"

He could practically hear the wicked grin spreading across her lips. He could see it perfectly in his mind—those pink lips curving upward to reveal a hint of white teeth, her vibrant blue eyes dancing with silent, untamed laughter.

"Remember what we told you," she purred. "Whatever happens next. *Do Not Let Go.*"

Suddenly, Captain Tennant's gruff voice broke over the shared frequency. "I've got a rider signature registered on the master terminal. What now Ryan?"

While it was a relief to know the Captain was still breathing in the communications room, it was profoundly horrifying to realize the man had absolutely no operational experience with this system. Talus was completely at the mercy of a blind grid, no steering, no manual brakes, and zero knowledge of how to safely disengage.

"Press the primary green toggle and give Tal a ride, Captain!" Ryan shouted.

Talus intertwined his fingers through the woven fabric of the strap, bracing for impact. He had a brief, terrifying vision of his hands slipping, his body violently flipping backward, and his face dragging along the silver floor at terminal velocity while his feet rocketed down the track. *This is an absolute—*

A low, hydraulic buzz vibrated through the tubing, followed by a violent, concussive surge of kinetic energy.

BOOM.

Talus was instantly ripped forward, his body shot like a slug from a railgun. A wall of pressurized wind slammed into his face with such sharp force he genuinely expected his flesh to be flayed from his skull by the time he reached the terminus. The sheer G-force tore at his muscles, his arms and legs screaming under the immense strain as he fought to keep his grip on the vibrating strap.

Through the serpentine, winding maze of the subterranean network he flew. And *flew* was the only accurate description. The speed was blinding, the air screaming past his ears in a deafening, chaotic roar.

"Are you holding up okay down there?" a voice suddenly echoed inside his receiver. "That was quite the majestic scream."

He could barely process the words. In the background, Anya

369

was laughing hysterically, while Ryan was making a thoroughly pathetic attempt to sound professional. Did these daft humans honestly expect a coherent answer while his body was being hurtled through a pitch-black labyrinth with no hope of decelerating until a man he'd never met and had no experience at the controls stopped him?

"Just hold on, Tal!" Anya shouted over the wind.

Because there are so many other options available?! he thought furiously.

Then, forcing his ancient mind to override the panic, he reminded himself to breathe. He relaxed his rigid posture, forcing his eyes open against the rushing air. The silver geometry of the tunnel blurred into an unbroken streak of light. It was terrifying. It was reckless.

It was utterly exhilarating.

He began to calculate the trajectory, adjusting his center of gravity against the high-speed turns. A fierce, primal spark ignited within his chest. This was what it felt like to be alive again. This bold, untamed rush was something he never could have experienced in his laboratory or at all. Not until two chaotic humans dragged him out into the world.

A genuine, breathless smile broke across his face. Yielding to pure impulse, he pulled his right hand free from the strap and thrust it out into the roaring wind, letting out a wild laugh. This was fun. Truly, beautifully fun.

"Alright, new proposal!" Talus called into the comms, a rare, vibrant lightness ringing in his voice. "I will give you one of our holographic communicators if you build me one of these tracks at the base!"

He knew Lily would have absolutely loathed this. She would have called him mad, reckless, and entirely irresponsible. She never had this sort of adventurous spirit, it was only Anya that could have ever given him an experience like this.

Laughter erupted over the comms, the humans clearly relishing his transformation.

'Sorry to burst your bubble, but you're approaching the

entrance," Ryan warned, his tone shifting back to business. "The automated dampeners are going to engage, and the moment you cross the threshold, your magnetic clips will disengage."

"Understood."

A flash of genuine disappointment hit him, but it vanished instantly as a sharp, frantic beeping began to detonate from his wrist. He couldn't safely activate the holographic display without risking losing his grip, but the frequency of the proximity alerts was accelerating at a disturbing rate.

He glanced ahead. The tunnel walls were flashing red on his peripheral sensors. He slammed his free hand back onto the safety strap, tucking his chin tightly into his chest, praying the shadows of his heavy black coat would conceal his identity from whatever was coming.

"I am not alone in this shaft!" Talus hissed into the mic, his voice dropping into a tense, commanding register. "You had better have that security door unsealed the millisecond I arrive!"

"Uh, copy that! Captain, did you copy that?!" Ryan panicked. "Unseal the secondary hatch the moment his rider icon clears the system tracker! It should be illuminating on your terminal right now!"

"Which damn button is it, Ryan?!" Tennant bellowed back.

"The orange one!"

"There are three different shades of orange up here!"

I am utterly doomed, Talus thought. He made a strict mental note to engineer an aggressive audio filter for his communications network the moment he survived this, if only to spare his ears from the terrifying reality of human incompetence. Listening to Ryan and the Captain bicker over basic controls was doing nothing but confirming he was in the worst possible hands.

He kept his head buried, chin tucked tightly into his chest, as the rapid pulsing on his wrist array locked into a solid, continuous death-wail. The proximity sensor was bleeding a deep, angry crimson.

Then, a sound tore through the rush of wind that had nothing to do with his comm link—low, gravelly voices echoing from an intersecting shaft, distorted and monstrous. The Others were close enough that they would be able to see him at any moment and if they did, he would expose the entrance to the base.

"Brace for impact!" Ryan shouted.

In the next instant, an invisible wall of electromagnetic dampeners slammed against his momentum. The sudden deceleration nearly ripped his arms from their sockets. A split second later, the magnetic clips on his boots violently detached with a sharp hiss. Stripped of his support, Talus went flying forward, tumbling across the silver floor before crashing hard against a reinforced bulkhead.

"Captain, open the damn door now!" Anya's voice screamed through his earpiece.

Talus pushed himself up, spinning around to face a massive, seamless wall. There was absolutely nothing about the silver paneling that distinguished it from the rest of the corridor. A flawless, military-grade camouflage job. He shook his head, thoroughly annoyed that his scientific mind was admiring the engineering while his freedom was actively on the line.

"Anytime now, Captain," Talus growled, his hand drifting to his coat pockets.

The Others were closing fast. Though he couldn't hear their thundering footsteps yet over the hum of the facility, the proximity gauge was bleeding back into the red. He wrapped his fingers around the cold, metallic cylinders Anya had packed into his gear.

He locked his eyes down the dark stretch of the tunnel, bracing for the onslaught.

PFFFF-CHHHHHH.

A loud pneumatic hiss erupted behind him. He spun around to see the seamless wall splitting down the center, revealing the interior of the Tigris facility. Talus dived through the opening, rolling onto the concrete floor inside.

"I'm through! Seal it!"

The response was instantaneous. The steel doors slammed shut with a concussive *THUD*, the locking bolts engaging with a mechanical snap. *At least the Captain is a fast learner,* Talus thought, exhaling a breath.

But the victory was short-lived. The beeping on his wrist flared back to life. He activated the forearm display, casting a map of the base into the air. A cluster of bright red hostile signatures was actively moving through the upper sectors.

"You've entered into the center of the primary maintenance shaft," Ryan instructed, his fingers flying across his own console back on the aircraft. "The communications room is located on the top platform. You'll need to navigate the access ramps to get to the top level."

Talus frowned, staring at the empty airwaves. "I was afraid of that. Tell your Captain to kill the lights, lock his perimeter door, and cease all transmissions. Do not give any indication that there is someone in that room. The enemy has already infiltrated the base."

He crept to the edge of the maintenance catwalk and peered upward. The Tigris facility was staggering in scale, an immense subterranean cavern crisscrossed by a dizzying web of structural ramps and platforms. On his arm display, dozens of dark figures were wandering across the upper tiers. It wasn't a coordinated execution squad; their movements were erratic, searching. They knew the base had been evacuated, but they were hunting for something specific.

"I don't suppose your blueprints feature an auxiliary route to the top platform?" Talus asked. "Something that avoids these exposed catwalks?"

"Just the central freight elevator," Ryan countered. "It's marked on your overlay, but activating it is going to pull every hostile in the sector directly to you."

It was a true assessment. Yet, Talus had an ace up his sleeve.

"Elan, are you monitoring this frequency?"

"Always, Talus," Elan's smooth, detached voice chimed in. "Cary is here as well. He refuses to leave, worried mother hen that he is."

"Talus? Are the humans still alive?" Cary's voice suddenly detonated over the link, loud and aggressively unhinged. "You better not have let them die, remember those fuckers die easily. You must protect them."

Talus pinched the bridge of his nose, feeling a massive headache forming. Cary was precisely the reason he despised personal communicators; the man lacked any semblance of operational boundaries and possessed a pathological need to insert himself into every crisis.

"I left the humans safely aboard the plane, Cary. So yes, they are perfectly intact," Talus snapped, his voice dripping with venom. "Right now, I am significantly more occupied with extracting an entirely different human who possesses an apparent suicide wish. So, if you don't mind... *GET OFF MY CHANNEL!*"

A beautiful, blessed silence followed. Talus let out a breath, highly doubting Cary would stay quiet for long, but grateful for the temporary reprieve.

"Elan I have the enemy being tracked on my computer," Talus continued, adjusting his pace. "but I need you to tap into their communicators. See if you can get a hold on what they are looking for."

As he spoke, his eyes swept the massive cavern. The freight elevator sat on the polar opposite side of the central chasm. He could make a run for it, but the moment the heavy gears engaged, the Others would know that someone else was in the base. He stared at his arm display, desperately searching for another tunnel system that was higher up that could offer a clean getaway. Once he got to the top platform there would be no time to waste. The faster he got in and out the better.

"Ryan, what is the closest way out from the communication room?"

"Right here" Ryan answered, a localized waypoint flashing green on Talus' holographic map.

It was structurally close to the hub, but a heavy cluster of red signatures sat directly in the bottleneck. This was rapidly becoming an extraordinarily terrible plan. Talus reached into his coat, feeling the cold metal of Anya's Fulgar charges. Effective, sure, but highly inefficient in a crowded space.

"Alright, instruct the Captain to maintain his cover," Talus ordered. "I'm advancing on the elevator vector. If we can pin that cluster of hostiles between us, we might be able to blind them with the charges and clear a path to the secondary tunnel. Ryan get the plane somewhere on the path of that tunnel."

"And if the extraction point is already compromised by immortals?" Ryan pressed.

"There are immortals everywhere. So we will deal with that problem when we get there." He paused, a sudden, blinding realization connecting in his mind, something he should have figured out before. "Patch your Captain's audio feed directly into my personal communicator. Let's eliminate the middleman."

"Hey! I am significantly more than just a middleman in this operation!" Ryan protested.

"Just give me a private channel to him, Ryan." Talus rolled his eyes. Humans were profoundly sensitive creatures.

"Talus?" Elan's voice returned, low and clinical.

"Report, Elan."

"I'm picking up localized chatter on their lower frequencies," the scientist reported. "But the syntax doesn't make sense. They keep referencing an 'Origin Location.' Whatever that means, their leadership believes the coordinates are stored within the top administrative suites. Taking the lift is your fastest option, but you will be a sitting duck once those doors part."

Talus froze, his blood running cold. *Origin Location.* He knew precisely what those words meant, but it was impossible for that data to exist here. This base was a secondary military stronghold; all primary evolution logs should have been vaporized under maximum security protocols.

He glanced at his forearm. The immediate sector around the elevator base had cleared out. It was a straight shot. Striding across the concrete platform, he couldn't help but marvel at the staggering architectural feats achieved by humanity before the collapse. He had assisted in the primary layout of these strongholds. Hundreds of them had been drafted when the global conflict shifted and Cobalt Bombs were no longer just theory. Bombs that unleashed an absolute nightmare upon the biosphere. Yet, even in the ruin, this place stood as a monument to human defiance.

He strained his ears, trying to see if he could make out any sounds from the immortals above him. It was time to confront the Captain.

"Line is live, channel 3." Ryan said.

Talus was immediately struck by an unsettling realization: Anya had not spoken a single word since he entered the facility. Either she was utterly furious with him, or she had vacated the aircraft. Both were highly probable scenarios, but he knew which one was an absolute certainty.

"Captain Tennant, do you maintain a secure perimeter?" Talus asked.

"For now," Tennant's gravelly voice rasped back. "But the corridor is entirely blocked. If Anya and Ryan have successfully cleared the facility, you need to abort this rescue, soldier. I am not worth risking an operative."

Noble, certainly. But a bit late to develop a conscience. "I am in full agreement with that assessment, Captain, but your subordinates are not. So here we are. If they followed my plan, they would be perfectly safe inside the aircraft—"

"Which means you have absolutely no idea where Anya is right now," Tennant interrupted cleanly.

"I suspect she is anywhere but where I ordered her to stay," Talus muttered. "But the faster I extract you, the faster I can drag her out of this war zone. Now listen to me: the hostiles have consolidated on the top platform. They are hunting for files regarding the Origin Location. That category of data should never have been routed to this facility. Every scrap of it was ordered destroyed."

There was silence on the other line. In that quiet, the scattered data points in Talus' mind instantly snapped into perfect, terrifying alignment. The story was starting to come into focus, not the complete text, but a very specific, damning chapter.

"You knew Anya was safe the moment we established contact," Talus said, his voice dropping into a deadly, accusing whisper. "You knew she had left the base. So why did you choose to remain in a compromised bunker? There is an asset here. Something you deliberately left behind and risked your life to reclaim. Anya wasn't your

376

objective; she was your cover story. Captain Tennant... What is inside your office?"

"No! I came back for my Rangers!" Tennant fired back, his voice cracked with defensive panic. "But... during our retreat from the Phoenix sector, a scout mentioned they had intercepted transmissions regarding the Origin coordinates. It was then that I knew I had left something behind that those immortal bastards should not have. So I came back to get it but they were already in my office. I retreated to the comms tower to find a way to reach Anya and Ryan for assistance!"

The freight elevator let out a soft electronic chime, arriving at the apex platform. Talus tightened his jaw. His conflict was waiting for him just beyond the steel barrier, and every nerve in his body was bristling with pure, unadulterated frustration. This was the exact brand of tight-lipped, bureaucratic arrogance that made him despise people. If they did not have plenty of redeeming qualities to make up for it he would probably let them all die in their holes.

"Captain, what is inside your office?" Talus demanded, stepping toward the front of the lift. "What do you have in there that could tell them about the origin location?"

"What do you know about the origin location?" Tennant snapped defensively "No one knows about the origin location!"

Defensive, arrogant, and thoroughly foolish. Talus genuinely couldn't comprehend why soldiers as fiercely talented as Ryan and Anya swore absolute fealty to this man.

The heavy steel elevator doors groaned, sliding back to reveal the top deck.

Talus froze. The platform was completely crawling with the Others. Dozens of massive, pale figures spun around instantly, their dark, venomous eyes locking onto him with terrifying focus. Right. He had spent so much energy cross-examining the human commander that he had neglected to formulate a practical tactical entry plan. *This is an exceptionally—*

"Get back in the elevator and close the door!" a fierce voice suddenly bellowed from above.

Anya. He knew there was no possibility she had stayed on that aircraft.

"Move it! Unless you want to spend the next half hour on the floor, get back in that elevator now!"

He didn't have a tactical alternative. The Others were already surging forward, their expressions shifting from cold malice to a bizarre, sudden curiosity. The lead immortal raised a pale hand, his gaze locking onto Talus' face as he uttered a single, breathless word.

"*Creator.*"

"No, call me Talus," he muttered, slamming his palm against the emergency door override. "'Creator' carries far too much of a tragic Doctor Frankenstein aesthetic."

The doors slammed shut just as the lead hostile lunged. A microsecond later, a blinding, concussive wave of blue electrical energy detonated directly outside the elevator shafts, the raw voltage arc-flashing through the steel seams. The lights in the cabin flickered before dying out completely.

Silence followed, broken only by the sound of structural snapping. Suddenly, the roof hatch of the lift was pulled clear, and a familiar, dirt-smudged face dropped into the opening, swinging upside down.

"Told you that you needed me," Anya smirked, her blue eyes flashing in the dark.

Talus exhaled a slow breath, his pride taking a hit. He didn't want to admit it, but yes, her chaotic intervention had saved him from a very messy captivity. Though he still maintained he would have drafted an elegant counter-strategy had he not been thoroughly derailed by her Captain.

"Your timing was adequate," Talus replied dryly, pulling himself up through the roof hatch to join her on the scaffolding above. "but you should have stayed on the plane. This is far from over and I have a feeling it is going to get much worse."

Anya tilted her head at him, and he found himself momentarily paralyzed by the curious, intense expression on her face. He should have been angry that she didn't listen, even though he expected nothing less, but instead the anger was fear. He needed her to always be safe.

It was no longer just because she was an asset, or because she possessed a fierce intelligence and compassion that set her apart from the rest of her fragile species. It was something much more terrifying to a man of logic. In her element, she was a force of nature, breathtakingly alive. He didn't just want to protect her for the sake of the mission. He wanted to protect her because the mere thought of losing that magnificent light left a cold, hollow ache in his chest.

They dropped down onto the catwalk, stepping over the twitching, paralyzed bodies of a dozen immortals. The air smelled heavily of ozone and scorched synthetic fabric. They made a rapid, tactical sprint toward the communications room.

"Will that surge have penetrated the reinforced bunker walls?" Talus asked, eyeing the device on the floor. It was a dense, spherical metallic core pulsing with residual static—a specialized disruption bomb engineered to completely overload the nervous systems of immortal biology. He needed to dissect the architecture later; structurally, its energy yield shouldn't have been capable of dropping an immortal force this clean.

"Honestly? I have no idea," Anya admitted, tossing another one of the devices into the air and catching it. "This is only my second time deploying it. The first was at Phoenix."

"A thoroughly comforting track record," Talus noted, catching the sphere as she tossed it to him, inspecting the configuration before slipping it into his own pocket. He noted the large combat pack strapped to her shoulders; she was infinitely more equipped for a rescue mission than he was. He had marched into a danger zone wearing nothing but a lab coat and a handful of her weapons, fully expecting his superior intellect to carry the day. Human traits were apparently contagious.

"It worked flawlessly at Phoenix!" she countered, her jaw tensing. "I just ran into a minor logistical complication at the exit."

"Well, I suggest we prepare for another complication if your toy took down your Captain," Talus said, halting before the reinforced security door of the communications hub. He rapped his knuckles against the steel. "Captain, disengage the seals."

"It's clear, Captain! It's me, Anya!

Talus couldn't help but shake his head. She was surrounded by a small army of paralyzed monsters who were going to regain their motor functions at any moment, trapped inside a compromised mountain fortress, and she was still entirely high-energy.

The lock disengaged, and the door slid back to reveal a pale, gaunt man with a heavily graying beard and sunken eyes. He did not resemble the legendary base commander Talus had constructed in his mind.

Before the man could speak, Talus gripped the Captain's vest and forcefully dragged him out into the corridor. "Your office, Captain. Move. And you will detail exactly what is secured inside on the way."

"Talus? What the hell is happening here?!" Anya demanded, sprinting to keep pace.

Talus raised a sharp hand, cutting her off. "It is not a question of withholding anything from you, Anya, but there is no time. I require answers before we breach the office." He shot her a hard, grounding look, trying to convey that he would unpack the entire truth once they were clear of the blast zone.

The Captain swallowed hard, his voice shaking. "Something from the *Mars Orion 3*."

Talus' fists clenched so hard his joints popped. *Stupid, arrogant, short-sighted creatures.* Always operating under the delusion that their own desires outweighed global safety. "Every piece of that ship was ordered to be returned so that it could be destroyed. Fate of humanity initiative, sounds pretty serious because it was. No one was ever supposed to touch a piece of that ship or ever find out where it crashed."

"This is his office, Talus." Anya interrupted, halting before a solid metal door stamped with command insignias.

Talus checked his forearm scanner, the thermal array painting the interior walls. "Five active heat signatures inside the office.

He looked down to see her fingers already woven into the pins of two Fulgar charges. She met his gaze with a sharp nod. A slow smile crept onto Talus' lips. He glanced back at the trembling Captain, who was drawing his own Fular with a pale hand.

"I go in first," Talus commanded. "you come around. It's a small space with zero cover. Stay low, I will ensure all their attention will be on me and their new treasure. With luck, they won't realize your presence until the Fulgar charges detonate."

"Why are you taking the point position?" Tennant demanded.

"Because she possesses a pathological tendency toward self-sacrifice and I do not maintain a high level of trust in your leadership at this moment, Captain."

Talus took a deep, centering breath. The attempt to calm his nervous system failed entirely. He threw his weight against the door, shattering the locking mechanism as he burst into the room, his voice instantly shifting into an unnervingly loud, cheerful boom.

""Well, salutations, gentlemen! I seem to be lost. I was looking for some friends of mine but they seem to have vanished. Any idea what they might have gone? No? Yeah it looks like this whole base has been abandoned, guess someone forgot to pass along the message. But what are you doing here? A bit far from home right?"

Apparently when barging into a situation without any plan at all, he took a page from Cary's book and adopted an entirely new personality. One that was cocky, confident and talked just a little too much.

"Creator."

"Nope sorry. Talus. And you are?"

He extended a hand, but the monsters stood like stone statues, their eyes boring into his chest.

"Well I guess I will just be on my way then, unless you have anything you want to give me. Something relating to the origin location perhaps?"

He looked around but still they remained frozen. Then, Talus noticed a subtle shifting in their irises—a rapid, rhythmic twitching. They weren't just staring; they were communicating across a neural network, exchanging information he couldn't intercept.

"Ah, you've managed the telepathic interface links then?" Talus mused, stepping closer to the desk. "Fascinating. It never ceases to amaze me how rapidly each group evolves technology to resolve their immediate survival deficits. Forced evolution within a single generation. Truly magnificent. Well... I must be going."

Talus gave a small nod.

Anya and the Captain rose up from the flanks like ghosts. Anya lunged forward, her Fulgar charge slamming directly into the neck of the nearest hostile, the blue current instantly dropping him. The Captain incapacitated his target a second later.

The remaining three immortals spun toward the noise. Talus lunged across the desk, driving his fist into the sternum of the third, overloading his cardiac rhythm, before pressing his own charged Fulgar into the creature's neck.

That left two. Anya vaulted off a filing cabinet, landing squarely on the back of a massive immortal, driving a dagger into his shoulder joints. But the final hostile had already cleared his sidearm, the barrel tracking directly toward her exposed chest.

"Anya, move!" Talus roared.

He threw his body across the gap, grabbing the assailant's forearm just as the weapon discharged.

BANG.

A white-hot spike of agony detonated through Talus' thigh. He let out a sharp groan, realizing too late that his instinct had been off. He should have forced the barrel upward rather than down.

Before the hostile could fire a second round, Captain Tennant drove a Fulgar charge directly into the creature's jaw, the electrical explosion sending the last monster crashing through the glass cabinet.

Talus slumped against the desk, gripping his leg.

"Well... that was stupid of me," he gasped. "Captain... the artifact. Where is it secured?"

"You've been shot," Tennant whispered, standing entirely frozen, pointing a trembling finger at Talus' trousers. The black fabric quickly soaked through with blood. Talus was glad it would hide the stain, ensuring no one would notice when, in just a matter of moments, his wound stopped bleeding altogether.

"Your observational skills are magnificent, Captain. Yes, I have been shot so maybe we should be more concerned about getting that piece and getting out of here before dozens of immortals are chasing us." Talus hissed, pulling himself upright.

The Captain snapped out of his daze, nodding frantically as he lunged toward the main desk. He slammed a concealed toggle beneath the mahogany rim, and a structural steel panel in the far wall slid back.

The vault was entirely empty, save for a single, ragged piece of industrial insulation cloth.

Talus scrambled to his feet, ignoring the fading ache in his leg as he tore through the pockets and gear of the unconscious hostiles on the floor. Anya and the Captain joined the frantic sweep, tearing the room apart, but they all came up empty.

"Was there anything else in this room? Any papers, computer discs or anything else relating to the origin location or the Orion 3 mission?" Talus demanded, his face inches from the Captain's. He wanted the commander to see the raw, terrifying fire burning in his eyes. He needed this man to comprehend that if he uttered another single lie or risked Anya's life to preserve some bureaucratic secret, Talus would personally toss him out to the Others.

"No just the artifact." Tennant shouted, his eyes wide with genuine panic. "It was secured right there! I swear to you, it has to be here!"

Talus took one last look around before shaking his head.

Talus took one sweeping look across the ruined office before letting out a sharp breath and turning away. "No. It is gone. Their leadership isn't foolish; they wouldn't leave an asset like that for a second. They had already breached the room when you arrived, Captain. They took the artifact immediately; the rest of these operatives were simply scrubbing the terminal for secondary files. We are out of time. Move."

Talus surged out the door, leading the sprint back across the apex deck where the paralyzed bodies of the immortals were already beginning to twitch.

"Ryan, do you copy? Is the plane stabilized over the tunnel hatch?"

"Yeah, I think I've successfully mastered this alien console of yours," Ryan's voice returned over the frequency, sounding breathless but triumphant. "Elan had Alton walk me through the primary flight controls. I'm holding position directly above the exhaust vector. I've dropped our coordinate beacon onto your tactical display. Is Anya with you?"

Talus vaulted over a structural rail, landing cleanly on the lower ramp. "Yes, Ryan. And thank you for the timely notification regarding her absence from the plane."

"I honestly thought it would be obvious." Ryan replied.

"Your sarcasm is noted, Ryan," Talus muttered, his boots pounding against the concrete as he sprinted down the incline. His comm terminal flashed to life again, but this time, the proximity signatures were registering directly within the lower transport corridor. They were running out of time.

They skidded to a halt before the massive vault doors of the secondary tunnel system.

"The extraction track is right through here, Talus," Anya said, lunging toward the manual control interface. Her fingers flew across the panel. "I'll initialize the unsealing sequence."

"Hold that, Anya," Talus commanded, grabbing her shoulder and pulling her back into the shadow of the bulkhead. "We have company on the other side of that threshold."

She froze, checking her own wrist-comm. "Dammit. They've bottlenecked the exit track. We either break through their line or neutralize them individually. But if we detonate another Plasma Globe in this corridor, the electrical arc will fry the primary pneumatic rails, and we'll be trapped down here."

"We could bypass the tracks and proceed on foot," Anya suggested.

"You wouldn't make it three hundred meters with that ballistic wound," Captain Tennant countered, his eyes dropping to Talus' blood-soaked leg. "You're running on pure survival adrenaline right now, but that muscle tissue is going to fail the moment your heart rate drops."

Talus let out a bitter laugh. He was rapidly developing a new regret for this entire endeavor. The only benefit of this mission had been discovering that the apocalypse was significantly more convoluted than he had realized. There was truly something to be said for blissful ignorance.

"There are four active signatures directly outside the hatch," Talus calculated, staring at his forearm display. "If we modify the disruption sphere's output, we can focus the kinetic arc into a tight, directional burst. It will neutralize the immortals at the door without bleeding into the pressurized lines. Then we initialize a high-speed launch and clear the secondary line before their reinforcements can intercept. Anya, can you program the guide rails to launch the exact second our boots lock on? We cannot afford any lag, and we cannot leave an operative behind to manually crank the grid."

Anya nodded fiercely, her fingers already tearing into the wall-mounted terminal. "I can override the launch timers, but I don't know how to alter the disruption Plasma Globe."

"I can do it," Captain Tennant interrupted, stepping between them and reaching for the metallic sphere in Talus' coat.

Talus narrowed his eyes, his hand clamping over his pocket. "You?"

"I assisted the primary engineering team that drafted these weapons before the attack on Tigris," Tennant said, his voice hardening with a sudden, quiet authority. "I was a weapons design engineer before they handed me a captain's commission. When you get too proficient at building things that kill, the military keeps promoting you."

Talus stared into the old soldier's eyes for a mere second before releasing his grip, letting the Captain take the sphere. He still had very little trust regarding for the man, but he didn't have an alternative at the moment.

As the Captain worked, Talus' mind raced through the available information. He had a natural habit of over-analyzing things that had served him well, but now it was only providing him with bad outcomes.

The Others were hunting for the Origin Location. But why? The location had been sealed and its coordinates purged to prevent humanity from unearthing the weapons that broke the world. But the

Others *were* the weapon. They already possessed the viral strain. Unless their biological sequence had suffered an evolutionary contamination. If their strain was decaying, they wouldn't know how to synthesize a stable strain without the original source code. They were hunting for a cure. But if that was their objective, why hadn't their leadership simply marched on his primary laboratory? Their high command knew where his original bunker sat. They would assume he held the master sequence. They vastly outnumbered his small circle of scientists; a direct assault would be child's play. Why choose the hard way?

"Override complete!" Tennant shouted, snapping the sphere's casing back into place.

"Launch grid is live!" Anya echoed, her hand hovering over the door release.

The dual declarations snapped Talus back to the present reality.

"Captain, unseal the hatch exactly three inches," Talus commanded, bracing his shoulder against the steel frame. "Anya will deploy the directional charge, the exact moment it clears the frame, slam the door shut. If that arc bleeds back into this room, we will all be paralyzed when the main force arrives." And given that the immortals on the catwalks by the elevator were already beginning to groan and push themselves off the floor, that arrival was imminent.

"Mark!" Tennant roared.

The heavy door cracked open. Anya blurred forward, slipping the modified sphere through the gap with a fluid, practiced motion. Tennant slammed his full weight against the seal, the heavy locking bolts screaming as they engaged.

A muffled, directional *THUMP* vibrated through the steel plates.

But as the resonance faded, a sudden, terrifying sound echoed from the dark corridor behind them. Loud, synchronous footsteps.

The main force was awake. And they were angry.

Talus spun around to see dozens of massive, pale figures emerging from the upper ramps, their eyes burning with a dark, primal fury as they locked onto his position. This was the exact nightmare scenario his brain had drafted.

"Get that door back open now!" Talus yelled.

"We don't know if the voltage has cleared the tunnel track yet!" Ryan shouted through the speaker.

"We have significantly larger problems to worry about, Ryan! Captain, unseal the hatch! We go now!"

The steel door groaned, sliding back to reveal the tunnel. Outside, the four hostiles were collapsed on the silver floor, their muscles spasming wildly from the focused charge. Beyond them, the silver guide lines were pulsing with a violent, unstable green light.

Behind them, a collective, deafening roar shook the concrete foundations of the cavern. Dozens of voices lifted in a terrifying, synchronous chant that echoed off the high ceilings.

"CREATOR!"

"Go! Clear the threshold!" Talus roared, shoving the Captain through the opening. "Anya, launch!"

They scrambled into the metallic corridor just as the first wave of hostiles reached the catwalk. Tennant threw his weight against the external controls, slamming the secondary door shut just as a dozen pale hands slammed against the reinforced steel on the other side.

Talus backed up against the vibrating bulkhead, his chest heaving. This had been an extraordinary excess of adventure for a single day. Yet, looking down the long, silver stretch of the tunnel, he had a distinct, inescapable premonition that their nightmare was only beginning.

"Move, move! Lock onto the tracks!" Anya ordered, snapping her safety strap onto the overhead rail.

"You won't be able to maintain your center of gravity on that line with a bullet wound in your leg, you fool" Tennant barked, his eyes focused on the dark blood on Talus' trousers. "The force will rip that wound completely open."

Talus didn't glance up as he slammed his boots onto the lower pneumatic rail. The internal magnets engaged with a loud, definitive CLANG.

"Your concern is irrelevant, Captain," Talus said smoothly. "The damage has already been repaired."

With a casual gesture, Talus pulled back the torn, blood-soaked fabric of his trousers. Beneath the ruin of the cloth, the skin of his thigh was perfectly smooth, pale, and entirely devoid of a single scratch or scar. The bullet hole had vanished completely.

The Captain stared down at the unblemished flesh, his jaw dropping as his eyes traveled slowly back up to meet Talus' cold, ancient gaze. His chest heaved, his voice dropping into a horrified, breathless whisper.

"But... that means you're one of—"

"Apparently, Anya listens to you about as well as she listens to me," Talus growled, shooting a glare toward her. He stepped into the Captain's space, his imposing frame forcing the older man backward. "She answered the call that *you* were too afraid to. She was safe with me until you decided to come back for the Mars Orion 3 piece. Which might have been admirable, Captain, if you hadn't been fool enough to leave it behind in the first place. Now *move!*"

The Captain's face hardened, but he didn't argue. Recognizing the sheer disaster unfolding around them, he turned, snapped his safety strap onto the overhead rail, and slammed his boots onto the lower pneumatic line. The magnets locked with a sharp, metallic *CLANG*, and a microsecond later, the system engaged, launching him down the silver corridor in a breathless rush of wind.

Talus immediately keyed his wrist transmitter. "Ryan, the Captain is on the pipe and heading toward your location. Anya and I are right on his heels. Prepare for extraction."

"Copy that. Ready and waiting at the primary tunnel terminus," Ryan's voice crackled back, tight with adrenaline. "This line feeds directly into the plane's recovery bay. The automated dampeners are connected to my console, so the transport grid will decelerate you automatically. You won't have to worry about a manual disengage."

That was marginally reassuring. It still promised a jarring, bone-rattling halt, but at least he wouldn't be thrown face-first into another steel bulkhead.

Talus turned to Anya. The roaring chant of the awakened army was still vibrating through the thick steel of the security doors behind them, but in the narrow confines of the silver tunnel, the world felt suddenly, intensely quiet. He looked into her eyes, a slow, genuine smile breaking through his stark demeanor.

"Ready?" he asked softly.

Anya looked up at him, her fierce, untamed smile mirroring his own. "Ready."

Together, they threw their safety straps over the overhead rail, clicked the heavy buckles shut, and slammed their boots onto the pulsing guide tracks. The magnets fired in perfect unison, and before the roaring horde behind them could breach the seal, the grid erupted with power, launching them both into the screaming dark.

29

Anya

There was none of the usual dread this time around with Talus riding the transit tubes. In fact, it was the opposite. Anya kept glancing back over her shoulder just to catch the rare flash of exhilaration on his face—a genuine smile that softened his normally harsh features.

Their trip to Tigris had broken every single expectation she had.

She had fully intended to save Talus from his own stubbornness, but she hadn't anticipated the raw, toxic hatred he harbored toward her Captain. It had something to do with the *Mars Orion 3* and the origin location, but none of the pieces fit yet. The moment they were securely aboard the transport plane, she was going to get those answers.

As they sped through the pitch-black tunnels, Talus periodically ducked inward, using his broad shoulders to shield her face and guide her down. Every time he shifted, she caught the blur of silent figures watching from the shadows of the catwalks. *Why were they calling him the creator? What did he have to do with the Others?* Every time his chest pressed against her in the narrow capsule, her heart hammered against her ribs and it wasn't due to the speed of their escape.

When they finally rattled to the end of the line, Captain Tennant was already waiting on the platform, an immortal soldier crumpled and twitching at his feet.

"What took you so long?" Tennant asked, casually kicking the body aside. "I thought I was going to have to zap the demon again."

Anya quickly punched the keypad, opening the hatch to the surface. A heavy cargo rope dangled down through the opening, and looking up, she met Ryan's grinning face. They had made it. All of them.

Glancing back down into the dimly lit tunnel, she saw Talus glaring daggers at Tennant. For a terrifying second, Anya wondered where her loyalty would lie if she were ever forced to choose between them. Looking at the grim set of Talus' jaw, she realized with a jolt that the choice wasn't nearly as clear-cut as it used to be.

"Come on!" Anya urged, her voice tight with rising anxiety. "I want to get out of here before the rest catch up!"

Talus snapped his head toward her. His piercing eyes locked onto hers with an intensity that made her breath hitch. Breaking the gaze just as quickly, he hauled himself up the ladder first, with Tennant right behind him. Anya grabbed the rough rope, feeling the heavy, rhythmic tug of Talus climbing upward directly below her, keeping pace in her wake.

At the top, Ryan hoisted her through the hull of the small

transport plane. "Good to have you back aboard, my lady. Now, let's see what you brought us?"

Anya let out a breathless, uneven laugh—partly at Ryan's familiar silliness, but mostly to mask the suffocating weight in her stomach. Everything was about to collide in this tiny cockpit.

"One Talus, okay not that interesting but bonus he can fly the plane." Ryan joked as he helped Talus into the plane, giving him an odd, wary look before turning to the hatch.

"And there we go!" Ryan forced a cheerful, theatrical tone. "The bounty, our Captain safe and sound. And hopefully so happy to be alive that he will completely ignore the fact that we disobeyed pretty much every order he gave us."

"Technically, Ryan, Tigris is abandoned," Talus said, his deep voice dropping into the cabin like lead. "He has no base to command. He is not your Captain anymore. He is not even a Captain."

The words cast an immediate pall over the cabin. Anya saw Ryan's shoulders instantly slump. She knew Talus was only trying to reassure them that Tennant had no authority left to punish them, but it simply hammered home how much they had lost. She couldn't imagine serving another leader. Yet, as she watched Talus slide into the pilot's console, a reckless thought crossed her mind: *If he isn't my Captain anymore, I might as well stay with Talus for good.*

She climbed into the co-pilot seat beside Talus while Ryan and Tennant strapped into the back. This time, Talus didn't waste any time. He punched the coordinates into the computer, flipped a row of primary switches, and then whirled his chair completely around to face the passenger seats.

"Alright, Captain," Talus growled, leaning forward. "These two risked their lives for you. I took a bullet for you, albeit nothing worse than I have done to myself but nevertheless irritating. You owe me answers, and you will give them to me now. I need to know why the Others are so interested in that piece and why they want the origin location."

Anya turned her own chair to face the back. Captain Tennant looked smaller now, hollowed out. Was it the weight of whatever mistake he had made at Tigris, or was it just the sheer, intimidating gravity that Talus radiated?

"The Others?" Tennant repeated blankly.

Anya's mouth dropped open. "Focus Captain, please. The Others are what Talus calls the immortals attacking us. I went to him to find an end to this hiding and fighting. Whatever he needs to know, you tell him."

She glanced at Talus, but his jaw remained set, his eyes fixed relentlessly on Tennant.

"I don't have the answers you want," Tennant snapped, a flicker of his old authority returning to his voice. "And why would I tell you anyway? You're one of them!"

Anger flared hot in Anya's chest. Talus had risked himself in order to save her Captain from an army of immortals, and Tennant still saw him as nothing but a monster. She opened her mouth to defend him, but Talus held up a sharp, silencing hand.

"I take offense to very few things, Captain, but that is one of them," Talus said. His voice was dangerously low, vibrating with a suppressed fury. "May I remind you that this is *my* plane, and I can easily remove you from it. We are heading to a base filled with people like me. People who remember the *Mars Orion 3* crash. They will be even less pleased to know you let the Others get a piece of it. You have no idea what they can do with it."

Anya frowned, looking between the two men. "What do you mean, crashed? The historical records say the *Orion 3* exploded during re-entry."

Talus shot a dark look at Tennant, who avoided his eyes and stared at the floor. He sighed, and had the same look he had on his face when they spoke at the coffee shop. He was debating what to tell her. If he thought that he was going to get away with telling her anything but the complete truth he was out of his mind. She could zap him and fly this plane home herself until he was willing to talk.

"The *Mars Orion 3* made contact with what we thought was an asteroid," Talus explained quietly. "They brought samples aboard and found microscopic lifeforms. Tiny, with an amazing potential for good…and bad. They were virtually immortal. They could withstand almost anything. When the ship went down, it crashed into the ocean. The lifeforms survived. The astronauts did not. The government scoured the crash site to recover every single cell to keep them a secret."

Anya swallowed hard, her voice soft and unsure. "How do you know this? You were there?"

Talus nodded slowly. "I was a biologist at the time, working with my father. He was on the *Orion 3*. He discovered them, and spoke of their limitless potential for mankind. He wanted it to be his gift to the world. When he died in the crash, I vowed to carry on his work."

'So what does this have to do with the Others?" Ryan asked from the back row.

'Don't you see?" Talus said, turning slightly. "Our base was where it all started. There were once dozens of us studying those creatures, amazed at their potential. But one person figured out that the lifeforms had these stem cells that could transform into any other cell, including human cells. All they needed was a little time to learn the new biomap. Mix the stem cells with a host blood and then inject that blood into the host. The stem cells do the rest and you have a race of immortal humans."

'So you're an alien?" It was not the most intelligent thing she had ever said but she could not help it. This whole story was more like a fantastic story than truth. And yet immortal humans existed, there had to be some explanation for it.

'I would not go that far. But the stem cells that make me what I am are certainly not from this planet. We always meant to go back, examine the asteroid, perhaps find out where it came from but then came the war. What is important right now is finding out what piece of the *Mars Orion 3* they have and prevent them from finding the origin location."

Tennant finally spoke up, his voice hollow. "The *Orion 3* had backup drives for all the research data. One drive was never recovered from the crash site by the recovery teams. My grandfather found it years later. It was a black rectangular box. He gave it to my father and my father gave it to me and told me it held secrets that needed to be protected at all costs."

Some job you did, Anya thought bitterly, catching the echo of her own frustration in the sudden tightening of Talus' jaw.

"There are still more questions than answers," Talus muttered, his eyes narrowing as he stared at the console. "I don't know if they truly understand what they have, or if they even know how to use it. But they want the origin location. They have to be planning something—and whatever it is, it cannot be good for the rest of us."

That was a terrifying certainty. The Others were already functionally immortal, and for all she knew they outnumbered the remnants of humanity. What could an unstoppable army possibly be planning? If their goal was to expand their numbers, how could they even do it? Anya had never heard of an immortal having children, and they were actively slaughtering humans instead of turning them. If they weren't building an empire, and they weren't reproducing, what was left? What else could they possibly want but absolute eradication?

"What do we do next?" Anya asked. She realized, without a shred of doubt, that she was looking to Talus for orders now. She trusted him deeply.

"Get answers," Talus said.

"Do you have a plan for that?"

"No," Talus admitted, his voice flat. "Not a clue. Other than asking them, of course."

Anya rolled her eyes at him, a knot of frustration tightening in her chest. They were in no better shape than they had been an hour ago. They were still completely blind to the Others' true motives, and they still had absolutely no strategy for how to kill them. Knowing exactly how much they didn't know wasn't helpful; it was terrifying.

"What about heading straight to the origin location?" Ryan suggested from the back, leaning forward between their seats. "Maybe we can beat them to whatever it is they're looking for. It feels like a much better option than knocking on the front door of the people trying to slaughter us and politely asking for their evil master plan."

Anya looked from Ryan to Talus, weighing it. It was a long shot, but it was a tangible goal. If they could gather intel at the origin site, they could return to Talus' base, map out a way to infiltrate the Others' compound, and finally figure out their endgame. And, of course, they could find a way to permanently eliminate them—because none of this mattered if they couldn't rid the world of them for good.

"So you're suggesting a total change of course, Ryan?" Talus asked, staring at the console as his fingers hovered over the grid. "We would have to ensure absolute radio silence. Our home base is on the way. We could make a blind stop, resupply, and find a way to retrofit this plane with stealth capability."

"You say that like it's easy," Tennant muttered.

Anya glanced back at her Captain, noting the deep disbelief etched into his face. She had no delusions about the difficulty of modifying a transport plane on the fly, but she also had zero doubt that Talus knew the exact people who could pull it off.

"If the Others have this kind of tracking capability, why doesn't the plane have stealth mode already?" Anya asked, a sudden chill settling over her. "Isn't it possible they're tracking us right now?"

Talus frowned, his brow furrowing as he stared out the front cockpit glass.

"We've never taken this craft far from the perimeter of our base," he said quietly. "Up until now, there was no reason for a stealth drive. But the soldiers we stunned at Tigris likely alerted their commander the second they woke up. Maybe even the exact moment they went down. We still don't know the full extent of their telepathic network. It is highly probable they are tracking our signature. For that reason, even if we do make it back home, we can't risk landing anywhere near the base. We will have to abandon the—"

"Talus. How nice of you to come out of the shadows."

The voice distorted through the cockpit speakers was cold, sharp, and dripping with malice. Talus went entirely rigid, his face turning incredibly grim.

"What are you planning, Cavalk? Why are you looking for the origin location?" Talus' voice was darker than she had ever heard it.

"Who is he? How does he know who you are?"

Her voice was hushed and whispered. She highly doubted he would give her an answer, especially now but she still felt compelled to ask. His face remained stoic but instead of holding his hand up to silence her, he placed his hand in hers. There was an odd sense of dread about that simple act from him.

"Talus, you know me better than that," the voice chuckled over the airwaves, a sound that made Anya's skin crawl. "Come down here and let's have a chat. Just like old times. Or, I will shoot down your pretty little plane."

A loud, piercing alarm blared through the cockpit. **Missile lock.**

Talus slammed his hands onto the manual controls, throwing the plane into a violent, stomach-churning bank. Anya gasped as a streak of white fire roared past the cockpit window, missing them by inches.

"The next one won't miss," the voice warned smoothly. "Come down, and I might just let the others fly away home."

Talus ran a hand through his hair, a rare flicker of desperation crossing his face. "You know I can't trust you, Cavalk. Just shoot us down. You know I'll survive it."

Anya's eyes went wide. "Talus, don't provoke him!"

"I would," Cavalk's voice purred through the feedback, "but it would be a waste. With a little persuasion, that female ranger on your plane could be very useful to me."

A dead silence fell over the cabin. Ryan and Tennant stared at Anya from the back. Talus slowly turned his head to her, his eyes burning with a terrifying, protective fury. Perhaps her brazen attacks against the immortals were not the smartest move. She opened her mouth to ask Talus what he meant by a little help because it certainly did not sound good for her.

"I will rip this plane apart myself before I let him touch you," Talus hissed.

The sheer desperation in his voice sent a shiver down her spine. Whatever Cavalk wanted with her, it was a fate worse than death.

In his hand was a comm-link, much thicker than his standard

device. Anya realized instantly that it must be heavily encrypted, shielded from whoever was intercepting their main channel. Talus pushed a small button on the side of the dense alloy band and gently slipped it over her wrist.

The unexpected tenderness of his touch made her chest ache. He didn't just hand it to her; he took her trembling fingers in his own, guiding her wrist upward until the tiny microphone was brushing against her lips. Her breath hit the metal in short, hot, panicked gasps.

Leaning in close, his shoulder pressing firmly against hers, he pressed his lips right against the shell of her ear. His voice was a rough, urgent ghost of a sound. "Whisper. Tell Elan our situation. He will know what to do."

Before she could even nod, Talus whirled back to the primary console, deliberately raising his voice to drown her out as he opened the main frequency to Cavalk.

"I have three rangers up here, Cavalk!" Talus barked, his tone dripping with mock defiance. "Three rangers who have outwitted entire armies of yours. It's a tragedy you intend to blow them out of the sky instead of forcing them to lead your forces. Is that why you desperately need the origin location? You're planning to scavenge for scraps in the dirt, hoping you might still find a few surviving creatures? Have you finally run out of your supply, Cavalk? Did you never figure out how to make more?"

Cavalk's harsh, mocking laugh boomed through the cockpit speakers again. The sound sent a frozen shiver down Anya's spine; she knew if she survived this day, that laugh would haunt her nightmares for the rest of her life.

Huddling down into her collar, she spoke directly into the encrypted wrist-unit. "Elan? Elan, please be there. God, please answer."

The line clicked, and Elan's voice came through, sharply alert. "Anya? What's going on? You sound terrified."

"We're in the SunSpear," she whispered, her voice so faint she could barely hear it over the sound of Talus' deliberate rants. He was talking in frantic circles now, doing anything he could to bait Cavalk and keep him from pulling the trigger. "One of the

Others—Cavalk—has intercepted our system. He has a missile lock. He's going to shoot us down, and Talus... Talus is actively telling him to do it."

There was a tense, agonizing beat of silence on the other end.

"I've got a lock on your coordinates," Elan said, his voice dropping into a steady, authoritative calm that did little to soothe her racing heart. "I'm sending someone to intercept. Talus will make sure you're safe till we get there. Just trust him."

Anya looked at Talus. He glanced back, raising an eyebrow in a silent question. She nodded. *Elan knows.*

Talus immediately flipped a series of override switches, cutting the automatic stabilizers. The plane bucked wildly, plunging into a terrifying, unassisted nose-dive.

"What is going on?!" Tennant yelled, thrown against his harness.

"Talus!" Anya screamed, playing along so Cavalk would believe the crash was real. Talus shot her a quick, approving glance.

"Talus! What trick is this?!" Cavalk roared over the radio.

"Looks like the plane beat you to it, Cavalk!" Talus shouted back. He grabbed a long Fulgar rod from the back and jammed it straight into the radio circuit. Sparks exploded over the console, and the line went dead.

"Everyone to the back, now!" Talus ordered, wrestling with the manual yoke. "I've crashed this plane enough times to know how to survive it. Grab the camouflage tarp. The second we hit, get out, get under it, and do not move until Cary arrives."

Anya unbuckled her straps, but she didn't go back. She stood frozen between the pilot seats, the deck tilting violently beneath her feet. "What about you?"

"Cavalk won't look for you if he thinks you died in the wreckage and he has me," Talus said, his knuckles white as he guided their descent toward a stretch of open valley. "Go to the origin location. Cary knows the way."

"No," Anya gasped, the tears finally spilling over and blurring her vision. She grabbed the collar of his jacket, her fingers locking into the fabric with a desperate, white-knuckled grip. "No, Talus, please, come with us! Hide with us! We can find another way, we can figure it out together. Please don't do this, you can't stay behind!"

"Anya, if you die here, who comes for me?" Talus' voice finally broke, stripping away his stoic mask to reveal a raw, desperate vulnerability.

He abandoned the controls for mere seconds, grabbing her by the waist and pulling her flush against his chest. Before she could plead with him again, his mouth slammed onto hers. The kiss was fierce, desperate, and filled with all the unspoken things that had been building between them since the moment they met. It tasted like panic and fire and a sudden, devastating heartbreak. He held her like he was trying to tether her to the earth, and Anya clung to him, pouring all her terror and growing love into him, sobbing into the kiss as she begged him against his lips to change his mind.

He pulled away, his breathing ragged, his forehead resting against hers for one agonizing second.

"You have to go," Talus whispered. His voice cracked under the weight of his panic, his fingers tightening on her arms with a fierce, trembling grip. He leaned in closer, his eyes wide and fractured with a desperation he could no longer hide.

"Listen to me, Anya. Cavalk is going to put me through hell. He is going to try to tear me apart piece by piece, and I will let him. I will take every single thing he throws at me. But the *only* way I am going to endure what he is about to do—the only way I survive it—is if I know you are safe. If anything happens to you I won't come back from it Anya, I won't want to. Please just this once listen to me and save yourself." Talus pulled Anya into his arms, burying his face in her hair for one final, devastating second before forcing himself to step back. He met Ryan's eyes over her shoulder, giving him a sharp, wordless nod that commanded him to drag her away.

"No! No, Talus, don't do this!" Anya cried out, her voice fracturing as she tried to lung forward again, her hands reaching wildly for his jacket. "We can make it out together! Please, don't let him take you! We can escape together, you promised we'd do this together!"

"Now, Anya!" Ryan shouted. He lunged up from the back of the plane, wrapping his arms around her waist and dragging her backward, out of the cockpit.

"Talus, please! *Please!*" Anya screamed, her fingers slipping from Talus' jacket as Ryan dragged her down to the back of the plane. Tears streamed down her face as she fought against Ryan's grip, her desperate pleas echoing over the roar of the engines.

"Brace yourselves!" Talus yelled, drowning out her cries as he threw himself back into the pilot's seat.

The ground rushed up to meet them. At the last possible second, Talus yanked the nose up, forcing the plane into a brutal belly-slide through the rough grass. The impact was deafening. The world spun. Anya's head slammed into Ryan's, a blinding flash of pain exploding behind her eyes as the solar plane tore itself apart and finally slid to a bone-jarring halt.

Groans echoed through the dust-filled cabin.

"Get out! Now!" Talus' voice commanded from the front, sharp and cutting through the ringing in her ears.

Anya blinked away the dizziness, forcing her eyes to focus through the haze of smoke filling the ruined cockpit. Talus' face was a mask of blood and bruises, but even as she watched, the deep cuts on his forehead were already knitting together, the synthetic cells working frantically beneath his skin.

"Talus, please," Anya wept, her voice a fractured, desperate plea as Ryan and Tennant grabbed her by the arms. She kicked out, her boots striking the shattered console as she fought to break their hold. "No! You don't have to do this! Let me go!"

Talus looked back at her over his shoulder. The chaotic alarms and sparking wires faded behind the soft, tragic finality in his eyes. He held her gaze, embedding the image of her face into his mind, before shifting his look past her to Ryan and the Captain.

"Keep her safe," Talus ordered, his voice dropping to a low, lethal gravity. "If Cavalk finds her, she's gone forever."

"No! I won't let him have you!" Anya choked out, the words tearing from her throat like a sacred vow, defying the hands that were finally lifting her off her feet. "I will come back for you! Do you hear me? I will come back!"

Talus gave her a small, breathtaking smile—a flash of pure, defiant warmth amidst the ruin. "I'm counting on it. Now run."

With a final, desperate surge of strength, Ryan and the Captain hauled her through the jagged hatch and threw themselves out into the tall grass, dragging her body away from the smoking, ticking wreckage. Anya fought them every inch of the way, clawing at the dirt, twisting her body around as her eyes locked onto the shattered fuselage. She wanted to break their grip. She wanted to run back into the fire. She wanted to fight until her knuckles bled, but as the distance grew, she couldn't even draw air into her lungs under the crushing weight of the agony ripping through her soul.

Suddenly, a deafening explosion shook the earth.

A shockwave of heat threw them to the ground. Darkness swarmed over her as Ryan threw the heavy camouflage tarp over their bodies, pinning her down.

"What are you doing?!" Anya shrieked, thrashing violently beneath the heavy canvas. "He's still in there! We have to help him!"

"He blew up the plane, Anya!" Ryan hissed, holding her down with all his remaining strength. "He had to destroy the evidence that we survived! He's immortal, remember? He'll live!"

"But they're going to take him! You don't know what they'll do to him!" She was sobbing hysterically now, her fingers clawing at the dirt, her chest tight with a desperation so profound it felt like dying.

Tennant placed a heavy, broken arm over her, his own face swollen and bleeding. "This was his choice. Be quiet and hold still ranger. You heard him, if we're found, there will be no surviving for any of us, Talus included."

Anya clenched her fists, biting her lip until it bled to stifle her screams.

Minutes ticked by like hours. Then, the muffled sound of a heavy truck approached, stopping near the burning wreckage. Muffled voices drifted through the air.

Anya desperately lifted the tiny edge of the tarp. Ryan tried to pull her back, but the raw, murderous glare she shot him made him freeze.

Through the smoke, she saw Cavalk walking around the flaming chassis of the plane.

"So, Talus," Cavalk's cruel voice echoed. "You'd rather kill three good soldiers than let me have them. You always were a genius. Just not smart enough to save yourself." Cavalk kicked something on the ground. "That looks painful. Time to go have that chat, old friend."

Two large soldiers dragged Talus out from the smoke. Anya's breath hitched in her throat, a fresh wave of devastation crashing over her. Talus' right leg had been severed below the knee, the flesh raw and horribly regrowing in real-time. His chest and right arm were a blackened mass of severe burns. He was entirely conscious, enduring the unspeakable pain without a sound, all to make the illusion perfect. All to keep her safe.

They hoisted his broken, bleeding body into the back of the truck like cargo. The engine roared, and the truck sped away, kicking up a cloud of choking dust.

Anya let the tarp fall, her tears wetting the dirt. She squeezed the comm-link on her wrist, her voice cracking with a deadly, quiet resolve.

"I will get you back, Talus. Just hold on."

The comm-link buzzed softly against her skin, and Elan's voice came through. "Anya, it's Cary. I'm on my way. Just hold on."

The apocalypse continues with Hold On, the second book in The Immortals Series